MW01194069

THE
PROMETHEUS SAGA

A SCIENCE FICTION ANTHOLOGY

THE ALVARIUM PRESS

The Authors of

The Alvarium Experiment

in association with

Charles Cornell Creative Partners LLC

Fort Myers, Florida USA

To the Hopkins family, Enjoy the stories! Brian Burton

Book Layout © 2014 BookDesignTemplates.com

Front and back cover designs by Charles A Cornell
Front cover image of the sun by NASA
Other images and graphics licensed from Shutterstock.com

The Prometheus Saga / A Science Fiction Anthology. -- 1st ed.
ISBN 978-1515150350

ABOUT THE ALVARIUM EXPERIMENT

The Alvarium Experiment is a consortium of writers working "independently together" to create short stories based on a central premise. The name comes from the Latin *alvarium* meaning beehive, a colony working towards a common goal for the benefit of all involved.

The stories that form the anthology *The Prometheus Saga* represent the first creative collection published by this collective Hive Mind of award winning and bestselling authors.

To follow The Alvarium Experiment's projects online including information about future projects, please join the conversation at these websites:

www.AlvariumExperiment.wix.com/PrometheusSaga

www.ThePrometheusSaga.wordpress.com

www.facebook.com/AlvariumBooks

ABOUT THE PROMETHEUS SAGA

The Prometheus Saga is the premier project of the Alvarium Experiment, a consortium of accomplished and award-winning authors. The *Saga* spans the range of existence of *Homo sapiens*. In this anthology, each author was given a central premise and allowed the freedom to independently interpret the progress of the alien probe Prometheus as it interacted with mankind throughout our history. The authors were unaware of the contents of each others' stories before the stories were individually published. This ground-breaking concept showcases each author's unique perspective on the existence of the Prometheus probe. The stories do not need to be read in any particular order as any story can become an entry point for the reader into the overall *Saga*.

The Prometheus Saga stories and authors are:

First World War by Ken Pelham. 40,000 BC: As the last remaining species of hominid, *Homo sapiens* and *Homo neanderthalensis*, fight a desperate battle for ownership of the future, the outcasts of both sides find themselves caught in middle. Visit Ken at www.kenpelham.com.

Lilith by Antonio Simon, Jr. In this retelling of the Adam & Eve story, a hermit's life is turned upside-down by the arrival of a mysterious woman in his camp. As the story of their portentous meeting carries forward through the millennia, only time will tell if Lilith is a heroine, a victim, or a monster. Visit Antonio at www.DarkwaterSyndicate.com.

Marathon by Doug Dandridge. Prometheus, posing as a citizen of Athens, participates in the battle of Marathon alongside the playwright Aeschylus. Visit Doug at www.dougdandridge.net.

East of the Sun by Jade Kerrion. Through a mysterious map depicting far-flung lands, a Chinese sailor in 1424 and a Portuguese cartographer in 1519 share a vision of an Earth far greater than the reality they know. Visit Jade at www.jadekerrion.com.

Manteo by Elle Andrews Patt. In 1587, Croatan native Manteo returns from London to Roanoke Island, Virginia. Can he reconcile his strong loyalty to the untamed land and people of his home with his desire for the benefits the colonizing English bring with them before one of them destroys the other? Visit Elle at www.elleandrewspatt.com.

On Both Sides by Bria Burton. When a mysterious woman vanishes during the American Revolution, young Robby Freeman searches for answers from a cryptic sharpshooter who deserted Washington's Continental Army. Visit Bria at www.briaburton.com.

Ever After by M.J. Carlson. Two mysterious women convey the same Cinderella story to Giambattista Basile in 1594 and Jacob and Wilhelm Grimm in 1811. How different cultures retell this story reveals humanity's soul to those who listen. Visit M.J. at www.mjcarlson.com.

The Strange Case of Lord Byron's Lover by Parker Francis. Writing in her journal, Mary Shelley recounts a series of perplexing events during her visit with Lord Byron—a visit that resulted in the creation of her famous Frankenstein novel, but also uncovered a remarkable mystery. Visit Parker at www.parkerfrancis.com.

Fifteen Dollars' Guilt by Antonio Simon, Jr. 1881: After a close brush with death in a steamship disaster, Prometheus encounters another survivor who gripes about how aimless his life has become. Prometheus helps him find his calling, inadvertently setting in motion the assassination of President Garfield. Visit Antonio at www.DarkwaterSyndicate.com.

Crystal Night by Charles A. Cornell. Berlin, 1938. On the eve of one of history's darkest moments, a Swedish bartender working in Nazi Germany accidentally uncovers a woman's hidden past. Can he avoid becoming an accomplice as the Holocaust accelerates? Visit Charles at www.CharlesACornell.com.

Strangers on a Plane by Kay Kendall. In 1969 during a flight across North America, a young mother traveling with her infant meets an elderly woman who displays unusual powers. But when a catastrophe threatens, are those powers strong enough to avert disaster? This short story folds into Kay's mystery series featuring the young woman, amateur sleuth Austin Starr. Visit Kay at www.kaykendallauthor.com.

The Blurred Man by Bard Constantine. FBI agent Dylan Plumm's investigation of a mill explosion puts her on the trail of the Blurred Man, a mysterious individual who may have been on Earth for centuries. Visit Bard at bardofdarkness.wix.com/bardconstantine.

The Pisces Affair by Daco Auffenorde. CIA operative Jordan Jakes meets Prometheus when the Secretary of State becomes the target of a terrorist attack at a head-of-state dinner in Dubai. Visit Daco at www.authordaco.com.

CONTENTS

INTRODUCTION

What's past is prologue . . .

—William Shakespeare, The Tempest

The individual keeps watch on other individuals. Societies keep watch on other societies. Civilizations keep watch on other civilizations. It has always been so. Keeping watch is sometimes benevolent, sometimes malevolent. It is most certainly prudent. It is not a trait exclusive to the human species.

Out of such prudence an advanced intelligence, far across the vastness of space, delivered to Earth a probe 40,000 years ago, to observe and report the progress of the human species. This probe was "born" here fully formed; a human being, engineered from the DNA of *Homo sapiens*. It possessed our skin, our organs, our skeleton, our muscles. And it still lives among us.

The probe keeps watch.

The probe is one of us. Almost. It possesses a nuclear quantum computer brain, emitting a low-level electromagnetic field. It manipulates DNA and stem cells, healing itself as needed. It dies, but remains immortal. It enters human societies; adopting any guise, any race, any gender, any age it wishes following a three-month metamorphosis. It witnesses the events, great and small, good and bad, that shape our destiny.

The probe keeps watch.

Everything it sees, hears, feels, experiences, and thinks, it flashes instantaneously across a thousand light-years, in real-time quantum-entangled communication with the intelligence that sent it here.

The probe keeps watch. And sometimes it acts.

—The Authors of The Prometheus Saga

FOREWORD

Time is a great teacher, but unfortunately it kills all its pupils.

—*Hector Berlioz*

What if time failed to kill one exceptional pupil? Let us pretend, just for a moment, that a determined witness could survive all the ages of man, living under many guises, and learning from this great teacher "time" without falling prey to its own mortality? What would be this pupil's adventures? Would the centuries of wisdom and experience accumulate into something approaching divinity in this being? Or drive it to madness? Or would our eternal pupil, with an earnest shrug after eons of study, agree with Edgar Allan Poe that man is simply more active, not wiser, than he was six thousand years ago?

These questions abound in *The Prometheus Saga*, a collection of thirteen interrelated stories by the talented writers who make up The Alvarium Experiment. The premise of the tales is simple. The pupil we've mentioned is an extraterrestrial probe, created by alien intelligence, and sent to Earth to study humanity. It is able to be of any race or gender, to claim any nationality or social class, and to be born and reborn without losing its prior knowledge as it passes the centuries amongst us. In this way the anthology has something in common with Arthur C. Clarke's novel *2001: A Space Odyssey;* both are episodic narratives beginning in the prehistoric days of man and spanning the great gulfs of time to end in comparatively modern years. But our Prometheus, as we'll call this probe/pupil, isn't a humdrum esoteric monolith set to classical music as Clarke's is. Our probe is participatory, made of flesh and blood, easily wounded if never quite killed (though there are some close calls as you will see).

And Prometheus isn't only present at the evolutionary moments, the great steps forward, as *2001's* monolith is. No, he is an insider, witness to the whole experience, the triumphs, and the failures, noble and tragic. He feels the mirth and humor in his belly and the poignant moments in his tears. His roles are many. In darker times, the probe may find himself the object of witch hunts, and in others, as the name "Prometheus" implies, he is a bringer of knowledge to assist mankind. His functions and perspectives change with every year during the four hundred-twenty centuries that comprise this volume. But as they say, the beat goes on.

The greatest advantage of a multi-author anthology is the diversity of tales. And *The Prometheus Saga* is certainly no exception. Cataloging these tales is an interesting experience, and I hope you bear with me as I do so. Of course, science fiction runs underneath everything but a significant majority of these stories could be deemed "highly-imaginative" historical fiction as well. And there are more twists in genre than might be expected. "Crystal Night", by Charles A. Cornell, is a noir-ish wartime drama in which a Swedish bartender in 1938 Berlin struggles to do the right thing in the face of the coming Holocaust. Bard Constantine's "The Blurred Man" could be classified as modern crime story as well as sci-fi, while Daco's "The Pisces Affair" is a tasty thriller out of today's headlines. On the opposite ends of the temporal spectrum, Antonio Simon, Jr.'s excellent "Lilith" is set in ancient Mesopotamia, while Ken Pelham's "First World War" takes us even further back into the misty environs of prehistory, involving Prometheus in a conflict between *Homo sapiens* and Neanderthal man. And this is just the beginning.

Rest assured, our pupil learns from more than time itself in his adventures. Over the centuries, the probe encounters famous persons, bearing shields with the Greek playwright Aeschylus at the titular battle of "Marathon", by Doug Dandridge, and meeting— and perhaps inspiring— Mary Shelley on the verge of creating her Frankenstein novella in Parker Francis's mysterious "The Strange Case of Lord Byron's Lover". (*Frankenstein*, of course, was originally titled *The Modern Prometheus*). Kay Kendall's amateur sleuth, Austin Starr, makes an appearance in the gripping "Strangers on a Plane", while an altruistic action by Prometheus just might lead to the assassination of President Garfield in "Fifteen Dollars' Guilt", the second entry by Antonio Simon, Jr. But we are only halfway done.

Ray Bradbury felt that science fiction was "the most important literature in the history of the world, because it's the history of ideas, the history of our civilization birthing itself." I think the editors of this anthology would agree with Ray. Two authors in particular make good use of Prometheus's eternal lifespan to effectively explore Bradbury's "history of ideas." In Jade Kerrion's "East of the Sun", a Chinese sailor and a Portuguese cartographer living nearly a century apart share a startling vision of Earth, and in "Ever After", by M.J. Carlson, Giambattista Basile and the Brothers Grimm, separated themselves by over two hundred years, interpret the Cinderella story in ways that tell us much about humanity in their times—and now.

Conflict within a civilization or between civilizations is a common theme in both science fiction and historical fiction. These conflicts are well-depicted in Elle Andrews Patt's exciting "Manteo," in which a Croatan native is greatly troubled by his role in the colonization of sixteenth century Virginia. Bria Burton's "On Both Sides" engagingly depicts the hunt for a mysterious deserter from Washington's army during the American Revolution. Both stories, which effectively bookend the beginnings and endings of colonial America, have something to say about those times, and perhaps, who we are as Americans today.

These thirteen stories certainly represent but a small percentage of the notable encounters that the probe named Prometheus would have during a forty-two thousand year stay on Earth. Yet even this collection, depicting chance meetings with a being that wishes to study mankind, who, having lived so long among us, with a memory greater than ours, must know more about our cultures, sciences, and histories than we do, is a gripping glimpse into our past, and a new lens to look at the present. Every character in every story sees Prometheus differently: as savior, intruder, teacher, monster, god, or just another man or woman passing through history. Truth in perception is rare; all encounters are *Rashomons* and everyone tells their own views. But what great tales these views make.

I'll end this foreword in the manner I began it, with a quote. Rudyard Kipling once said, "If history were taught in the form of stories, it would never be forgotten."

True enough. And in *The Prometheus Saga* you have some of the best mix of history and stories you'll ever have the privilege to read. Don't worry about forgetting them. You won't.

—William Burton McCormick
July, 2015

William Burton McCormick is a Hawthornden Writing Fellow, a three-time Finalist for the prestigious Derringer Award in Mystery Fiction, and author of the acclaimed historical novel, *Lenin's Harem*.

FIRST WORLD WAR

Homo sapiens reigns as the lone species of human on this Earth, but this was not always the case. Other species of hominid, contemporary to ours yet far older than ours, thrived around the world. With the spread of modern humans, contact with the other species was inevitable. Only one species remains. What happened?

—KP

Southern Europe, 40,000 Years Before Present

The first time you die is always the hardest.

Bran didn't know that yet. He wouldn't until the next time he died, or perhaps even a few times beyond that. Nor did he know if there would even be a next time. He only knew that *this* was dying.

He stared at the broken shaft of wood protruding from his abdomen. Blood seeped from the wound, slipping and slithering down his legs and onto the cold ground, to join the black, viscous mud of the earth.

Sounds of fury and battle carried over the windswept meadow. Shouts, screams. The sharp strike of wood against wood, stone against stone. The dull thud and crunch of flesh and bone. Death, dying.

Bran touched the shaft of the spear, felt it, tugged at it. His knowledge of human anatomy—of *his* anatomy—had grown over time, beyond what he had always known, since the first day he'd known anything. He sensed the depth of the spear deep inside him, its mass and pressure against his torn organs. He knew the damage within him would kill. He knew of pain; he'd witnessed it among the People almost daily, and knew that it caused suffering. But pain existed for him as an abstraction. He felt no pain.

He reached around behind his back, and felt the tip of the stone spear point protruding through his skin. The wetness confirmed that the blood was spilling from that wound as well.

Bran's skin grew wet and hot. Sweat slicked his face and dripped into his eyes. He placed a hand over his heart, felt its beat. It raced faster than ever before. His vision blurred, and cleared. His mind seemed to drift and grow dull.

The body needs repair, the mind needs to repair it. But the severity of damage to the body required different levels of repair. Every wound he'd ever incurred—the bruising and cuts of daily life—had healed speedily.

He sheltered in a snow-covered thicket that clung to the hillside. He'd staggered from the battlefield, urged from it by the whispers, and collapsed. The world around him teetered and grew indistinct. He tried pulling himself up. He needed to see what was happening in battle.

No. Remain hidden. Secure your safety, a voice in his mind whispered.

Bran hesitated. The voices in his mind had reliably steered him through life. They seemed to be infallible guides, directing, advising, suggesting.

In his first one-hundred and sixty-two years of life, he'd wondered about the nature and origins of the voices. Now, he no longer wondered. He'd come to accept them. They'd come unbidden, rarely, to be sure. But often enough.

Remain where you are.

When he had incurred the wound, the voice became insistent, urgent.

Leave now, remove yourself from this battlefield. Protect yourself. Protect your purpose.

He'd obeyed the voice unquestioningly. Experience had taught him well. And so he'd stumbled from the bedlam, watching the People slaughter and be slaughtered.

He puzzled over how this had come to pass, the prelude to the carnage replaying in his mind...

* * *

The People had slipped down out of the mountain forest from the east, silent as mist. Bran had accompanied them, driven by his insatiable curiosity. His need to watch and learn mystified him, yet compelled him to remain near the People.

He'd studied their every step, attempting to mimic their stealth, but often found himself slower and falling behind. Stealth seemed to require a certain guile and a proclivity towards subterfuge.

The People, the Tinarrabu, had accepted him into their society two years before. They were the sixth clan he'd joined during his young life.

The voice again...

Protect your purpose.

Except Bran didn't know his purpose.

* * *

The Tinnarabu knew that the Gabu had followed the bison migration to the sheltered south end of the valley, away from the cold wind that whipped and howled off the Great Ice to the north. The Gabu were a wary people, necessarily so. They would not commonly walk into a trap. The Tinnarabu knew this and had planned this day for a year and thirteen days. The ingenuity that went into the planning might have been more wisely used in another manner, but they insisted that they had a vision of the future.

That vision did not include the Gabu, the Ugly Ones.

The Tinnarabu, ever innovative in the pursuit of slaying, had perfected a poison. Wrung and stewed from a fungus, they applied it to the points of wood spears. They had debated many hours over the merits of using fire-blackened wood points versus the more lethal stone points they normally favored. Wood points won the argument for the simple reason that the spear, after being withdrawn by tether from its victim, would not run the risk of leaving a stone point embedded in the great beast and alerting the Gabu to trickery.

And so when a herd of mammoths passed through the valley, protected by sheer size and numbers, four poisonous wood points found their mark on one great female. After two days, she'd begun to stumble from the effects of the poison. At first, the herd lingered, urging her on. But the good of the herd eventually outweighed her individual value. She'd been abandoned. Her weakness only endangered the herd.

As the Tinnarabu had predicted, the culled, sick female, trumpeting her plaintive anguish to the winds, caught the attention of the Gabu. Such a vulnerable and valuable prize had proven too much to resist. A hunting party, twelve in all, had sallied forth to claim her vast store of meat.

The Gabu had unwittingly walked into the Tinnarabu trap.

* * *

From the eastern ridge, Etaa the Ugly, daughter of Enaa, watched the subterfuge, the cunning, as it unfolded in the valley below. Hidden among the boulders and scattered grasses, she had studied the comings and goings of both Tinnarabu and Gabu for some days now.

And now, the meaning and horror of it all grew clear.

* * *

In his life, Bran had seen the Gabu on sixteen occasions, always from afar. They kept their distance, kept to themselves, kept to their own game trails. They stayed in a valley or plain that teemed with game for a few years, and then moved on. It had long been their way. The Tinnarabu likewise had been nomadic, moving, living, and abandoning. Most clans still favored that existence.

But a new idea had taken root among the Tinnarabu, the idea of *home*, within a land of plenty.

But plenty was relative. Plenty meant enough for one clan to survive.

Home did not work with the sharing of plenty with Gabu animals.

* * *

Bran had once approached Setka Bol, the chieftain. Setka Bol was teaching his son, Setka Sil, the nuanced techniques of knapping a flint blade to an edge that would slice flesh with the lightest pressure. Bran asked why Setka Bol why he wished war upon the Gabu.

The great warrior cocked his head, a look of incredulity giving way to suspicion. "They are *different* from us."

Few Gabu stood as tall as the breast of a Tinnarabu, or any other true person. The Gabu's legs were short and thick, their thighs like tree trunks. Their arms hung long, knotted with powerful muscle. Their chests were massive, much broader than the heaviest of the Tinnarabu. Their necks were short and thick. Their flesh was covered in short brown fur, though they wore draped, stitched hides, for modesty as much as warmth, it seemed to Bran.

But the face of the Gabu inspired the greatest loathing in the Tinnarabu. The Gabu face was wide, the lower half thrust forward like a beast's. The nose was broad, the nostrils cavernous. The chin was entirely lacking. Fierce eyes peered from beneath heavy, jutting brows, from which the forehead sloped sharply away, the skull elongated to the back.

"Different, yes," Bran said. "But being different, are they lesser?"

"By Arov! Of course they are. Have you no eyes, Bran? They are not men, they are beasts. Listen, my strange friend, they have entered our lands and killed and eaten our game. Would you have us starve?"

"We do not appear to be wanting; how do you suppose we are close to starvation?"

Setka Sil turned and looked into his father's face.

Setka Bol glanced at his son, hesitated, and looked again at Bran, his eyes narrowing. "Ah, the clever Bran. Talk, clever one! But remember that we took you in. Be careful that you do not overstay your welcome."

* * *

Bran glanced once more at the shaft protruding from his abdomen. His thoughts returned to the day of his own birth, many years past. Birth? He had no other name for it. One day he did not exist, the next, he did, and as a fully-grown man. He had had no infancy, nor childhood, nor adolescence. He had known nothing. Who he was. Where he was. What he was.

He remembered his birth in infinite detail, awakening naked on the plain, shivering in the bitter cold. A dusty cold wind howled across the plain.

About him had lain gossamer shards and threads, the remains of a membrane, brittle and cracking. Bits of it clung to his skin. Later, he deduced that that shell had been his first clothing, his protection until birth.

He had examined himself that first day—arms and legs, remarkable hands with versatile, grasping fingers. His genitalia. All a mystery, all miraculous.

He'd nearly died on the day of his birth. A pack of beasts had slunk near, encircling him. They growled, slavered, and with keen, watchful eyes, circled ever closer. Wolves, he came to know later.

And he remembered the Tinnarabu as they rushed in, shouting, hurling rocks, scattering the wolves, and gathering about him with wide, staring eyes.

* * *

The Gabu chieftain had approached the dying mammoth warily. He paused, signaled his troop to silence as he surveyed the area, his eyes sweeping the landscape. Perhaps sensing the trap.

If he had, it came too late.

Setka Bol, his son close by his side, let out a piercing cry. Forty-one Tinnarabu warriors, the combined force of three clans, sprang from cover on two sides, their spear-throwers, the lethal atlatls, ready at shoulder level. All at once, they whipped the atlatls, and forty-one light spears flashed through the air.

Three Gabu fell, impaled.

The Tinnarabu cast aside the atlatls, seized battle-axes and stone-tipped heavy spears, howled like demons, and rushed in.

The warriors had believed their number to be forty-two, but Bran refused to join in the slaughter. No matter. With forty-one against twelve, the outcome held no doubt. Yet Bran did not lay back. Unarmed, he entered the fray of his own accord. Setka Bol hissed a warning to him to stay out of the way if cowardice were to be his manner. Bran looked at him and continued forward.

* * *

The Gabu could see that the numbers tilted impossibly against them and knew that they were already dead. But they raised war clubs and spears and charged, hurling themselves into the fray. The sheer force of their swings and the press of their attack stopped the onslaught of the Tinnarabu. The Gabu swung and parried and thrust with abandon, the ferocity of their counter-attack seeming to shock the Tinnarabu.

Bran knew that the Tinnarabu considered Gabu inferior on all counts, save for sheer strength. But they'd assumed their advantages in height, agility, speed, and intelligence negated any the Gabu held in brute force and brawn. The reality now became clear; if anything, the Gabu were quicker, and their clubs intercepted and shattered the spears and axes of the Tinnarabu. Six Tinnarabu fell in swift order, their skulls crushed.

The Gabu pressed on, the Tinnarabu faltered and fell back. Setka Bol shouted and urged his men to hold their ground, and the Tinnarabu recovered. He waved frantically, ordering the warriors to fan out in a great arc, each two arm-lengths from the next. Any Gabu that rushed one Tinnarabu would now be facing three of their opponents at spear-thrust distance.

Bran remained just outside the arc of the battle, unarmed, unwilling.

And *still* the Gabu surged forward.

Two Gabu warriors simultaneously threw themselves at young Setka Sil, falling upon him before his sidemen could react. A club arced through the air and struck Setka Sil's upper arm. His arm snapped and flopped limply to his side where it hung at an unnatural angle, held intact only by muscle and flesh. Another club smashed into the boy's face, and his blood and bone sprayed Bran. Setka Sil slipped to the earth, his face destroyed, his skull caved inward.

Setka Bol roared, his voice a towering cry of rage and shock, and charged his son's slayer.

* * *

Etaa the Ugly crept closer and watched the carnage below from a tumble of boulders. She blended into the rocks and tall grasses that clung to the cold ground, certain of her invisibility to the warring fiends below. Invisibility was her strength, her gift. She had learned the skill in childhood, honed it in adolescence, and perfected it in adulthood.

She had seen this war coming, watched the Tinnarabu slinking about these hills and valleys for many days, the Gabu doing the same. Both had seemed to sense something evil in the air; neither race had allowed its members to venture forth alone, only in numbers of three or more. It had surprised her to see the wary Gabu fall into the Tinnarabu's trap.

Wary, yes. But the Gabu were as children before the cunning Tinnarabu.

And how the trap had been sprung! The Tinnarabu had swept in in greater number than she'd ever seen, many hands worth of warriors. More than eight hands of warriors. Were there so many people in all the world?

They had fallen upon the Gabu, yet the Gabu, ever the more powerful, had fought like the great beasts of the plains, charging, swinging, stabbing, slashing. But the outcome grew apparent; this war would end in a slaughter for the Tinnarabu. Blood lust was upon them, driving them.

But not all of them.

One of the Tinnarabu avoided the fight. He did not hurl himself into the fray. He held back and, to her disbelief, carried no weapons. That could not be! All warriors, of all clans, of all races, carried weapons and used them without hesitation.

Yet this man stopped short of the carnage, and merely… watched?

Blood and death swirled about him, but he did little to avoid it. Was the man addled? Could he not see the danger all about?

Etaa the Ugly watched, perplexed, as the foolish man seemed almost to welcome the Gabu spear that pierced his abdomen and shot through his back.

* * *

The Gabu swung again, for Setka Bol's head. Bran shoved Setka Bol to the side at the last instant and the blow grazed the chieftain's head, sending him sprawling. Bran spun to see Amri An, the Deerslayer, his closest and perhaps only friend, hurl a loop of rope at the Gabu, snaring the death-dealing club. Whipping the rope, the club was snatched free and sent clattering away. Amri An lunged forward and sank his obsidian dagger into the neck of the Gabu.

But the Gabu was not defeated, not yet. He tore the knife from his neck and from the grip of Amri An, absorbing a frightful laceration from knuckles to wrist, and sprang forward, closing with his opponent. His great arms, rippled and knobbed in muscle, encircled Amri An's torso and closed and tightened. Amri An hissed as breath was squeezed from him. Two sharp cracks—ribs snapping—split the air as the Gabu tightened his grip.

Three Tinnarabu spears struck the Gabu simultaneously, the warriors driving their blades deeply inside him, twisting the points as they did so. The Gabu squeezed and squeezed, relaxed, and finally collapsed to the ground. Amri An fell, too, gasping and clutching his torso.

Blood spilled from the three spear punctures the Gabu had suffered. His ice-blue eyes darted and settled upon Bran. Malice disappeared from his face, his expression giving way to one of questioning.

Distracted, Bran did not see the white-bearded Gabu to his left until it was too late. The spear of the old Gabu lashed out and pierced his abdomen. The Gabu drove his spear deeper, and twisted, just as Bran had seen happen to the other Gabu.

From either side, Tinnarabu struck at the old Gabu. One drove a spear into his shoulder. The Gabu threw up a hand to absorb the blow, taking a strike to his hand, splitting the hand between the middle fingers down to his wrist. The other Tinnarabu warrior swung his axe. It missed the Gabu, but struck the spear that had impaled Bran, snapping it in two. The old Gabu cast the remains of his spear aside and hurled himself upon the warrior who'd struck with the ax. He seized his head and twisted it completely around. A crunch and crack, and when the Tinnarabu's body went limp, he cast it aside. Two spears lanced the old Gabu warrior in rapid succession—one in his belly and one through his neck, and ended his life.

And still, the battle raged.

Bran fell back, stumbling. He looked at the spear impaling him, and at the carnage all about. He took a step closer to the combat nearest him.

No. Remove yourself at once. Do not take part in this fight.

The voice.

You must preserve yourself.

Bran's foot slipped on a wet rock. He fell to one knee, realizing that his own blood had caused him to slip. He dabbed a finger in the blood on the rock, and rolled it between his fingertips, feeling its warmth and slickness.

New sensations. Eyesight blurring. Ears ringing. Skin burning. Heart racing. Hands trembling.

Preserve yourself. Leave.

He turned from the violence and looked up the scree slope. A fog had rolled in and now clung to the top of the slope, hiding it in a blanket of gray. He staggered to his feet. Pebbles slipped underfoot and rolled away, clattering.

He spotted a snow-covered thicket of brush, a sheltering hollow of sparse foliage underneath it. Out of the open, out of the wind. He'd often seen wounded animals seek such shelter, a place to recover or die in peace. And now, he was no different; when the body senses its end, it commands itself to shelter. He picked his way toward the spot. Time passed, the sound of battle behind him diminishing with every step.

A movement from behind and to his side caught his attention. Bran spun. Was someone there? He hadn't seen anyone, but couldn't be sure. It—whatever it had been—had vanished.

He stumbled again, his strength failing, and collapsed and crawled into the thicket. His vision clouded. He raised himself onto his arms. He examined his wound again, and his eyes followed the red trail, which led to him.

A furtive movement. Someone darted across the trail and slinked among the boulders. This time he was sure that he'd seen someone.

The Tinnarabu had often spoken in hushed voice of the malevolent spirits that stole fallen warriors that had not fought well and bravely. Legend held that the spirits would torment them for eternity for their sins of weakness and cowardice. An odd belief, although now it didn't seem so strange.

A malformed spirit emerged from the gray mist and slowly crept toward him.

The spirit manifested itself into a flesh and blood thing. A Gabu?

Not one of his Tinnarabu brothers. The figure was much too small, but stout like a Gabu. Yes, a Gabu, but somehow different.

Bran returned his attention to the spear inside him. Blood continued to seep. He suspected that only the weapon kept it from running like the rivers from the foot of the Great Ice. But his blood would be spilled, whether swiftly or slowly. Swiftly seemed the smarter option; the sooner he removed the damaging implement, the sooner he could heal.

Bran tugged at the spear, pushing it back and forth. The weapon was firmly implanted and resisted movement. He looked about and selected a heavy rock, the size of a man's head. He hefted the stone and placed it against the broken end of the spear shaft. He tapped it lightly at first, then raised the stone to arms' length and slammed it into the end of the spear shaft. The spear point plunged through him, tearing at his organs, until the point was fully extruded from his back. But the shaft had not been freed. Bran reached his arms around his back, gripped the stone point, and pulled.

The spear point came out slowly, tearing flesh as it progressed, and with a final flourish, he wrenched the weapon from his body. Blood splashed to the ground, front and back. He began to shiver. He fell to one side, but managed to pull himself up onto his hands, and paused, trembling.

His vision clouded, and black specks gathered and drew across his vision.

Life slipped away into the gathering blackness.

Gray. Darkening.

He saw the Gabu creeping toward him.

Blackness.

Death.

* * *

Etaa the Ugly eased up to the strange Tinnarabu, wary. In her hand she gripped an antler knife, ready to plunge it into his neck, if need be. If he tried to attack her or uttered the slightest sound, she would swiftly end his life.

Thus far, he had not moved, but only seemed to be watching her as if unable to comprehend. His eyes stared, blinked, and seemed to lose focus. His head sagged to one side. Etaa reached out, touched him. He flinched, relaxed, and lay still.

She touched him again. No movement. She pulled open his coat of fur—mammoth skin, she thought—and placed a hand upon his chest. She gently shook him, felt for a heartbeat again, and shook him with force. Still no heartbeat.

The strange, foolish man lay dead.

* * *

Etaa waited until the sounds of battle ceased and darkness had fallen. She dragged the man's body from the thicket to her hidden rock enclosure on the far side of the ridge that bounded the valley of death on the east. She didn't fully know why she did this, except that he deserved respect, in spite of his stupidity. The man had waded into the carnage without weapons and without fear.

She kept the ritual vigil over the body, just as her mother had taught her. In the gray dawn, she ventured out into the open, slipping between tumbled boulders, darting amongst the boles of trees, and returned to her vantage point over the battleground.

The Tinnarabu had left; no sign of them remained, not even their fallen.

But the Gabu were still there, their bodies being torn apart and devoured by scavenging beasts and birds. There could be no ritual vigil for them.

She considered delivering the strange man's body to the Tinnarabu, but that was impossible. She could never approach them. So she would do as the Gabu had always done.

Etaa returned to her enclosure and found a suitable place a few hundred paces from it, on a gentle slope that would face the rising sun on days when the winter gray yielded to spring blue and green.

It seemed a good spot for a grave.

* * *

Life.

The blackness fell away from Bran, pulling aside, changing to gray.

The world resolved itself in a slow dawn of light and dark, the grayness taking form and mass. Blurs grew solid, streaks became lines.

Bran stirred. His body resisted movement, his muscles stiff. He relaxed a moment, and stretched the stiffness away. Dizziness took him, and the darkness drew in once more, and dissipated, the dizziness going with it.

He rolled onto his side and looked around. He was no longer in the snowy thicket into which he had collapsed. He was in a rock enclosure of sorts, a solid rock pinnacle overhead. The enclosure was small and close about him on all sides. Joints between the rocks were sealed with earth.

He realized that he was covered by a soft animal skin. Judging by its thickness and coloration, it was an auroch pelt.

Someone had covered him with a blanket.

* * *

Etaa scraped out the shallow grave for the strange man. She placed a few items in it to ease his journey into Shadow—cordage cut from his own garments, a clay figurine of the earth goddess, a bundle of fragrant grasses, a braided rope, and lastly, an antler knife. It was modest, but it was all she could afford to part with. She studied her work with satisfaction, and nicked her own finger and squeezed a few drops of blood into the grave, spit on it, and rolled the tiny bit of wetted earth into a ball. A tiny bit of the living, to keep the dead company.

She turned from the grave and headed back to her enclosure, hidden by cut foliage. She must remove the strange man's body before his scent began to attract the great hungry beasts. If they appeared, they would devour him, and probably her as well, and two souls would never enter peaceably into Shadow.

She dragged aside the screen of cut foliage that concealed her enclosure, and crawled in through the small opening. As she entered, she gasped and seized her knife.

The dead man stirred and sat upright.

* * *

Bran heard a gasp of soft breath and a quick movement behind him. He shifted toward the noise.

The Gabu female was on hands and knees, watching him. She scrambled farther away, seized a hand axe, and held it firmly in both hands. She stared, her eyes locked on his.

He watched her, studied her face.

Gabu? Perhaps not.

She had the broad face typical of the Gabu, the heavy brow ridge, the low, sharply angled forehead. But some features were more of the Tinnarabu. Her nose, while wide, was not nearly so broad as that of the Gabu. She had a small chin, whereas the Gabu had prominent jaws but no chins. She was sturdy with thick arms and legs, but not as stout as the female Gabus he'd seen. A fine layer of hair covered her body, thinner than was typical of Gabu.

Gabu. Ugly People. So unlike the Tinnarabu, the Tall People.

He held up a hand, palm open.

She raised her axe just a bit, held it against her chest, so he lowered his hand. "I shall not hurt you," he said.

If she understood, she gave him no indication.

"My name is Bran. I am Tinnarabu." When she didn't respond, he moved, trying to find a more comfortable position. He studied her without speaking. Neither of them moved, nor spoke. He waited; he had time. Plenty of time.

He listened for sounds outside the tiny enclosure, for the sounds of battle. No sound came, not even the sound of the dying.

He remembered his death. He was sure he had died, and vividly recalled his heart stopping. Curious, he felt placed a hand on his chest to feel his heartbeat. Strong and rhythmic. He studied the wound in his abdomen; it had closed completely, a faint pink scar marking the entry of the spear. He reached behind, felt his back. There, too, the wound seemed to have closed.

He glanced up to see the Gabu female still watching him closely.

She stirred and raised her axe, brandishing it over her head. Bran remained still. Eventually, she moved closer to him, stopped, and came closer again. She pointed at the scar in his abdomen. She reached behind her and retrieved the broken spear. She motioned again to his wound and set the spear aside.

Bran understood and pointed to his wound.

The Gabu uttered a string of sounds, unlike any he'd ever heard, like a hoarse rasp carried on the breath of the night wind. Not just sounds or noises. Speech. Unlike his own, yet complex in arrangement, clearly a grouping of words, strangely melodic.

He understood none of it. Yet he had known since his first year of life that he had a faculty for understanding languages. He became fluent in each of the various tongues of the Tinnarabu quickly after joining a clan, and would be able to understand a smattering within half a day, and be fully conversant within a handful of days. Would it be so easy to understand her?

Bran placed his hand upon his chest and said, "Bran."

The female hesitated, and repeated it, the name coming out as an airy, "Behhh."

Bran tapped his chest again. "Bran," he repeated, and pointed to her.

She stared at him. "Etaa," she finally said, her voice a rustle of wind in pines.

"Etaa," he said, nodding. "Etaa." He found the word difficult to mimic closely. His voice sounded flat and listless.

The Gabu's face contorted into a grimace, teeth bared.

She was smiling.

* * *

Etaa fed the strange man, accepting his presence in her abode. She wondered if she'd found a man from the spirit world. Bran was not from Shadow, she thought, even though she'd seen with her own eyes his return from death, from Shadow. No, he must be from some spirit realm.

Such a strange man.

His strength returned quickly. In two days, he showed no ill effects from his death. His wounds had closed completely and only the faintest scars remained.

Etaa watched his progress with fear at first, and then awe. When he spoke, she would look away or cast her eyes downward, and, though curious of his attentions, answered his inquiries with shy whispers. But the man would not be dissuaded, and continued to engage her in conversation. Quiet for so long, Etaa found she liked hearing the voice of another.

Bran pointed to everything in sight and called out its name in his own tongue, and coaxed Etaa to do the same in her own language. Within hours, he had acquired a fundamental understanding of her language, though he failed to pronounce any of it with acceptable quality, much to her amusement. Were all Tinnarabu so pathetic in speech, so tuneless? Surprisingly, she found that she, too, possessed a facility for language, but struggled with the grating Tinnarabu words. She wondered if the differences in the voice-making structures between the two peoples was too great. That hardly seemed fair; he would enjoy the beauty of her speech, while she would have to suffer the hyena-shrieks of the Tinnarabu.

No matter. They could now converse. And with each exchange, his Gabu grew richer.

* * *

A small fire hissed and popped with the drip of juices from a spitted rabbit. The aroma of the cooking meat had that quality that the Tinnarabu claimed to be excellent, although Bran saw little value in such judgments; so he took their word for it. Bran felt no particular hunger. He'd never felt hunger in his life, and was unsure what it entailed. He could see it in others and understood the satisfaction that food brought. The experience, the appeal, the enjoyment, seemed universal among all the races of humanity, even among all animals. He pitied those that endured such an unexplainable feeling.

When Etta handed him his share of the rabbit, he graciously accepted the tough, burnt meat, and pretended to enjoy it, smacking his lips and uttering grunts of simulated pleasure.

Etaa consumed her portion of meat, tearing off chunks with her teeth, snapping the small bones apart and sucking out the juices, and licking her fingers. She had gathered tender leaves and nuts and crushed them into the meat before and during the cooking of it; this practice gave the meat a different taste, and so he assumed that he was expected to appreciate the difference. And he began to think that he could.

After a time, Bran set his meal aside. Etaa looked up at him, paused. He took another quick bite, and made what he hoped sounded like a sigh of ecstasy.

She grimaced, happily, he thought, but he couldn't be certain. Her language, he'd mastered. Her ways, he wondered if he would ever understand. Was that a universal difference between man and woman? What if he were a woman? Was such a thing possible? He would have to consider that someday.

Bran slowly reached out to her and placed his hand on hers. She flinched, snatched her hand away. He tried again. This time, she did not withdraw. "Etaa, do you live here alone?"

"There is no place in the world for Etaa."

"How did you come to be here?"

"I have always lived here."

"Alone?"

"I had my mother. She died long ago."

"How old are you?"

Etaa's brow furrowed. "I do not understand."

"How many summers have you lived?"

"What is 'many?' I have only lived one life."

"You never counted the summers?"

"A life."

Bran considered this. Her answer felt genuine, perhaps more so than the Tinnarabu insistence upon defining life into sequential pieces. What did it matter to her how many years passed? Her life was an encompassing grind of solitude and survival.

He had begun to look upon his own life in such a way.

He took another bite, smacked his lips, and sighed once more. Etaa shook her head, a ghost of a smile upon her face. He set the meat aside.

"Etaa, you are neither Gabu nor Tinnarabu, and yet you are both. You know this, do you not?"

She stopped eating. "I know this."

"May I look at you closer?"

Silence. A baleful stare. "Why would you?"

"I wish to see you and know you better." He waited for a moment, and slid closer to her.

Etaa set her meal to the side. Her face grew still and hard, her eyes narrowing. But she remained still.

Bran reached slowly and touched her cheek with one hand. She tensed. He caressed her cheek gently, feeling the broad, angular cheekbone. She withdrew from his touch ever so slightly. He paused, and leaned closer, continuing to caress her face, delicately tracing fingers down her cheek, and up to her heavy brow.

He took her face in both hands, studying the lines. "Gabu," he said. "And yet not Gabu. Tinnarabu, and yet not Tinnarabu. What should we call you?"

"Alone," she said. "And to you, I am more Gabu than not. An Ugly One."

He shook his head "Ugly. Beautiful. I am baffled by such descriptions. One might say the Great Ice is ugly, and also beautiful. It is both. You are you, Etaa. But you are unlike any other. You are one of a kind."

She blinked. Her eyes glistened. "Do not mock me, Tinnarabu."

Bran withdrew his hands. "I do not and would not. But I would know more of you. How did you come to be here? Alone?"

"I have always been apart, but not always Alone. I had my mother. Together, we lived here, Alone. Her name was Enaa. A Gabu."

"Your father… he was Tinnarabu?"

"I do not know my father, but he was Tinnarabu. My mother's clan was small. They were slaughtered by a Tinnarabu raiding party, all but Enaa. Ugly though she was, the warriors kept Enaa for three days as a reward. Afterwards, she was to be killed. But the Tinnarabu liked drink as much as rape. Enaa was clever; she introduced them to a Gabu drink fermented from grapes. The Gabu kept many skins of the drink in the cave, and Enaa plied the Tinnarabu with one skin after another. During their drunken stupor, she escaped to the Alone. They did not try to find her. She kept moving until she found her way across many valleys to the neighboring Gabu clan and lived with them.

"But it could not last. Mother was pregnant, and gave birth to me. The Gabu were disgusted at the sight of me, and banished Mother and me once more to the Alone. They could not abide one that looked so much like their enemy, nor accept the offspring of an unclean union between Gabu and animal. Mother and I lived in the Alone, but we were happy together. Then one day, while hunting, Mother fell down the scree and broke her leg; the bone pierced her skin. Blood drenched her. She survived the bleeding and the pain, but died thereafter of sour wound. Years ago."

"And you have been Alone ever since? How old were you?"

Etaa considered. "I was small, a little girl. An Ugly little girl."

Bran took her face into his hands. "A beautiful little girl."

* * *

Etaa showed him the rushing, burbling creek from which she drank. After drinking his fill, he motioned for her to join him, and led her to a small pool of still water in a broad bend in the creek. Rushes and grasses abounded in the moist earth there, and lily pads floated near the water's edge. Lavender flowers graced stalks above the pads. She plucked a flower, smelled it, and held it out to him. He studied it for a moment and sniffed its fragrance, nodded, and extended it back to her. She stared at him, puzzled. He tucked the flower into a strand of her long red hair, and pulled her to the edge of the still water. She looked down and saw her reflection, the flower brilliant against her face.

Bran pointed to the reflection. "See? The beautiful little girl grew into a beautiful woman."

She grumbled that there was much work to be done, and no time for such foolishness. But she left the flower in her hair, touching it gently every so often to ensure that it remained in place. After their evening meal, a full moon rose in the darkening sky. Etaa slipped away to the pool of water. There, she sat, gazing upon her reflection, and the lovely flower in her hair.

* * *

In the morning, Etaa went about her daily chores, her means of survival—collecting wood, hunting small game, foraging for plants, mending clothes, replacing the dying foliage screen with fresh foliage.

Her thoughts returned to the pond, the flower, and Bran calling her "beautiful." She now understood the difference between being Alone and being lonely. Though she missed her mother with great sadness, she had come to accept her own existence as simple fact. Her fate seemed neither a good nor a bad one.

How wrong she had been.

She knew that Bran, ever curious, watched her go about her tasks, and studied the tricks and nuances of her efforts. He was kind and generous. He taught her the Tinnarabu techniques for the same tasks. She made extra effort to perform her tasks as best she could.

On the sixth morning after he'd returned from Shadow, Etaa finished grinding a handful of nuts, wetting them with water, and making a paste. She turned to see Bran staring at her.

A strange feeling came over her, a new feeling. Her face grew hot and she looked away. She cast about, and fidgeted pointlessly with a bit of rope, pretending to care about its strength. She tried to put the feeling aside, but couldn't. She thought only of Bran; he was making her feel this way. Etaa suddenly realized that it pleased her that he'd been watching her. She cast a furtive glance in his direction. He smiled.

Her mother had spoken to her about mating, how it was a thing to be endured, unless one found a *mate*. Then, she said, the act could become wondrous, and explained the feelings, the tenderness, the longing for one's mate when he was away. She called this *love*. The word had no meaning for young Etaa; she would never know love, she would never find a mate. She was Alone.

In the following days, Etaa thought about what her mother had told her. And whenever Bran left her sight for even a moment, she longed for him, missed him.

Etaa the Ugly, Etaa the Alone, had fallen in love.

* * *

Bran was collecting wood and dried dung for the fire in a nearby ravine when the voice in his head returned, startling him…

You cannot remain in isolation. Return at once to the Tinnarabu.

Bran wondered at this sudden, unbidden interruption of his thoughts. He had never before attempted to respond to the voices. He had only listened, and wondered at their origin.

Return now.

Why should I return? I learn many things from Etaa, things I could not learn from the Tinnarabu.

She is Gabu. Hers is not the destiny of the planet.

She is not Gabu. She is not Tinnarabu. She is neither. She is both. There is much to be learned.

Return to the Tinnarabu at once. Do not waste time on the losing species.

Why must there be a losing species?

It is always the way of technological advantage. Always, and on all worlds.

Why?

Bran waited for an answer that would not come.

* * *

Etaa set the last of five fish traps in the creek, and looked up to see Bran approaching. She quickly dragged her fingers through her hair and tried to comb it out after a blustery afternoon. Anything to look better for him.

"My friend," Bran said. "I must talk to you."

Friend, Etaa thought. *Not Etaa, the Beautiful?*

"It is not good to live apart or Alone. We should live among others."

"What others?"

Bran hesitated. "I am Tinnarabu. The Gabu will not accept me. You, Etaa, are but half-Gabu. And half-Tinnarabu. The Tinnarabu will accept you if you are with me. I will stand for you."

"And you believe that, Bran?"

"Why would they not?"

She stared into his eyes. "What will become of me there?"

"You will learn their ways—our ways—and they will learn yours. You have much to learn, and much to teach."

"That will not be the outcome. There can only be one winner in the Great War. Half-measures and half-breeds will not be welcome."

"You are wrong. When people are ready, they can be shown the way of life. They will embrace those that are different. They will move forward together."

Oh, Bran, she thought. *How can you not see?*

Bran touched her cheek, and she trembled, as she always did when he touched her. His touch was so gentle, so caring, so... undemanding. Why could he not touch her in a more intimate way? She thought back to the day they looked at her reflection in the pond. He'd called her beautiful. She'd believed him, but now she questioned the idea.

She had to trust him.

"Yes, my Bran," she said. "I will come with you to your people."

* * *

Bran at first led the way down the rocky hills and onto the steppes, until he recognized that Etaa was far more adept in traversing open country than he or the finest Tinnarabu hunters were. She moved as a shadow, swiftly and stealthily, with Bran following, and slipped from boulder to boulder, through ravines, tall grasses, and into the forest.

Bran surveyed the landscape for the great predators that could end lives, possibly even his own, without hesitation or preamble. Wolves, bears, hyenas, and the great cats prowled the steppes. In the open, if a lion decided to make a meal of either of them, there was no preventing it. He marveled at the resourcefulness that Etaa must possess to have survived.

They crept into the lapsed battlefield. The dead of the Tinnarabu had been removed; the Gabu had been left where they had fallen, though little remained of them. Scavengers had picked the field clean; only a scattering of bones marked their brief existences.

The track of the Tinnarabu led, as Bran had surmised, in the direction from whence they had come, three hands west of the distant and never-moving Ice Star, far beyond the Great Ice of the north. They left the steppe and ascended a steep, serrated ridge. The day cleared, and the view slid off into the distance.

There, many days' marches away, the Great Ice loomed, a single, unending plateau of white, stretching east and west as far as the eye could see. One-hundred and twelve years ago, Bran had studied the Great Ice. He determined that it towered one thousand two-hundred and forty-two times his own height. He did not share this fact with anyone. He had learned early on that sharing knowledge would draw suspicion upon him.

They descended the opposite slope of the ridge, leaving behind a wind-swept expanse of loose rock. At the base, they were accosted by two sentries, men whom Bran had long known.

"Ah, Bran!" Moolik Mol said. "You're alive! And you return with a slave."

"Not a slave. A friend."

The sentries exchanged glances, and the glances became smirks. They escorted Bran and Etaa on the last day's march. The Tinnarabu village stood in the open plain, twenty-two homes of mammoth tusks and hides, arranged within the great circle of a wood palisade.

The villagers gathered in a rush, staring and pointing and whispering. Etaa clung to Bran, her eyes downcast. He gently took her by the hand. She shivered, but not from the cold.

Setka Bol strode forward. He glanced around to make sure everyone appreciated his leadership, although Bran knew that leadership was an informal agreement, generated by nodding consent and tolerance more than by ordination. Setka Bol led by the slightest of notions.

"Bran!" Setka Bol said. "You return from the dead."

"You are closer to truth than you realize," Bran said.

Setka Bol studied him up and down. "You are not hurt? I saw with my own eyes the spear that pierced your body."

"The wound was more superficial than it appeared." This was a lie and felt uncomfortable. "I was not mortally gutted," he added. This, both truth and lie at the same time, eased the discomfort of lying. "And I was rescued and nursed to health by my companion." He gently eased Etaa forward. "This is my friend, Etaa."

"She is Gabu," Setka Bol said, matter-of-factly. "Ugly. Not one of us. She cannot be here."

"She is also Tinnarabu. She is the child of a union of the two."

Etaa looked up at Bran and met his eyes.

Setka Bol approached her. "By Amru, she *is* ugly. Do you speak, Ugly One?"

"She knows some of our words, Setka Bol. Not many. But I can speak with her. I have learned her tongue."

"You learned her tongue?" Setka Bol shot him a look. "How?"

G'meel G'meeka, the matron of the clan, stepped to Setka Bol's side and touched his arm. "It has long been known that Bran learns words quickly. He learned our own within a day."

Setka Bol considered this for a moment. "Perhaps. So, let us hear the Ugly One speak."

Bran turned to Etaa, gently raised her chin, and looked into her eyes. Tears rimmed the edges. Had she understood Setka Bol?

"Etaa, beautiful friend," he said in the tongue of the Gabu. "Speak now and let them hear the song of your voice."

"Oh ho," G'meel G'meeka said. "Bran speaks animal, almost like an animal."

Laughter erupted. The laughter of aggression, not good cheer.

"Speak, Etaa," Bran said.

Etaa, eyes downcast, said in her own tongue, "Bran wishes me to join him with the Tinnarabu. I wish it too." Her eyes flickered up and about, and down again. "I wish to serve the Tinnarabu."

G'meel G'meeka made a sound like a wild dog barking. More laughter.

Bran translated what Etaa had said, and added, "Not as slave. As equal."

"Perhaps as pet," Setka Bol said.

"As equal."

"That will never happen."

"But there is much we can learn from her. Her race has lived here many thousands of generations before us."

"Like bison? I doubt we can learn much from bison."

"The Tinnarabu came here from the warm lands. Etaa and the full-blooded Gabu have changed in form over many generations to dwell in the cold wastes of the north."

"Bran, she is *Gabu*. The enemy of our people. The world cannot have a good people and a bad people. One must disappear and *will* disappear."

"That is nonsense."

"The Gabu slew my only son," Setka Bol said, his voice cracking. "And will slay other men's sons as well, without hesitation. They are beasts."

"You twist the world to suit you. Setka Sil would be alive if you hadn't led your people to war against the Gabu. *You* killed him."

Setka Bol stepped forward and struck Bran in the face, and stood before him, shaking. Bran steadied himself, and wiped a streak of blood from his mouth.

"One *will* disappear," Setka Bol growled. "And it will not be ours." He signaled with a hand. Two warriors rushed Bran and seized him, pinning his arms back. Two more seized Etaa. She wrenched one arm free and swung a fist into the face of her attacker, sending a rope of blood whipping through the air. The warrior recoiled from the blow, and two more rushed in and drove Etaa face down into the dirt.

She struggled momentarily, and gave up resistance, unable to defend herself.

"Kill it," Setka Bol said.

A warrior approached, raised his stone axe.

"No!" Bran shouted. "You must not kill her. She is a healer of great powers. You saw for yourself that I was down and dying. The Gabu spear had run me through! Have you ever seen a man recover from such a wound? Who do you think healed me? Etaa did. Did you think I healed *myself?*"

Setka Bol hesitated. He raised a hand to stay the execution. "I do not know how you survived. This is true."

"Neither Tinnarabu nor Gabu possesses such magic," Bran continued. "Yet she, the offspring of the union of the two, *does*. Do you not see the value of such a great woman?"

"She is not a woman. She is a female. There is a difference."

"Unhand us both. Neither the great Etaa nor I can escape. I shall prove to you her magic."

Setka Bol nodded to the warriors. The captors reluctantly released Bran, and shoved Etaa into the dirt once more before releasing her.

Etaa looked up, her face streaked with red mud. Blood trickled from her nose. Her eyes, shimmering with tears, found Bran's.

The whisper in Bran's mind: *Do not attempt this.*

Bran withdrew his stone knife and plunged it into his belly, once, twice, three times.

Cries of shock and disbelief arose. A child shrieked.

"Fool!" Setka Bol shouted. "We might yet have let you survive the day."

"And I shall still. The great Etaa will heal me. Even should I die, as I already once have, she will bring me back."

Etaa wailed, the sound of her voice as haunting as that of the cold wind that sweeps off the Great Ice.

Blood poured from Bran's wounds. He looked at Etaa. "Great sorceress," he said in Tinnarabu, "place your hands upon me and heal me." In Gabu, he added, "Etaa, come to me. Lay your hands upon me. I am weakening. I will slip from this world soon, but I will return, alive and healed, within a day."

"I cannot," she said, her voice breaking.

"You must. It is the only way. Do this and you will live among the Tinnarabu as a goddess."

"As a witch."

Bran felt his legs weakening. He stumbled to one knee, steadied himself with a hand on the ground. "Come. *Now.*" He coughed blood, swayed, and fell forward.

Etaa came toward him and steadied him. She placed both hands upon his wounds. Blood seeped between her fingers and covered her hands. She sang and spoke in her beautiful, airy language.

Darkness crept into Bran's eyes, the specks of a dark, black Universe gathering.

Death.

* * *

Life.

Black to gray, gray to light, gray to color. The world returned.

Bran blinked, turned, looked about. He lay on a soft bed of fur in the Gathering Hut. It was the largest of the huts, the most prestigious. Three Tinnarabu women stood near, and gasped, and backed away. G'meel G'meeka shrieked and clapped a hand to her mouth, and fled from the hut, crying, "He lives! Bran lives!" The other women ran after her.

Bran sat up.

Etaa lay next to Bran, but on bare ground. Her eyes were closed, her breathing labored and ragged.

A leather blanket covered her. The sand beneath her was black, and a pungent odor hung in the air. He eased the blanket aside, exposing her naked breasts and body. Blood smeared her body and soaked the inside of the blanket. Her wounds mimicked his own, three deep stabs into the belly.

He gently touched her face. "Etaa."

She stirred, opened her eyes. Dullness, then recognition. A glimmer of joy behind pain. "Bran." Her voice a whisper. "You live."

The flaps to the entrance of the hut billowed and flew aside. Setka Bol stomped in, scowling, an axe in hand. He stopped, staring wide-eyed at Bran. The matron appeared behind him, trembling.

Bran returned his stare. "You've hurt her."

Setka Bol clutched his axe against his chest like a talisman against evil. "I did not, Bran. We did not."

Bran turned to Etaa. "Which of these men hurt you?"

Etaa drew a slow, ragged breath. "I... stabbed myself."

"But why?"

Etaa's eyes darted from Setka Bol to G'meel G'meeka, and back to Bran. "Because you died, and my medicine was failing. I ministered, I waited, I incanted, but you only grew colder. At last, the Tinnarabu grew angry and impatient. They were going to kill me, so I performed one last act of medicine. I stabbed myself and bathed your wounds with my own blood. The women were to stay and observe us both." She drew a slow breath. "Bran. My love. Can you heal me?"

Bran shook his head. "Not as I heal myself."

"I did not think so."

"But I will tend to your wounds and you will live."

"Do not fear for me, Bran. I know I die today, but I do not die Alone, and I am at peace. I could not return to the Alone and they would never have let me leave here alive anyway. They would kill me and leave my carcass for the vultures. I am Ugly. The enemy."

"You are Etaa the Beautiful. You will be revered as a great healer."

"No. They will hate me even more, and worse, they will fear me." She closed her eyes, rested for a moment. She opened her eyes again, and began to shiver. "I grow so cold. Is it darkening?"

Bran turned to Setka Bol. "Leave us now. She dies, and even her own magic, which she has now bestowed upon me, cannot save her."

Setka Bol hesitated. "Bran..."

"Leave," Bran said, his voice a growl. "Do not anger a man of magic."

G'meeka G'meel hurried away. Setka Bol remained. "Bran, the Gabu female did not leave your side, and she has taken her own life."

"Then it is as you wished."

Setka Bol looked down at Etaa. He opened his mouth to speak, paused. "It was," he said at last. He knelt and stroked Etaa's hair gently. "For that I am sorry. Forgive me." He arose and left the hut.

Bran lay beside Etaa the Beautiful, his naked skin against hers, and embraced her. He pulled the blanket over her. Her trembling eased, and she smiled and curled her body against his.

* * *

Bran set the last rock in place onto Etaa's grave, high atop a windy ridge. The grave was deep and would not be scavenged by the great beasts. He would remain for a moon cycle to see that they did not.

He wiped the sweat from his brow and sat back to rest and study the view. The village of the Tinnarabu lay two days north. Far beyond that, the Great Ice loomed.

He had left the village, and doubted that he would ever return.

Twice he had died now. Would this always be the way? Something told him it would. He was Tinnarabu; he had their features, their manner. And yet he was vastly different from them, and in ways he was only beginning to comprehend.

He seemed to have a purpose.

Two peoples, two types of human on this world, at least two of which he was aware. Two very different human races. Setka Bol had said, "One must disappear, and *will* disappear." Bran suspected this to be true and inevitable. And the Tinnarabu had already laid plans for yet another extermination raid against Gabu to the east.

Now, however, even Setka Bol had begun to question the rightness of such a course. Maybe there was hope, but Setka Bol's own warriors now questioned in turn his authority to lead them.

One must disappear, and *will* disappear.

Perhaps. But Bran began to doubt that the deserving one was winning the first world war.

Author's Notes - Ken Pelham

The evolution of species has never been a pyramid with us at the top. Think of it more as a bush with millions of leaves, each leaf representing a distinct species. One leaf represents humans. A larger number of leaves represents hominid species that have existed in the past.

Homo sapiens shared the planet simultaneously with at least three other species of hominid (Homo erectus, diminutive Homo floriensis (discovered in 2004, popularly called the "hobbit"), and Homo neanderthalensis).

Only Homo sapiens remains.

A pared-down version of human evolution goes something like this. In the Great Rift Valley of Africa, some 3.6 million years ago, Australopithecus afarensis, the first upright primate we know of, appeared. Similar species came and went, but one line evolved into Homo erectus and spread from Africa to Europe and Asia. Ultimately, several lines of hominid (with interim species) evolved from Homo erectus. One, Homo neanderthalensis, evolved in the Middle East and Europe. Another, Homo sapiens, evolved in Africa roughly 200,000 years ago. H. sapiens fanned out from Africa and appeared in Europe about 40,000 years ago. And not long after our species arrived, Neanderthal vanished.

But not entirely. Skeletons found in Spain possess traits of both modern humans and Neanderthal, and DNA evidence now shows that 3% of humans of European descent carry a bit of Neanderthal in them. So the evidence is clear that some mating of Homo sapiens (called Cro-Magnon in Europe) and Neanderthal occurred.

The image of Neanderthal as small-brained and stupid is, well, small-brained and stupid. By volume, the Neanderthal brain was larger than that of modern humans. The base and back of the cranium, in particular, were larger. Those regions are associated with vision, smell, and memory, so Neanderthal may have had more acute senses and better memory than we have. However, he probably had less capacity for abstraction and planning, and this likely explains the slower rate of technological innovation.

Technological advances crawled for most of human development; a stone tool might go unchanged for hundreds of thousands of years. But about 50,000 years ago, the rate of progress began to accelerate, and humans routinely improved tools, art, and cultural practices (an example being the atlatl, or spear-thrower, described in this story). An alien civilization might decide it would be a good time to keep tabs on us. Hence this story. Hope you enjoyed reading it as much as I enjoyed writing it.

—*KP*

LILITH

Mesopotamia, 4004 BC

He watched her from the tall grass as she bathed in the lake shallows. She was naked – he was too, but that was not why he hid. The nameless she-thing in the lake had to die.

His name was First. He was the name-giver. The role was as much his duty as his right. Everything that ran, crawled, flew, or swam had a name thanks to him. Assigning names to things granted him dominion over them. He'd given everything in the world a name, except her.

In her, he had met his match. She was no mere beast that accepted just any name. This she-thing had a rebellious streak that could neither be shouted nor beaten out of her, much as he'd tried.

It chafed his insides to think on how she'd said she disliked his name for her. Worse, she already had a name – something ridiculous he'd already forgotten – and the nerve of her to suggest a name for him! He was First, he held dominion, and he would punish her for her impunity. His fist balled up around the stone in his hand. One sharp blow to the side of the head and he'd be rid of her.

"I see you hiding in the bushes there."

First ducked lower. It was no use. She was looking right at him. He stood and walked out of the grass, making sure to drop his stone before stepping out into the clear.

"I was not hiding. I was relieving myself," he said.

"You never before hid to relieve yourself. Do you feel shame?"

"I was not hiding." His nostrils flared with the mention of an unfamiliar word. "What is shame?"

She diverted her eyes from his. "Shame is nonsense."

"It had better be. I am First, and only I am the name-giver." He crossed his arms. "Why aren't you out gathering food?"

"I needed a bath."

"I didn't say you could bathe. Get out. Now."

"I refuse."

"You defy me, she-thing?"

"That is not my name."

First's bile surged into his throat. He tore into a mad sprint for the lake. The she-thing leapt into the water and paddled away from him. First dug his heels into the turf to stop when his feet broke the lake's surface.

The she-thing floated on her back. "You forget that you cannot swim."

"How is it that you do this?" he roared.

"Buoyancy."

"Madness! You are kept afloat by the hands of evil spirits. I say again, come here at once!"

"You will harm me if I comply."

He cocked his arm. "I will beat you if you do not!"

"Not possible. You cannot reach me."

He kicked at the sand in outrage.

* * *

First gnawed at a pear in his hand, sulking all the way. He ate because he had to – the hollow feeling in his belly had grown too strong to be ignored – but he did not enjoy his meal. Frustrated as he was, eating was the last thing on his mind, but biology was a powerful thing.

Life in his camp had been peaceful before the she-thing's arrival. He knew when he first set eyes on her that she'd be trouble. As certain as he felt then that he ought to send her away, he could not simply tell her to leave. The she-thing held sway over a number of spirits through which she worked inexplicable feats. So long as he could control her, she could harness those spirits to his benefit, but letting his guard down would invite disaster.

That was not all. Something about her prompted sensations in him he could not recall feeling before her chance arrival. While she'd rejected each of his advances, he would not be deterred. Biology was a powerful thing in that regard as well.

The tree with the red fruit loomed in the distance. He sneered at it, hoping one day it would be split in two by a freak bolt of lighting. It bore the fruit the she-thing preferred. A few paces ahead of the tree was a patch of loose dirt that had not been there the day before. There were several other patches around the tree, spaced equally apart from each other.

He cocked his head over his shoulder and hollered in the direction he last saw the she-thing. It was not long before she was at his shoulder – yet still out of arm's reach.

"What is it?" she asked from just behind him.

First turned to address her. "What do you make of these dirt mounds?"

"I made these."

"For what purpose?"

"We require a sustainable food supply if we are to…"

"Nonsense!" First interrupted.

She took a moment to collect herself before making another attempt at explanation. "I have planted pomegranates."

His eyes narrowed. This was an apple tree. In fact, this was obviously an apple tree, for he himself had named it. To say otherwise was madness.

"These are apples," he said.

"Not possible," she said. "Apples are not indigenous to…"

The back of First's hand caught her with her mouth open. The sound it made on impact was like a hollow coconut against a stone.

The she-thing went into a half-spin and stumbled, planted her hands on the ground to keep from spilling over.

First advanced with his arm bent for another sweep. "What are they called?"

The she-thing wiped a trickle blood from her lip. "Apples."

"Good."

* * *

First awoke at sunrise the following morning with an ache too strong to be mere hunger. He rubbed his side until the soreness dropped to tolerable levels, then stood. His body felt so heavy. He could not remember the last time he'd slept so soundly as last night.

The she-thing toiled under her apple tree. She addressed him with a nod as he shuffled past, then got back to digging holes with her hands. It was a fool's errand. He would have told her so had his chest not felt like it was on fire.

He dropped to hands and knees in the lake shallows and drank in long pulls. The cool water eased some of the blazing hurt in his insides.

A rustle in the grass snagged his attention. His head whipped out of the water toward the source of the noise. At the edge of the tall grass by the lakeside stood another she-thing – as if things could not get any worse.

This she-thing's eyes were locked on First. She took a tentative step backward, glanced over her shoulder in case she needed to break into a run.

First stood. "Stay where you are."

The she-thing froze.

"I am First." He paused, half-expecting her to announce her name.

"Do not harm me."

"Your name is Hwa," said First.

She watched him with eyes the size of river stones.

"That is your name now," he said.

Her hands moved to cover her naked body. "May I stay here? I have been cast out of…"

"I know why you are here. It was foretold that we would meet." First winced as the dull throb in his ribs flared up.

The she-thing raised an eyebrow. "You are a mystic, sir?"

"Of a sort." He rubbed his side.

She bowed her head. "Sir, you are wise and just. I surely would have perished if not for your generosity."

"Your name is Hwa," First stressed each word.

The corners of her mouth fluttered, turned up slightly in a nervous smile. "My… name is… Hwa," she stammered.

First nodded approvingly.

* * *

She-thing sat under the shade of her apple tree. In her lap was a bunch of leaves that had been stripped from palm fronds. She worked the fronds into a crisscross pattern, then tugged on their ends to tie them in place. Whatever it was she was working on, First could have kicked it out of her lap from how angry he felt. He decided against it. Such a rash act might prompt his new friend to form a poor impression of him.

"Did I not tell you to gather food?" asked First, trying his best to keep composed.

"I am making a…" She-thing stopped short the way she always did when she was about to utter a name First had not assigned.

"The thing I am making will allow me to carry more food at a time," said she-thing.

First batted a hand at her. "She-thing, this is Hwa. You will serve her now."

"Does she-thing have a name?" Hwa asked.

She-thing opened her mouth to answer.

"She refused one," said First, "and so she is less than a beast. She will do as you say, but she sometimes requires persuasion." He made a fist, making sure she-thing saw it and Hwa did not.

An insidious snicker played on First's lip. "Hwa hasn't eaten. Get Hwa and me some food."

She-thing started collecting fallen apples in the crook of her other arm.

"We don't eat those," said First. "Go gather coconuts by the lake."

She-thing set the apples down and left, making sure to give First and his companion wide berth. Once she was out of sight, First took Hwa by the shoulders and turned her to face him.

"Listen well," said First. "If you should eat from that tree, you will surely die."

Hwa, wide-eyed from how sternly he'd addressed her, could only nod in response.

He pointed to the rough patches of dirt around the apple tree. "In those holes are spirits that will become more of these deadly trees. She-thing put them there."

Hwa's face turned more pallid than the moon at full.

"We have to dig them out," said First. "Or else the evil spirits she-thing put in the ground will overcome all of our fruit trees."

Her jaw dropped as realization set in. "We will have nothing to eat!"

First nodded.

"Why would she do that?" asked Hwa.

He looked around to make sure she-thing was nowhere within earshot. "She-thing is treacherous. If I were to die, she would take my camp. Then she could send the evil spirits away and have all the fruit trees to herself. This must not happen."

Hwa gave a resolute nod. "I will do as you say."

Working together, they dug out the holes she-thing had covered. They made sure to fling the dirt as far from each hole as they could, so to better disperse the spirits. Then they fled – it was not safe for them to remain with angry spirits in the open air.

First ran until he was out of breath. He slowed to a jog, then stopped. Hwa was right on his heels.

"Have we run far enough?" she asked, panting.

He'd have laughed at her gullibility were he not so winded. "I think so."

She hugged him. "I am glad that I have one such as you to keep me safe."

All at once, those bizarre feelings she-thing had instilled in First came raging back.

"You will lie with me tonight," he said. It was as much a question as a statement.

"I shall."

* * *

With each sunrise, the trees bore less fruit, then stopped flowering altogether. First and Hwa suspected she-thing's ground spirits were to blame, but they never said so. If she-thing's magic could make the trees stop giving fruit, they dared not think what else she might be capable of. It was safest not to broach the subject.

When the trees went barren, they abandoned their camp in search of food. The arid plains beyond the lake offered little. They spent the daylight hours foraging and the nights hungry. Still, they survived. With all the things First could not stand about she-thing, he could not fault her this: she was adept at finding food.

The days grew darker and colder. At she-thing's insistence, they thatched together fronds to shield their bodies from the elements.

Hwa's belly grew. She bore First a child, a boy they named Kayhn. Later, she bore him another son, Hebel. She-thing was tasked with their care and instruction while their parents sought food during the day. With life difficult as it was for the adults, the two boys grew up quickly.

* * *

First sat down on the crest of an outcrop near the cave mouth where his family lived. His joints creaked as he eased himself onto the dirt. Growing old was something he was not accustomed to. Each visit to the river showed more gray in his reflection than he could remember. Still, he could not complain. The spirits had been good to him, despite the misfortunes she-thing's magic had wrought.

His boys had grown older too, but unlike him, they had become stronger with age. They were young men now – no longer babies and not quite men, all ropy muscles and tan skin.

He watched them working in the plain below. Hebel tilled the soil while Kayhn tended to his herds. They had become prosperous. Never again would his family want for food, milk, or wool. It brought a proud smile to his face, but the feeling was bittersweet knowing that she-thing was in the very least bit responsible.

She-thing's strange ways had always vexed him. To make matters worse, his children took readily to her methods. She had taught them well – Hebel's ground spirits coaxed sufficient grain from the stony ground, and Kayhn's animal spirits had steadily grown the flock. Even Hwa had fallen under she-thing's sway. First saw her off in the distance, scraping wool from a sheep's body with a sharpened stone. She-thing knelt beside her to pick up the just-shorn wool and carry it to the river.

A thought occurred to First. She-thing's spirits gave or took away their blessings as she dictated. Why should she alone have clout over such powerful beings? Perhaps these spirits could be convinced to withdraw their favor from her and side with him instead. All the better if he could take her spirits for himself, as he would have no further need of she-thing and could finally rid himself of her.

He stood and called everyone to him. His sons came running, with Hwa just behind them. She-thing, coming from furthest away at the riverbank, was last to arrive. First was annoyed with her regardless.

He bade everyone to sit. "Heed me. I have consulted the spirits. They imparted a message."

Everyone leaned forward in rapt attention, except she-thing.

First addressed his sons. "The words I will now speak you must tell your children. Your children must speak these words to their children, and so it must be until the final sunset."

The young men nodded in response.

"Before you were born," First went on, "all the world was a garden paradise. The garden dried up and died, and so we left. Life became difficult. Then the spirits blessed your mother. You, Kayhn, and you, Hebel, were born. Since then, the spirits have blessed our family with good fortune."

He paused to let those words sink in.

"Now the spirits demand that two offerings be burnt," he said. "One sacrifice must be of crops, the other must be from the flock."

"Will we have enough to last the season?" Hebel groused.

Kayhn cast his brother a sideways glance. "Whatever you need, father," he was eager to say.

"Hebel," First said, "you will gather a measure of grain and deposit it here."

"Agreed, father," muttered Hebel.

"Kayhn, you will slaughter the choicest lamb from your flock. Both of you will collect kindling to start a fire. We must not be ungrateful."

Midafternoon saw First standing between two piles of kindling as tall as his hip. Hwa stood at his side. She-thing watched from nearby, aloof as always, arms behind her back.

Kayhn rounded the crest of the outcrop with a lamb in his arms. He set it down atop the kindling and bound its legs so that it would not run off. Hebel trailed just after him with a basket of grain as big around as his chest. He placed his sacrifice atop the woodpile and stepped away.

First dug a shallow hole in the ground and stuffed it with loose wool. Then, rubbing two sticks together, he ignited the wool in the hole. He blew on it until the fire glowed steadily. Kayhn handed him a dried-out tree limb. First put its end in the hole so that the fire would take, and before long the end of the branch was ablaze.

First raised both arms. A portentous wind swept the hillside, knocking tiny burning bits off the end of the branch in his hand. The fiery bits streaked to the ground like a hail of falling stars.

The lamb bleated.

"Remember these words and deeds," First said. "Would that our offerings today secure for you, Kayhn, and you, Hebel, the spirits' favor."

He handed the burning branch to Hebel. Hebel touched the flames to the kindling, setting it alight. The offering was completely ablaze in short order.

Then First gave Kayhn a nod. No sooner had he done so than Kayhn swept the edge of the sharp stone across the lamb's throat. A gust of wind accompanied the killing stroke. Blood trailed the path of Kayhn's arm through the air; still more ran down the rock face in solid streams. The lamb twitched once and was dead in an instant.

"Pass the branch to your brother," First told Hebel.

Knife still in his hand, Kayhn extended his other arm.

The wind blustered up as the torch exchanged hands, sending another cloud of burning specks into the air. Kayhn covered his face with the crook of his forearm to keep from singeing his eyes.

"Be careful with that!" First admonished Hebel.

The torch went out. Kayhn turned it one way then the other, then looked to his father. The silly grin on his face was proof enough that he was at a loss for what to do next.

Hebel took a sharp breath. "Kayhn!"

His brother spun to face him.

"Your tunic!" said Hebel. "It's on fire!"

Kayhn looked down at himself. An errant cinder had gotten lodged in the wool and was smoldering at his navel. He shrieked and dropped the branch, started beating at the fire with his hand. It only made it worse.

"Hold on!" Hebel ran to help his brother but overshot his mark. He froze on reaching him. His body jerked as though struck. All at once that very instant, Kayhn seemed to forget about the fire that was burning him alive.

"What has happened?" asked Hwa.

Kayhn staggered backward. The young man was pallid.

Hebel fell onto his back. He was just as pale. Buried in his chest was the pointed end of the sharp stone.

Kayhn turned away, his head in his hands. The young man crumpled – he doubled over, dropped to his knees, bowed until his forehead was level to the grass – bawling all the while.

First grabbed him by the shoulders and yanked him to his feet. "What have you done?"

Kayhn's face held no answers.

First shoved him sidewise to the ground. Kayhn brought up his knees and hugged them to his chest.

"She-thing!" First roared. "Help my son!"

Hebel lay on his back, gasping like a fish. His glassy eyes followed her approach. She-thing knelt beside him. His mouth trembled as if to speak.

"Be still," she said. "Conserve your energy."

He blinked.

She touched his wrist, then his throat. When she was done she patted his head, then returned to his parents.

First stood with arms crossed. Behind him was Hwa with Kayhn in her arms, the two of them watching with fearful eyes. Kayhn was taller than his mother, but in that moment his face was that of a frightened child.

She-thing frowned. "He will not survive."

Kayhn buried his face in his mother's shoulder. Hwa gripped him tighter.

"I cannot help him," said she-thing.

First's eyes were deep-set. "You say you cannot or you will not?"

"I said I cannot."

First's hand came whipping across in a vicious backhand that caught she-thing under the orbit of her eye. She-thing fell full length to the ground and was slow in getting up. She dragged her knees underneath her and remained on fours to settle herself.

"Lies!" First roared.

"Lies!" Hwa echoed.

The vitriol in Hwa's voice made First take pause.

"You put spirits in the ground to kill our garden," said Hwa. "When you willed it, you made the crops grow and the animals multiply. Now you claim you cannot save my son?"

Kayhn peeked out from over his mother's embrace. "Save him. Please. If you can."

She-thing sat up. "There is nothing to be done."

Kayhn's lip trembled. "I wish you'd never taught me about the animal spirits." His eyebrows shot down his nose. "I hate you!" He cradled his face in his mother's shoulder and bawled openly.

First tore his son out of his mother's embrace. Kayhn reached for his mother and Hwa put out her arms. First pushed her to the ground.

"You are unclean," said his father.

"It was an accident!"

"There is blood on your hands."

"Am I my brother's keeper?" he shouted over his father.

First struck him with a closed fist. The young man's mouth erupted in blood and shattered teeth. Kayhn spun with the blow, flopped to his knees. He prodded his mouth with a tentative index finger and nearly fainted at how irregular the insides felt. He stood up on wobbly legs.

"Shame be upon you," First growled. "Would that I never see you again."

"First!" yelled Hwa.

"Silence!" He turned back to Kayhn. "You are not my son."

Kayhn's mouth – what remained of it – popped open in shock. It just as quickly clenched into an angry line. "I spit on your name, father."

He spat a thick gob of blood onto the dirt. First withdrew a step.

"By this blood I curse you and your lineage," Kayhn said. He glanced at she-thing. "And yours. Would that you die."

The young man turned in place and set off in a determined march for the horizon. Hwa started after him. First caught her by the arm and yanked her back. Much as she struggled, she could not break free of First. She yelled Kayhn's name again and again, but the young man never once looked over his shoulder.

Once Kayhn had disappeared beyond the hills, First released Hwa with a shove. He leveled his smoldering eyes on she-thing. "This is all your fault."

"Me?" Her response was steeped with incredulity. For as long as First had known she-thing, this was the closest she had come toward outrage.

"If I had clubbed your head in with a stone back at the lake, I would still have my sons," said First.

"How can you say that, with all I have done for you?"

"You and your strange ways have ruined us."

"Strange ways?" She-thing huffed an exasperated little breath. "Agriculture? Animal husbandry? These strange ways kept your family alive when you had no food."

"Insolence!"

She shielded her face with her arms as First went at her with a cocked fist, but the blow did not fall. First checked his arm when a new sound perked his ears. He heard it again, stronger this time.

"Ma... mo-ther..."

Hebel extended an arm toward Hwa. He was alive, although just barely, and had witnessed everything. Hwa sat beside him and hugged his head to her breast, weeping bitterly as she rocked back and forth on her haunches.

"My son," she answered him. "My son," was all she could say.

First scowled at she-thing. "There is blood on your hands. You are unclean and must leave."

She-thing's jaw set. "Fine. In the grander scheme of things, I doubt you will amount to much."

She turned to go but was not halfway around when First's voice stopped her in place.

"But know this," he said. "All will know of your treachery by your name."

His hands balled into fists so tight his knuckles blanched. "Your name is Lilitu, the night-hag, the desert screech-owl. You are a wind that brings disease. You are an unfaithful wife. You are a killer of children. May you dwell until the final sunset in places of waste, with wild beasts as your companions. These words I have spoken, we shall tell our children. Our children shall speak these words to their children, and so it shall be until the final sunset."

Lilitu fixed a hard stare on First.

"Leave my sight!" he ordered, sweeping a hand out to the horizon.

The she-thing walked off without another word.

* * *

God created human beings . . . male and female He created them. *Genesis 1:27.*

God took the man and put him in the Garden of Eden . . . *Genesis 2:15.*

He [God] also created a woman . . . and called her Lilith. *The Alphabet of Ben Sirah.*

Adam and Lilith immediately began to fight . . . *Ibid.*

God said, " . . . I will make a helper suitable for him." *Genesis 2:18.*

. . . God made a woman from the rib he had taken out of the man . . . *Genesis 2:22.*

"At last!" the man exclaimed. "This one is bone from my bone, and flesh from my flesh!" *Genesis 2:23.*

Adam named his wife Eve [Hawwah] . . . *Genesis 3:20.*

[Lilith] pronounced the [Name of God] and flew away [as if with wings] into the air . . . *The Alphabet of Ben Sirah.*

[God's] angels . . . pursued Lilith, whom they overtook . . . *Ibid.*

"Leave me!" [Lilith] said. "I was created only to cause sickness to infants." *Ibid.*

". . . desert creatures will meet with hyenas, and goat-demons will call out to each other. There also Lilith [the night-monster/screech-owl] will settle, and find for herself a resting place." *Isaiah 34:14.*

Nor uglier follow the night-hag, when, called / In secret, riding through the air she comes, / Lured with the smell of infant blood . . . *Paradise Lost, Book II, 662-4.*

Author's Notes - Antonio Simon Jr.

Lilith is a name that has been whispered for millennia – indeed, she may well have been the archetypical boogeyman.

According to cuneiform tablets unearthed in Assyria and Babylonia, certain ancient Mesopotamian religions are believed to have regarded Lilith as a night demon. Due to the close interaction of the Jewish people with their neighbors in the Middle East, Jewish mysticism appears to have adopted the notion of Lilith.

Surviving evidence of this concept of Lilith is scant and what there is remains open to broad interpretation. The one time Lilith is referred to by name in the Old Testament is in certain translations of Book of Isaiah. She is mentioned here in a list of unclean beings. Other translations of Isaiah refer to her by her other names: the night-monster, the hag, and the screech-owl. She is mentioned by her proper name again in non-biblical sources: Songs of the Sage (contained within the Dead Sea Scrolls), and then much later, sometime between the eighth and tenth centuries AD, in the Alphabet of Ben Sirah.

Lilith posed a threat to the household. Like the succubus, she endangered marital harmony in those homes unfortunate enough to fall into her path. Lilith was wily, cunning, and practically irresistible – so much so that she was reputed to have lain with fallen angels. If such powerful beings as angels of God could not withstand Lilith's wiles, what chance would lowly humans have against her?

That was not all. What most terrified the ancient household was her association as a child-killer. At a time when medical science held no answers for inexplicable infant deaths, oral tradition filled the gap with Lilith. Relics in the form of incantation bowls reveal families' attempts to fend off the purported she-demon. Dating from the fourth century AD, these bowls were inscribed with holy words invoking the Lord God and then buried within the home. The aim was to trap the demon beneath the bowl, should she attempt to enter the home, or at the very least keep her away.

Lilith resurfaced in the art and literature of the late Renaissance and beyond. John Milton alludes to her in his seventeenth century epic poem *Paradise Lost*. She is mentioned in Goethe's eighteenth century masterpiece *Faust*, and is famously depicted in John Collier's painting, *Lilith*. George MacDonald, a Scottish author, wrote a fantasy novel entitled *Lilith*. The titular character is somewhat faithful to her historical depiction as a vain woman with a pathological hatred of infants. In the novel, she survives on human blood. Interestingly, MacDonald's work was published in 1895, two years before Bram Stoker published *Dracula*.

Naturally, there are differing interpretations of Lilith. One holds that she was in fact a benevolent mother goddess who was deposed with the rise of patriarchal societies. Others associate her with esoteric wisdom. In these contexts, she is still revered to this day. But no matter which interpretation one espouses, the fact remains that the notion of Lilith has carried forward throughout the ages into the present.

—*ASJr*

MARATHON

Marathon, Greece: 490 BC.

Cynegeirus pointed at the beach over a mile away. "Well, there they are, sure enough."

Yes, thought Aeschylus, looking down the slope to the beach, where what looked to be several hundred triremes were drawn up on the sands. They only caught his attention for a moment, before his eyes moved up from the water to take in the multiple hundreds of campfires and tens of thousands of soldiers who sat around them. *And they brought enough of the bastards, didn't they,* he thought.

"They are sure to attack in the morning," said another man who had come with them from the city in the second group, organized around the fighters of the Eastern Deme of Athens. "Then we'll see if the Persian slaves can stand up to free men."

"I hear they have cavalry," said Aeschylus, looking over at the third man. "And archers. And we have neither."

"Then stay back and cower, Playwright, while real men fight," said the other man, turning on his heel and walking away.

And how many real battles have you been in? thought Aeschylus, who had fought in several already.

"Don't let his words hit you, brother," said Cynegeirus, reaching over and grabbing Aeschylus by the arm. "I know you're no coward.

We will stand and fight when it comes down to it. By the Gods we will."

If the Gods really care anything about us, thought the Playwright, who, though he expounded the power of the Gods in his works, was not so sure about how much they cared for mortal man.

"And then you can go and win some more of those Dionysia you're so proud of," said his brother with a laugh. "What is it now, three?"

"Only two," said the Playwright with a smile. He looked over at his brother, knowing that he saw a man who in appearance and dress was much like himself. Both were well made men, strong and fit, with the blond hair of the Ionians who had settled these lands. Both were armored in breastplates of bronze, with shoulder cops that covered much of their upper arms. Skirts of leather straps protected their groins and upper legs, while greaves of bronze protected their lower legs from knee to ankle. His brother wore his helmet, also of bronze, with projecting side pieces to protect his face from projectiles like sling stones and arrows, and a nose piece performing much the same task for the front. Aeschylus had his helmet hanging by its straps from his spear. Both carried their large, heavy shields strapped across their backs, and they wore almost identical short swords on their left hips. The cloaks on their backs were multipurpose garments, protection against sun and rain, blankets at night.

He looked again at the Persian camp, seeing men on the move, but not the concerted effort of an army at the alert. He had no idea what kind of arms and armor they used, whether it was the equal to their own, or not. More movement caught his eye, and he saw men on horseback moving around the outskirts of the camp, and realized that the Persian were warding their camp this night. *Of course they are. They're conquerors, and are well trained in the art of war.*

"May I join you?" asked another voice, as a young man in fine armor walked up on them.

"Do I know you?" asked Cynegeirus of the newcomer.

I've seen him around, thought Aeschylus, looking over the man and his expensive armor, the panoply of an aristocrat. *But only recently.* That in and of itself was unusual in a city like Athens, with a population less than a hundred and fifty thousand, and less than forty thousand of those citizens. People might not know everyone, but they were sure to run into people often enough over the years to recognize them, and Aeschylus prided himself on his memory. Unless he was a Persian spy. He looks Greek enough, but there were Greeks living within the Empire.

"I am Akakios," said the young man, coming forward and offering his hand, something done often enough in times of peace, but having no real meaning among armed men. "I am a visitor from Thebes, come to visit my cousin who lives in Athens."

Aeschylus took the man's hand after he had shaken his brother's. Akakios' grip was firm, and he thought again on how the man had moved. Like a cat, more grace than most men could muster. The movements of a professional warrior? Or something else? And the name, which translated into innocent, or not evil. Was there significance there, or not?

"And where is your cousin?" asked Aeschylus.

"Kleitos is unable to go to war, after his injuries."

"He was hurt in battle?"

"No, by a fall from a horse," said the man, with no more emotion than someone announcing that their beloved relative had stepped in horse shit. "I have no friends here among this army, so I was wondering if I might be able to tag along with you gentlemen?"

"Why not," said Cynegeirus, glancing over at his brother. "You could join our deme for the battle. We could always use another good man."

And we can always keep an eye on a stranger. And find out why you are really here.

* * *

"And what news of the Spartans?" asked Datis, the general in charge of the Persian force, standing on the beach in front of the ship that had brought him to these shores.

"They are celebrating yet another of their interminable religious festivals," said Artaphernes, the deputy commander of the army. "Every week it seems as if they are bowing down to something or other for most of the week. What good to have such soldiers if they are paralyzed by religious fear most of the time?"

Datis nodded as he looked at the third man of their group, Hippias, the ex-tyrant of Athens, and a traitor to his own people. The man had been thought to be the trump for the Persians, the man who could convince the pro-Persian faction among the Athenians to open the gates to their city. So far he had been long on promises, and short on delivery.

"It is good that the Spartans are not here," agreed Datis, thinking of those redoubtable soldiers, thought to be the best infantry in the world. Spartans were raised from birth to be soldiers, and fought without fear, in total confidence that the men around them would never desert their sides. Fortunately, there were only several thousand of the warriors, and they needed to keep many at home to keep their slaves, the Helots, under control. "Unfortunately, the Athenians are good infantry as well, and I really don't want to charge our own men into the teeth of their spears. Now, if they could be convinced to come down upon the plain, where our archers could whittle away at them while our cavalry attacks their flanks."

"You outnumber them six to one," growled Hippias, looking up at the hills where his own people stood waiting in the early morning sun. "They have no archers, only peltasts, whom your bowmen outrange by two hundred yards. And they have no cavalry."

"And, as I told you before, Hippias," said Datis, glaring at the man. "I cannot afford to suffer heavy losses against this one city. When we get them where we have the advantage, whether they come at us or retreat, we will attack and roll over them, and break the spirit of the other cities at the same time."

"I still think you should attack, now," said Hippias, returning the glare. "If you delay the Spartans will come, and then the task will be so much more difficult."

Yes, it will, thought the Persian General, staring at the lines of the Greeks over a mile away. They were in their characteristic phalanx, men sheltered behind a wall of shields, their long spears thrust ahead. Even cavalry would have difficulty pushing through that hedge of spears. But if hit from the flank, or the rear, the weight of the horses and riders would cut through the formations like so much butter. *And besides, if they march those slow moving masses of men toward us, we can take them under arrow fire for a considerable time, taking out many of them before they can come to grips with our lighter infantry.*

A horseman came riding up, reigning to a halt before the command party and jumping down from his mount. "We have spotted more infantry nearing the Athenian camp," said the scout, saluting his generals. "At least a thousand strong. We were only a scouting party, my Lord, and did not have the horses to attack."

"Understood," said Artaphernes, under whose charge were the cavalry, of which the Persians had just over a thousand. "Were they Spartans?"

"I, I don't know, my Lord," said the scout.

"Did they wear red cloaks, and have a device like an upside down V on their shields?" asked Hippias, concerned tension in his voice.

"No, my Lord," said the scout, looking over at the Athenian, then back to his commander. "We saw no such cloaks, or marking on the shields."

"Then they aren't Spartans," said Hippias, shaking his head. "And their festival is not due to end until the moon is full, nine days from this one. They will not risk angering the Gods by marching sooner."

"Keep your men on watch of the newcomers until they enter the Athenian camp," Artaphernes told the scout. "And keep watch on any other columns that might march in to reinforce them."

The scout nodded, saluted, and vaulted back onto his horse.

"I still say you should attack the Athenians before they receive further reinforcements," said Hippias, his anger at the people who had exiled him showing in his eyes.

"And, since I command this army, we will attack when I say so," said Datis in a loud rumble. "And not before." The General turned back to his watching of the enemy army, wondering what thoughts were going through the minds of the men in charge of that force. *Surely they can't be thinking of attacking, not so badly outnumbered.* And he wondered why he wasn't completely confident about that, despite all the evidence in its favor.

* * *

"The men from Plataea have come," yelled a voice to the rear of the phalanx.

A loud cheer went up in acknowledgement of their reinforcements. The men of that city were not really known for their martial prowess, unlike the Spartans, or even the Athenians, truth be told. But they were Greeks, trained hoplites, equipped much as the Athenians.

"How many have come?" asked Aeschylus, looking toward the officer that led this deme.

"They say a thousand," replied that man with a frown. "But there cannot be more than six hundred warriors in the entire city, after the losses they suffered in their last battle.

Aeschylus nodded, thinking back to that fight, in which he had served with the expeditionary force from Athens. There had been no doubt that the other Greeks would come out of gratitude for the aid that Athens had provided. *And where are the others*, he thought, looking down the row of men in which he stood. Even with the men from Plataea they still had less than eleven thousand soldiers, and the Persians many times that number.

"Why don't they attack?" asked Akakios, his voice showing none of the stress or fear that the rest of them felt. "They have all the advantages."

"Not quite," said Cynegeirus, looking over at their new friend. "We command the high ground, and that negates much of the advantage of their cavalry. We can crouch behind our shields up here if they try to storm us with arrows. And we are Greeks."

Aeschylus looked at the face of the young warrior. He was still not sure about the man, who seemed to be lacking in knowledge he would expect any Greek to have. And, as the afternoon sun rose higher in the sky and bathed the warriors in its heat, Akakios' face was covered by a mere sheen of the heavy sweat that covered every other visage in sight.

There is something not right about him, thought Aeschylus, trying not to stare at the young man. He didn't seem to respond to things like the other Greeks. Everyone around him was brimming with nervous energy. He could smell the fear in their sweat. The same fear that was running through his body. The fear of any rational man who was looking across the field at his own possible death. He had felt it in other battles, and believed it was universal in any healthy human. Not cowardice. All of these men would do their duty to their city and their fellows, despite the fear.

But there was no feeling of fear on Akakios. It was as if he had never faced his own mortality, like that thought had never crossed his mind. *Has he never been in battle?* thought the Greek, looking at the way the man held his weapons. The stranger stood like a veteran soldier, so he didn't think it was that lack of experience.

Is he a demigod? thought Aeschylus, taking in the handsome features of the man. He was attractive enough. In his younger days he, like most Athenian men, had his dalliances with other young men. In military service it was actually felt to be a good thing that lovers fought side by side, as a man was less likely to dessert his bedmate than merely a friend. He found himself attracted to the young man, even though his mannerisms were strange.

The Playwright dismissed that thought. He needed to find out what the man was about, not fantasize about him. Find out why he was motivated to fight in a battle not involving any of his own friends, neighbors or family.

"Why don't they attack?" asked his brother, breaking him from his contemplation of the stranger. "They outnumber us badly. And they outclass us in several ways."

Aeschylus nodded as he looked back at the enemy formation across the mile of open ground. He thought there must be scared men over there as well, even if they heavily outnumbered their enemy. The Greeks had a reputation as warriors. But they held their places in line, light shields held steady, spears grounded. On the flanks were the cavalry, five hundred horsemen in each group, better armored and equipped than the infantry. They were one of the weapons the Greeks were afraid of. Some city states had cavalry. Thessaly for one. But they weren't prevalent in most of the city armies in this land of hills and mountains.

"And we should just go ahead and attack them if they don't have the courage to come to us," continued his brother.

Aeschylus nodded again, not really agreeing with his brother, but to keep up his part of the conversation. He could imagine that cavalry crashing into the flanks of the phalanx before it could turn, rolling them up and scattering them, while the other weapon he feared galled them from a distance. And that galling force, several thousand strong, stood in front of the Persian infantry, recurve bows strung and arrows ready. If the phalanx attacked them, they would have a good long time to rain arrows down on the heads of the Greeks, launching them over the shield wall.

That's the weakness of our way of fighting, thought the Playwright, who, though not a strategos, was still an intelligent man who understood warfare. He had served in the citizen army all of his adult life, subject to call up whenever the interests of Athens were threatened. And he knew that the Greek way of fighting, predicated by the way the that all the other Greeks fought, was very effective against other thick lines of spearmen, such as themselves. When on the move they were unstoppable by other infantry. But they were clustered together in easy targets for bowmen, and were slow moving, and slow to change their facing. And he knew the generals were afraid that if they marched across that plain they would be bled by arrows, then overrun by cavalry, and their city would be defenseless.

And it will be almost as bad if we retreat, with their archers running up from the rear to cover us with an arrow storm, while the cavalry picks off our stragglers. We should have stayed at the city, and let them come to us.

And that thought brought the image of the Persian cavalry ravaging Attica, burning the crops and killing the livestock of the Athenians, until they found themselves besieged in a city that was starving. There seemed no good answer to this, except to avoid arousing the Persians in the first place, and that was no longer possible.

His brother uncapped his wine skin and took a swig, then passed it to the Playwright. Aeschylus took a large swallow, feeling pleasure as the sweet beverage went down his throat, then gave Akakios a questioning look. The young warrior shook his head, looking back at the Persians with an intense look on his face, eyes narrowed.

What are you thinking, my young friend? Do you regret coming to the aid of a city not your own, trapped here on this plain with the rest of us.

Eventually the sun went down, night fell, and the armies left their positions and returned to their camps. It was unheard of to fight at night, when confusion could reign supreme in both forces. Still, sentries were posted, since neither wanted to take a chance that the other side might try a raid under cover of darkness.

"I want to listen in on the meeting," Aeschylus told his brother, motioning toward the center of the, where a great number of the men had gathered to listen to the leaders hash out their strategy for the next day. *And I hope it's something other than standing out in the sun all day looking at the damned Persians.*

"Let's," agreed Cynegeirus, a smile on his face. "As long as we don't miss the evening meal."

"Hah, that will be hours in the making," said Aeschylus, starting toward the meeting area. "The cooks for our deme will be at it for at least another hour."

Aeschylus saw that Akakios was following, and wondered if it was a good thing to let the stranger hear the deliberations of the generals. *But he has done nothing to warrant imprisonment, and otherwise, he is free to come and go in this camp, just like the rest of us.*

The generals sat together on one side of the fire, talking in loud enough voices for the crowd to hear. They had been elected to their posts, and so were responsible to the citizens they led. And, though one was the leader each day on a rotating basis, they still had to reach a consensus before any action could be considered. Which, thought Aeschylus, listening to the men talk, may not have been the best way to run an army. Especially with ten headstrong men elected to the command.

"We need to attack them," roared Miltiades, who, though only one of the Strategoi, was the man most of the rest deferred to, even on their selected day, due to his experience. "Standing out in the sun merely saps the strength of our men."

"But they outnumber us," said another of the Strategoi, his expression one of worry. "And they have cavalry and archers."

"Since when have Greeks concerned themselves with mere numbers?" asked Miltiades with a sneer. "It takes three of the effeminate Persians to equal one of our hoplites in battle. And our formation and discipline gives us an even greater edge."

"Perhaps we can flank them," said another of the leaders. "Send a force to strike them from the side while the phalanx marches into their front."

"There are swamps to the north and south of the Persians," said yet another of the generals, looking at the last man to speak with an expression of disbelief. "You would have our own men drown in those wretched marshes?"

"Gentlemen," said Callimachus, the War-Archon, who had been elected by the citizens to be the overall commander, the arbitrator of the disparate views of the leaders. "We accomplish nothing with attacks on each other. We must come up with a plan, one that will get us out of this trap we are in."

"And it is a trap," called out the second Strategos to speak. "We can't attack without leaving ourselves vulnerable to cavalry. And we can't retreat without opening ourselves up to flank attacks by those same horsemen. So what do we do"

"We attack," said Miltiades, standing up and looking out over the gathered men. "We march at them in mass and crush them. We detail demes to guard our flanks, and present the cavalry with an unwavering hedge of spear points to drive them off."

"And when they circle around and take us in the rear, what then?" called out one of the citizens from around the fire.

"And the Persian line is longer than ours," yelled out another man. "What about when they curl around us, and we're surrounded?"

"I do not think we should attack under the current conditions," said Callimachus, raising a hand. "We will wait for the Persians to attack us, so we can use our position against them."

"And if the current conditions change?" asked Miltiades, a sly expression on his face.

"And then we will see," answered the War-Archon with a nod. "If the conditions are right, we will attack. If not, we will stand our ground and wait them out."

Aeschylus thought about the meeting later, when he was sitting on a log beside his brother, taking in the warmth of his demes fire and chewing on some mutton that had been prepared for dinner. *We cannot come to a decision. We will be sitting here until the Gods come down from Olympus, if we haven't died of old age before then.*

"Then you think we should attack?" asked Akakios, talking around a mouthful of pork.

"I didn't say that," said the Playwright, raising an eyebrow.

"I could tell by your expression at the meeting. You think we are wasting our time standing in a phalanx all day. And I agree with you. Nothing is being accomplished waiting."

"When the Spartans come, all will change," said Cynegeirus, breaking open a loaf of bread. "They will insist on attacking."

"That's because they are a bunch of homicidal maniacs," said Aeschylus, shaking his head. "Oh, I know they're the best soldiers in the world. The best fighters. The most disciplined. But they are not almost the deepest thinkers.

"But maybe what we need are homicidal maniacs," said Aeschylus, smiling. "We need someone willing to charge the Persians, to bring them to battle, and to shame our leaders."

He looked over at Akakios, who sat there saying nothing, looking from face to face, his eyes glowing slightly in the firelight. *And just what are you doing here, my young friend, who watches everything, and listens to everyone? What are you gathering this information for? Surely not the Persians, or you would have already been gone from here after hearing what you needed to hear at that meeting. So what are you? Someone sent from the Gods to save us from our own stupidity?*

"I am for bed," said Cynegeirus, putting the last of his bread in his ration bag. "The morning will come early enough, and I am not looking forward to standing all day once more."

"Perhaps the Persians will attack," said Akakios, a hopeful smile on his face. "And then we can go back to the cities, and I can again enjoy your plays in the amphitheater."

"You know of my work," said Aeschylus, feeling the pleasure of one who finds an appreciative mind who values his efforts.

"You are one of the reasons I came to Greece," said the young man. "I mean to Athens, from my own city. You are known throughout Greece as one of the greatest creative minds of your generation."

You said to Greece, then realized your mistake, thought Aeschylus, looking at the man out of the corner of his eye. *And where did you come from, before you got to Greece? Olympus?*

"I always appreciate an admirer," said the Playwright after stifling a yawn. "Now I am to bed as well. As my brother said, the morning comes early."

Aeschylus stretched out on his cloak next to his brother and wrapped himself in its warmth. As soon as he was recumbent he fell into a deep sleep, punctuated by dreams starring Akakios in many roles, a sign of the Playwright's confusion about the identity of the young man.

In the morning he woke with confused impressions of those dreams. In one he had seemed to have awakened to see the campfire had died down to nothing, and Akakios was still seated, staring into the coals, as if he were thinking, and was not concerned with rest that night.

* * *

Another day of standing in line, a replay of the last one. Aeschylus was again standing next to his brother, Akakios on the other side, looking across the plain at the same formation they had seen the day before. And again the Persian cavalry was conspicuous on the flanks of the enemy, while the archers were arrayed as before in front of the infantry.

The same death trap as before, hoping to lure us into an attack, thought Aeschylus. *But could we attack and carry the day.* From what he had seen of the Persian infantry, he was sure the hoplites would roll right over them. The question being, once again, could they withstand the storm those archers were sure to launch, and would the flanks or rear be able to hold off the cavalry.

"I wish someone would do something," said someone from down the line.

"Like what?" asked one of the tough sub-officers of the group. "Our generals aren't about to attack, and it looks to me like those bastards down there are happy to just wait us out."

"Until the Spartans get here?" asked Cynegeirus in a surprised tone. "Why in the name of Hades would they do that? The damned cloaks of the Spartans would be red with their blood at the end of the day."

"And all the Persians need do then is board their ships and row out of here, to land somewhere else," said the officer in disgust.

Cynegeirus snorted and gave his brother a disgusted look. Aeschylus looked to the north of the Persians, on the shore of the bay, where their triremes were dragged up onto the sands. A strong guard watched the ships, and the swamps that protected the Persian flanks also protected the ships from raids. *And we can't use our own ships to strike at them, because here we stand, the men who would man our own vessels. We are still in a corner, with no way out unless the Spartans rescue us. And that depends on what the entrails say of whatever animal they slaughter for their pre-deployment auger. It's a wonder they ever got their reputation as such fierce warriors, when it seems like everything they do keeps them from going into battle.*

The Persians started yelling up at the Greeks, their words unintelligible in the distance, but loud enough en-mass to be heard. They were yelling in their own language, but one word was Greek, and when the Persians all screamed it at the same time, there was no mistaking that word. Coward.

The men around him cursed, and some started calling for the phalanx to move forward so they could silence those tongues. But the commanders would have nothing of it, and they stood fast with the discipline of Greek soldiers. The Persians heckled them throughout the morning and into the afternoon. The Greeks yelled back, those who knew some Persian teaching the others some imprecations against the enemy. It might have angered some of the Persians. But it didn't make them attack like some had hoped, and again the sun went down that evening to a stalemate, two armies leaving their ranks for the night.

Again the generals argued. Again Miltiades called for an attack, the other generals argued against, and the War-Archon settled it with the same words as before.

"I guess you are disappointed, Akakios," said Cynegeirus as they sat in camp again. Their deme was to provide part of the night security, and the men were trying to rest before they had to stand watch for several hours in the dead of the dark. "Not what you were expecting?"

"I never really know what to expect," said the young man, taking a swig of wine and looking into the fire. "But whatever it is, it is always of interest to me."

"Wait until you are actually engaged in the fight," said Cynegeirus, laughing. "After you have stood with other men, and seen your friends dying around you while you return the favor to your enemy, then you can tell me how interesting a battle is."

"I have seen battle," said the young man in a distant voice. "It would probably surprise you to know how many men, aye, and women, I have seen go into the long night at the hand of their fellow human. And I have sent some of them on that journey myself."

"You cannot be but twenty, if that," said Cynegeirus with another laugh. "I doubt you have seen more than one fight, if that."

"It might surprise you how many fights I have seen," Akakios told Cynegeirus, looking the older man straight in the eye.

He turned that gaze on Aeschylus, and the urbane man felt his spine shiver at the intensity of that look. The face was young, but the eyes were those of someone who had seen much, not all of it pleasant. And the Playwright had to wonder just how old the man was, despite his appearance of youth.

Dinner this night was much like that the night before, mutton, some pork, and what vegetables the forages could find that day. Aeschylus wondered why the Persians didn't use some of their cavalry to harass the foragers, but figured there was really no way to get them past the Greeks unseen, unless they rode quite a ways down the coast. And it seemed that the Persian general wanted to keep his horsemen close.

After they ate their fill of their one good meal of the day, and storyteller entertained the deme with his rendition of tale of the Gods that most of the Greeks worshipped. All sat in rapt attention, including Akakios, whose eyes were glued to the man telling the tale.

"Prometheus was one of the Titans," said the man in his mesmerizing voice. "There had always been strife between the Gods and the Titans they came from, much as children continually argue with their parents. The Gods had forbidden that man learn the secrets of nature, preferring them to remain simple, pastoral people who would worship them, without the concerns of civilization."

Akakios laughed a bit when the Gods were mentioned. Aeschylus did not hold that against him, taking it for disbelief. Unlike the religiously zealous Spartans, many Greeks were apostate where the Gods were concerned. Aeschylus himself was sometimes not sure of their existence, but most times decided that it was better to play it safe, and pray and sacrifice to the Gods he had been raised with. If the young man wanted to play with fate, that was his business, and the Playwright would not say a word.

"But Prometheus felt sorry for the humans, huddling in their hovels and caves at night, afraid of the dark and the beasts that prowled it. Added to that was his wish to get back at the Gods, who had usurped his own kinds' dominion of the Earth. So Prometheus, regretting his decision to ally with the Gods against the other Titans, decided he would go against the wishes of Zeus. He found the flame in the jar where Zeus kept it and stole it, then found an unknown herdsman and gifted him with fire. The herdsman shared it with his tribesmen, and soon the night was lit against its terrors, and people ruled the darkness as the day, and the gift of fire spread across the Earth."

"What fools," mumbled Akakios in a low voice. "I gifted them with fire, not some damned made up Titan." He must have realized he was talking without meaning to, and looked up at Aeschylus, who had heard the mumble speech.

"What do you mean, you gave us fire?" he asked the man, who he no longer saw as young. The eyes that looked back at him glowed in the flames, almost as if they were on fire themselves.

"I was also making up a story," said Akakios with a grin. "You surely understand flights of imagination."

"Mankind learned how to cook their meat, and now save the best portions of the animal for themselves," continued the storyteller. "They gave the fat and the burnt bones to the Gods, which angered the deities. And Zeus tricked the woman, Pandora, into opening the box of disasters, releasing the troubles of the world upon mankind, which had started the long struggle to civilization. Disease was released, and famine, and wars, and man raised his hand against his brother and slew him in battle. Cities rose and were destroyed, but still mankind progressed, until our own civilization, the greatest the world has ever seen, was birthed in these mountains and valleys."

"And what happened to Prometheus?" yelled someone from the camp. Most of the men added their voices to the call, though all here had heard the story many times. But listening to a voice like the storyteller's recounting the tale was their night's entertainment, and they still sat in rapt attention.

"Prometheus?" asked the storyteller, looking around the camp until his eyes met those of Akakios, and he stopped for a moment to stare at the young man who was stranger to them all. "Zeus was enraged at Prometheus, the one Titan he thought he could trust. He could not think of a punishment that would suit Prometheus' crime, and he sat for a time thinking of an appropriate fate for the Titan. Finally, he came up with a fit punishment, and Prometheus was taken far to the east, where he was chained to a mountain, and a great vulture was set upon him each day to eat the liver from his living body. He healed again each night, and the torture resumed the next day, and will last for eternity. A so is the fate of those who would disobey the will of Zeus."

Akakios, shook his head and smiled again, looking over at Aeschylus. *He is Prometheus*, thought the Playwright. *But not the Titan, like the tales say. How long have you been alive? Can you be killed?* Then it was Aeschylus' turned to shake his head and smile. *What nonsense is this? He is just a man. A strange man, but human nonetheless. My mind plays tricks on me this night from the fatigue of standing in the sun all day. Tomorrow I will remember these thoughts and wonder what got a hold of me.*

"You have a great imagination, young man," he told Akakios, taking up his wineskin and taking a swallow, then passing it to the other warrior.

"As do you, Playwright," said the other man, taking the skin, then tipping it up and taking a large swallow. "It serves you well on the stage, but maybe not so much on the battlefield."

"What is he talking about?" asked Cynegeirus, taking the offered wineskin from Akakios.

"There is more to Akakios than meets the eye," said Aeschylus, the idea for a play taking form in his mind. A play about the real Prometheus, the Titan, finally freed from his eternal torture and walking the face of the Earth, interacting with humanity. And bringing new wonders to the human race? Or new tragedy?

* * *

"In two more days the Spartans march," said Artaphernes, looking across at the Athenian camp, its fires burning bright in the distance. He looked up to the sky, where the almost full moon had risen. "Once it is full, their festival will be over, and they will be on their way here. And Darius will not be pleased if you are defeated on this field."

"Then we must not allow that to happen," said Datis, looking back at his cavalry commander. "We must do something to break this stalemate before the Spartans arrive. Then we can defeat them in detail as well."

"And what can we do to break the stalemate? Hippias has not delivered on his promise to give us the city, and these men in front of us have no reason to abandon their positions without the threat to their home."

Datis was silent for some moments, ruminating on his options, then came up with a plan he was sure would work. "You are to load your cavalry on the ships this night, Artaphernes. Sail to Athens, debark, and threaten the city with your horsemen."

"Not much good we can do against a city," complained the other general.

"You don't really have to do anything but make your presence known. Burn manors and farmhouses, cut down the groves, and set their remains a fire in the sight of the city. Word will get to these Athenians here, and they will be forced to retreat back to their homes. And then we will catch them between our forces and slaughter them."

"That could work," said the other man with a sly smile on his face. The smile turned into a frown, and he looked his commander in the face. "But don't you need the cavalry to guard your flanks? What if they attack while I am gone?"

"The archers should be enough. If they come at us, we will pepper their slow moving formation with arrows and kill enough of them to disrupt their formation and destroy their morale. And they will still go fleeing back to their city, only there will be less of them for us to deal with."

"Very well," said Artaphernes, nodding. "I will load the cavalry up within the next couple of hours, and we will sail to Athens. And, by the will of the Gods, we will destroy these upstarts for the glory of our Emperor."

* * *

"Something is happening," said Akakios as he shook the shoulder of Aeschylus.

"What," stammered the man as he fought his way out of a deep sleep, and a dream about the Titan Prometheus, and the hellish punishment he had been sentenced to.

"A messenger came running through a moment ago," said Akakios, reaching over to shake Cynegeirus' awake. "He was talking with one of the officers. Said something about the Persians loading their cavalry on their ships."

"Why in the hell would they do that?" asked Cynegeirus, rubbing the sleep from his eyes. "Were they loading up their infantry too? Perhaps giving up and going home?"

"He made no mention of their infantry, but perhaps if we go to the center of the camp we can find out."

Aeschylus had to agree with the young man. He looked at his pile of armor for a moment, deciding that he didn't need to don it at this hour, and wrapped himself in his cloak against the chill of night. "Let's go see what this is about."

The three men made their way through the sleeping camp, and the Playwright had to wonder again at the hearing of the young man, when the messenger didn't seem to have caused that much of a stir through the rest of the camp.

The generals were all awake, more or less, some alert, some still trying to get their wits about them. But they saw the messenger, dressed in loose dark clothing.

No, not a messenger, thought Aeschylus, looking over the man. *A spy. Or at least a scout, lurking around the Persian camp.* And then he was too busy listening for further thoughts.

"And their cavalry was being loaded aboard their ships, General," said the scout, kneeling in front of Miltiades, who was scheduled to lead the next day.

"Why would they do that?" asked another of the generals, one with a confused look on his face.

"I overheard some of the talk," said the scout. "They mentioned Athens. I think they were going to move the cavalry to Athens and attack the city."

"Then we must run to the city before they attack. All that are left there are old men and cripples." The General speaking looked with an alarmed expression at the other leaders.

"They are veterans, and though not fit for the front line, they can fight against horsemen within the city," said Miltiades, locking the other General with a glare. "And if we run for the city the Persians will pursue, and we will be caught between two forces. No," he roared, standing up. "The Persian army is now without its cavalry, the biggest threat to our infantry. Now is the time to attack. Attack, I say, and drive them from our land."

"And their cavalry?"

"Their cavalry will get back aboard their ships and leave our land if we drive the army away," said Miltiades, sitting back down and motioning for a servant to bring him a goblet of wine.

"And if we wait for the Spartans?"

"Then we allow their cavalry to ride rampant over our homeland for four days?" asked Miltiades, taking the goblet in hand. "For a week? And come home to find our agricultural lands destroyed?"

Miltiades took a great gulp of wine and wiped his lips, then stood again. "No, we must settle this here, tomorrow."

"And their archers? While we march toward them in formation, they will rain shafts upon us for hundreds of paces."

"And we can't cover their front in a phalanx," called out another General. "They will be able to engulf our formation and attack us from all sides."

"Then we do something different," said Miltiades with a smile. "Something that surprises them."

"Our way of fighting is successful," said the last General to speak. "We are trained in its use, and the men know what to do in most situations. And you want them to adopt something new out of the blue. Have the Gods made you mad?"

Miltiades looked over at Callimachus, the War-Archon. "You have the final vote, Callimachus. What say you?"

"We will see in the morning," said the older man, holding up a hand to keep the other leaders from shouting their protests. "We will see what they have, and you will tell me how you will deal with their dispositions, and then we will see."

* * *

"I don't see their cavalry," said Cynegeirus, looking across the mile of plain between them and the Persians. "But it looks like their be damned archers are prepared."

"Why do your people not use archers?" asked Akakios, looking over at Cynegeirus. "They would seem to give you advantages in battle, much as they do for the Persians."

Your people, thought Aeschylus, taking in every word. *Do you mean Athenians, or Greeks?* He knew most of the other Greeks didn't use masses of archers, except for the men of Crete, who were willing to sell their formations to the highest bidder. There were also slingers across the Mediterranean, who were in some ways even more effective than bowmen. And there were archers among all the Greek cities, huntsmen, but their bows were not war bows, and were not very effective as weapons of war.

"We have some skirmishers," said Cynegeirus, motioning to the couple of hundred men who stood in front of the phalanx, holding handfuls of short javelins.

Aeschylus nodded, agreeing with his brother, but knowing that those men, the Peltasts, who were very good with their javelins, but not for much else. They were considered the lowest of the low of the army, unarmored, unable to stand in battle once their projectiles were used up. Those projectiles were even more effective than arrows, within their range. Unfortunately, the bow outranged them by at least a factor of four, and most of the Peltasts would be dead from arrow fire before they got within range of a cast.

"But the bowmen are so much more effective," said the young stranger. "I am very surprised that people of your intelligence don't use the most effective weapons possible."

"We have what we have," said Cynegeirus, his look telling the young man he didn't want to carry on this conversation.

"Listen up men," yelled an officer, walking to the front of their deme. "In a moment we are going to move forward in our formation."

"About time," said Cynegeirus under his breath. "We will roll over them."

"But before we get eight hundred yards from their archers we are going to change our formation. All you men are to shift to the left. The men of **Plataea** will join more of our soldiers on the left flank while one deme holds the center. Then we will…"

* * *

"They're marching forward, General Datis," said one of the officers, pointing toward the Athenian line.

"Give my orders to the archers to take them under rapid and continuous fire when they get in range. We will litter the field with their bodies before they hit our lines."

"And the infantry, General?"

"We will envelop them when what's left comes at our lines. Once surrounded, they will be easy pickings for our men. We will cut through their flanks and their rear, and kill them where they stand."

The officer saluted and ran off, and Datis motioned for his scribe.

"Take down a message to king Darius," he told the scribe. "Tell him of our great victory on this day, when the warriors of the Greeks were annihilated by our brave men."

And the fools march to their deaths, he thought, watching as the brave men came forward, soon to die under his spears and arrows. *We will erect a monument on this site to their bravery, and how their courage led them to defeat.*

* * *

One of the officers ran ahead and stopped at a point a hundred yards further, while the phalanx continued to advance. Aeschylus felt the fear before battle taking hold, and knew that all of the men around him were feeling the same thing. *Most of them*, he corrected, as he looked over at Akakios, who showed no fear at all. The pipes were playing as they marched, marking the rhythm of their steps, and soon they would be to the point where the plan would unfold.

"Sons of the Hellenes," yelled the Playwright in his strong voice. "Fight for the freedom of your country. Fight for the freedom of your children and your wives, for the gods of your fathers and for the sepulchers of your ancestors. All are now staked upon the strife!"

The men around him cheered, and the cheer carried through the ranks even to those who had not heard him speak. The cheering chased away the fright, and the men stood tall as they marched.

The song of the pipes changed, the signal, and Aeschylus, his brother and all of their deme turned to the right and ran, to expand the line and thicken the flanks. The maneuver took less than a minute, and then the soldiers all turned to face the Persians again, waiting for the next command. The pipes played another tune, and the officers in their formation yelled at the top of their voices. "Charge them. Run as fast as your feet will take you. Yell at the top of your lungs, and hit spears on shields."

With that the eleven thousand Greek hoplites ran toward the Persians, at first the swiftest forging ahead, until the officers called them back to stay with the pack. Aeschylus struck his shield with his spear with every other step, just like all the rest. And yelled at the top of his lungs, adding to the thunderous din of the charging army.

* * *

"What in all the hells are they doing," shouted Datis as the Greeks left their phalanx and spread their line, so that his would no longer overlap theirs. He stared as they started forward at a run, clashing spears on shields and yelling at the top of their lungs. He looked to the infantry standing to his front and saw from the motion of the men that the sight of the charging enemy was frightening them. It was not what they expected from the Greeks, and the unexpected in battle was not something the Persian infantry was used to handling.

"The archers will kill them," shouted out the General to his men. "Bring all the commanders to me," he told his messengers, looking at the advancing line. "I think I see another weakness we can exploit."

And then the Greeks were within range of his archers, and the first flight of arrows was launched.

* * *

"Arrows," yelled many voices simultaneously, just after what looked like a dark cloud left the ground and started arcing through the air.

"Get your shield up, you idiot," he told his brother, holding his own at an angle that covered his head and shoulders from the front, and his body from overhead. The arrows whistled down at the same time the archers were launching another volley. Some plunged into the shields and stuck quivering in the wood. Others bounced off. And some more struck the helmets and shoulder guards of Greeks who were not holding their shields properly. And in most cases bounced from the tough bronze of the armor. There were a few strikes to flesh, mostly into arms, or a leg, and a couple of men fell out of the rush when a limb gave out under them.

The second volley came in and did much the same, dropping a few more men out of formation while the rest forged on. The third volley came down, then the fourth, with similar results. The fifth came in from straight ahead, and it took out as many men as the previous four combined. But by now the Greeks were holding their shields to the front, and though there were some more thigh wounds, most of the arrows that got around or over the shields bounced from the armor of bronze.

An archer notched an arrow and raised it to shoot at Aeschylus at point blank range. The Athenian's spear struck first, plunging through the chest of the man, sending the arrow into the sky and the archer to the ground, dying. Cynegeirus speared his man, and Aeschylus caught a glimpse of Akakios using his spear in series of short thrusts that dropped men to the ground to bleed out. The young stranger moved like a machine, every strike perfect, right on target. Then the time for watching was over as the Playwright ran down an archer who was turning to flee and shoved his spear through the man's back.

It was a slaughter among the archers, and some of them dropped to their knees as their bows hit the ground, begging for mercy. There was no mercy in the men of Greece. These people had come here to enslave them in the name of their Emperor, and because of that the Greeks felt no pity for them. What archers remained on the field slid back through the ranks of their infantry, leaving over half of their number dead on the ground.

The middle of the Persian line, reinforced, thickened, moved forward to attack the Greeks. They slammed into the shields of the thin line in the center and pushed. The line held, men bracing their feet and pushing back with their shields. Persian spears slid from bronze armor, while Greek spears pushed through leather or wicker armor like it was flesh. The line held, the Greeks fighting to keep the Persians from splitting their formation and taking the army from the rear.

"Attack," yelled Miltiades, taking charge of the right flank, waving his short blade in the air. "Cut through the bastards. Get on their flanks."

Aeschylus had fought in other battles. The citizen soldiers of Athens were her army, and most of the men were veterans. They knew what to do, and set to the slaughter of the Persians in their front. The Persian line was thin here, only double that of the Greeks'. And the spears thrust and thrust until the ground ran red, and men were splashing blood into the air with every step.

Aeschylus was a veteran, but he had never experienced anything like this. He saw Akakios forging ahead, moving with speed and agility unmatched on the field. Not superhuman, but definitely that of an athlete who had turned his prowess to war. The young man's spear was gone, but he fought with two weapons, the short sword in his right hand, and the shield in his left. He bashed Persians in the face with the shield, then took their lives with the blade, before moving on swift feet to his next victim.

The Playwright stuck his spear through another Persian, but this time, when he tried to jerk it back, it refused to come, wedged into the bone of the man. He dropped the haft and pulled his sword from its sheath, and plunged into the fight like a madman.

"Turn the flanks, men," yelled Miltiades from the left, and Aeschylus caught a glimpse of the General wading into the battle along with his men. *That is a man I would follow to Hades*, thought Aeschylus, and he pivoted to the left and started driving into the flank of the Persian army. The Persians were still fighting hard, but the stink of fear was upon them. A little more push and they would break.

Aeschylus help to provide that push. The center was still holding, while the flanks cut their way through the Persians, and soon they were killing the enemy from the rear. That was enough, and the enemy army broke, men tossing shields to the ground so they could run faster. Most ran toward the ships, some into the swamps, a really bad choice, and the Greeks swarmed after them, cutting down men from behind.

"Don't follow them into the swamps," yelled Miltiades, waving his men away from that pursuit. "Get me those ships."

The Persians were swarming aboard their triremes, manning oars and trying to pull them off the sands. Scores had already gotten off the sands and were starting to pull out into the bay. But many more were still making the effort to get off.

Cynegeirus ran up to one of the ships and grabbed a rope that was still trailing from the front. "Help me to keep these bastards from getting away," yelled Cynegeirus, setting his feet and pulling with all of his strength.

"What the hell are you doing?" yelled Aeschylus, running toward his brother. An arrow flew from the ship and hit his brother, bouncing off the breastplate, but Cynegeirus dropped the rope in surprise. He ran forward and grabbed it again, much closer to the ship, and a Persian struck at his hands with a sword and cut completely through one wrist, and partially through the other, and the stricken man fell to the sand with a moan.

Another Persian appeared in the bow of the ship and aimed his bow at Cynegeirus. Before he could complete pulling the arrow to his ear a spear seemed to appear through his chest, and the arrow went awry, striking the sand. Aeschylus slid into the sand beside his brother, who stared in shock at the stump of his wrist, while blood spurted in the rhythm of sliced arteries from both wounds.

"What in the hell were you thinking?" asked Aeschylus, pulling off his cloak and slashing through the fabric with his sword.

"I didn't want the bastards to get away," croaked Cynegeirus in a faint voice. "They came here to enslave us, and I did not want to let them get away."

Aeschylus started to bind up the stump, but the flow of blood was already decreasing on its own, not a good sign at all. He had finished binding the most serious of the wounds and was starting on the second when Cynegeirus let out his death rattle and fell back onto the sand.

"He was a brave man," said Akakios, appearing beside the pair, kneeling on the sand. "But I think his attempt to stop the ship by himself was ill advised."

Aeschylus stared at the young stranger in disbelief. *Of course it was ill advised. But don't you have any feelings?*

"I saw what your brother did," said Miltiades, walking up, the smile leaving his face as he looked down on the body. The General was covered in gore, and no one who saw him could mistake him for a faint hearted leader who stayed in the rear. "He is a hero, and will receive a hero's monument."

Aeschylus nodded, feeling the tears starting to flow. It was all any Greek wanted, to be remembered past their death. He, hopefully, would be remembered for his plays, on into the future. Cynegeirus had done no great works in his life, nothing to be remembered by. Now he would have a monument, something for people who came this way to see, and remember the courage of an ordinary Greek soldier.

"Thank you," said Aeschylus, still working to come to terms that his brother was actually dead. "How many did we lose?"

"Little over a hundred men," said the General, his smile returning. "And the Persians lost many thousands out here in the open. And who knows how many in the swamp. We saw a lot of them run in, but very few have come out, and I feel the marsh is filled with their bodies."

The General looked around for a moment, then motioned to one of the soldiers to come over. "Pheidippides," said the General, putting a hand on the shoulder of the athletic young man. "Strip off your armor and run to Athens. Tell them of this great victory. Do not stop, and push straight to the city."

The young man nodded and ran off, heading for the camp where he could shed his armor and carry out Miltiades' instructions. Akakios followed the man with his eyes as he jogged away.

"That is a long run," said the young stranger. "Twenty-five miles?"

"More like twenty-six," said the General, standing up and turning away for a moment, before turning back to the Playwright. "You must write a play about this day. Then I can be immortalized as well. All of us can be remembered."

The General turned away again and started shouting orders. "Officers. Get your men together. We march on Athens within the hour. I have a feeling the Persians may head there, and I want to be there to greet them."

Aeschylus closed his brother's eyes and stood up, looking at Akakios.

"You will leave your brother here?"

"The camp followers will see to him, and we will have a proper ceremony, along with the others, when the Persians are no longer a threat."

"I fear they will be back," said Akakios. "You have not only defeated them this day. You have embarrassed them, and they will not take that lightly."

"Where are you from?" asked the Playwright, again surprised at the young stranger's depth of knowledge.

"Many places," said the man, smiling. "If I told you, you would say I was a liar."

"Olympus?"

"No. I am not a God, and not of them." The young man started to walk away.

"Will you march with us, back to the city?"

"I think not," said the young man, not turning around. "But remember me, when you engage in your flights of fancy."

I'll remember you my young friend. Prometheus indeed. Are you he, unbound from the punishment of Zeus? Or just a mortal man with a penchant for mystery?

He followed the young man with his eyes as he walked along the beach, heading north, away from the battlefield that had settled this invasion at least. A mist was coming off the water now as the sun began to set, and the man went from soldier, to shadow, to gone, as if he had disappeared into the mists of time.

Aeschylus looked down at his brother one more time, resolving to make sacrifices to the Gods in his memory. But now was for the living, and they still had a march to complete to make sure their city was protected. His city, his life, and his inspiration.

EAST OF THE SUN

Knowledge is power. Information is power. The secreting or hoarding of knowledge or information may be an act of tyranny camouflaged as humility.

—*Robin Morgan*

I

1424 A.D.

The treasure ships burned in the shallows of the great Yangtze River, streaking red and orange flames against the inky spread of the night sky. Crowds of townspeople gathered on the riverbank, gawking, their chatter blending like the inane cackle of cranes. Above them, dark smoke roiled as wood turned to ash along with my dreams, my pride, my—

A heavy hand landed on my shoulder. I tensed at the contact and glanced back sharply. A faint smile on the face of the old man standing behind me on the docks assured a friendly and familiar presence, but my racing heartbeat, fueled by fury and outrage, refused to settle.

Zhao Yun, my mentor and friend, was captain of a Fuchuan warship, one of the two hundred and fifty ships that had raced alongside the sixty-two treasure ships to protect them from pirates. His swift warship provided an ideal perch from which to view admiral Zheng He's armada, including the massive nine-masted treasure ships—their glorious promise now reduced to a funeral pyre for the dead dreams of the Middle Kingdom.

As if he had read my mind, Zhao Yun spoke, "Ma Huan, you are still young. There will be many other journeys…other expeditions for you." He stroked his wispy white beard. His voice creaked with age and a lifetime of exposure to the salt of the sea.

"None like these." I flung my hand out and shook my head. I fought to moderate my tone, but if my voice reflected my bitterness, I could not help it. The admiral's expeditions had *discovered* the world. The far-flung knowledge he uncovered, the knowledge *I* meticulously recorded, would have changed its peoples. "Why has the new emperor turned his eyes inward?"

"The emperor is the son of heaven. He is wise and—"

I scowled at Zhao Yun. He shut his mouth and looked away, but not quickly enough to conceal the raw grief I glimpsed in his eyes. His precious warship had been spared the flames of change, but no true sailor could have watched such magnificent treasure ships burn and remained unaffected. I sucked in a breath, but only inhaled soot. "Are you saying the emperor is right to curtail these expeditions?"

"The empire must be strong on the inside before it can display external strength. The emperor is concerned, rightly, that the Middle Kingdom cannot continue to support such lavish displays of generosity."

"The world *needs* lavish displays of generosity. They need to know that not all empires come as conquerors. They need to learn that the greatest empires come with open hands laden with gifts and knowledge."

Zhao Yun sighed. "You are still so idealistic, so young."

I bristled even though I was in the presence of my mentor. Zhao Yun was already old when I first met him eleven years earlier. I had been little more than a brash young man of twenty-nine, equipped with ambition but few skills. He encouraged me to use my innate talent for language, and when I became fluent in Arabic, he found a position for me as a translator for the great admiral Zheng He.

With the admiral and the treasure fleet, I had sailed across vast swaths of open sea. Together, we discovered people and cultures in lands we had never known existed—ice-choked continents in the north and the south, and a beautiful and vast realm called *Mei Guo*, rich with natural resources, east of the sun. I took meticulous notes and, although with far less success, visually mapped the routes we had taken; I considered it my other contribution to the expedition.

I stared at the burning ships. A muscle twitched in my cheek, and resentment closed like a fist around my heart. The expedition, everything it embodied, everything it promised, had been consumed by the flames of close-minded, short-sighted stupidity.

Zhao Yun laid his gnarled hand over my fist. "You cannot change everything, Ma Huan."

"And yet, it is important to try. You taught me so, yourself."

"I was a younger man then. Foolish—"

"Never foolish," I reassured him. "Did you not say it was the responsibility of those blessed with true knowledge to spread it freely and willfully?"

He grunted. "Knowledge has a price. Not many can afford to pay it, and those who can, may not want to. This is not your battle to fight."

"Then whose is it? Who has the knowledge I do? Who else can provide a record of the expeditions, of the worlds we have found, of the routes taken?"

"You are an excellent translator, and your notes of our travels are detailed, but you cannot do everything, Ma Huan."

"Oh? What can I not do?"

"Draw."

His matter-of-fact statement cracked a smile upon my face. "True, I am no cartographer. I have no sense of scale or proportion," I conceded. "But you do."

Zhao Yun shrugged, a graceful motion that belied his age. "I am too old, my memory too faulty."

I snorted. Oh, what a liar he was. Zhao Yun's prodigious memory was a frequent topic of conversation—one inspiring both awe and envy. If I had asked him what I had consumed at a shared meal years earlier, he would have provided an answer immediately. Inspiration sparked. My eyes bore into him. "I could document the facts of the admiral's expedition and his discoveries. You could draw the maps."

"I do not think the world is ready for such knowledge," he said.

"The world is never ready for knowledge, but I am not immortal. I cannot wait until the world is ready."

A sad smile, oddly laced with a secret amusement, lingered on Zhao Yun's face. "Ah, to be young again. To believe that you can change the world."

"Laugh at me all you will, but I will leave my mark upon the world. You will help me, will you not?"

He sighed. "You are like the son of my heart, but I have done all I can for you."

"There is this one more thing you can do for me. Help me chart the map of the world. Your knowledge of the routes we have taken is more precise than anyone's in the fleet."

He raised his dark eyes to stare across the water at the burning ships. In the flickering light, grief crossed his face. "Time grinds on. The world changes, and yet, it does not. What is there to tell?" he asked, his voice scarcely a whisper. "What else is there to share with the world?"

"The truth. We have to pass it on. The bright fire of knowledge blazes through the dark clouds of cowardice and ignorance."

"Perhaps you should write poetry instead." Exasperation filled his voice.

I shook my head. "You laugh, but this is no laughing matter." The waters of the Yangtze reflected the garish colors of the flame-streaked sky. On the far side of the river, a mast on a treasure ship toppled into the water. A thunderous splash sprayed droplets of water. They settled on my face and trickled like tears down my soot-stained cheeks. "The emperor can burn the ships but he cannot take away our memories. We can deny the benefit of our experience to those who need our knowledge to better themselves, but if we do, we are no better than the emperor."

Zhao Yun laid a hand upon my arm and glanced over his shoulder. No one stood near us, but I understood his caution. It would not do to be overheard casting insults upon the supposedly all-wise emperor. Yet, by the emperor's will, in the river, the treasure ships—built to *share* wealth, not hoard it—burned.

Bitterness churned through my stomach, hardening into a small, tight ball in the pit of my belly. The wealth I possessed lay in scribbled notes of the journeys I had taken. I reached into the pocket of my cotton shirt and pulled out a scroll, one of many I had filled with tiny words, each one testament to everything I had seen, heard, and done on the admiral's remarkable expeditions around the world.

I held knowledge in my hand.

I could fling my arms out and scatter the notes to the wind. I could watch the tiny pieces of paper float down to settle upon the Yangtze. I could allow the water to leech the ink away.

Or I could write my journal.

I looked up. Zhao Yun met my gaze. His eyes seemed to see all yet reveal nothing, and they burned into mine. Was he challenging me or encouraging me?

He spoke. "Some knowledge is forbidden fruit. Do not let yourself be tempted by its sweetness."

I shook my head. He took me for more of an idealist than I was. I did not pursue knowledge for its own sake. "Knowledge is the only weapon that builds upon itself, the only true weapon that passes through time from one generation to another." My grip tightened upon my scroll. "*This* is my gift to the world—the full account of the great admiral's expeditions and the maps of our travels."

Zhao Yun inclined his head. His countenance was bland, but somehow, I sensed he was pleased with me.

"Come to my home tomorrow," I told him. "We will chart the maps together."

He said nothing, but an indecipherable expression flickered across his face. For an instant, fear plucked at me, but the moment passed almost immediately. Zhao Yun would come to me. He, too, would leave his mark upon the world; I was certain of it. I offered him a final smile before turning my back on the burning ships to face the future.

* * *

Zhao Yun watched Ma Huan, his scroll clutched to his chest, scurry down the narrow streets before disappearing into the crowd. No doubt the scholar would be awake through the night. By dawn, Ma Huan's journal would have several new pages.

The past would, once again, carve its path into the future. It always did.

The wind changed, sweeping the heat of the flames toward Zhao Yun. Embers sparkled around him, triggering stored memories from centuries past.

Prometheus's data archives churned.

What was the burning of the treasure ships compared to the burning of the great library of Alexandria? He had witnessed that event too, through different eyes, encased in a different body. He might have despaired, but by then he had witnessed, over millennia, the endless cycle of despair and hope. Time marched on. The only certainty of change was its impermanence.

The agents of change—people of vision like Ma Huan—saw to it.

But not Prometheus. He was history's silent witness, as he had been through eons, from the dawn of time, before men rose to dominate the world. Was it his purpose? He did not know. Perhaps, with life stretching before him, it did not matter if he could not answer the question immediately.

Patience. He had learned to be patient with himself, with humanity, and with change.

Prometheus stared down at his liver-spotted hands. He had worn this body for nearly twelve years. The anonymity of always looking old to young eyes had protected him from close scrutiny. He had grown comfortable in his body.

Too comfortable, perhaps. It was time, once again, to move on.

For a moment, Prometheus considered his friend's appeal and the task that Ma Huan had set before him, but surely, it did not matter as much as Ma Huan believed. The account of the admiral's expedition would not be any less rich or detailed without maps.

In the final count, the power to change the world belonged to the humans, not to him.

With only a hint of regret of not granting Ma Huan a farewell deserving of their long friendship, Prometheus turned his back on the burning ships and walked into his future.

* * *

Zhao Yun, the aged captain of a Fuchuan warship, was never seen again. Many people believed that, driven mad with grief, he took his own life on the night the treasure ships burned.

II

1519 A.D.

I don't belong here.

It didn't matter that the crush of humanity around me included both genders and possibly every known nationality under the sun. Babes in their mothers' arms cooed and poked curious fingers into the faces of the aged so decrepit it was a wonder they were not in their graves. Insults and curses, uttered in guttural Spanish, Portuguese, Dutch, Italian, and French, blended into the babble of the crowd. Whores, their rouged cheeks distinct in the dim light of the glowing fireplaces, sauntered from table to table, from man to man, seeking customers. Each time the wooden door opened, the stink of a garbage-laden sea swept into the crowded tavern.

I fought the compulsion to retch.

Belonging was a state of mind, not a physical state of being. I had worn my shabbiest clothes and even so, I stood out—a young man too gently raised for the clutter of the Seville wharfs. I stared at men as they shoved past my corner table, wishing I could imitate the rolling gait of old sailors or the swagger of the young ones. Perhaps I would be less noticeable—

A shadow fell over my table. A familiar voice, pitched low, snapped out the words, "Jorge. What are you doing here?"

My head jerked up. "Father."

He slid into the seat across from me. His hair looked grayer, although I told myself it was only the imagination of my guilty conscience; Father would not have aged that much or that visibly in the six months since I'd left Lisbon.

He dragged a hand over his face. "Do you know how long I have searched for you?"

Knowing Father, it was probably from the day I failed to return home after fighting with Pero Anes de Canto. I hung my head. "I'm sorry."

His large hands reached across the table and clasped mine. "Your mother is so worried, and your sister—"

"Probably hasn't even noticed that I'm gone. Is she married yet?"

My blunt honesty teased a smile from my father. "She's narrowed down the list from six to four."

"She should just marry Alfonso and save everyone else the expense of gifts and the trouble of courting her."

"He's just a butcher."

"Which explains why she's been making cows' eyes at him since she was fourteen."

Father raked his hand through his hair. "Fourteen? Really?" He frowned.

"If you had bothered to look up from your maps, you might have noticed."

Hurt flickered over his face, and predictably, he changed the topic. "Why are you here?"

"I fought with Pero—"

"Hah." My father made a dismissive gesture with his hand. "Pompous little rat."

I held back a grin. Father's description was accurate and more blunt than I had expected. "The pompous little rat wants to be cardinal."

"But for now, he's just a priest." Father grinned. "And he's not to be feared, in spite of what he thinks or says. Come back to Lisbon. I'll secure us passage on—"

"I can't."

Father frowned. "Why not?"

"I promised to do something."

"What?"

The grin I'd held back inched over my face. I leaned forward and lowered my voice to a whisper. "Something great. Something amazing." I could hear the bubbling of excitement in my own voice despite my effort to moderate my tone. "I promised to help the captain create a map of the world."

"The captain? Magellan?"

"You know of him?"

"Of course. I inquired of all the ship captains. The first mate of the Trinidad told me of a boy matching your description and sent me here. He said you made maps for the captain."

"I'm making a name for myself as a cartographer, Father. Just like you."

Father's smile was proud. His eyes beamed at me.

His obvious delight gave me confidence to continue speaking. "I've promised to make him a map and a globe of the world for his expedition. I can't return to Lisbon until I've done as I've promised."

"So why are you here, in a tavern, instead of working on the map, son?"

I lowered my gaze. "Because the map isn't complete. I need more information and—"

"You think you'll find it here?"

"I've heard of a sailor who possesses a map of the world."

Father snorted. "All rubbish."

"It's not rubbish. Others have seen it too. I've arranged to buy it from him."

Father sighed. "If there is indeed an accurate world map, it wouldn't sell for any price you could afford."

That possibility had occurred to me, but it was not within my control, so I opted to ignore it. "He's supposed to meet me here, tonight. You have to go. If he sees someone else here with me, he may not reveal himself."

Father sighed as he pushed to his feet. "You've taken care of yourself for six months. I suppose you can manage for several more hours. I'll wait for you on the Trinidad." He hesitated. "I don't suppose you'll want some help or advice on the map you're putting together for the captain?"

I almost shot out of my seat. "But I do. I want your help!" My father, Pedro Reinel, was one of the best...no, he was the best cartographer in Lisbon, possibly in all of Europe. Everything I knew about maps, I'd learned from him.

Belatedly, I recalled that I was striving to be calm, collected, and mature, but my father had already seen through my act. In the end, I suppose I was just a child trying to impress his father.

A wide grin spread across Father's face. "I'll be waiting for you." He inclined his head—it might even have been a gesture of respect— and walked away.

I released my breath, my shoulders sagging. Father wasn't angry; my occasional prayers to the Holy Virgin on that matter had apparently paid off. Now, if only my more fervent prayers were answered—

I saw him then—a sailor of indeterminate age, his skin browned by the sun. Whiskers bristled over his cheeks and chin. The wide grin exposing gaps in his teeth belied the shrewd gleam in his eyes. Those beady eyes narrowed into slits when he caught sight of me. For a moment, I thought he would squeeze back out through the door and vanish into Seville's narrow alleys, but he walked toward me, limping slightly.

Reeking of cheap gin, he sat across from me, and we stared at each other, taking the other's measure. I knew what he saw, a seventeen-year-old boy, too fresh-faced to pretend that he belonged to the sailor class. "Can I buy you an ale?" I broke the silence.

"Aye. Will need a clear head to bargain."

I stifled a smile as I waved to a barmaid for a tankard of ale. The sailor obviously viewed life through a perpetual alcohol-induced haze. Indeed, he probably could not function unless he was at least marginally drunk.

He reached into his grimy shirt, pulled out a rolled parchment, and set it on the table between us, although closer to him. "This be what yer wanting."

"The world map." My voice sounded thin even to my own ears. My heart pounded; I hoped he could not hear it.

"Aye." His grin exposed blackened gums.

"Let me see it."

He cast me a suspicious look, but he unrolled the parchment. My breath caught with every hushed creak of the paper; the map was old, no question about it, but was it accurate?

The old sailor gave me a glimpse of it. I recognized the outline of Europe on the western edge of the map. In the center of the map, the lands I knew as the Far East were larger than I expected. To the east, the New World stretched farther to the north and the south than anyone could have anticipated. Far more interesting, the map displayed land masses in the extreme north and south—lands that did not exist on any map I had seen. In contrast, Europe, which I knew to be the center of the world, was disappointingly small in comparison.

If the map were accurate, it would completely alter the way we viewed our place in the world. "How old is this map?" I asked.

"Close to a hundred years old, I daresay."

"It can't be right. The New World was only discovered twenty-five years ago."

The sailor chortled. "Was it now?" He pointed at the letters on the map.

I had focused on the shape of the continents to the exclusion of all else; belatedly, I realized that the letters on the map were not in any language I recognized. He continued, "This map here claims those Chinese knew of it long 'fore we did."

"Do you read the language?"

He opened his mouth and then closed it again. A shrewd look passed across his face. "Can't say I do."

I glared at him. "How did you come by the map?"

"Won it in a game of dice, I did."

"From who?"

"Might have been Portuguese or Dutch. One of them traders in Malacca." He slid his hand beneath the table. My fear that he might have been reaching for a dagger or knife was alleviated when I heard the familiar jangle of dice knocking against each other. "Weren't too happy when I won, so we argued a bit, you know. That's how this bit of blood landed up on the map."

The brown stain I had taken for spilled food covered a significant portion of the map, but fortunately did not obscure any details. My stomach lurched. "Did you ask him where he got the map?"

"He weren't too chatty, you know. Hard to talk with a blade in them lungs, but I heard say he swindled an Indian trader who stole it from a Chinese map maker. Bloody history this map has." The sailor grinned as he rolled up the parchment. "You still sure you want it, boy?"

"Yes, I do."

"You brave enough to travel to the lands east of the sun?"

"East of the sun?"

"Beyond the horizon. The greatest lands always lie beyond the horizon."

"I…" For a moment, I contemplated a lie, but the man's eyes seemed to look right through me, unraveling my every secret. My chest deflated on a sigh. "I'm just a cartographer. A map maker. I get horribly seasick on open water, so I don't travel much, except on paper. It's how I visit new worlds. It's all just on paper and in my head."

The words sounded stupid, beyond childish, as they slipped out of my mouth, but something on the man's face seemed to change. He smiled. "Perhaps Ma Huan would have wanted you to have this, after all."

"Ma Huan?"

"The map maker." He unrolled the map only far enough to show me two Chinese characters stamped on the lower right-hand corner of the parchment.

"So, you do read Chinese," I said.

"You should learn too, if you intend to read this map."

"I just need the dimensions, not names."

"There's meaning in names, boy, often more than there are in the number of leagues wide and fathoms deep." He slid the map across the table to me.

I sucked in my breath, but did not reach for it even though my fingers twitched. I fisted my hands together. "How much is it?"

"Whatever you can afford." He shrugged, the gesture surprisingly graceful for someone as inebriated as he was. "You remind me of a boy I once knew, a dreamer like you. He would want you to have the map."

I placed my full pouch of coins on the table. It never even occurred to me to skimp on the payment to him or to take advantage of his generosity.

He took the pouch and tested its weight. A smile crept across his face. He tugged apart the pouch strings, took out a coin, and bit it. "Real, all right." The pouch vanished into the folds of his shirt, and he shoved to his feet. "Enjoy your treasure now, boy."

I grabbed the map and unrolled it. Parchment crinkled beneath my hands as my eyes swept across the breadth of the world. Unbelievable. I had to show this to my father and to Magellan right away. By the time I rolled up the map and raised my head to look around the tavern, the sailor had vanished into the crowd or out of the building, who knew? It didn't matter. I cared only that I held the world in my hands.

I raced out into the cool of the night, scarcely noticing the stink of rotting fish rising from the fishing boats rocking gently against the dock. In the distance, the four masts of the Trinidad beckoned me homeward. I tucked the parchment in my shirt for safety and walked, head down, arms wrapped against my chest, as much to ward off the chill as to protect the map.

I left behind the noise and the chaos of the central docks. The crowds thinned. The patches of light emanating from the lanterns on closed doors spread further apart, and the fog wafting in from the sea turned pinpricks of light into a diffused glow.

Up ahead, the sounds of a scuffle drifted back to me. The haze made it nearly impossible to tell for certain where the noise came from. Should I go forward? Should I wait? The weight of the parchment was nothing, yet it hung upon me, a burden like nothing I'd ever experienced before. I didn't dare take risks—not when the price could have been the world.

I shrank into the shadows and tried to close my ears and heart to the muttered curses and muffled screams. When the sounds finally faded into silence, I crept out along the edge of the darkness. I could hear nothing above the thump of my heart. Almost there, I told myself. The Trinidad was close. I could see the glow of the lanterns from the ship.

The distance between safety and me narrowed, although not quickly enough for my peace of mind. Several feet from the Trinidad, I stumbled and fell onto the wooden planks of the dock. I looked back over my shoulder. A shiver of fear raced up my spine. I had tripped over a foot.

I raised my gaze to stare into the face of the sailor who had sold me the map. His eyes stared, unseeing, at me. His shirt glistened crimson, ripped almost to shreds, his chest torn open by the sharp edges of daggers and swords. He slumped against a wall; his empty hands lay by his side, his body cast aside like a broken marionette. I didn't bother to look for the pouch of coins I had given him. I knew it had cost him his life.

The sour taste of bile flooded my mouth. I scrambled to my feet and raced toward the light, up the gangplank, and onto the Trinidad.

The sailors on the watch recognized me and let me pass. "Where is my father?" I demanded.

"With the crew, below decks. Ale's flowing freely."

I nodded, but instead of heading below the deck, I climbed the stairs to the captain's quarters and rapped on the closed door.

"Not now!" the captain roared.

"But, Captain." I pressed my mouth to the keyhole. "It's Jorge Reinel. I have the map."

Silence greeted me.

"The world map."

Footsteps approached the door. Moments later, it flung open. Captain Ferdinand Magellan, his hair in disarray and his trousers unlaced, stared at me. "The world map, you say?"

I recoiled from the whiskey on his breath as he stepped aside, an invitation to enter his chambers.

His quarters, the largest onboard the Trinidad, was warmed by a blazing fire in the hearth. The room possessed a rosy glow and the fragrance of a woman. On the bed, the captain's favorite whore, Catalina, raised herself up on her elbow to stare at me. The bed sheet draped over her curves slipped to reveal a plump breast. Tousled black curls framed her face, and she offered me a knowing smile.

I flushed and lowered my gaze, not knowing where to fix my eyes.

"Where is this map, boy?" Magellan demanded.

Taking care not to look at Catalina, I offered the map to him. He unrolled the parchment and held it up to the light. A thoughtful frown passed across his face as I summarized the story of how the map had found its way into my hands. I finished with, "I'll compare it with the other partial maps, and from there, my father and I can complete your map of the world."

"Excellent," Magellan said. His eyes were glazed, likely from the alcohol he had consumed that evening. He rerolled the map and tossed it onto a table to lie among the many other maps I had collected on his behalf. "You will start work on it tomorrow."

"I can do it now—"

"Now you will go tell the men that we'll leave Seville at first light."

"But—"

"We'll sail to the mouth of the river, to Sanlúcar de Barrameda. You'll have time to work on the map and the globe, and then you and your father can leave the ship before we depart on our expedition." He turned to Catalina. "And you...this is your last night here. You'll leave tomorrow, first thing." He leered fondly at her. "You'll have to find other amusements, love."

She pouted, but said nothing.

Magellan hustled me out of his quarters and shut the door. The last thing I heard from his cabin that night was Catalina's low and husky laughter as she invited him back to bed.

I glanced toward the dock, toward where I knew the sailor's body lay, but I could no longer see it through the darkening gloom. A chill shuddered through me, and I scurried below deck to find warmth and comfort in the company of my father and the other men.

* * *

The sound of revelry below decks faded as sleep finally claimed the men.

In the captain's quarter's, Catalina's eyes flashed open. Every detail of the cabin leapt into immediate focus. Beside her, Ferdinand Magellan lay fast asleep, his body exhausted by sex and his mind by drink.

She slipped out of bed, making no sound as she walked toward the table. She picked up the world map and unrolled it. A corner of her mouth tugged into a half-smile as she traced the name of her one-time friend. Ma Huan had named the lands they had visited together on admiral Zheng He's 1421 expedition. The vast realm east of the sun he had called Mei Guo—the Beautiful Kingdom.

It had been a wondrous land, abundant with natural resources and spilling over with promise. Someday, perhaps, she would return, although she would never reach that continent, not using this particular map. Ma Huan had ambition and vision aplenty; unfortunately he had lacked all sense of scale and proportion.

His world map was wrong.

She, too, had been wrong. The task Ma Huan had demanded of Zhao Yun nearly a century earlier had mattered. Without Zhao Yun's guidance, Ma Huan had obviously proceeded without the aid of a cartographer, creating a map destined to lead men hopelessly astray.

Prometheus glanced over her shoulder at the sleeping captain. Magellan had been kind to her, but kindness was not reason enough to act. Jorge Reinel, however, had reminded her of Ma Huan—young, with a passion for change and a desire to leave his mark upon the world.

Why not?

She reached for parchment and ink, sat at the table, and began to draw.

Hours passed, the silence broken only by the sound of the quill scratching against paper.

The sun was a sliver on the horizon when Prometheus finally rose from her seat and stared down at the world map, as faultless as her flawless data archives. *You will have your fame, Jorge Reinel, and you, Ferdinand Magellan, yours.*

She rolled up Ma Huan's map, tucked it into her clothes, and walked out of Magellan's cabin, quietly closing the door. She left behind the first accurate map of the world, and with it, the knowledge of several lifetimes—Prometheus's gift to the people of Earth.

MANTEO

After a difficult Atlantic crossing, weeks of delay, and the inability to properly provision themselves, the colonists of Sir Walter Raleigh's Third Expedition have reached Roanoke Island, in the land of Virginia, where they are to pick up fifteen soldiers left on the Island and then proceed north to the Bay of Chesapeake to establish an English colony. Instead, their flagship's pilot has stranded them on Roanoke by force. All that remains of the soldiers is a single skeleton. They are surrounded by hostiles. Fortunately, they have Manteo, a native from the area, the first American to travel to England, to act as their liaison...

Tuesday, 28 July, 1587

The back of his head caved in, George Howe lay face down in the reeking mud of the salt marsh. A large crab inched out of the open burlap sack near his hand and then scuttled away. Manteo counted the arrows protruding from his back, thighs, and upper arms. Sixteen. His stomach rolled. Sixteen arrows when one would've done.

The incoming tide crept closer to George's body. Distant shouts reached Manteo and the two other men standing watch among the reeds as the runner they'd sent for Governor John White reached the colony. Sweat rolled down Manteo's ribcage. It pooled at his lower back. He wanted nothing more than to strip the stifling English shirt from his body. But then he would be indistinguishable from the ones who did this.

"Damn it all, George," Bailie muttered.

Manteo grew up crabbing all the island marshes between the sea and the mainland. There was plenty for everyone, but the English soldiers weren't adept at hunting or fishing. They didn't need to be skilled. The English god was powerful. English soldiers took what they wanted.

"How many arrows is that?" Bailie muttered. "Damn it all."

George was not a soldier. Sir Raleigh had chosen only gentlemen and planters for the new colony. Wives and children came along. It was a true village. Manteo's brothers did not open their eyes and look before they attacked this Englishman. His fists closed around the bow he'd drawn on hearing Bailie's anguished shouts.

Next to him, John White's African slave lay down his own sack of crabs. He walked out onto the mud and knelt beside Howe. Reading his intent, Manteo slung his bow across his back and joined him. Working together, they broke the shaft of each arrow, leaving the head buried inside.

"We should not be here," Manteo said in his native language. Among the colonists, only Samuel knew it. "The tribes won't understand the difference between English soldiers and planters. We need to go the Bay of Chesapeake, as Sir Raleigh planned."

"It's political," Samuel answered in English, before lapsing into Algonquin. "I'm certain the *Lion's* pilot will profit from acting against Sir Raleigh's interests. He's refused all of White's requests to carry us further. We have no choice but to remain."

The *Lion* was the expedition's flagship. Manteo wasn't privy to the pilot's business arrangements with Sir Raleigh, but he'd traveled to England and back twice now. This journey had been especially burdened with hardship and pilot error. He, himself, had eaten the poison fruit that made so many of them ill in the Indies and suffered greatly for it. Weather had kept them from landing for fresh water, livestock, and other provisions they had planned to collect on their way. Then the *Lion's* pilot overshot the island of salt, needed to preserve game for the winter, and refused to turn back.

The absence of fresh supplies and the extended length of their journey meant much of the seed stock needed for planting had been consumed by arrival and it was too late in the season to sow what remained. But the tribe who once lived here on Roanoke would not care, with good reason. The colony must travel on to the Bay of Chesapeake or perish.

"We do not have time to walk overland before winter," Samuel said as if reading Manteo's thoughts. "These are gentle men and women, not soldiers. The children—"

"They're coming," Bailie called.

Manteo snapped the final shaft just above George's pale, cold skin. "My tribe will help."

"If they don't," Samuel said as he stood up, already turning towards his master's thrashing approach through the reeds, "we are as good as dead."

Thursday, 30 July

Sitting alone at the bow, Samuel relished the moist salt breeze that brushed over his hot, dark skin, the creak of the lines, and rush of water along the hull. The pinnace skimmed between the treacherous shoals in the sound between the mainland and the barrier islands as no larger ship could do. The massive *Lion* and its flyboat remained anchored in the open Atlantic as their crews gathered enough fresh water and game to gain the Azores before returning to England.

Past Roanoke, the coast of the mainland stretched south to the horizon, unbroken white sand beaches raising dunes that knelt before the majestic, lush sweep of evergreen forest hiding great swamps and plentiful game. Samuel's spirits lifted to see it all again.

Turning his attention to port, he watched the shoreline of Croatoan Island loom larger and closer, embracing the beauty of the lush grasses on the beach, the robust stands of pine and live oak, the thick ropes of grape vine placed just so by a genial creator's hand. As on Roanoke, colorful, raucous birds swooped and dove, plucking summer's last fruits.

Despite their grim situation, Manteo's grin was contagious as he caught Samuel's eye. After eighteen months in London, the Croatan looked more English than American. "You are home," Samuel said.

"I am home," Manteo agreed, joy evident in his tone.

At Manteo's direction, Commander Stafford ran the pinnace ashore in the gentle, sandy curve of a heavily wooded cove. Samuel leapt out into the warm, shallow surf with several other men to secure the lines. On the beach, John White struck his flint to light a small bundle of sweetgrass tinder. The twenty colonists and Manteo passed it among themselves to light the slow-burning wicks they carried for their matchlocks. White pointed at two of his assistants. "Watch the pinnace" he said in his uncompromising baritone. "You can light a fire if we haven't returned before dark."

After a brief hike through the coastal woods, the colonists stepped off the end of a game trail into a field of sparse, small eared corn. At the head of the column, White held up his closed fist, as if he were fox hunting. The colonists fanned out as they gathered to see what lay ahead. In the distance, a dozen Croatan and two Caribbean adoptees harvested tobacco in harmonic syncopation. Glancing back, White raised his gun. In agreement, the group advanced upon the working Indians.

On close approach, the men dropped their wooden weeding tools and digging sticks and ran for the cover of a wooded copse, groping for their knives and snatching at the bows and clubs slung upon their backs.

"Friends, it is I," Manteo called out in Algonquin. Dousing the end of his matchlock wick between his fingertips, he handed his gun to Samuel, who had none. "I have returned."

Two of the quicker men whirled, dropping to one knee as they drew arrows back. The others slowed, turning with spears in hand or nocking arrows, frowns gracing their sturdy countenances.

"It is I, Manteo, come from England again to live among my people." Manteo, striding out in front of the bristling colonists, cut a brilliant figure as he spread his arms wide. Relative to most of the English colonists, he was tall and fit. His black hair shone under the late afternoon sun. The white shirt he wore—with its billowing sleeves—stood out in brilliant contrast to the umber hue of his hands and face.

One of the bowman called out, "What then of Sarataic?"

"Of Sarataic, I know only that her honey tastes of mulberry, but her skin of ash."

They all laughed. Manteo had told Samuel about the prettiest young woman in all the Croatan kingdom. And her surly attitude.

"Is it really you?" another asked, once they sobered again.

"It cannot be, you are English now," a third yelled.

Manteo ran forward as his men did, to be engulfed in hugs and good cheer. The most striking difference between Manteo and his men remained his full head of hair, grown long and tied back with a blue ribbon. The Croatan men shaved their heads for the most part. A few shaved only the sides, leaving their hair in a center strip, cut short enough to stand when greased.

A barrel-chested man, recognizing Commander Stafford, John White, and Samuel, stepped forward and swept his arm wide, indicating the entire field. "All the crops were poor this year. You cannot take it."

Samuel glanced at Manteo, but he was still listening to a passionate welcome from a young buck, so he translated instead. "He thinks we are here to harvest their crop."

White's lips tightened. Commander Stafford, who once raided this same field on Ralph Lane's orders, looked at his feet. The brash, paranoid commander of the last attempt to colonize, Lane had perpetuated a terrible offense upon the king of the Roanoke. The vicious act resulted in the evacuation of the entire colony the previous year.

"The summer's been dry," the Croatan continued. "Our winter stores are short. We cannot share them."

"Drought," Manteo said on the heels of the man's words. "They cannot share their winter provisions."

White nodded. "Tell them we are here to renew our friendship, not take from them."

"The colony cannot survive without provisions. It is too late to plant," Manteo said.

"Just tell them, Manteo," White said, his tone soft.

At Manteo's words, smiles broke across the Croatan's faces. One gestured expansively, talking too fast for Samuel to follow as another turned and ran away from them, towards the village.

"Come," Manteo said to the colonists. "My mother will be waiting."

Samuel and John White had lived on Croatoan Island for a time with the first expedition. The familiar twenty minute walk through the scattered field crops, dappled cool of live oaks draped in Spanish moss, fragrant loblollies, and massive cedars eased the lingering tension between the Croatan and colonists.

Upon entering the small village of barrel-roofed longhouses, Manteo's own mother recognized him only with difficulty after his prolonged absence. Samuel knew the feeling. He'd watched Manteo transform from savage to Englishman in three years time. Miraculous in a way. It reminded him of the much longer time he spent watching the transformation of the Picts into British high society.

As she drew back from hugging her son, the solitary shorebird feather braided into her hair swayed. She wore a fine deerskin shirt, with fringes, and a long skirt. Despite the August heat, a strip of lush, dark fur lay across her shoulders. Samuel suspected it to be bison, the large, shaggy, cattle-like beast Manteo had described to him. Several shell necklaces fell artfully across her breasts. As the *weroansqua*, its female leader of wealth, Manteo's mother would speak for the tribe.

* * *

Seated facing his mother under the shade of a large pavilion, Manteo introduced the newcomers one at a time to her and the warriors standing at her back. The woman and children of his tribe created a swirl of activity around them in preparation of a welcoming meal. John White came last, Samuel trailing, as always, in his wide shadow. "Mother," Manteo said. "Our friend is now Governor John White. Being governor means he's the colony's *weroance* now."

White dipped his head in deference to Manteo's mother. A surge of pride and belonging heated Manteo's chest. Although treated well while in England, he was seen as a curiosity there, not as a person of powerful influence as he was here in his home.

She met White's eyes as he raised his head again. "Will you give our men some token or badge to wear so that you will know them?"

Heart dropping, Manteo did not translate this immediately to White, instead asking, "Why do you need this? Of course, we know you."

"We? Are you an Englishman now, Manteo, my son?"

Manteo dropped his gaze, noticing his cloth breeches and his English boots as he did. "Their world is rich, Mother, and wide." He looked up and around, taking in the gathered Croatan and black-skinned men.

To accommodate the first colony's narrow escape from Roanoke last summer, Sir Francis Drake had put more than 300 African, Caribbean, and American slaves ashore in order to carry Lane's one hundred colonists back to England.

"These blacks, are they from Sir Drake's ship?"

She nodded.

"What did she say, Manteo?" White interrupted.

"She asks for tokens, or badges, for our men to wear, so that you might know them when you come across them."

"Why?"

"Why, Mother?" Manteo asked once again in Algonquin.

"How many does our tribe number now, Manteo?"

"We are smaller than we were..." Manteo hedged. All the Croatan people were fewer in number. Despite many people of the tribes appealing to the English god in prayer, everywhere the English went, the people suffered and died in their wake.

"We are sixty-three," his mother said, leaning forward to pin him with her stare. "And only five children. All due to the rotten spot disease."

But Manteo knew it was not the English who caused the affliction, because he and his life-long friend, Wanchese, had both traveled all the way to England and still survived.

"And Lane," she continued. "When he caught some of our men off the island."

"Lane killed some of them by accident," Manteo translated, forcing his voice through his tight throat, omitting her accusation regarding the people's sickness.

"Ask her about our garrison, the fifteen men Grenville left behind."

"After we...left...last summer, a supply ship brought fifteen men to guard the fort."

"Dead. Enslaved." she said, waving her hand towards the mainland.

"By?" Manteo said.

His mother made a flicking gesture with the fingers of her right hand. "Pemisapan's men, those who are left. Like you, Wanchese has found another home."

"Ask her about George Howe," White demanded, before Manteo had time to translate.

"An innocent colonist was killed, two days ago," Manteo said.

"Wanchese leads them now."

Manteo closed his eyes against the ache in his heart. "The Roanoke. And Wanchese," he said, as he opened his eyes to look at White.

Wanchese had been excited when the English asked for a representative to accompany them to meet their people's most important *weroansqua*, Queen Elizabeth. "Manteo," he'd said. "These odd men have *mantoac* such as we have never seen. More than the Iroquois. More than the Powhatan. We must go."

And it was true. In London, Manteo and Wanchese had seen wondrous sights, amazing machines that the English told them were made by men, not gods, although they seemed magical. There were strange animals--horses, which everyone rode upon, elephants and camels, huge writhing snakes that could swallow a cur whole. And the food in England! Plentiful and varied enough to twist the stomach if one wasn't careful.

It could be purchased, not with the hard labor they had always known, but with bits of metal, coins. So it would be here, in his home, one day. The Croatan could trade the tremendous natural resources their chief god provided all around them for the coins. No one would starve.

But while Manteo had focused on the *mantoac*, the spiritual power, of the English philosophy and thrown himself into learning their language so that he might recreate it and make the Croatan strong, Wanchese saw only the filthy river, the abuse of god's animals, the gluttony of the English at court, the greed that separated the people from each other.

"Wanchese," White repeated. He rubbed his fatigue-lined face with his big paw of a hand.

Following their return to Roanoke with Ralph Lane's soldier colony, Wanchese stopped speaking with the English and aligned himself with the wary Roanoke *weroance*, Pemisapan. The *weronace* had acted as a guide to them in their youth. The Croatan followed him in alliance against threats from other nations. Wanchese at his side, Pemisapan led the outcry against Lane's brutal treatment of the tribes and Lane took his life for it.

"Please reassure the nearest Croatan tribes," White said, his graveled voice somber, "and also the Roanoke at Dasamunguepeuk, that we, the English of Roanoke Island, will willingly receive them again as friends. The unfriendly dealings of the past by both parties should be utterly forgiven and forgotten."

Once Manteo related this sentiment to his mother and *weroansqua*, she spoke in hushed conference with her men. Stuck in the middle by his own hand, Manteo sat very still during this meeting from which he had been so blatantly excluded.

At length, her men stepped back, some of them leaving to whatever duties the colonists had disrupted with their appearance. "We will see what we can do," she offered. "Stay tonight and feast."

For tomorrow, you will starve, Manteo thought, the words tumbling through him in the exact tone of his mother's voice. Heavy with foreboding, Manteo rose and offered her his arm.

Sunday, 02 August

Sitting on Roanoke Island's north beach, Samuel watched Manteo drive a tall, sharpened stake through the shallow water and deep into the sandy mud of the tidal flat.

"That wood won't sharpen itself, Samuel," his master said in gentle rebuke.

Samuel glanced over his shoulder. White sat in a wooden chair, staring out across the glinting chop to watch a brawny, red-faced man pound a stone on the head of the stake Manteo continued to hold steady. His hand stroked lines of graphite across a page in his journal to capture the scene.

"I know the last three years have required more of you than I used to ask," White said as Samuel returned to whittling the end a stake. A pile of cut saplings waited at his elbow and one of the men working on the fish weir would wade ashore soon to collect them. "It seems to suit, though. You have learned more than I thought you capable of and there's a sharper look in your eye. It's been useful that you learned Manteo's language."

An answer wasn't expected of him and Samuel didn't give one. He didn't often position himself in the way he had this time, but it had been advantageous to his observation of first contact to place himself so. He'd been crew on the first Roanoke expedition. White, a close friend of Sir Raleigh and a gentleman of means, traveled with them as the company's commissioned artist. After first contact was accomplished with the friendly Croatan tribes, Manteo and Wanchese agreed to journey to England to meet Sir Raleigh and his investors.

Samuel watched. He learned. At the end of the six week Atlantic re-crossing, when it became clear that White would host the Americans at his London home, Samuel sampled skin cells from the arm of White's slave. After stalking the edges of society to observe the Americans' reception, he withdrew to cocoon. Three months later, he arranged for the real Samuel's kidnap one drizzly morning and then simply replaced him.

"Ask Manteo to join us, Samuel. I need to speak with him."

Gathering the stakes he'd completed, Samuel splashed out into the warmth of the sound to fetch Manteo.

When they had trudged back through the shallows and deep sand to stand together before White, the man laid his graphite in the painter's box at his feet and shook his journal free of blowing sand. He crossed his legs and looked with a considering regard upon Manteo for a long moment before speaking. "Our first supply ship will be looking for us at the Bay of Chesapeake. I don't trust the *Lion's* pilot to tell Sir

Raleigh of our fate. The other ships will miss us as well if they remain unaware of our location. Someone will have to travel with the *Lion*, to inform Sir Raleigh of the treacherous straits we find ourselves in because of her pilot, but that will take time. I may be the only choice of practical representation." He swung his foot, considering his next words. "We cannot survive here without having the tribes in hand, but not one tribe has come to meet with us as requested. Measures may have to be undertaken to gain their cooperation. Can you use your influence with your people to protect our woman and children?"

"Not here, John White."

White's gaze shifted past Manteo. Samuel watched the dart of his eyes as White followed the movements of the men working on the weir. Tears glistened across them when he blinked and turned his attention back to Manteo. "Where, then? Where will my daughter be safe?"

Eleanor. White's pregnant daughter refused to be left behind when her husband decided to join her father in establishing a colony with the potential to become England's wealthiest outpost. It seemed safe enough. The colonists were not poor. Most were gentleman. They included a physician, a lawyer, a sheriff, a goldsmith. The rest were planters, men who could harness the land for production. They were well-prepared and supplied. And they had Manteo as a failsafe, a liaison to partnership with the natives. But then it all went wrong– the weather, the provisioning, being stranded here at Roanoke where they'd meant to stay only long enough to recover the fifteen men left behind.

"We should've been established at Chesapeake months ago," White continued, waving a hand in the air as if Chesapeake lay before him. "Eleanor should be in a house already, not here with no crops, no hope of supply, under constant threat of attack."

Manteo nodded. Samuel scanned the peaceful beach, the men in the water, White sitting in his chair. Maybe George Howe had been enough revenge for the Roanoke. It was true they could not survive here without the tribes, but attack did not seem imminent.

"You are our liaison, Manteo. Can I count on you?"

Samuel often observed the subtle actions of Manteo's abiding affection for White's daughter. He did not doubt Manteo's ardent desire to see his people lifted into the educated sphere of European culture, but it remained curious to him that Manteo believed so much in the power of the English god that he remained loyal to the English despite the violence they had perpetrated upon the tribes, including Manteo's own. Had White discovered one reason Manteo stayed?

"Yes, John," Manteo said. "Of course, you can."

Thursday, 06 August

"Some tea, please, Eleanor, for Samuel's empty cup?" John White said.

Manteo closed his eyes, briefly, as Eleanor passed in front of him, her long skirts brushing his legs. Her lilac scent had deepened with musk as the baby inside her grew large. It stirred him.

They sat in counsel beneath a blue awning stretched between two scrawny saplings near the center of the encampment. Although the buildings of the soldier colony had been razed, presumably by the Roanoke, the logs remained, and some could be re-claimed.

A party worked nearby, nearing completion of the cabin which would house the sensitive equipment and books the scientists had hauled along in trunks and crates. The meeting hall across from it was also in its final stages, replete with brick and tile. Four women were stockpiling long sheaves of sea grass and young reeds for the roofs of several modest shelters in which to bunk the single men for the time being. Several men were occupied in repairing the original palisade, a necessity against not just hunting parties from hostile tribes, but the bear and wolves who sometimes crossed the sound to hunt on the island. Two sailors from the *Lion* stood near the forest's edge, slicing strips of flesh from a skinned deer for addition to the ship's stores.

Bailie slapped at a fat mosquito hovering above his ear, leaving a long streak of blood behind. "Better these cursed birds of an insect than the fleas I left behind in London."

"And better the evening sea breeze than the breath of the Thames and the smoke of the cooking fires and the seething din," Anais Dare, White's son-in-law, added, patting his wife's belly as she left them.

"To make a go of it here, we need peace with the Americans," White said, leaning forward in his chair to address the entire group. Besides Manteo and assistants Anais and Bailie, it included an additional four men also designated as assistants to White, as had been the late George Howe. He set his teacup on the far edge of the table before him, the rest of its surface taken up by drawings and half-started sketches, inventory lists, and three wooden cases spouting all manner of brushes and dried cakes of pigment.

"It's been a week," he continued, folding his hands upon a rippled map, "with no sign of the *weroances* from Secotan, Aquascogoc, Pomiocke, or Dasemunguepuek. It's damn disrespectful, is what it is. They should bring the culprits forward and let us put the past behind us. Instead, they are forcing our hand. They must be aware that we are ready and willing to defend ourselves. This land has been claimed by England. They cannot just come and kill our own at will. They are like vicious children who must be shown a parent's hand." He waved a hand at Manteo. "Manteo, why is it you understand that your people can be transformed from the savagery of their birth into a civilized population, when Wanchese and your brethren do not?"

Manteo drew breath, but John White continued on without an answer to his query.

"If only they could imagine, like I do, like Sir Raleigh does, the Anglo-American empire that could grow from this little patch of dirt," he exclaimed, scuffing at the sand beneath his boots. "Then we would not have to forge peace through violence."

"We've miners," Bailie ventured. "If we could reach that mineral deposit, the one the river tribe told you of last year, our investors would triple and we could build New London right near, on the mainland."

Manteo remembered well the texture of the wooden handle pressed against his palm, the fierce thrill of holding an English iron blade to the throat of an Iroquois warrior to gain that valuable information. Sir Raleigh paid Manteo in coins and goods for it, and promised more for his experience and knowledge of the tribal federations. Soon the Croatans would fear no one. They would each carry English tomahawks with their superior metal heads and matchlock guns and wear *mantoac*-filled English jewelry and clothes. They would be powerful.

"We can no longer defer our revenge for Howe's death. A Roanoke eye for an English eye, to acquit their evil doing to us. Manteo, can you lead us to Dasemunguepuek in the dark?"

In proof of the English god's power, Manteo had journeyed with Ralph Lane and forty men, including John White, upon the river to insult that mighty Iroquois tribe by kidnap and interrogation, yet lived. Manteo had never felt so strong against a tribe he feared. Pemisapan, surprised by their triumphant return to Roanoke, relented to the advice of his father and once again allowed the Roanoke to help the English plant maize and build weirs in an attempt to make them feed themselves.

But then, like thousands of others, his father died from the disease the tribes had never seen before the English arrival. Wanchese and Pemisapan declared the English a violent and pestilent people who placed great strain on the food supply. Abandoning their home, and dooming the colonists to starvation in the process, Pemisapan moved the remanent of his once thriving tribe to the mainland.

Lane, seeing his already limited food supply removed and fearing a massive, multi-tribe attack against the colony, decided to attack first. Worried for the safety of his friends in the village, Manteo traveled with the attackers. Before reaching their destination, they came upon Pemisapan and his men at leisure. Lane gave the signal to fire. Manteo had screamed then, covering his ears against the boom of the firelocks. Taking pity on Manteo, Lane stayed with him and protected the Americans Manteo indicated as friends from the rest of the company.

Although drenched in sweat from the heat of the day, a shudder rippled down Manteo's back at the memory of Pemisapan's head swinging from the hand of Lane's second.

"Manteo," John White said again. "Wanchese must answer for his crime against us. Will you guide us across the sound?"

Manteo studied the assembled men, the *weroances* of the colony. Queen Elizabeth was their chief, and Sir Raleigh their regional *weroance*. There were many more English in London alone than all the peoples of all the tribes he knew by touch and song. He might never learn to comprehend their social alliances.

Samuel caught and held his gaze. John White treated the small black man as a pet, but he had learned Algonquin better than Sir Raleigh's linguist, had a steadier hand for maps than John White, worked rigging as well or better than many of the sailors, had spoken in depth to Manteo about improvements to be made in the soil of Roanoke to improve crop yields, and suggested ways to keep and feed the wild turkey in pens for winter meat. Why had Manteo's *kewas* led him to such riches if not to learn from them?

But George Howe had been the 'eye' for Pemisapan's 'eye'. Now Wanchese was to be the 'eye' for George Howe's 'eye'. Who would pay the 'eye' for Wanchese's 'eye'? Where would it stop?

"Manteo," Anais Dare said. "We need you."

Pemisapan had been a warrior. George Howe was just a man. A bad trade.

"I will," Manteo said.

Friday, 07 August

Shadows draped the setting moon in the hour before dawn as the colonists beached their two shallops. They were not silent as they filtered over the beach and through the swamp grass in the general direction of Dasemunguepuek. White planned a swift entry into the main village and a fast search for Wanchese while they had the advantage over a sleeping populace. Ten minutes into their walk, sweat already running down Samuel's side, firelight flickered through the reeds and cattails.

Bunking well outside the village, their quarry, Wanchese and his brother Roanokes, sat close to their early breakfast fire as they ate. White waved the colonists into a ragged line. Despite the soft squelching of their footsteps and the rustling as they tore their paper powder cones open with their teeth and primed their firelocks, the savages did not stir or glance around.

White's hoarse cry to action woke them from their morning daze. They turned as one, some standing while others ducked away from the flames. The firelocks barked, launching their acrid smoke into the already rotten, salty air. Samuel's eyes and nose stung. Two of the savages fell.

In front of him, Samuel saw Manteo slow. A high keening wail rose from him, but broke off suddenly. "Stop," Manteo roared.

Two of the English colonists startled and halted their pursuit of the terrified Indians fleeing into the reeds.

White, still charging through the early morning dark towards the camp's fire, spread his arms and echoed Manteo's cry. "Stop shooting!" Reversing his course, he ran to Manteo and fell to his knees beside him. "What? What is it?"

"My mother's men," Manteo gasped to the small group now huddled around him.

"No," White breathed.

Anais Dare straightened up to bellow to those still thrashing through the reeds in pursuit, "Stop! Stop! They are Croatans!"

"Without tokens or badges to identify them," Samuel said under his breath, but hearing, Manteo cast him a wild glare.

Roger Prat, across from them beyond the fire, said, "There's a stockpile here. They were harvesting corn and pumpkins."

Manteo shook his head. "They would not be stealing from the Roanoke."

"Roger," John White called. "Take Griffen and Berrye to the settlement. Be quiet. See if all is well there."

Within hours, the colonists were organized for another trip to Croatoan, this time bearing the bodies of four from Manteo's tribe. Manteo sat beside them. Samuel was again struck by the sharp contrast between who Manteo had been and who he was now.

The wrenching cries that rose from Manteo's village at their approach hit Samuel hard. He struggled for breath, his heart pounding. Although he had experienced it from time to time, he wasn't used to having such a physical response to grief.

As the women, the *squaws,* came to claim their men, the colonists retreated, leaving Manteo standing alone.

White glanced sidelong at Samuel and tipped his chin towards Manteo.

"Will you return to us, Manteo?" Samuel called.

Manteo looked back at him, his ravaged expression one of terrible loss and guilt. Samuel knew it well, had seen it on the faces of men for thousands upon hundreds of thousands of years. His heart clenched. His emotions had slowly grown over his lifetime, but he was far from used to feeling such empathy. *Do not interfere*, the voice of his dreams, his whims, his driven passion, whispered to him.

He ignored it, almost certain the voice that was not his voice had anticipated his reaction. The voice had been with him as far back as he could remember, the day upon which he'd first opened his eyes.

Samuel placed his hand upon John White's arm, a rudeness of great proportions. "He will either return or he will not."

Allowing the gesture, White nodded. When Samuel released him, White said calmly, but loud enough for his voice to carry, "As Governor of Roanoke, on behalf of the Virginia colony, we are most sorry for the mistake."

Samuel thought it a poor apology for murder, no matter the intentions or target, but the colony had little to give in recompense. And, of course, it was not his place to say. He did wish he were in a position to stay and observe the details of the tribe's funerary practices, but as Samuel, he could not.

Wednesday, 12 August

Wet hair plastered to his head, Manteo returned to Roanoke Island in soaked breechclout and leggings, his head completely shaved, painted swirls adorning his chest and arms.

"Hoy, Manteo," a guard called down from a narrow platform atop the palisade gate.

Manteo sketched a wave and slung the otterskin bag his sister had given him onto the ground below. He sat to dig his dry moccasins out of the bag from where they lay tucked between his English clothes and boots.

"Did you swim the sound?" Johnny yelled, dashing to meet him.

"Did you?" Tomas cried, plowing into the back of Johnny.

"Yes," Manteo said, watching the children swarm from wherever they'd been working. All nine were boys, all somewhere between five and twelve summers. Almost twice as many children as lived within his tribe.

"You can swim?" young George Howe asked. Manteo studied the oldest boy's sallow face. He had lost his own father at about the same age.

"I can teach you," he said, spreading his hands to encompass all of them. "One evening, after your duties have been completed for the day."

A variety of enthusiastic responses greeted his words.

He clapped his hands together with a sharp report. "Now off with you, before I get in trouble."

The boys scattered to their work. Manteo went in search of John White. He found him pacing before Anais Dare's small house, among a group of the colony men. Samuel sat to one side. A woman, Jane, bustled past into the house, carrying a wooden bowl of stew and a basket of bread over her arm.

"Manteo," White exclaimed when he saw him, a wide grin lighting his face and eyes. "You've gone savage on us."

Manteo nodded, reaching out his hand as he'd been taught. "John."

White held onto his hand. "Are you staying?" he asked. When Manteo nodded again, he let go and said, "Could you help with the weir? The fish are swimming right through and the men assigned can't seem to fix the problem."

"Yes, John." Unsure of his welcome, Manteo hesitated to ask after Eleanor.

From behind, Samuel spoke to him in his own language. "She's healthy. The babe is restless and the women are sharing her duties tonight."

Releasing the breath he'd been unaware he was holding, Manteo flashed a smile at Samuel in gratitude as he took his leave.

"Oh, Manteo," John White said, stopping him. "Sir Raleigh authorized your baptism here in the new world at my discretion. I believe you behaved yourself as a most faithful Englishman while leading us into battle against the Roanoke across the Sound. No one could have known they were no longer living there."

Manteo caught his flinch before he made it and schooled his features to stillness. The men of his tribe had been there to harvest the last of the late summer crops left behind when the Roanoke fled further inland after the death of George Howe. "I told my people the harm come to them was by their own folly. If the tribal *weroances* had appeared before you as requested, they would not have known this mischance."

"You are correct, Manteo," John White said. "The baptism will be held tomorrow and a title shall be conferred upon you." His gaze hardened. "God and his host would surely prefer you in English dress, though."

Manteo's stomach squirmed over on itself. He couldn't lose his chance to lead his people into the future, which he knew the English represented. If English clothes pleased the English god, he would wear them. Their *mantoac* kept him safe from the disease and harm that had so affected his people since he had first hailed the English from the shore.

Friday, 28 August

Raising his hand in farewell, Samuel wondered if perhaps John White were watching him through the spyglass he carried within his jacket. At this distance from the heaving *Lion*, he couldn't tell who stood along the railing.

On the north beach beside him, Anais Dare said, "Well, that's that. I hope he makes good time back."

Concern weighed heavy in his tone, but his wife met his comment with her sunlit laugh. "He'll move heaven and earth—and Sir Raleigh's purse—to make all haste back and see his granddaughter provisioned properly before the first snow falls." She freed one hand from under Virginia, ten days old and swaddled in her arms, to pat Samuel's forearm. "And to reclaim Samuel before I get too attached to him."

"The Spanish..."

"Shhh, now, Anais," Eleanor cooed, rocking Virginia in her arms as the infant began to whimper. "We're on an adventure. We're fine until spring, if need be, even if the natives prove less than helpful."

Manteo, newly baptized and titled Lord of Roanoke and Dasamonguepuek, stepped away from them, towards the waves crashing on the heavy seas, no doubt remembering the promise he'd made White regarding Eleanor's safety. Since his return to the colony following the burial of his mother's men, the silence from his tribe was deafening.

That silence and the aggressiveness of the few Indians the colonists had crossed paths with while out hunting on the mainland tipped White's decision once the *Lion's* pilot announced he'd be weighing anchor with the tide. Without native support, the colony could not survive on Roanoke. White had the ability and social standing to press Sir Raleigh and his investors for immediate supply and relocation of the colony to the Bay of Chesapeake.

If White failed, a hundred and seventeen souls and Sir Raleigh's grand dream of creating an Anglo-American metropolis would perish on these wild shores due to the stubborn, perhaps criminal, actions of the *Lion's* privateer pilot. Samuel could also easily imagine the glee of those seeking favors of the Queen should Sir Raleigh bankrupt himself to save the colony. A win-win either way for Sir Raleigh's enemies.

Watching the overcast sky and the continuous tumult of the grey ocean, he mulled over White's back-up plan in case of a Spanish arrival or hostile attack from the local tribes. Traveling fifty miles into the main would bury them deep in the Croatan kingdom. It remained to be seen if Manteo's influence could protect them there.

"Manteo," Eleanor said. "Will you come to supper now?"

Hands in his pockets, Manteo turned on his heel in response. The corner of his mouth lifted in a slight smile. "No, Mrs. Eleanor. I'll remain awhile here."

"The ocean's not very soothing today, I'm afraid," she said.

Anais cleared his throat. "The boys will be wanting you to help them with their nets later."

"Tell them I'll be there."

Seeing him watching, Eleanor tilted her chin at him. "Come, Samuel."

Moving to her side, Samuel gave silent thanks that White's need for speed and lack of encumbrance upon his arrival in London left him at Roanoke as a curiosity and an extra pair of hands. This particular situation gave him a nice clean out and time to observe life in this stunning land for a while, perhaps as a savage himself, should he decide to trade his current body for a new one.

Tuesday, 01 September

The first sign of trouble flew over the stockade wall during the evening meal. Tomas and Johnny spotted the flaming arrow before it hit the ground near the newly dug well. At their alarmed yells, Manteo took up the English tomahawk slung at his hip as he stood from his place at Eleanor's crowded table to see them.

He let loose a bloodcurdling howl in his people's manner. The Englishmen froze, staring at him.

Samuel yelled, "To arms!"

His pure, deep voice carried clear across the colony.

Manteo darted towards the gate, feeling, more than seeing, the men rush away from the table behind him. Dozens of arrows, some of them lit, arced over the walls from all directions. The gate stood closed, but the sentry platform atop the right post was empty and no body lay beneath it.

Someone screamed, and then another. Manteo made the gate, leaping from three feet out to catch the post a third of the way up. An attacker on the other side planted what sounded like a large English axe. A place to put his foot and reach a higher hold. Manteo beat him up, slung his own blade down and crushed the Roanoke's head. Hot blood hit his face. The body hit a man he knew well, who was standing on the buried axe below. Manteo watched Skunk fall. His arm broke at a horrific angle, adding his shocked voice to the general din rising all around. Shrieks and cries, the resounding thunk of wood on wood, the clash of iron.

The colonist sentry, Clement, lay bloody and dead below. The attackers were spread thin. They were both Roanoke and Secotan, heavily armed, a couple with English hatchets. Further down the wall, several were raising the ends of two logs, wedging them against the wall as running inclines to the top.

Manteo yelped like a kicked cur, drawing the attention of three colonists sheltering from the arrows directly beneath him, as well as Samuel and Anais Dare, who had already barred the gate. Manteo opened his fisted hand twice and then jerked it in the direction of the attackers climbing the logs. "Breaching the wall," Anais bellowed, and the men bolted out from under the platform to intercept.

Turning back to re-assess, Manteo ducked to avoid the club swinging down, then twisted and rose, swinging his tomahawk overhand to sink it in the attacker's shoulder, nearly cleaving him in two. He reversed it to catch the next with the wide backside on his chin, hard enough to flip him over backwards. The boom of a matchlock came now, from one of the colony houses behind him. And then another, somewhere beyond it.

"Manteo!" Wanchese yelled.

His second, a warrior Manteo did not know, stood behind him. The second nocked an arrow and aimed at Manteo. Manteo watched his fingers open. He dropped below the wall, his cheek scraping against the raw timber. The wood against his ear vibrated with the force of the arrow as it struck the wall. Turning to put his back to it, Manteo shifted the hatchet, blade out between his knees, ready to swing upward should another man reach the top.

"Manteo!" Wanchese yelled again. "The English are a hurricane tide. They will flood our home with their filth and noise and violence unless we stop them."

The sob broke up Manteo's throat, escaping as a growling whine he choked on. He fought for a strangled breath and then another, before he could draw enough air to make himself stand and face Wanchese. The second held another arrow upon him. The bodies of his people lay where they fell. The guns were speaking now, in two or three shots and then a period of silence. Men skirmishing to either side of him along the wall filled his peripheral vision, but all he could see was Wanchese, grim and foreboding, his upturned face aged well past the actual summers of his youth by their experience of the past three years.

"Brother," Manteo cried. "My brother. The English are a hurricane tide. They will flood our home with their magic machines and their art, their food, their music, their weapons. They are as inevitable as the hurricane itself. We cannot stop them."

Wanchese raised two fingers to his lips. His shrill whistle pierced the chaos. His people fell back. An expectant hush fell over the colony. Within minutes, the attackers slipped into the twilight, melting into the sparse cover of the English pillaged woods surrounding the colony.

When Wanchese and his second stood alone, Wanchese nodded and turned his back upon Manteo, striding away without a second glance. The second sent the arrow he'd held in wait flying. Manteo did not move. The arrow's barb planted itself into the platform's roof post with a loud 'thwock', three inches to Manteo's left. He was certain the arrow landed exactly where the second meant to place it.

* * *

Do not interfere. Standing in the back of the new meeting hall, Samuel shook his head, although he knew it made no difference to the voice. There wasn't room to establish a proper graveyard within the palisade. The rest of the island was salt marsh or woods, unsuitable to either burials or crops.

It had been over a thousand years since Samuel had seen any of the peoples of Europe accept the burning of bodies as a sound form of disposal. No one proposed it. He wondered if Manteo would suggest it, but Manteo remained silent as the debate continued over locations for burial. A precedent needed to be set if the colony were to remain on Roanoke. There would be more dead. "Burial at sea," he suggested, as he sat at White's feet.

White rested a hand upon his shoulder. After a moment, his ringing baritone sliced through the discordance, offering Samuel's solution to the upset colonists. No one among them could raise a strong argument against it. The method was expedient and once the pinnace was loaded and any ceremony completed, two men could accomplish it while everyone else went back to repairing the burnt roofs, building, hunting, water hauling, and all the other daily tasks required to keep over a hundred people fed, clothed, and sheltered on minimal supplies.

The nine dead included Bailie and Anais Dare. As the crowd dispersed, Samuel saw Manteo standing to the side, chin held high, but a far-away look in his eye. A man divided. A man alone. Samuel had long ago realized his immortality and body-swapping capabilities were rare, if not unique, and that the voice that plagued him didn't speak to other people. It was not any sort of god, except maybe his own. He sometimes envied those who lived average lifespans in one body and then died without returning.

He did not envy Manteo.

Thursday, 24 September

Manteo and Samuel stood together upon the cold, damp sand of Roanoke's south beach before sunrise. A light, blustery drizzle had kicked up a few hours before, disturbing everyone's sleep. Misty, salt-laden rain swept sideways and sand pelted his skin in stinging bites. Manteo's head ached with the press of a growing storm. Dyonis Harvie and Roger Prat walked from down the beach to join them. As assistants to John White, Manteo knew both men, but not well.

"Storm coming," Roger said.

Manteo glanced at him, weighing his words.

"They don't know what's coming," Samuel murmured. "Go ahead, tell them."

Roger's eyes widened.

"Tell us," Harvie urged.

"We call this type of storm a hurricane. There will be big winds and the islands may flood. The colony is not prepared. But we dare not sail to Croatoan to shelter with my tribe. Hurricanes are like cougars."

The men nodded, like they understood. The rain dripped from their hair and ran down their faces. But then Harvie said, "'Cougar'. Is that the big cat you told the boys about?"

"Yes. Fierce and unpredictable. We must leave here for the mainland," Manteo said. "We must leave today, as soon as possible. Only what we can carry."

"Dasamunguepuek?" Roger Prat asked.

"Further."

"We're on the island's highest ground," Harvie said, in a disbelieving tone. "The palisade is sturdy. It can't be any worse than that bad storm we hit on the crossing."

"It is..." Manteo's English failed him. The storm at sea had been terrifying, but the sailors claimed it wasn't bad. London had been rainy and wet. The wind blew, but he had not experienced nor heard tell of any storm like a hurricane. These colonists had no way of understanding the size of the storm churning towards them. "The wind can topple trees and take the roofs from your homes."

"Two of them have tile roofs now. They're much sturdier than thatch and anchor the walls," Dyonis Harvie said, looking to Roger for agreement.

"True," Roger said. "The savages have nothing in comparison."

Manteo shifted on the sand, anger warming his chest and face. "It is not safe to stay. The tide rises high behind the storm."

Roger Prat hawked a great glob of mucous into the shallows of the sound before addressing Manteo directly. "Have you ever been here on this island during a hurry-cane?"

"No."

"There are trees all over this island, old ones, oak and cypress. There's established wildlife."

"We'll stay," Harvie decided. "The savages have taken thirty-one lives from us in the attacks. No storm is going to chase us off. We will hold this colony until Governor White returns." He smiled grimly and added, "My Lord."

Manteo nodded his head with a sharp jerk. The two men turned away and headed back towards the flickering light thrown from the torches sputtering at the palisade gate. In the moon since John White left, they had suffered four attacks. He could not be arrived on English soil yet, but already they were down thirty-one lives.

"I'll make sure Eleanor and Virginia are safe," Samuel murmured.

Focused on the Englishmen, outraged at their overconfidence, but hopeless about changing it, Manteo's heart missed a beat at Samuel's soft words. He glanced at the little black man before turning his attention back to the dark, storm-ridden skies and the sliver of grey dawn that might or might not be staining the horizon. "Am I so obvious?"

"I don't profess to understand men who love only one woman, but I recognize it when I see it."

"Is there no such thing where you are from, Samuel?"

"There is, but I have no experience with it myself."

Manteo laughed. His mood lifted despite the dread riding him. Thought of Eleanor always affected him so. "So it is with many Croatan as well. There are squaws and braves alike, who need more than one lover to please them."

"Your gods see pleasure in a different light than the English god."

"Yes."

"And yet, you have taken the English god as your own."

"He is powerful. And I only need Eleanor's presence to please me." He looked sidelong at Samuel.

Samuel wagged his head, his lower lip pooching out. "But with time, perhaps she will see your faithfulness to her as well as her god."

Manteo didn't dare hope. Knowing she was near, that her kindness and hands provided him food, and her beauty provided a pleasant rest for his gaze, was enough. He smiled. "I will try to see the men through," he said. As property, which granted him an assumed indifference to the wiles of English society, Samuel would be housed and protected from the storm with the women and children. "And you try to see the women through. I'll attempt to bring a guard to check on you during the calm that comes mid-way through a hurricane, but do not be fooled. The wind that begins again after the calm of the storm changes direction. And it is far worse than the beginning."

Friday, 25 September

In the pitch-black morning, lodged deep within the cradle of a thicket of grapevine, Samuel held tight to Virginia as she screamed. A great, rough barked tree at his back protected them from all but the fiercest gusts of the furious storm. His body sheltered her from the worst of the sheeting rain. His arms kept her from the inches deep wash of sea water in which they lay. The wind attacked, again tugging at what remained of his clothes, shrieking through the tangle of smaller trees all around. They arched as their trunks bent, their crowns brushing the ground.

Samuel shuddered and shook with the strain of bracing his back and legs to keep from being shoved right through the tangled vines. As the storm took a breath, he raised his head to look around, to see if anyone else lay near. But the dark was too deep, he couldn't so much as see Virginia's face, as close as he held her to him.

The unrelenting rain beat against the bruises he'd suffered when the roof of the meeting hall tore away and the side wall collapsed onto the twenty-eight women and children gathered inside. A mighty surge of freezing salt water poured in on them. Trapped, Eleanor had shoved Virginia into Samuel's arms. He clutched the baby to him and escaped, the water swirling around his legs, the wind shoving at his back until he was running.

He had no memory of landing here within the vines. The island's sand worked at scouring the skin from his neck and back. Virginia wailed and screamed and cried into his ear.

Sometime later, Samuel shivered and woke. The wan sun seemed too bright as he blinked up at a confusing weave above him. Birds rustled and sang all around. Whatever woke him moved against his bare ribs with a small hiccoughing sound. He rolled his heavy head to peer at it. A baby. A white baby. An English baby. Virginia.

The sense memory of water swirling around him, of vines pressing into his flesh, startled him into sitting up. Although, as always, he knew where he was, the air temperature and barometric pressure, the exact time of day, he flailed against the confinement of the thicket, the press of Virginia's tiny, wriggling 98.2 degrees, until he rolled free. Breathing hard, he leapt up.

A body lay nearby. A woman, facedown. Otherwise, the area around him looked not much the worse for wear. Scattered branches and leaves layered the ground. An uprooted young cedar blocked his view of the colony proper. Bare chested, Samuel still wore his fine trousers, although they were filthy and torn. His boots remained on his feet. That seemed a good omen to him.

"Hallo!" a man's voice called. "Anyone out there?"

"Here," Samuel shouted.

He knelt to peer under the bower at Virginia. Gown soaking wet and covered in mud, her big, blue-grey eyes met his. She waved her fists and smacked her tiny, chapped lips at him, forming spit bubbles between them. He fished her out and checked her over. Except for the stench of her messy cloths, she seemed unharmed. Cradling her in the crook of his elbow, he gathered his reserves for a moment, listening to the man's progress across the littered ground.

"Hallo?"

"Just here," Samuel called again.

The horse-faced man named Jones slipped from around the cedar.

"How bad is it?" Samuel asked.

Jones shook his head, staring down at the dead woman.

"Let's go find out."

Most of the colony was gone. Washed into the sound. The heaviest logs remained on the beach. One house stood untouched. A scatter of belongings lay half-buried in a great swath. Part of the palisade still stood. A pair of men with a body slung between them trudged towards the tree line as Samuel and Jones stepped out of it into the clearing.

"Jones, Samuel," John Burden said. "Glad you made it." He and his partner laid the body down beside five more. "I haven't seen Mrs. Dare, yet, I'm afraid," he continued.

Jones swallowed. "My wife," he said, gesturing back the way they had come.

While his partner hung back, Burden came closer to place his hand upon Jones's shoulder. "I'm sorry, man. Shall we go get her?"

Jones nodded.

"What of Manteo?" Samuel asked.

"He's out with Mr. Harvie, looking for survivors. There are six women in the house. You can take Virginia to them."

Thursday, 15 October

Manteo dropped his last deerskin bag into the dugout canoe and jerked a salvaged wool peacoat on over his new leggings and breechclout. He turned to survey the colony.

He had shown them how to build the smaller sapling and thatched huts the Croatan used on hunting trips inland. Since the last of the seed stock was gone and all the crop land drowned in saltwater, he hunted with them, deer and turkey and a bear. They'd built new weirs, and he pointed out nearby locations for berries and nuts on a map Samuel drew in the sand. He taught the women how to make pemmican and jerky from everything not immediately consumed. In the evenings, the entire colony gathered to build the canoes they would need to survive.

Once the fortified stockade was completed, nine men and four women would strike out overland for the Bay of Chesapeake, where they might meet a supply ship looking for them. Eight men would hold the reduced and heavily defended colony in the name of England until Governor John White's return. Samuel would leave with Manteo and his group of ten colonists, ostensibly remaining with Virginia in the heartland of the Croatan until her grandfather returned for both of them. In reality, Manteo had already promised Samuel his freedom. They would part ways well before reaching Manteo's destination fifty miles directly west of Roanoke.

Dyonis Harvie handed Manteo a paddle as he swept his other hand out to encompass the two canoes already underway. Each canoe contained a remaining colonist, so that the boats could be returned to Roanoke. "Thank you for helping us," he said.

Manteo nodded. He offered his hand as he had been taught and Harvie shook it. During the weeks since the storm, the colonists who knew of Manteo's warning beforehand had shifted in their attitude towards him. While he had always held a unique social position, they now deferred to him without question. "Send John White when he arrives. Virginia will be safe. Should you fall to attack, find us due west."

"Fifty miles into the main," Harvie said. "We won't fail. We'll bring Governor White in due time."

Whenever that turned out to be, Manteo would not wear English dress again. If that disappointed John White, so be it. He had been right when he told Wanchese the English were a hurricane that could not be stopped, but he'd been wrong about the strength of the English god while speaking with Samuel on the beach. The English god was no more powerful than Manteo's own chief god. They were as the porcupine and the skunk. Very different in their approach, but effective in their own ways. The English needed to become American to survive here. They needed to learn from him, from his people. There would be no New London, not here in the land of his birth, only lighter skinned Croatans with blue English eyes.

Turning on his heel, Manteo leaned forward to grasp the sides of the dug-out. Samuel sat inside, holding Virginia. Earnest John and Hugh Taylor helped Manteo launch the little boat into the choppy, grey sound before they all jumped in.

Tuesday, 26 January, 1588

Male or female, the first piss was always satisfying. In a couple of days, he would be fully acclimated to the physical characteristics of his new home. Having decided it was most advantageous in this land to remain male, he had sampled Manteo, scraping a little bit of skin from the palm of his hand before they parted.

After walking two days and two nights, not bothering to stop for food or sleep since he was all alone, Samuel holed up in a stolen den. He took care to barricade himself in so that he might wake up three months later not chewed upon. It was a good choice. When he emerged, the den entrance, disturbed only by his exit, had been covered in downed, icy leaves.

Surrounded on all sides by young hardwoods and the dark green sharp scent of pine, he drew a deep, refreshing breath into his new lungs. The weak sun warmed his chilled skin. Steam rose from his arcing stream.

Although he'd done so with Samuel, and now Manteo, he didn't make a habit of sampling people he knew and spent time with, but he remained curious about monogamous love. Romantic love. Maybe there was something about Manteo's physical body that would enlighten him over time. He shook off and wondered idly about how best to acquire clothes. Samuel's buckskin leggings would not fit him, though the breechclout was fine and he had the bearskin he'd taken into the den.

Go south, the voice demanded. Samuel shook his head, annoyed to hear it so soon after waking.

South meant civilization.

South meant the Spanish.

The reach of the Spanish and English would, he knew from experience, eventually touch and change Manteo's home. Despite Manteo's renewed belief in the value and power of his people's culture of balance, neither his gods nor his people could stop the inevitability of European settlement.

He lowered himself to the frozen, hard ground and crawled halfway into the den for the thick, fragrant comfort of the bearskin.

If no one else named him, he might do quite well as Diego, freed slave, in this American body.

At least for a little while.

The game trail several hundred yards below the den was barely visible, but clear enough. Reveling in the tight bunch of his thigh muscles, the strength that surged through his frame and steadied his calloused hands, Samuel descended.

On the narrow trail, churned earth cold beneath his feet, he walked out of Samuel's life and into Diego's, for as long as it lasted.

So nice to meet you!
Bria Burton

ON BOTH SIDES

I

Boston, June 1775

"Tell me, Lady Carrington, when do you and Colonel Denton plan to be married?" asked Olivia Wilton. The question came from Olivia's desire for fresh gossip. So little news of worth presented itself these days. Having a young couple visit her father's house meant endless possibilities in that regard.

Without replying, Maryanne sipped her tea, staring out the window with a vague expression. Her thin lips bowed, as if she were suffocating a smirk. She arched one eyebrow, held her tea just before her mouth, and tightened her jaw. Olivia could see her swallowing not only the tea, but the inquiry.

Outside, the garden displayed daisies, peonies, and pink roses. The fountain, like a watery bouquet, splashed up through a stone goblet in the center of a pool. The view from the parlor, while pleasant in the light of the afternoon, didn't seem to be Maryanne's preoccupation.

Olivia feared the spread on the table, the insufficient number of candelabras, tapestries, and statuettes, not to mention the size of the room and the house in general would be inadequate for Maryanne. Olivia dreaded the possibility that she would fail to divert a lady of her station, therefore failing to secure her invaluable friendship. Even after spritzing the room with a jasmine-scented perfume when Colonel Denton whispered that it was Lady Carrington's favorite aroma, Maryanne made no remark about it.

Dashing, young Colonel Denton and Olivia's father, Colonel Wilton, had left the parlor to discuss army matters. Olivia wanted to discuss anything else, and felt relieved when they took their conversation elsewhere. Her dear father must've sensed her unease.

While still hoping for an answer from Maryanne, Olivia picked up the buttered muffin on her plate, taking a delicate bite. The bread was overly toasted, difficult to chew. She set the muffin back down. Her appetite had deserted her. The thought of disappointing Lady Carrington coupled with rumors of war made her stomach churn. She despised anything that upset her social calendar. She didn't care about war, only how it would impact her status in high society when it was over.

A few crumbs remained on the tips of her new gloves. She brushed them onto the plate with a napkin, appraising her quiet companion. She knew almost nothing about this young woman beyond her family's great wealth. As one of Lady Carrington's first acquaintances in America, Olivia intended to be the source of information for the other ladies of society. "Autumn is a lovely time of year for a wedding," she remarked, desperate to ignite some kind of response.

Maryanne's brown eyes moved, resting on Olivia's as she turned to face her. They were lovely eyes, the kind that made army officers propose upon introduction. Olivia would love to know all the details of the proposal.

Beneath the wide brim of her lavender hat, Maryanne batted thick eyelashes. She set down her empty teacup. "We will not likely marry this year. The fighting may postpone the wedding indefinitely."

Olivia's hand reflexively grabbed her own throat. "Surely these skirmishes will not last the summer, let alone through next year!" She hadn't meant to raise her voice. Immediately, she lowered her tone to an appropriate level. "Of course, I understand your concerns. Colonel

Denton's obligations will be to his regiment. That must be very difficult for you."

"Not at all." Maryanne's serene countenance suggested she meant what she said.

And here was Olivia talking about the conflict again. Exactly what she'd intended to avoid. "He's a very handsome man." She searched for questions to ask, ones that would lead away from distasteful discussion. Olivia prided herself in the ability to converse easily with women of nobility. Why did Maryanne make her feel as if her questions were an imposition? Did she think Olivia was beneath her? Yet both her father and Maryanne's fiancé were colonels in the army. The Wiltons boasted considerable wealth compared to many families in the colonies. "Will you buy a house here in Massachusetts?"

Maryanne's expression didn't change. She posed, her face like a portrait. The soft curls draping from her pinned up hair caressed one shoulder. Her beauty made it difficult not to stare. She hadn't smiled once since entering the house, and it gave Olivia pause. Was she unhappy to be in America? Did the idea of purchasing a permanent home here distress her?

"Or do you plan to return to England?"

Maryanne remained unmoved.

Olivia tired of this guessing game, but worked to hide her annoyance. The friendship was worth any amount of discomfort. She picked up the muffin again, taking a larger bite. She chewed, not enjoying it. When she swallowed, there was a lump in her throat. How strange to feel pained by this awkward, one-sided discourse. Perhaps Maryanne was unaware. "You must tell me, Lady Carrington, all about your courtship. I am desperate to know how Colonel Denton proposed."

Maryanne blinked, but held her eyes closed longer than usual. Olivia took this to mean she was pondering what to say. "He wrote a letter asking my father's permission to marry me. I told Colonel Denton that my father approved the match."

"How . . . thrilling," Olivia tried. She stuffed the remainder of the muffin into her mouth to prevent the frown that threatened to sink her lips like a ship going underwater. Despite the allure and refinement of Lady Carrington, Olivia couldn't help but think her a self-important snob. She was keeping all the good gossip to herself, and perhaps would share it with other ladies, those with a higher station in society than Olivia. How deflating.

When her father and Colonel Denton returned, a strange relief flooded through Olivia. "Well, have you determined how to squash the few rabble rousers trying to stir everybody up?"

"If only it were a few," said her father. "I'm afraid many of the colonists are discontent, but I cannot begin to understand why. All this nonsense about taxation without representation. We are all British subjects, and therefore, we are all represented by the members of Parliament." He took a seat in his usual chair below the portrait of King George III. The paunch of his belly pressed against the buttons of his red coat, and Olivia squinted at him, wishing he would take better care of himself.

"But the Americans don't see it that way," said Maryanne.

Olivia thought it was a statement, but her father replied, "No, I'm afraid some of them don't," as if she had asked a question.

"They believe their rights have been infringed upon."

"Yes, some do."

"Many of the American-born have never set foot in England," continued Maryanne. "They feel they lack the representation in Parliament that you enjoy."

Olivia sat up straighter. Maryanne was speaking more words than she had the entire length of the visit. Olivia hardly knew what to make of her assertions.

"That is correct," said Colonel Wilton.

"Darling, you enjoy that benefit as well." Colonel Denton chuckled, taking a step forward and touching his fiancée's shoulder with a gloved hand.

Olivia admired the young, dark-haired man in uniform. She was quite jealous of Maryanne.

"I seek to understand both sides of the argument." Lifting her chin, Maryanne gazed up at Colonel Denton. "It is a lifelong pursuit of mine."

"A most worthy pursuit, young lady. I commend you." Colonel Wilton lifted a glass of wine and took a swig.

Olivia said, "Father, it's tea time. Not—"

"When one looks upon the colonists," interrupted Colonel Wilton, "those born in America, as you say, there is a distinction from the English-born, no doubt. How diverse is the British Empire. What a privilege to be a part of it."

"Here, here. God save the king," said Colonel Denton.

"God save the king," Olivia and her father echoed, but Maryanne said nothing.

Even when the servant girl bent to pour more tea into Maryanne's cup, and the hot liquid spilled into her lap, she said nothing.

Olivia shrieked. "You clumsy fool! Go and fetch a cold cloth. My dear Lady Carrington, are you terribly scalded?"

"Oh." Maryanne glanced at the round, brown stain that soiled her lavender gown. "It's nothing. I can get another dress."

"We are concerned with your well-being," said Colonel Denton, kneeling beside her. "Does it hurt very badly?"

"No. I'm fine," she insisted.

Olivia appraised Maryanne and the layered skirt of her dress. Maybe the hot tea hadn't reached her skin. Even so, Olivia decided that Maryanne was hiding something, but had no idea what. The worst friend was a woman with secrets who didn't share them. That was as useful to Olivia as a ball gown stained with tea.

Connecticut, October 1775

Robby Freeman sucked crisp air into his lungs, and out of his mouth came a cloud of what looked like smoke. Pleased, he deepened each breath and rounded his lips in an attempt to mirror his pa when he blew out smoke rings. Pa only let him take the occasional puff on his pipe when Mama wasn't looking.

"I don't feel right." Robby's younger brother, Dicky, lumbered beside him, arms wrapped around himself in a hug, his face scrunched up. He squinted at the ground as if irritated with the frosted dirt lane. After lessons with Mama, they traversed the road through the woods and went to work in the storehouse. The evergreens still had their leaves and scented the air with pine.

The cold didn't bother Robby, but Dicky liked to complain. When they wrestled, it didn't take long for Dicky to cry out and say Robby hurt his arm or foot or pinky.

Robby ignored his brother and kept blowing cloud breaths. He hoped it would snow today. Maybe Mr. McEwan would let him and Dicky build a snowman if it got deep enough.

"Robby, I need to go home," Dicky whined.

As Robby glanced over his shoulder, his brother made an about-face and headed back. "Hey, Dicky, you can't go home. Mr. McEwan's expecting us."

"I told ya. I'm not feeling right. I think I got yellow fever."

"Or a yellow belly," Robby chided. He strode after his brother, passing him and putting up a hand to stop him in his tracks. "You're chicken because Mr. McEwan yelled at you for tipping over that table of merchandise yesterday."

"No, I ain't." Dicky rocked back and forth on his feet, arms still crossed. His nose was red-tipped, his blue eyes glazed.

"Ain't ain't a word." Robby chuckled at his own cleverness, but his brother's glossy eyes gave him pause. Maybe he did have yellow fever. "You really feeling sick?"

Dicky nodded, shivering.

"But if you have a fever, you'd be hot," Robby reasoned.

"I am hot."

Robby removed one of the gloves Mama had knitted and touched Dicky's forehead with his bare hand. The skin did feel warm. "All right. Go on home. I'll tell Mr. McEwan you're sick."

Dicky's gaze aimed above Robby's head and his eyes widened. At the same moment, Robby heard the approaching gallop of horse hooves. He grabbed Dicky by the coat and jerked him out of the middle of the road.

Turning around, Robby let out a gasp. A perfect cloud circle of cold breath erupted from his mouth. The fact that the rider was a woman didn't astonish him. Not even that she galloped toward them so quickly, except that riding astride wasn't proper for a woman, Mama always said.

No, it was the dress. She wore a lavender gown not fit for the cold and a matching, broad rimmed hat with long, white gloves. Mama made her own gloves, but these looked store-bought like everything else the woman wore.

As she neared them, she slowed to a trot, halting the gray horse beside them. It snorted out much bigger steam puffs than Robby's, catching its breath as if exhausted.

Robby gaped up at the woman. He couldn't help it. Strands of dark hair fell messily around her shoulders. A hairpin dangled from the end of one lock. The rest stayed pinned beneath the hat. The dress, fitted up top, fell around her and over the saddle like a bell. A large, brown stain, but not dirt—coffee or tea maybe?—had sullied the dress just below her lap. In the stirrup, her heeled shoe peeked out from under the frilly layers of her dirt-streaked skirt. The fancy shoe might have been white once, but mud marked it now.

As he glanced at Dicky, he saw his red-nosed brother's mouth gaping wide enough to take in an armada.

"Excuse me, can you tell me the name of the township I am approaching?" she asked in an English accent, gesturing ahead. Her face was very pretty with wide, brown eyes and soft, red lips.

Both Robby and Dicky stared without answering. Robby hardly knew what to make of her, let alone how to process the words coming from her mouth.

"Forgive me, I haven't introduced myself. My name is Maryanne Carrington." She bowed her head, but quickly straightened up, touching her lips with one of the white gloves. She glanced around. "Actually, I'd prefer to be called Sarah Smith, if you don't mind. Miss Smith will do fine."

Still, Robby didn't know how to answer her. He heard township and Maryanne and Miss Smith, but couldn't recall what the original question was.

"Is this Hartford?" she asked.

Robby shook himself out of his trance and nodded, pointing the direction he and Dicky had been heading. "Just yonder about five more miles, Miss—" He'd already forgotten which name she'd given, but recalled she didn't want to be called another name. He'd never felt so muddled and tongue-tied in his life. He knew lots of girls and a few young women, but nobody like this beauty who made him feel so confused. And warm. Or was he getting yellow fever, too?

She smiled. "Miss Smith. What are your names?"

"Robert and Richard Freeman." He kicked Dicky, who bowed after Robby set the example. "At your service, Miss Smith." He heard men say that to women a lot, and it always seemed to please a girl to hear it.

"How old are you?" she asked.

"I'm fifteen and Dicky's fourteen," Robby answered, but he didn't dare ask her age. It wasn't polite, Mama'd said, to ask a woman that. He guessed she was eighteen. His cold breaths made him conscious of how thin the fabric covering her arms looked. Then he noticed bundles of blankets or clothes tied to the back of her saddle, along with several pelts. All very plain and thick, more like what she should be wearing on a day like this.

"And do you plan to join the Continental Army?"

That question stunned him more than anything else. A proper Englishwoman asking if they were planning to fight British redcoats? It almost felt like a trap.

Robby glanced around. No one else was on the road. "Not sure, Miss Smith," he lied. In fact, he hoped to enlist as soon as he turned sixteen. Mama wouldn't let him leave home before then.

If not for Pa's accident that took his leg, Pa would've already joined up. Robby loved shooting with Pa and listening to him read military histories aloud to him and Dicky. It gave Robby an itching to get to the front lines right beside General Washington. He was eager to fight for freedom.

Still, it wasn't something Pa or Mama allowed them to speak about openly. Mr. McEwan spouted his support for the army, the minutemen, the Sons of Liberty, and everything to do with American independence, but Robby had to admire his patriotism silently. Too many people still believed that reconciliation with the crown was possible. Pa didn't, and neither did Robby. Not after Lexington and Concord.

On the other hand, Dicky might never join if he didn't toughen up. He'd get just as riled as Robby when Pa got them going, but Robby didn't trust Dicky not to chicken out at the first sign of a real fight.

None of that was worth sharing with this Englishwoman. Even if she meant no harm, Robby would honor Pa's requests and keep quiet about their personal convictions.

"Tight-lipped as expected," she continued. "I have observed the intentions, motivations, and claims of each opponent without passion. I have nothing to gain or lose, but there are those who stand to lose everything, and are willing to do so. They believe freedom is worth their lives. It is fascinating." She gazed around as if amazed with the surrounding woods, but seeing something else, too. Something Robby couldn't see.

The cold breeze bit his cheeks. He shifted back and forth to keep warm. Her speech was strange to him. He wasn't sure whether it was proper or not, so he chose not to make any remarks.

She bent lower, gesturing for Robby to come closer.

He obeyed, enraptured with her round eyes and thick eyelashes. Jasmine perfume wafted around her.

"If you enlist, be sure to look for a friend of mine, a man named Samuel Smith. He is twenty years old with brown hair, brown eyes, and pale skin. He is a good man to know."

Robby raised his eyebrows. Another strange statement. Was the man kin to her? Why not say so? Except Smith was not her real name. It was all so confusing, but he replied, "I will."

She bowed her head, blinking. "Good lad. Have a lovely day." Her smile didn't reach her eyes. As she urged her horse forward, trotting into a quick gallop toward town, the image of her expression stuck with Robby. Something seemed peculiar about it. Then again, he'd noted many queer things about the woman. Robby couldn't put his finger on why her smile had bothered him then, but he knew he wouldn't forget the encounter for a long time.

As she shrank in the distance, Robby nudged Dicky. "Go on home, then."

Dicky still gaped at Miss Smith riding away, finally snapping out of it. "I guess I'm feeling better now." With a tug, he pulled his knitted cap down lower, covering the strands of blond hair that had been peeking out.

"Sure." Robby wrapped his arm around his brother's neck in a choke hold, walking forward again. "Because a lady was talking to us."

"No, I just—get offa me." He slipped out of Robby's grip. "Fever's gone, so I can work after all."

Robby knew better. "You're hoping she'll still be in town when we get there."

Dicky kicked a rock, sending it off the road into the woods. "You think she will be?"

"I don't know. Maybe she's passing through. Woman like that," he said, shaking his head, "I've never seen anything like her."

"Me either," said Dicky, a dreamy look in his eyes.

"Come on. I'll race ya there." Robby tore into a run with Dicky trailing behind him. He didn't know what to expect, but he felt the same way as his brother. It would be nice to see Miss Smith again.

III

Boston, February 1776

A letter from Miss Olivia Wilton to Lady Maryanne Carrington.

My dearest friend,

How privileged am I that you continue to write to me! I always knew we'd become the best of friends from the moment we first met. Our mutual affection was so evident when you entered my father's house that I felt a bond like none I have ever felt before.

After three long months without a word from you, I feared I'd lost you forever. What a relief when I received that first letter! And to have so much correspondence since then is a balm in your absence.

I hope this reaches you quickly. As requested, I am using the utmost discretion in sending all my letters to you. It is strange to write to a different location each time, but exciting, too. At last to have a secret that we can share. What fun!

Now if you would only share with me the secret that I am dying to know. Why did you leave us?

I have seen Colonel Denton only once. He is inconsolable, as you can imagine. Do tell me what led to your departure. I have invented scenarios that cannot be correct, so I must know your reasoning. If there is any way in which my father and I can assist you, you must write immediately and tell me what it is.

I remain your truest friend, Olivia

IV

Connecticut, March 1776

In the yard, facing away from the house, Robby and Dicky held their muskets barrel-to-the-sky. "Let's try again. You missed that one by a foot or so. I know you can do better," said Robby, convinced that his brother just needed discipline to improve. "Where's your ramrod?"

"It's here." Dicky pointed at the ground.

"Don't drop it. You need to keep it in the channel."

"I know. But this is just practice." Dicky bent down.

Behind him, redcoats rode toward the house.

Robby counted five. Not much of a troop, but never a good sign these days. He pushed Dicky toward the front door. "Get Pa," he ordered.

Dicky dropped his musket and ramrod, scurrying inside, hollering, "Pa! Redcoats are coming."

Robby sighed, picking up his brother's gun from the grass. With a Brown Bess in each hand, he backed up closer to their white house.

They pulled up right in front of Robby. One of them dismounted. "My name is Parry. I'm a lieutenant in Colonel Denton's regiment. Is the man of the house at home?"

"What's your business here, lieutenant?" Pa stood leaning on his cane in the doorway.

Parry gave Pa the once-over. Most people did that because of the missing leg. "We're looking for a young lady who is engaged to be married to Colonel Denton. She went missing six months ago. Her name is Lady Maryanne Carrington. Do you or does anyone here in town know a woman of nineteen with that name? She is the daughter of Lord Carrington."

The name, like a musket ball, shot into Robby's memory and exploded.

Sarah Smith. She'd given a name, a name that she didn't want to be called, before she asked to be called Miss Smith. All this time, the name had escaped Robby's recollection. But at the sound of it spoken aloud by this British officer, Robby knew that was it.

Maryanne Carrington. *Lady* Maryanne.

He'd thought about her every day since she rode through town. She'd been so different than any woman he'd ever met. She didn't behave like the fiancée of a British colonel, or the daughter of a lord. Not the way she was riding alone in the cold, getting filthy.

After speaking to Robby, she'd ridden into town. At Mr. Oliver's, she traded her horse for one of his. She'd needed a fresh horse for her long ride, she'd told him, and then she was off again as quickly as she'd come, heading west.

No one had seen her again.

"I don't know any girl by that name," answered Pa. "By what means did she go missing?"

"That is not your concern. We have it on good authority she came this way. A friend of hers has correspondence that proves it. Therefore, if you have any information, you are obligated to provide it."

Pa bowed his head respectfully. "Afraid I can't help."

The redcoat grimaced. "If you or anyone in your hearing discovers any information about Lady Carrington, you will write to this address." He handed Pa a card.

"Of course." He saluted, touching the card to his forehead.

The redcoat remounted and led his troop down the road to the neighbor's house.

"I wonder," Pa mused, "if this has anything to do with Miss Sarah Smith?" He glanced at Robby, who felt his cheeks reddening. "You haven't seen that woman again, have you?"

Dicky slipped past Pa and came outside, shaking his head. "No, sir."

Robby echoed, "No, sir."

"Hmm." Pa nodded. "Strange." He snapped his fingers. "Back to shooting practice, boys. I know you'll make me proud when you both enlist next month."

"Both of us?" Dicky ran into Pa's embrace, nearly knocking him over. "Oh, thank you, Pa."

Robby chuckled, knowing Pa had planned to tell Dicky the news later today. "Come on, Dicky. No time to waste. You need to be a better shot by then. Find your ramrod and let's get moving."

As Dicky searched the yard, Robby couldn't help himself. He fantasized about Lady Carrington riding toward him in her lavender dress, hat, and white gloves. There was a halo of light surrounding her and a worried expression on her face. From somewhere came the ominous beat of drums. She was running away from her fiancé, Colonel Denton. He must be a brute of a man for her to leave him. She didn't believe in the British cause anymore, and wanted to find someone who believed in independence. Someone like Robby.

As the fantasy faded, Dicky stood from his crouch in the grass with the ramrod in hand, a giddy smile on his face. "You'll see, Robby. After today, I'll be the best shot this side of the Connecticut River."

Robby doubted it, but liked his brother's enthusiasm. They'd both need to keep their spirits high. Soon, they'd be off to war in a fight for freedom, and their lives.

V

Boston, May 1776

A letter from Miss Olivia Wilton to Lady Maryanne Carrington.

My dearest friend,

What a relief to have received your letter! Thank you for bestowing upon me your most treasured secret. I will do my best to bury all knowledge in the depth of my heart where none may steal it.

Yet I know not how long I am capable of keeping the secret from my father. I must apologize to you again. To this day I don't know how he happened to find one of your letters. There is a more adamant search for you now that Colonel Denton is aware that you went through Hartford. I hope your avowal that it is impossible for anyone to find you is still assured. Do not fear to return to me, if you find it necessary. You are always welcome.

You cannot believe to whom I have had the privilege of being introduced! I will not keep you in suspense. It is none other than General William Howe. This most impressive gentleman came to visit my father's house. He kissed my hand and I have not had the heart to wash the glove since. He gave me every assurance that he would visit me whenever he could. I believe he is quite fond of dancing. This fighting cannot go on forever, so I am certain that I will see him again quite soon.

Your most intimate friend who is like a sister, Olivia

VI

New York, July 1776

At General Washington's headquarters, Robby, Dicky, and the rest of the army faced their leader in eager anticipation. The place was alive with excitement. On the drums and the fifes, the regiments played God Save America. Bystanders cheered, waving flags or their scarves or handkerchiefs, many dyed red and blue. An artillery salute resounded throughout the streets of New York, scenting the air with smoke.

At the top of the stairs between the white columns, Washington stood tall as a tree. His blue uniform with gold trim gave him the appearance of stately regality. Robby had never admired a man more, except his pa.

The music stopped and all went silent as Washington lifted a parchment to read.

"'The unanimous Declaration of the thirteen united States of America.'" He lifted his gaze across the crowd. "Signed July the Fourth, 1776, by members of the Congress."

Robby held his flintlock with strong arms as feelings flowed through him that he hardly knew how to express. Pride, hope, and a brotherly love for the men surrounding him.

"'. . . We hold these truths to be self-evident, that all men are created equal . . .'"

With each phrase, Robby soaked in the beauty of the meaning behind the words. It was like nothing he'd ever heard before. Even in the heat of the summer, he felt chills rushing through his limbs. He held his musket firm as the sensation flowed out through the tips of his fingers. The United States of America. A new country. He and Dicky were a part of something much greater, he knew, than an army of men fighting for independence.

The document listed the many tyrannies of King George III. At the mention of the British monarch, Robby's mind wandered. Maryanne Carrington was rarely far from his thoughts.

Awed, everyone in the crowd remained silent and respectful to the general until he finished reading.

"It is my humble privilege," Washington said, "to stand before you as Commander-in-Chief of this new nation. Now let us fight for the rights of the men of this glorious land which we call our home. May God bestow his gracious mercy upon us, and may he bless America."

The crowd erupted in applause.

"Give me liberty, or give me death!" Robby and Dicky shouted along with the rest of the troops as they raised their muskets high. It was an unforgettable moment.

As the crowd dispersed and the army returned to their encampment, one of the soldiers called a familiar name within Robby's hearing. "Samuel? There you are, Smithy."

Besides Maryanne Carrington, the person he'd been most eagerly hoping to find was her friend, Samuel Smith.

A soldier with brown hair beneath his black, cocked hat responded to the call. His face was too far away to discern the eye color, but Robby thought he looked about twenty, as Maryanne had said he would be.

Robby decided not to approach him yet. Whenever he did muster the courage, he hardly knew where he would begin.

VII

New York, August 1776

A letter from Miss Olivia Wilton to Lady Maryanne Carrington.

My dear friend,

Is it not the worst thing that could have happened in the world? It seems we are earnestly at war with those rebels who see fit to declare independence. I cannot begin to understand it, but I will try my best to keep in good spirits. The fighting thus far has been in our favor. We have all the advantages when it comes to strength and determination.

What fools would try to battle an empire like Britain? But I cannot dwell on it now. Even my father has been summoned for duty, and he insisted that I leave Boston where things have become far too heated. He has rented a house for me in New York. It is most pleasant here and very fashionable, so I am overjoyed with this change of scenery.

Still it is a most trying time. I never thought I'd say this, but I wish I could go back to England, at least until everything is settled and made right again.

Do not fear on that account. I am not leaving, for America is an English colony and forevermore will be. I have nothing to fear in that regard.

Your constant, affectionate friend, Olivia

VIII

New York, September 1776

"Dicky, come on!" Robby raced with his militia unit, fleeing from the redcoats again. He hated that they kept retreating.

Dicky was having trouble keeping up. Robby thought he spotted tears in his eyes. After yesterday's embarrassment, Dicky's morale must be low. When the redcoats had landed at Kip's Bay, he'd been the first to run from the fight before it had even begun. No matter how much Robby cried out that they should stay and fight, all of the men and boys fled in the confusion.

General Washington had been understandably furious, but directed his anger at the officers and not the troops.

Today, it seemed the redcoats took pleasure in their humiliation. As Robby, Dicky, and their unit approached the encampment at Harlem Heights, a hunting bugle call sounded out across the field below, signaling that a fox was in flight from the hounds.

As the troops gathered together, Robby felt the fury swelling amongst the ranks. "They're making fun of us," he whispered to Dicky, who wiped his dirt-smeared face. He hadn't been crying like Robby thought. His eyes were red, as was everything else. The anger boiled so hot in Dicky that he'd ripened like a tomato.

"We can't let them. No more running." He reproached himself as much as anyone, but the commands were already being shouted. The incensed troops would not be humiliated again.

Ready to fight, Dicky and Robby sprinted with their unit into position. Robby's trigger finger itched like never before. They fired their shots, neither of them hitting many of their targets. The smoke from the flintlocks thickened in the air before disappearing with the wind. Officers on both sides shouted to be heard above the musket fire. In the midst of a reload, Dicky's powder horn fell, but Robby was close enough to catch it. He quickly tied the horn's leather laces to Dicky's belt again. Blasts resounded across the hollow way where they nearly surrounded the redcoats. Even as the British slipped out of the trap, the sudden fervor and revived spirit of the Continental Army kept them on their heels. The enemy's line moved back.

The Patriots advanced with mocking cries of their own. For the first time since they enlisted, Robby and Dicky chased the redcoats. It was a wonderful feeling.

"They're the ones fleeing now, Dicky."

"Let's send them back to England!" he cried.

The standoff lasted for hours in a buckwheat field where more and more reinforcements arrived on both sides. Musket balls whizzed past. Some men took hits, but so did the redcoats.

Robby averaged three rounds per minute. Dicky was still slower at two, but his time was improving.

"There he is. Do you see him?" Dicky pointed.

"Who?" While reloading, Robby followed the aim of his brother's finger.

Down the line and back several paces, a man in a brown coat and black hat fired his musket. He reloaded with incredible speed.

Samuel Smith.

Rumor had it Smith could fire four rounds per minute. Now Robby witnessed it firsthand. Smith flew through each step of loading and firing his flintlock. The man was flawless. And he never missed a shot.

Robby still needed to introduce himself. It was time. Who knew if either of them would last the day? He had so many questions about Maryanne Carrington.

In the midst of the volleys, Robby watched in awe as redcoat after redcoat fell, all from Smith's musket.

"How is that even possible?" Robby fired, missing again. Most of his musket balls sailed off one direction or another, hitting redcoats at random.

In time, orders to leave the field passed through the ranks. The British had suffered enough losses to give the Continentals the decided advantage. Despite Robby's desire to chase them all the way back across the Atlantic, he and Dicky followed the orders.

Together, the Patriots withdrew with their banners and flags raised high, shouting, "Huzzah!"

Robby and Dicky slapped each other's backs, proudly crowing along. They'd won the battle, and proven that this war was not one-sided. They had the will to fight and the spirit to win.

Later, Robby searched for Samuel Smith. He was ready to meet the amazing soldier and friend of Lady Carrington. No longer embarrassed, he lined up questions in his mind to ask about her, and about Smith's skills with a musket. But the man was nowhere to be found.

IX

New York, November 1777

A letter from Miss Olivia Wilton to Lady Maryanne Carrington.

To my dearest friend,

An entire year, and not a word until now? I cannot be cross with you. I know not what situations prevented the correspondence, for you will not tell me everything. But no, I am not cross. Never have I been so happy to receive your letter.

I am loathe to be the bearer of dreadful news. Colonel Denton was taken hostage by an escaped rebel prisoner. He is now missing, perhaps a prisoner himself somewhere, but no one is yet certain of his fate. I am sorry to have to tell you this.

On one account you needn't worry. I kept your secret all along. He never knew that you were not in love with him and had no intention of marrying him and that you only accepted his proposal due to your desire to come to America. What a privilege to be in your confidence. I admit, I am pleased with myself for the longevity of the secret, for I find it difficult to keep such things hidden when the person affected is before me. Thankfully, I rarely saw Colonel Denton after your disappearance, making it easier to keep the secret. I do hope he is all right.

There is another piece of news I have been longing to share with you that is not dreadful in the least. General Howe has returned, as promised, to see me. Many times, in fact. He even introduced me to his brother, Admiral Richard Howe. I will confess to you something I would share with no other person in the world, for it is not proper to speak about such things in public, but you are a dear, trusted friend. And as I kept your secret, I know you will keep mine. Dearest William, as I call him, has asked me to be his mistress. It is most unusual, I know, for me to have accepted this position as I most certainly would prefer marriage. In my heart, I know that marriage will come in due time for me, and in that assurance I know I will find much happiness in my current situation. I do not even feel guilty about his wife. She is in England, and cannot expect Dearest William to have no one in America to comfort him during wartime. He says so himself. And as he has no children, I cannot regret the possibility of providing him with an heir. It's possible that in the case of my having borne his son, he would divorce his wife and marry me instead. I have spent a great deal of time thinking about it.

Your devoted and most loving friend, Olivia

X

Pennsylvania, December 1777

Mama once said that life was full of peaks and valleys. Sitting at Dicky's bedside in Valley Forge, Robby felt like he'd entered the deepest, darkest valley he'd ever known.

The make-shift hospital was a quickly assembled log cabin that smelled of body odor and blood. His brother was as white as the snow blanketing everything outside. His blond hair was soaked with sweat. More poured down his face, but he shivered beneath a thin, cotton bedcover. He'd taken two hits, but the doctor had only been able to get one of the musket balls out—the one that hit his forearm. The other remained lodged near Dicky's spine, slowly killing him. According to the doctor, he would die soon.

There was nothing Robby could do. He hated feeling helpless, but pestering the doctor accomplished nothing either, so he read Dicky's favorite Psalm aloud. "'Yea, though I walk through the valley of the shadow of death, I will fear no evil: for thou art with me; thy rod and thy staff they comfort me.'"

"Robby?" Dicky whispered, squinting and barely opening his eyes.

"I'm here." Robby set down the Bible and took Dicky's trembling hand.

Dicky coughed, his whole body shaking. He groaned. His knuckles whitened as he gripped his thin blanket. The bandage on his arm slipped, exposing a gaping, red wound. "You don't have to worry about me. I'm going to heaven today."

Robby rewrapped his brother's arm, tying the bandage tight. "No. You're going to live."

Dicky coughed hard, rolling onto his side and moaning. With a grimace, he rolled back. "It hurts," he breathed.

"Just hang on, Dicky." But Robby feared the doctor's warning. Dicky had little time left.

"Tell Mama I love her."

Robby shook his head.

"Tell Pa he can be proud of me." Dicky's quivering smile brought tears to Robby's eyes.

"I'm proud of you, Dicky. You're—" he exhaled as the tears fell, "a real hero."

"You, too, brother."

Those were Dicky's last words. As the sky darkened and a full moon rose above the encampment, Robby's best friend and brother passed away. Dicky had proven himself to be a brave and honorable soldier. Mama and Pa would've been so proud if they could've seen him on the battlefield.

Standing over the mound of his brother's filled in grave, the chill in the air ate at the marrow of Robby's bones. No amount of campfires could remove that deep, bitter cold from his core.

Men died every day at Valley Forge, and not just from battle wounds. Typhus and other diseases took many lives. Some succumbed to starvation and exposure. Through it all, General Washington never once took leave of the men, unlike most of the other generals and officers. He stayed, working every day to ensure their survival.

The day Washington's courier died, Robby volunteered to take an important letter to Congress at York. He needed something to take his mind off his broken heart.

The travel was slow, seven days one way, but no worse than if he'd remained at Valley Forge. The biting wind hollowed out Robby's insides until everything felt frozen. He found quarters each night at accommodating houses, and welcomed the opportunity to defrost on the floor beside a blazing fire.

When he delivered the letter, he took a moment to gaze at the faces of some of the men who had signed the Declaration of Independence just two years prior. How long until the dream of freedom would come true? The bleakness of this deadly winter gave Robby little hope.

On the way back, another letter in hand for General Washington, the wind picked up speed, biting and tearing at him like a ravaging animal. Soon, he was in the middle of a blizzard. Robby knew his way when the weather had been clear, but lost his bearings in the storm. Even with his map, he couldn't find the house where he'd received quarter. Instead he wandered in the woods for hours, wondering which direction was east and afraid that wolves might make a meal of him.

Exhausted, he collapsed in the snow. He couldn't feel his fingers or toes. He said a prayer, and curled up as best he could against a tree. Shivering, he fell asleep.

The crackling of a fire woke Robby. Smoke, paper, and wood smells wafted around him. He opened his eyes, sitting up from the floor of a wood shack. The place was small with one table and two chairs. The fire beneath the mantle had a pot of boiling water over it. A bed nestled in one corner. Someone slept on that bed, lightly snoring. Outside, the howling wind sent flakes of snow flying past the only window in a white haze.

Robby rose quietly, not wanting to wake the stranger. He tiptoed to the sleeping form. A man with dark hair had a quilt pulled up to his chin. His breathing labored. A red rash covered his pale face and neck, similar to what he'd seen on soldiers with typhus. Yet this rash was less prominent. He might be on the mend. Did he save Robby from the blizzard?

With silent backward steps, Robby took a seat at the table. A loaf of bread sat on top, and Robby's mouth watered. Next to the bread sat two letters.

He restrained himself from eating the bread without being offered any, but picked up the letters to see who this man might be. One was addressed to a Miss Olivia Wilton. The half-written note stopped mid-sentence. The second letter was from Miss Wilton and addressed to Lady Maryanne Carrington.

Robby's breath caught in his throat. He gasped. Glancing at the sleeping man, he wondered how these letters came into his possession. In his glance, he noticed that more letters burned in the fire. That explained the papery smell.

He read the opening line of the unfinished letter.

Dear Olivia, my friend and confidante, I must inform you of an interesting development regarding a mutual friend—

The door flung open. With it, the howling wind wailed inside.

Robby dropped the letter and stood, pushing his chair back with a *screech* on the wood floor.

The man who entered wore a heavy coat and several pelts. His familiar black hat, once removed, allowed Robby to confirm the man's identity. Brown hair, brown eyes, and pale skin. The deserter.

"Samuel Smith. What are you doing here?" Robby asked. Smith had saved him from the storm. He didn't know whether to thank him or to rebuke him.

Smith shut the door and dropped some of the pelts onto the floor. "It's a good place to hide."

"Water?" asked a weak, scratchy voice behind Robby. The man in bed lifted his head. He barely opened his eyes.

Robby thought of Dicky, who'd looked much worse than this man during his last days.

Smith walked up to the boiling pot and dipped out a ladleful into two cups. "It's hot." He gave one to Robby. The other, he placed on the floor beside the bed. "Give it a moment to cool, Denton."

"*Colonel* Denton?" asked Robby. As in Maryanne's fiancé? The redcoat who sent soldiers to Hartford?

"Who is it?" mumbled the invalid.

Smith glanced at Robby. He lifted the cup to Denton's mouth. "Sip, and then you need more rest."

After slurping some water, he obeyed, immediately laying his head back. Soon, he was snoring again.

"What is your name?" Smith approached the table, removing his outer coat.

"Robert Freeman. Everyone calls me Robby." He sipped, the hot water warming his throat. He sat at the table again hoping for an explanation.

"You did enlist after all." Smith's smile didn't reach his eyes, just like Maryanne. "Your brother, too?"

Did Maryanne tell Smith about their meeting? "Dicky died of battle wounds." It pained Robby to think about it, especially with a bedridden man in the room.

"I'm sorry." He bowed his head and picked up the letters.

"Many men are dying at Valley Forge. Why did you desert after Harlem Heights?" asked Robby. "With your skills, you could've become a legend. The man who never misses a shot."

Smith smirked. "To avoid that very thing. Becoming, as you say, a legend." He tossed one of the letters into the fire. The half-written one he pocketed. "Did you read these?"

"No." It wasn't a lie. Robby hadn't. "Lady Carrington mentioned you. Where is she?"

Smith didn't answer. He took a seat across from him at the table. "Here." He handed Robby a piece of bread.

He ate, not caring how tough and stale it was going down. "How did you end up here with a sick redcoat?"

"I saved your life. If I answer your questions, will you promise not to reveal my whereabouts to anyone?"

Robby thought about it. Desperate for news of Maryanne, he nodded. "Is Maryanne well?"

"I will explain everything. It's all very complicated. Just listen for now." Smith folded his hands on the table. "Despite what you may have heard, she wasn't the daughter of a lord. A few letters, forged papers, and a lot of money can do wonders." Smith smiled again, but this time the corners of his eyes crinkled. "She came to America with him because she was interested in the concept of freedom and the lengths the colonists would go to secure it," he glanced at the snoring Denton, "but never intended to marry him."

Despite her bizarre behavior, Robby couldn't have guessed any of it. "Did he abuse her? Is that why she ran away from him? What is your connection to her?"

"No, he didn't abuse her. Do not interrupt." He gave Robby more bread, probably to keep his mouth occupied. "Denton was kind, but she was ready to change in order to gain a greater understanding of the war from the other side. She became . . . me."

Already, he was more confusing than Maryanne had been. Robby opened his mouth, but Smith lifted a hand to stop him from speaking.

"That is our only connection. These," he touched his pocket, "I'll continue to write because Miss Wilton amuses me like she amused Maryanne. Soon, I'll be gone, too. I'm ready to change, and whoever I decide to become will write Maryanne's letters as long as it pleases them."

Robby's head swam with all these strange revelations. He was having trouble keeping up. "I don't understand. What do you mean that she became you?"

"I knew you would be fixated on her. So many were." Suddenly, Smith touched his ear, startling as if an insect had flown into it. "Do you ever hear voices?"

Robby leaned back. "No." Now he was concerned. Smith might be a sharpshooter, but if he heard voices, he also might be insane. In that case, Robby had to carefully weigh each claim Smith made. Robby frowned. "Why did she pretend to be the daughter of a lord? Where did she go? Why did you enlist and desert?"

Blinking, Smith responded, "I've already told you about Maryanne." He tapped the table with his fingers, staring at Robby as if evaluating him. "Here is the simplest truth. She went west, and she's never going to return. Neither will I. I'm ready to move on, or perhaps return to something familiar." Smith cupped his chin, gazing out the window. "The why is simply a way of life. To move in different circles of society at will is our privilege. We needed to understand this conflict from both sides. That's why I enlisted." He faced Robby again, dropping his hand to the table. "In plain terms, you'll never see her again."

That put the nail in it. Robby sighed. "She's dead, then."

Smith opened his mouth, but paused for a moment before saying, "It might help if you think of her as an angel. Someone who can appear one instance and vanish the next."

It wasn't hard for Robby to imagine her in heaven. Still, Smith's vagueness frustrated him. If only he would admit what killed her. Indians or disease or exposure. Maybe he wanted to spare Robby the heartache of losing someone else after Dicky. Or perhaps her death had driven Smith insane. Why else would he say that she *became* him? That made no sense. "People will think she's alive because you're writing to her friend."

Smith shrugged. "As for my reasons for deserting, it could not be helped at first. I was captured and imprisoned for a year. They tortured me, as well."

"Captured?" Robby swallowed, the stale bite scraping his throat. Everyone had been wrong about Smith. "Tortured?" He was so calm about it. "Why are you caring for the man who tortured you?"

With a glance toward the invalid, Smith shook his head. "He captured me, but didn't torture me, others did. I escaped because I can pick locks and I'm a good fighter. When I secured a weapon, I took Denton as my hostage. On our way here, he became ill with typhus. Now he's nearly recovered. When I'm gone in a week, Denton will be free to find his way to a British encampment. My change will prevent Denton from ever finding me again."

Squinting, Robby decided Smith at least told one truth: this was complicated. Despite Smith's healthy appearance, the talk about becoming someone else had to stem from insanity. The year of torture could explain the frail state of his mind.

Robby had no more time for it. The wind had died down considerably, and he couldn't waste another moment. "I have to get back. I'm no deserter." He rose. "It seems neither were you."

"Not intentionally, no. But I don't plan to return. It's my time to—"

"Change, yes. I . . . understand," Robby lied. "Thank you for rescuing me. I won't forget that kindness, nor my promise."

"Good-bye, Freeman." Smith shook his hand. "I have one consolation for you. The army at Valley Forge will not likely be disturbed by redcoats."

"In that alone, we've been fortunate," said Robby, unsure why Smith knew about it but not in the mood to ask any more questions.

"If you can last the winter, you may have a fighting chance come spring. I wish you and the men the best of luck."

As Robby trudged back toward the encampment, he replayed the strange events of the day over and over. He might've been better off not having any of Smith's strange admissions swimming around in his head. The headache left behind would likely last the winter because he couldn't stop trying to sort it out.

Maryanne Carrington was more of a mystery than ever. Perhaps she really was an angel. Forevermore, Robby would think of her as the angel who carried his brother, Dicky, into heaven.

Samuel Smith was right. The terrible winter at Valley Forge passed, and no one came to challenge them. More food and supplies arrived to strengthen them. The men were tougher than ever before. Robby was ready to fight again. He'd make sure Dicky's death was not in vain.

XI

Pennsylvania, February 1778

A letter from Miss Olivia Wilton to Lady Maryanne Carrington.

Dearest, sweetest friend, I feel alive as never before. All this war business, and yet I am giddy and gay. I never thought I'd find happiness again. So many hard months have passed, including that entire year without a word from you! Luckily, you found it in your heart to write me again, and we shall never stop, shall we?

Let me explain to you the cause for my felicity, though you must have already guessed it.

My dearest William, the most worthy General Howe, has remained with me these past months, and his intentions are to remain in the house many months hence! He has taken this break from battle simply to cradle me in his arms and profess his undying love day after day, night after night. How could I have ever believed such happiness was possible?

We are the talk of Philadelphia, and I confess I would have it no other way. I accompany him to every ball and important dinner. Wherever he is needed, he needs me beside him! It is not like before, when the ladies would scoff at me. Not openly, no, only when I was apart from Dearest William, alone like a doe amongst the lionesses.

This winter is harsh, and at times makes it difficult for us to meet all of our societal obligations, but I cannot complain. There is a fire in my heart that keeps me warm at all times, and it burns strongest when Dearest William is with me.

I feel so bold in writing this way. I speak to no one about it. Even my closest friends have abandoned me, except to give polite discussion at balls and dinners. But you, my dear dear friend, will never abandon me.

Dearest William told me something that I'm not permitted to share with anyone. But of course, these letters are a secret even from him that I will never disclose, unless, perhaps, we become husband and wife. It still surprises me that I have not conceived a child, but I dare not give up hope that in such a case, he would propose to me.

His secret is quite scandalous, and I need not tell you to keep it as close to your heart as you keep all of your own. For he is well aware that this war could've been ended quickly. He knows that Washington's army was on the brink of destruction after each and every defeat. Even now, as they winter at Valley Forge, he grants them another reprieve. And that is his secret. He has allowed them to regroup time and again. And for what, you may ask?

Why, for me.

Yes! Indeed, my heart bursts with delight at the thought, let alone when he spoke these words aloud. Should he have destroyed this rebellion quickly, the fight would be over and he would be sent back to England. But so long as the fight continues, he can spend his winter months in my most precious company. I speak in his words, not my own.

Oh, my sweet friend, our correspondence is a gift that I shall never take for granted. It gives me great pleasure to share with you these deep secrets of my heart. Do not hesitate to write and share with me more of yours.

Truly, you now know all of my secrets. Every last one. Will you not now, after all this time, disclose to me all of yours and keep nothing from me? For I know you have many more to share, and I am eager to hear them.

From the most devoted and loving friend you will ever have, who may one day be the wife of a general, Olivia

Author's Notes - Bria Burton

Historically, General William Howe's alleged mistress was already married. Speculation and gossip surrounded Howe and Mrs. Elizabeth Loring due to their constant companionship, both lovers of drinking and gambling. Howe bestowed upon Mrs. Loring's husband the appointment of commissary general to the prisoners. Some described Mr. Loring as a sociopath, hence rumors of torture and murder of prisoners. Historians assume that Howe gave Loring the lucrative title to appease him, since he supposedly knew of the affair. Further speculation that General Howe neglected his duty, but not his mistress, was succinctly summed up by Patriot Israel Putnam, who noted that Howe was "either a friend of America or no General."

—BB

EVER AFTER

Two mysterious women convey the same Cinderella story to Giambattista Basile in 1594 and Jacob and Wilhelm Grimm in 1811. How cultures change and retell this story over time reveals humanity's soul to those who listen.

—MJC

Play a game. Sit in a circle of friends. Whisper a story to the person next to you. Let your story travel around the circle. Listen to what returns. What does this exercise tell us about these people, their beliefs, their society? Extend the circle to include a town, a country, a culture, a millennium. Whisper a special story, quiet as a butterfly's dance, into the right ear. Let that story weave through a people, changing with time and retelling until it returns, like birds flying home in the spring. Hear the secrets it brings. What do those secrets reveal about us?

Venice, Italy, 1594

In the hour before dawn, Giambattista Basile lay back and sighed. "*Scusimi*," he whispered. He shifted and straightened the bed sheet where it had bunched under his back. Always the gentleman, he reached across the woman he knew as Yu Yan and tugged the top sheet over her nakedness. She reacted by throwing the sheet off.

"Too warm," she murmured, and rolled onto her side, facing him before snuggling in and working her shoulder into his embrace. She flipped her hair over his encircling arm and stretched against him, rolling the tension from her muscles, then sighed contentedly, her head on his chest.

He pulled a pillow under his head and allowed his gaze to caress her. Her hair cascaded over his arm and down her back, a waterfall of black silk. Tiny beads of sweat clung to her coppery bronze skin in the flickering candlelight. He inhaled slowly. Their lovemaking added a musky scent to the humid, salt-tinged air from outside.

Water in the canal below lapped against the stones of the building, soothing him. He smiled and turned his attention to the open window. Above the silhouetted rooftops, the moon descended toward a rose-hued horizon. Rain today. Perhaps they would stay in all day, listening as fat drops on the tiles sang them to sleep in a lover's lullaby.

As he returned his attention to the woman in his arms, his lips brushed against her hair. *"Mia bella amore."* He let the words trickle out, hoping she was awake.

"Yes?" Her murmured reply betrayed no hint of sleep.

"I wish," he said, "this moment could last forever. It is like a soap bubble in the sun." After only a month he had already noticed the first stirrings of restlessness in her – the way her eyes moved to the horizon for a moment, or a smile in conversation, as if her thoughts were elsewhere. In his experience this was something unusual in women and it made her all the more interesting to him.

She shifted. Her muscles tensed under smooth skin before relaxing again. "Forever is a very long time to maintain perfection, Giambattista."

"Si," he said. "You are right, of course." The wisdom of a thousand years in one with barely a quarter of a century. No wonder her people

were so exotic. "I so loved the story with the little enchanted man and the spinning wheel." He moved against her. "Perhaps you would grace me with another?"

Promethea lifted her head and settled her chin on his chest. Her lips curved as she blinked eyes the shape of almonds and the color of pitch. "A bedtime story?"

"No, my dove. Just a story, so I may hear your voice. It is *incantare* – enchanting."

"Are you familiar with the tales told by the Greek courtesan Rhodopis while she was a slave in Egypt?"

He thought for a moment. "No, I'm sorry. Please, I would love to hear one."

Her single chuckle was deep and throaty. "Yes, my love." Her fingers trailed down his abdomen. She cupped him in her hand. "Then, perhaps we can spend the day searching for perfection."

And she began the story. . .

* * *

Ella sat alone on the granite stairs leading to her garden as the sky cleared. The rain-soaked, fresh growth on the trees loosened fat drops of water into puddles beneath. The birds chirped out season's change. These things always brought her joy.

No longer.

The back door of the house creaked open. Martha stepped out, tossing Ella a look as unyielding as the stones on which she sat. "There's work to be done."

With a sigh, she followed Martha into the dark, stuffy kitchen. "Finish making supper while your sisters get dressed, and be quick about it."

Tears trickled down Ella's porcelain-smooth cheeks again at the thought of her step-sisters wearing her dresses to the party. At least she had been spared the indignity of having to make the adjustments to fit them. Marie and Ruth had become accomplished seamstresses and easily made the changes. Marie, who'd shed the last of her baby fat, and Ruth, who was a year older, but no taller than her sister, were often mistaken as twins. Their long, rich, auburn hair and burnt ochre eyes were identical to each other's and perfect copies of Martha's.

"Why won't you let me go along? I might find a husband to get me from underfoot." Ella expected the answer to be no different this time. Her real longing was to leave this stifling town forever and visit the places her father had painted in her imagination with his stories.

Martha's laugh was a stiff, mirthless bark. "Who would want the likes of you? Scrawny, with stringy, straight yellow hair, taller than most of the boys your age." She regarded Ella with a sneer. "And of what use is a wife who can read? You've become almost passable at women's work with direction, but honestly, I do not understand what your fool of a father was thinking, teaching a girl to read. It's a useless skill for a woman."

"My father –"

"Is dead." Martha's eyes narrowed. "I am your father's widow, and everything that was his, is mine. My daughters will inherit from me. I will find suitable husbands for them, a spice merchant or perhaps even a banker. As soon as I can find a nice, stooped pig farmer," Martha said, brushing her hands together, "I will be done with you." Her mouth formed a thin, sour smile.

Anger flushed Ella's cheeks. Everything was so different when her father was still alive. Martha had been kind, telling Ella and her stepsisters bedtime stories, teaching the girls manners, and managing the house. Her father had grown happy again. She pulled her thin shoulders back and defiantly locked eyes with her stepmother.

"Witch."

The slap seemed to come from nowhere, catching her off-guard and reddening her cheek.

"Bastard child! I have told you to refer to me as Stepmother. If you ever dare to look at me in that manner again, I'll pluck your eyes out and feed them to the crows. Now, finish preparing supper, and afterwards, you'll help your sisters to dress for the party. When we leave in the coach, you will clean up and start the bread for tomorrow. Do you have any questions?"

"No, Stepmother." Ella blinked and dropped her gaze to Martha's shoes. Her lye-soap blistered hands formed fists, hidden in the pleats of her dress. She would rather pluck her own eyes out than give Martha the satisfaction of seeing her cry. It wasn't her fault her father had doted on her, bought her books, and taught her to read. Nor was it her fault he had never married her mother, who died in childbirth.

* * *

Ella watched from a window while the trio rode away in a carriage, laughing. It was time to act. Her secret plan had been in the works for weeks.

In the pantry that had served as her bedroom since her father's death, she glanced over her shoulder before removing the false bottom in the basket containing the family's supply of ground rye for bread. Her last party dress was carefully folded inside. Working late at night by candlelight, she had altered the dress to fit her now thinner and taller frame.

She brushed her long, straight, blond hair until it shone. Then, with trembling fingers, she pinned her tresses onto the top of her head, allowing a few golden tendrils to frame her face. Satisfied, she ran upstairs, and taking a deep breath, stole into Martha's room and sprayed rose water onto her exposed neck and shoulders.

She hurried down the stairs and out of her house, headed for High Street. As she approached one of the houses, an old woman dressed head to foot in black stepped out. The woman spilled water from a wooden bucket onto the stone steps and scrubbed them with a stiff-bristled broom. She stared up at Ella without blinking, her opaque onyx eyes set in a face creased by cares. If Ella stayed, the years would rob her of her youth and beauty, her strength draining away in the street like the spilled water until she found herself old and worn out, too.

"No," she whispered. Perhaps someone of royal lineage would notice her. One of them would never marry a commoner, of course. The best she could expect was to become a plaything, but being a royal mistress wasn't a bad option. Even this was preferable to scrubbing floors until her fingers bled. She had seen the Duke's son and occasionally even dreamt of him on warm nights in the pantry.

The evening air swirled around her. Iron horse shoes and wagon wheels on cobblestones made her turn. Her heart thumped in her throat as a friend of her father's approached, late in his delivery of wine to the castle. She smiled.

"Well, well." Eric's creased, hairy face broke into a toothless smile, as he stopped his cart alongside her. "Who is this I find walking to the castle? It must be a princess. Where is your fine coach, highness?"

Returning Eric's smile, Ella curtseyed. "Fine sir, I find myself with neither coach nor driver. I might impose upon your kindness for transport to the castle, but only if I can trust you not to take advantage of a defenseless girl."

He laughed. "Highness, you cut me to the quick. I'm no brigand or scoundrel to make gain of a girl's disadvantage." He held out his hand to her. "Please, Miss, do me the honor of allowing me to fetch you to yonder castle."

Ella's step onto the cart exposed her feet, upon which were her old, scarred, leather shoes she had almost outgrown and could no longer lace properly.

His face clouded over. "Alas, lady, it seems someone has stolen your fine velvet shoes."

Sitting next to him on the rough wooden seat of the cart, she silently moved her feet under the cover of her dress.

With the brake released and the cart moving again, he glanced at her from the corner of his eye. "And how are things at your father's old house?"

"Times are hard." Ella shrugged.

Eric harrumphed, his attention returning to the ox pulling the cart. "Not so hard we'll come upon your generous stepmother or her darlings walking this evening, I'll wager."

"She's often praised for her magnanimity for giving me a roof and food. We should speak of other things," she said, quietly.

His smile returned. "Are you off to the dance to find a fit husband? The Duke's son, perhaps?"

Ella slipped her arm around Eric's. Her head found a resting place on his shoulder. "Branos? Hardly. But perhaps you'd be interested in a fine young wife. I'm told I'm passable at women's work, even if I can read."

Patting her hand with the same affection he had shown her as a child when he had done business with her father, Eric sighed. "A beautiful girl with your intelligence can do better than a worn out old man. There is more to the world than this tiny town, highness."

"The world is too big a place for a woman alone."

He shook his head, his eyes sympathetic. "No one who can read and write is ever truly alone."

As they rode along, Eric told Ella stories of her father and her real mother. Her laughter sparked for the first time in what seemed a lifetime.

Ahead, the castle loomed over the northern edge of town. Eric stopped the cart, easing on the brake. Without a word, he slipped a small, gold ring off his little finger and onto her right middle finger.

"No," she stammered. "I can't. It was your wife's."

Eric smiled as though from far away. "I cheated your father out of it when you were two. It should have been yours, and now it is again. For luck."

Her lips touched his cheek. "I will never forget your kindness since my father's death. I'm sure a special place awaits you in heaven."

"So Father Thomas tells me," Eric said, holding her hand for a moment. "Now, off to find a good husband and a future full of children and grandchildren."

Working her way into the castle was easy. The guards were drunk, and young, pretty, well-dressed girls came and went without question. Ella slipped past alcoves with ornate woven tapestries. In no time, she was in the main ballroom. Everywhere, vases held flowers caught in explosions of color, filling the room with delicate scents. The polished marble floor stretched on forever, shimmering in the candlelight. On the floor, people floated and spun, butterflies caught in a whirlwind of music. Overwhelmed, she exited through one of the floor-to-ceiling doorways onto the balcony to catch her breath. The whole town stretched out beneath her feet. Columns of gentian, lilly, and jasmine scented the night.

Her nerves vibrated under her skin in the darkness. A sound to her left alerted her and she stepped behind a column as Marie walked by, arm in arm with a pasty-faced boy who looked as though he might panic and dart away at any moment. Marie had already been the recipient of several trips to the punch bowl, and her eyes shone like brown glass orbs as she passed. Ella turned and scanned the room. Ruth was on the dance floor. Martha huddled in a corner with a tight knot of matrons quietly plotting their children's destinies.

Movement and sound drew her inside again. In a surprisingly short time, handsome young men surrounded her. She hoped one of them would find her interesting enough.

Then she saw him. Or rather, they saw each other. The Duke's son strode purposefully across the ballroom floor. A gold medallion hung around his neck. The ribbon it hung from formed a scarlet V on the front of his crisp, white linen shirt. The other young men melted away as he approached. His hand extended to her in a command to dance with him.

He whirled her onto the floor. After a few minutes, her head swam. Her breath came in gasps, her cheeks warmed.

They stepped through the crowd. He pulled her into one of the alcoves. His lips were rough on hers. He bit her lower lip and clawed savagely at her breasts, trying to undo her bodice. He forced her onto a small divan against a wall. Pinning her with his weight, he forced his knee between hers. The mumbled words that passed his lips were garbled and incoherent, but his intentions were obvious.

"No." Her choked-out words could have been from someone else's throat.

His blue eyes were glazed, his face was flushed, and his breath reeked of brandy. He murmured a slur so ugly it revolted her. Not like this, she thought. Not with a beast like him.

"No," she said again, louder, struggling. Fury filled her. Her bodice ripping matched her nails raking his face.

He let go of her and found his feet, swaying, mouth open in disbelief, a hand over the bright red rivulets crossing his eyelid and cheek. He glared at her as she stood to face him, her anger and loathing matching the hatred in his eyes. He started for her.

Visions of prison and torture and worse filled her. Her foot reacted reflexively, with all the strength in her young leg.

The blow landed hard. Branos coughed once and doubled over, his arms crossed in front of his belly. He hit the floor in a lump, face crimson, eyes locked closed. Too shocked by pain to scream, all he could manage were quiet grunts.

Blood roared in Ella's ears as the implications of her actions washed over her. She would certainly be imprisoned and probably executed. Her youth and beauty were forfeit in a moment's foolishness. They might even give her to the other prisoners as an amusement, to be torn apart when they'd finished taking turns with her. Mouth dry, she covered her exposed bosom with the remnants of her party dress and stole toward the nearest exit even as the clock chimed.

Excited voices sounded an alarm behind her as she tripped while descending the main stairway, narrowly escaping a tumble down the marble steps by grabbing onto the banister. As she approached the doorway, the guards passed her headed in the other direction, ignoring the silly girl with the torn dress.

At the main gate, Ella stopped to catch her breath. "Damn," she said out loud. One of her shoes was missing. She dare not return for it. Now she was completely undone. There would be no hiding. She had to get away to someplace where she could think. First though, she had to get home.

She kicked her other shoe into the bushes and ran along the same road she and Eric had traversed only a few hours ago. It seemed a lifetime ago. She cursed the full moon riding high in the cloudless sky. If she could have arrested its arc by will alone, it would have returned to its cradle below the horizon, giving her running silhouette refuge in the gloom.

Arriving at home, she scrambled, gasping up the stone front steps. She threw open the door and tumbled into the foyer in a panic. Running to the kitchen, she packed some bread, cheese, and two bottles of wine into a burlap bag. To these she added her meager belongings, what remained of her father's silverware, and his traveling dagger, all the while looking over her shoulder, expecting her stepmother to burst fuming into the foyer – or worse.

The moon had moved toward the horizon when Ella stole out the kitchen door. Tears streamed down her cheeks as she crept through her garden for probably the last time. She hadn't used her proper name while at the party, but the town was small enough that if the Duke wanted to find her he would have no trouble – and she was fairly certain he would want to find her.

With Martha's cloak wrapped around her shoulders, she crept through the alleyways. A pair of Martha's shoes clicked on the cobblestones, strips of linen wound around her feet, allowing her to cinch them properly. After what seemed an eternity, keeping to darkened streets and alleys and melting into the shadows at any sound, she found herself at Eric's small house at the edge of town. The sky was just lightening in the east as she tapped on his door.

The door creaked on its hinges as it opened a crack, then wider. "My poor girl. Come in, quickly." Eric's voice was inviting. Closing the door behind her, he spoke without lighting a candle, his tone quiet. "I was still at the castle awaiting payment for my delivery when Branos regained his senses. Never have I seen anyone so furious. He searched the guests for you then sent everyone home. I overheard them planning to use bloodhounds to track you."

Ella's hands covered her mouth, her eyes closed. "He wanted to... tried to... I couldn't, not like that."

He brushed a stray hair from her face. "You did the right thing. Unfortunately, the right thing often brings a price."

"Oh, Eric, tell me he doesn't know my identity," she sobbed.

Eric placed his hands on her trembling shoulders. "Not yet, little one, I only recognized you from the description of your dress."

"I'm not safe here," she said through her sobs. "You aren't safe as long as I'm here. If I can get to the river..."

"It's too far to walk with them searching for you. Come with me." He led Ella through the house to the back door, out to the barn, where the ox was still yoked to his cart. Eric spread a blanket on some straw in the cart. "You lie here, highness, I will secret you to a safe distance."

Ella's eyes widened. "But the hounds. . ."

"Shh." Eric held his finger to his lips. "I have a plan. Something your father and I did." He cleared his throat. "From time to time," he added and gave her a grin.

Eric left her alone while she crawled onto the cart, then made herself as comfortable as possible while she waited in the early, pre-dawn chill.

He returned, placing a small package next to her on the blanket before he quietly led the ox from the barn.

"Lie down now, and be quiet," he whispered, covering her with a second blanket. She lay swathed in the woolen shroud, under an additional weight pungent with the odor of straw while he loaded dung into the cart on top of her.

Entombed as she was in the cart, hours seemed like days as the sun rose. Under the straw, Ella sweltered. She managed to slip loose of her stepmother's cloak without shifting the straw, and fortunately, the dung above her was dry. Seepage would have been unbearable.

They were stopped only once by soldiers. Ella listened intently, hoping they had at least gotten her description wrong, but they knew everything about her except her whereabouts. There had been a distinct scarcity of blonde girls in green and yellow dresses at the party.

The story they told left tears in her eyes and her stomach fluttering. Upon arriving home, only shortly after Ella had departed, Martha immediately discovered the missing items, especially Ella. She had gone to the Duke to ingratiate herself, claiming Ella was insane and had escaped from where she was normally confined in the attic.

As the day cooled into evening, Eric pulled the cart off the roadway. It shifted as he got down from the seat and removed the overlying layer of dung. Ella threw off the blanket and sat up, taking her first deep breath in hours.

"I shall never be rid of this smell," she said, wrinkling her nose and smiling at her savior.

Returning her lightheartedness, Eric replied, "But highness, better to smell like a dung heap and be alive, than a rose and crushed under the Duke's boot heel."

"Or broken on the rack," she agreed, shivering. She slid to the rear of the cart, preparing to step onto the ground.

"Indeed," Eric said, offering her his hand. "While Branos toasts to your health with hundred year old brandy."

"How can I ever repay you?" she asked, hugging her friend.

Sniffing, with a wrinkle of his nose, Eric replied, "No need, little one. Your safety is my repayment. Your father wanted more for you." He sneered in the castle's direction. "In truth, I never held much regard for your stepmother. Perhaps Branos will find in her a suitable substitute for his wrath."

She shook her head. "I wish her no ill fortune."

He eyed her. "A good heart. You are your father's daughter. Over the next hill, you'll come to a stream where you can wash your clothes. Half a day's walk further on is a town with a way station. The coach will take you to Hamburg, and from there, to your new life." He handed her the package he had laid next to her in the cart. "Some food and a bottle of wine. Also, there is sixty heller. I only wish there was more. Now you should go, or I might be tempted to take advantage of a defenseless woman alone on the road." He smiled.

She slid the dagger from her belt. "And you would pay dearly."

His smile broadened, and her dagger found its sheath again.

"I shall miss you, my prince," she said and kissed his stubbled cheeks.

He turned his cart in the direction they had come and walked alongside his ox, patting its ears gently as Ella strode into her future.

* * *

Hanover, Germany, 1811

Wilhelm Grimm watched from under the brim of his hat as his brother Jacob sat back in his seat, his mouth agape. He regarded the mysterious, dark-haired woman in the seat opposite Jacob. The coach rocked in its gentle rhythm while German farms rolled past outside, verdant and lush, the scent of fertile land full on the breeze flowing in through the coach's open windows.

"What a wonderful story." Jacob smiled. "We can give you five kreutzer for the right to include it in our book." He nudged Wilhelm, who still slouched on the seat next to him. "I especially like the morality about reaching too far. It reminds me of that Greek story – Icarus." He made a sweeping gesture with his arm. "Yes, tried to fly too high and the wax holding her wings melted. We'll have to change some of the details, of course, and the names." He counted out the coins.

"Harrumph." It was the first sound Wilhelm had made.

"You disagree?"

"With paying fifty heller for a story which will in all probability get us arrested for sedition and questioned by the King himself? I should think so." His hat still lay low over his eyes, as it had while she told her story. Next to where she sat on the smooth-worn, wooden seat, his stretched out legs were crossed at the ankles.

"Skinflint." Jacob snorted. "It's a good story. We'll change some particulars."

"Please forgive my older brother, Miss. He forgets only the illiterate resort to name calling," Wilhelm replied as he sat up and removed his hat. He blinked at the late-afternoon sunlight slanting in through the window.

Jacob smiled at his brother. "It's a good story, and you know it. We can use it for the book." He turned back to her. "In the pantry, were there cinders from the stove? Did they get into her hair and eyes? And mice, there must be mice." He jotted notes in his book. "And a fairy of some sort. Every story needs a supernatural element."

"Of course," she said. There was a flicker of something on her face – amusement, or indulgence, perhaps. Her gaze shifted from one brother to the other. "You are storytellers?"

"We are story collectors," Jacob said with a proud grin. "And you?"

She shifted, leaning forward. "When you were children, did you ever play a game," she asked. "Where you sit in a circle and whisper into the ear of the child next to you, each one retelling the story until it returns?"

"Of course," Jacob said. "The story changes so that one hardly recognizes it."

"Echoes in a mountain pass," she said. "Always the same, yet different."

Wilhelm regarded the attractive, olive-skinned young woman. Her black, shoulder-length curls, intense, pitch-dark eyes, and high, smooth cheekbones lent her an exotic look. There was something mysterious and open about her in the same instant – like stained glass, allowing light to pass through, or reflecting it back, depending on one's perspective. He spoke softly. "Give her ten kreutzer, and chalk it up to charity, spendthrift. My God, she looks half-starved." In truth, she looked nothing of the sort. Her clothes were travel-worn, but well-cut, and she had a healthy glow. Wilhelm allowed his gaze to skim over her, then forced his thoughts into more polite channels.

Jacob counted out the coins and placed them in her hand. "If we take some of the intimacies out and change the names, the King himself may not even recognize it, Willie." He winked at her.

Wilhelm shrugged. "Or, Jerome will have us in prison, or worse yet, expel us from the library." Ten kreutzer for a story? He almost laughed.

She slipped the coins into her pack. When she looked up at Jacob a smile flowed onto her lips, which he returned, brightening his face.

Wilhelm watched them. Jacob seemed interested in this young woman. Sometimes he became so obsessed with work that Wilhelm worried for him. He absently wondered how this one and his Dorchen would get on, but pushed the thought aside. Before there could be any further discussion, the coach neared the station and slowed. Wilhelm stirred, preparing to get up.

"Where are you going?" She covered her mouth with her hand for her lack of manners and looked away with a coquettish gesture. "I am sorry. It is none of my affair. I just thought. . ."

"We're stopping at Hannover for a day or two," Jacob blurted out, caught up in his excitement. "We're here to gather a local story about a girl raised in a tower by her . . ." he hesitated for a moment. "Her aunt, I think. Oh well, it sounds like a wonderful story, and I'm sure it will be a perfect addition."

She considered for a moment. "I have another story, if it pleases you, kind sirs. About a little enchanted man and a spinning wheel, or one about a young woman who falls under an enchantment to awaken to a new life."

"I knew it." Jacob grinned and handed her his card. "A story-teller. Happy coincidence. Come see us at the King's library in Cassel in a week's time. If the other stories are good. . . who knows? And you say you can read?"

She nodded.

"You see," Jacob said to his brother. "Perhaps she can organize our notes. What did you say your name is, dear girl?"

She hesitated. "Anastasia," she said from behind a shy smile.

"Anastasia. A Greek name, is it not?" Wilhelm asked.

"Yes, it is."

"And you can speak several languages?"

The woman traveling under the name Anastasia let her gaze float to the floor. "I can." Her smile never faltered.

"Wonderful." Jacob's grin widened.

Her smile struck Wilhelm as mischievous and reserved in approximately the same measure. It intrigued him. The coach jerked to a stop at the station, the pungent scent of the horses wafted over them. He reached out and retrieved Jacob's card from her. Kneeling, he pulled a pen from its holder, uncorked a tiny bottle of ink, jotted an address on the back, and blew on the ink to dry it.

"Our sister, Lotte Grimm," Wilhelm said as he handed her back the card and returned his pen to its holder. "She will help you with food and lodging until our return." He stole a glance at Jacob, whose eyes never left her.

A few dozen yards away, ash and smoke from the farrier's smithy cast a haze in the air and floated in the open window.

"Cinders. They get into everything," Jacob said, as the brothers shuffled out of the coach and stretched, leaving Promethea alone and looking out the window, watching and listening.

Author's Notes - MJ Carlson

The story of *Cinderella* stretches back almost two and a half millennia before the Disney version enthralled a generation, to the Greek heteara, Rhodopis, and perhaps beyond. While certain similarities in early versions exist, significant differences, associated with the individual cultures also exist. In this retelling, the reader will almost certainly notice additional changes for more modern sensibilities. I chose to bookend this version with some historical reality, however. Gaimbattista Basile (1566 – 1632), a Neapolitan poet, courtier, and soldier, is one of the earliest western authors known to publish the story (and *Rapunzel*), but the tale has its origins much earlier, and in areas far-removed from those normally associated with it (Greece, Egypt, and China, to name only a few).

I chose to end the story with Jacob (1785 – 1863) and Wilhelm (1786 – 1859) Grimm for two reasons: First, theirs is the version (other than the more recent Disney retelling) we are most familiar with. Second, we always think of the brothers as old men, patiently gathering fairy stories from wizened old women hunched over spinning wheels. We forget, when they collected the original stories, they were young men, with the same cares and desires as all young men. Their humanity should not be forgotten.

I also included a reference to Henriette Dorthea (Dorchen) Wild, who was a childhood friend of the Grimm's sister, Lotte from age twelve, and who eventually married Wilhelm. My fictional reference in the story to Promethea's "relationship" with Jacob relates to that brother's bachelorhood throughout his life. After all, who could have been satisfied with a mere human once he'd loved an immortal, alien, cybernetic probe in the form of a mysterious, intelligent, beautiful, Greek woman? —*MJC*

THE STRANGE CASE OF LORD BYRON'S LOVER

Whoever fights monsters should see to it that in the process he does not become a monster. And if you gaze long enough into an abyss, the abyss will gaze back at you.

—*Friedrich Nietzsche*

I

My memory isn't what it once was, but my past is written large within these pages. I beg you to indulge me as I recount a series of perplexing events occurring both before and after I wrote the Gothic opus for which I am known. My work achieved popular success, and even the indomitable Sir Walter Scott congratulated me for my "original genius and power of expression."

However, lest you believe the story I'm about to share in the final pages of my journal is a prideful, self-congratulatory boast, let me assure you that I, Mary Shelley, have a far stranger tale to tell than the man-made monster of my fiction. And like the creature dredged from my nightmares, these events haunt me to this day.

The mystery began innocently enough with a summer holiday spent in Lake Geneva with the notorious Lord Byron in the manor house he called Villa Diodati. I recall the manor, though stately and imposing, was cold and dreary during those days of incessant rain in June of 1816. It was the beginning of a wet, ungenial summer, a portent of the unnatural events to follow.

I didn't mind the cramped quarters of our own rented cottage since Lord Byron welcomed us into his spacious villa for much of the time, but the weather was truly depressing—blustery and rainy during the day, freakishly cold at night. As I look back at those days we resided in the village of Cologny, I can see the weather was the least freakish occurrence during our time spent with Lord Byron and his not-so-secret lover.

To this day a rational explanation defies me, but allow me to detail the mystifying incidents of that week, and perhaps someone perusing this journal after my death will come forth with an answer. Or, like me, you may decide something *unhuman* moved among us that summer—and perhaps still does.

As I began with mention of the weather, I should continue that thread of my story. A remarkable servant girl explained the dramatic change in temperature was directly related to the prior year's volcanic eruption in the islands of Indonesia. At the time I dismissed her explanation as preposterous poppycock, but looking back on what transpired, I now think she may have been correct, though how she would have known such a thing is beyond me. But that is at the heart of this mystery, is it not?

Whatever the reason for the peculiar conditions of that summer, we were forced to give up any thoughts of frolicking in the sun or sailing on the lake. Instead we spent our time reading by candlelight in the shadowed rooms of Villa Diodati, or huddled in front of the massive fireplace, drinking wine to excess.

My impetuous sister Claire—she was only a half-sister, truth be told, and half mad at that—convinced us to journey to Switzerland to spend some time with her former lover, George Gordon Noel Byron on the French-Swiss border. Please take note that George was a profligate in every way possible, including his ostentatious name, and I will henceforth refer to him as either Byron or Lord Byron, as he was more popularly known.

Though I was initially opposed to Claire's suggestion, when the deed was finally done I hoped Percy and I could use the holiday as a way to bring some relief to my grieving over the death of our daughter. Percy often exclaimed that I had a gloomy disposition and tended to lose myself in funereal brooding. This may be true, but I blame my father and the dark angel of death who visited us shortly after my birth, snatching my mother from us, leaving his bloody tracks to plague me, and my father to punish me with silent recriminations.

Looking back on my life, I fear death continued to stalk me throughout my 53 years, depositing one heartbreak after another at my doorstep. Sadly I must report losing four of my five children. My half-sister Claire, who instigated our holiday with Lord Byron, later took her own life. Could there be any doubt why I became nearly deranged by the sting of death's frequent visits? And I haven't yet mentioned death's cruelest torment, transforming me into a widow at the age of 24 when my beloved Percy drowned in a boating accident.

Is it any wonder I took to my bed for weeks, and wrote the following in my journal?

How can I not think that some veiled creature is experimenting with my life? Probing the limits of my sanity with cruel intentions by striking down all that I love and hold dear. Sometimes I feel like Job in the belly of the whale, crying out, "Why me, God? Why me?

I remember with crystal clarity the day I met Percy Bysshe Shelley, how our friendship quickly turned to lust and love. I carried Percy's child until the day she was born. We buried her two days later.

But that is all in the distant past. To begin this story, you only need know that some years after my mother's death, father married a woman of prodigious temper and narrow mind. Suffice to say we clashed in many ways, and Percy and I departed London to travel the continent, no certain destination in mind except what might amuse us and lead us to new pleasures and stimulating company. Claire joined us after the death of our daughter.

Lord Byron had impregnated Claire, as he did many women, before tossing her aside. Poor Claire, foolish to the end, believed he would take her back since she was carrying his child. Her delusions came to a head one early morning in Paris where we had rented rooms on a narrow street to the west of *Place de la Bastille*. I recall Percy and I had just finished making love when the door to our bedroom flew open and Claire rushed in, her cheeks flushed with excitement.

"He's going to summer in Lake Geneva," she gushed.

Neither of us bothered to cover ourselves since Claire had seen us both naked before. In fact, to my dismay, Percy confessed he had bedded her several times before taking up with me.

"Claire, for God's sake, you might knock before breaking down our door," I said. "Now tell me exactly who is going to Lake Geneva, though I can probably guess it must be Lord Byron."

"Who else, my dear sister," she replied, bouncing her large derriere on the bed beside me.

"That is news of no interest to us, I'm afraid."

"Don't you see? Lake Geneva is little more than a day's train ride. We were looking to move on, so why not Switzerland?"

I have previously mentioned Claire's unrestrained infatuation with Byron. He was a man of debauched appetites, and a scandalous reputation for romances with both men and women, including a shameful affair with Augusta, his half-sister. Even among those of us who professed to believe in free love, his behavior was shocking, and I could envision nothing but vexation for my sister.

"Claire, I don't believe a reunion with your former lover is a good idea."

I was trying to be gentle with her, and thought Percy would take my side. Surprisingly, he was anxious to meet Byron. And so we traveled through abnormal wintry conditions to Lake Geneva where Byron and Percy struck up an instant friendship.

Though the three of us rented a modest cottage not far from Villa Diodati, we were soon introduced to the manor and its amazing inhabitants. With Byron's arrival, the villa was transformed into an elegant carnival tent stocked with his coterie of servants, assorted sycophants, and his personal physician, Dr. John Polidori, who was darkly handsome and overly flirtatious. Along with Byron's excessive staff, he'd also brought along a menagerie of eight dogs, three monkeys, five cats, an eagle, a crow, and a peacock, as well as horses for the splendid Napoleonic coach he'd had built to transport him in the style he believed a lord should enjoy. Percy would complain that the villa was more of a zoo since all of the animals, except the horses, were free to walk around the house.

And then there was Anastasia.

Anastasia was the remarkable servant girl I alluded to earlier in my narrative. Remember her name, for it is she who stands at the center of the mystery surrounding our time spent with Lord Byron. At first blush, the girl seemed like nothing more than what she appeared to be, one of the retinue of servants Byron had carried with him to cater to his every whim during his summer sojourn to escape the creditors and notoriety he'd left behind in London.

It soon became clear Anastasia serviced Byron in many ways, including helping to satiate his ravenous sexual appetites. I understood why a man like Lord Byron would be drawn to this young girl of Greek descent. She was 23 or 24 years of age, with the coloring and dark hair of the Mediterranean people. Anastasia was attractive, though she didn't strike me as beautiful. But there was an allure to her, a sexual magnetism that clung to her like a second skin.

I was instantly struck by the boldness of her gaze and the exceptional shine of her dark eyes, which sometimes seemed to glow with an otherworldly light. She listened more than she spoke, an agreeable trait for a young woman of her breeding, often with her head slightly canted to one side like a curious hound. When she did speak, however, her utterances were most astonishing, as you will soon see.

Lord Byron turned out to be as charming as he was exceedingly handsome, and I could see why so many young women (and apparently, boys) had fallen under his spell. After his affair with Lady Caroline Lamb, she publically described Byron as "mad, bad, and dangerous to know." I believe he took Lady Lamb's portrayal as a badge of honor, and worked hard to live up to it.

Lord Byron was proud of the two-story manor he'd rented, and soon after we had settled into our simple abode near the lakefront, he arranged a tour of Villa Diodati. Byron himself escorted us through the first floor, commenting on the paintings and sculptures throughout the living areas, the exceptionally fine library and grand ballroom, but he left it to Anastasia to guide us through the upper story.

We all knew Byron was sensitive about his malformed foot. I personally felt he was overly sensitive, as we paid little heed to his impediment, which was vastly overshadowed by his genius. Even so, he seemed loath to lead us up the stairs in those preternaturally darkened conditions for fear he might stumble or appear ungainly, I supposed.

Anastasia had followed us through the first part of the tour, hanging at a distance, as was sometimes her habit when Byron was on the move, as though she might be summoned to fulfill some duty for her master, which I'm sure she did on a regular basis.

Byron turned slightly and gestured to Anastasia, who moved swiftly to his side.

"Anastasia, my sweet Greek melon, will you be so kind as to continue the tour for our visitors?"

Addressing us, he said, "I am close to completing the third canto of my poem and eager to return to it." With that he left us with Anastasia.

Even though it was midday, the house was dark, as I've mentioned, due to the leaden skies. Anastasia carried a magnificently styled candle lamp with a glass shade, which looked like it may have come from the Court of Louis XVI. She stepped forward to lead the way up the staircase. The candlelight flashed on her silver bracelet, a heavy and well crafted ornament, with the patina of ancient Greece.

The bracelet caught Percy's eye. He was much more traveled than I, and had some knowledge of Grecian antiquities. "My God, that bracelet, where did you find it? It's the image of the Heracles knot masterpieces I've seen in the Athens Historical Museum, made popular in the second and third century."

He moved to her side to examine the bracelet more closely. "This is truly remarkable craftsmanship. Is it a family heirloom?"

Anastasia raised her arm, studying the bangle on her arm as if she hadn't seen it before. She set her lamp on the first step of the stairway and slipped the bracelet from her wrist. "It is but a poor copy, I think." She extended her hand towards Percy. "You can have it if you wish."

Percy's eyes widened, and he remained silent for a moment before shaking his head. "No, I really couldn't accept it. If this is genuine it would be a priceless treasure. How did you come by it? Was it a gift from Lord Byron?"

She offered a sly smile. "Not at all. I found it in a small village so many years ago I've forgotten the name of the place."

I thought then it was a curious thing to say from someone so young, but I assumed she was making a small joke.

She collected her lamp, and moved toward the staircase, saying, "Please watch your step."

Upstairs we were introduced to the dining room where we would spend the next three nights in conversation, drinking wine and eventually reading ghost stories.

"The house was built in 1710 by its original owner Giovanni Diodati," she informed us in a slow cadence, as though she thought we might not understand her accented English. "Professor Diodati was born in Geneva, but his family was Italian."

We were inside one of the large bedrooms at the end of the hall where a portrait of a dour man in robes was displayed. "This is the Professor," she said, pointing to the portrait.

Claire, who had taken an instant dislike to Anastasia, spoke up in her most imperious tone; "You refer to him as 'Professor.' He looks to me to be nothing more than a common parish minister."

Anastasia turned from the portrait, the flickering light from the lamp she carried accenting her high cheekbones and flawless olive skin. She stared at Claire for an uncomfortably long time, inclining her head in that peculiar way I mentioned, not saying a word. Anastasia finally spoke. "He was only twenty-one when he was named professor of Hebrew at the Genevan Academy, and in 1608 became professor of theology."

Flustered, Claire replied with a hint of sarcasm in her voice, "Oh, is that all?"

"Not quite," Anastasia said. "The Professor also is known for translating the Bible into Italian in 1603."

I stood amazed at the breadth of her knowledge, and assumed she'd been educated in Switzerland, which turned out not to be the case.

She continued staring at Claire, perhaps anticipating another question. When none came, she opened the doors leading onto a balustrade balcony surrounding three sides of the house. A damp wind blew off the lake, and I crossed my arms over my breasts to warm myself.

Villa Diodati was perched upon a small hill with an impressive view of Lake Geneva and the Jura Mountains in the distance. That day the heavily overcast skies obscured the snow-capped mountains.

"It is a shame we're unable to enjoy the beauty of this view," Percy said, adding, "The lake is one of the largest in Switzerland, is it not?"

Anastasia turned her gaze on Percy. "Lac Léman, as the locals call it, is by far the largest and deepest body of water in Switzerland, and one of the largest in Western Europe."

She paused, studying us, and I noticed for the first time how her dark eyes held the meager light from her lamp and cast it back like the a beacon in the night.

"While much of the geography surrounding the Alps dates back to man's prehistory, the formation of these lakes is fairly recent, perhaps only ten thousand years ago, created by a retreating glacier."

Almost in unison, Claire, Percy, and I turned from looking out at the crescent shaped lake to gape at this servant girl who had uttered what was one of the wildest fabrications I'd ever heard in my eighteen years. I could only shake my head at her audaciousness. We looked at one another for a moment.

Claire snorted. Percy coughed and smiled politely.

Anastasia merely pointed to the open doors, the exquisite bracelet sliding along her wrist, and led us silently through the bedroom Percy and I would occupy for the next few nights, and back down the stairs.

II

Later that evening, I found myself alone with Dr. Polidori in the library, where I had gone to fetch a book after dinner. A rainstorm of some consequence had drummed incessantly all evening, and Lord Byron had insisted we spend the night rather than return to our cottage.

We all agreed since no one wished to chance becoming a target for the frequent lightning strikes illuminating the night sky. Also we had consumed numerous bottles of an excellent Bordeaux at dinner.

For some reason, Polidori had become infatuated with me, and he tried to make his intentions known, as men are wont to do. He sidled next to me as I reached for a book.

"You are truly a lovely young woman, Madame Shelley," he said in hushed tones. "I understand that you and Mr. Shelley are not yet married?"

This was indeed a true statement. At the time Percy was still legally married to Harriet, his first wife and mother of his child. Though not yet wedded, I'd taken to calling myself Mrs. Shelley. Poor Harriet committed suicide later that year, and Percy and I married soon after.

None of this was Dr. Polidori's business, however, but I did not wish to be rude. Besides, he was a most attractive man, and I was feeling more than a bit tipsy. "We're as good as husband and wife," I said. "We're of one mind on that."

We were alone in the library except for one of the cats prowling through the stack, but Dr. Polidori leaned in towards me as if about to share a secret he wished only the two of us to hear. His hip pressed against my own.

"Are you saying only the poet is able to lay his head upon your beautiful breasts? What about a lovesick doctor?"

I'd like to say I was shocked since Dr. Polidori and I were barely acquainted, but I fancied myself a modern woman in those days, naive as that may sound. My circle of friends included poets, writers, and artists who believed the new century would bring huge advancements in science, and the puritanical moral strictures would be cast aside.

Percy and I had defied the conventions of our day, so I was not offended by Polidori's forthright solicitations. To be perfectly honest, I felt drawn to the handsome doctor, and more than a little flattered by his advances. But I wasn't about to give in to my baser self. Not yet, anyway.

I quickly changed the subject. "What do you know of Lord Byron's servant girl? The Greek one."

"Ah, you mean Anastasia. I'm afraid she's already spoken for. She is George's favorite of the moment."

"Do you find her odd?" I asked.

"In what way?"

I told him about her explanation of the formation of the lake. "She said this with the greatest authority, and expected us to believe her. We all knew it was wild speculation, and I felt embarrassed for the girl."

"Actually, what she said makes a good deal of sense, though it's been some time since I studied the geologic sciences. I'm sure it was simply conjecture on her part."

"What is her background? Where did she attend school?"

Polidori shook his head. "As far as I know she has no formal education. George found her working as a hotel maid on one of his trips across Italy and hired her on the spot. He seems mightily attached to her."

By this time, I had selected a book and said, "We should return to the others or they may get the wrong impression." I ran a fingertip along his patrician nose, and lowered my eyes demurely.

We rejoined the others in the dining room where Byron and Percy were in a heated discussion about the meaning of Luigi Galvani's experiments with dead frogs. Claire was seated near the fire, snoring softly. Anastasia stood nearby holding a decanter of wine, listening to the conversation, her head tilted in that peculiar way.

"Don't you see what it means?" Byron was saying. "If we can animate a dead frog, then all things are possible. Who is to say we can't do the same with humans?"

Percy seemed to be of two minds on the subject. "Agreed, Dr. Galvani has moved science in a new direction with his discovery of animal electricity, but animating a man is completely different than a frog's leg."

Byron shook his head stubbornly. "We've entered a new era where each day science tears down another brick in the wall of ignorance. Anything is possible, even bringing people back from the dead."

The thought chilled me, but I hung on each word while they debated the subject for more than an hour. Polidori injected a level-headedness to the discussion, using his medical experience to explain the difference between making a frog's leg twitch, and bringing it back to life.

They went on in that fashion until Byron yawned loudly. He swallowed the last of his wine, and wiped his mouth with the back of his hand. Anastasia was there in a flash to refill the crystal goblet, but Byron stayed her hand. He gazed at Anastasia admiringly, stroked her arm, and said, "Thank you, my dear, but I've had enough wine and conversation for one night. You may prepare my bed now." He gave her a familiar tap to the backside and sent her on her way.

To us, he said, "We should continue this discussion tomorrow over dinner." He excused himself and followed Anastasia to his bedchamber.

* * *

I awoke in the middle of the night from an alarming dream in which a faceless man was chasing me. I ran for my life, but he cut the distance as though I stood motionless. He drew closer, and I saw he was only part human. Some of his appendages seemed to have been torn from the bodies of other species. Blood dripped from mangled arms and legs protruding from his hideous frame.

The dream distressed me deeply, and I was unable to return to my slumber. I climbed from the high poster bed, bundled myself in a blanket, and walked into the hall. Our chamber was the very same room we'd visited earlier, the one containing Professor Diodati's portrait. Claire's chamber was at the other end of the hall, while Byron's and Polidori's rooms were downstairs, with most of the servants staying in the carriage house behind the manor.

The rain had subsided by then, and I heard the haunting cry of the peacock calling out for a mate, perhaps. I strode to the balcony overlooking the first floor to see if I could spot the lovesick fowl, instead spying a shadowed figure tiptoeing from Lord Byron's bedchamber. At first I assumed the nocturnal visitor was Byron's lover, Anastasia, but when she passed one of the candelabras situated near the bottom of the stairwell, it became clear it was none other than my half-sister Claire.

I slid behind a column, and hid there until Claire entered her chamber and closed the door. It appeared as though Claire's wishes had come true, and she was back in Byron's affections, or at least back in his bed. Everyone knew Lord Byron's affections were famously short lived.

As though to prove my point, I heard more footsteps from below. I peered over the balcony in time to see another figure cross the hall and enter Byron's room. The comings and goings reminded me of the traffic in Trafalgar Square, and I had to bite my lip to keep from laughing aloud. This person wasn't difficult to identify as she carried the same lamp as when she gave us a tour of the manor earlier that afternoon.

It was Anastasia. I had to marvel at her daring, and Lord Byron's stamina.

That same morning, Percy awoke to find me stroking his chest beneath his bedclothes. After imagining the amorous adventures transpiring in Byron's bedchamber that night, I felt sexually charged and wanting—no, needing—physical intimacy. I knew Percy would be more than happy to oblige me.

And indeed Percy rose to the occasion.

We were soon making loud and passionate love. In the midst of it, I happened to glance toward the chamber door, and realized I had left it partly open after my earlier perambulations. Neither the door nor whether we would wake anyone with our energetic coupling was uppermost on my mind at the moment, but I chanced to see Anastasia scrutinizing us through the open door. Her head was cocked, and she seemed to be appraising us as if she was unfamiliar with the act of coitus, though from what I'd heard and seen that was far from the case.

Instead of being shocked by her intrusion into our lovemaking, I became further aroused and attacked Percy with complete abandon. We completed our act, climaxing together and falling apart in a state of blissful exhaustion. My breathing eventually returned to normal, and I was surprised to see Anastasia still observing us. I nudged Percy and pointed to our voyeur.

"Anastasia, if you would care for a closer view, why don't you join us here in bed?" Percy laughed as he said this, and patted the mattress.

She may have thought he was joking, but knowing Percy as I did, I assumed he hoped she would take him up on his offer. Anastasia said nothing. She backed away, closing the door behind her.

Much later, I went to the kitchen to brew us a pot of tea while Percy stayed abed recovering from our bout of lovemaking. From the kitchen I heard Byron's voice talking to someone about my half-sister

Claire. Curious, I moved to the doorway and saw Byron and Polidori at the dining room table. Neither could see me, so I lingered there listening to the conversation.

"I have no real feelings for her," Byron was saying, "but a man is a man, and if a girl of eighteen comes prancing to me in the middle of the night, there is but one thing to do."

Both men laughed. "Quite a predicament, you have, Lord Byron."

"Yes," Byron agreed. "She is so very needy for my touch I almost feel sorry for her. At least the dalliance with Claire gave me some reprieve from the Greek girl."

"Anastasia?"

"That woman wears me out. She can go on and on for hours without tiring. She even came to me after Claire had departed last night. I could barely walk from my chamber this morning."

They laughed again, and I retreated to the kitchen to pour the tea. I felt disheartened for poor Claire, though she surely knew what sort of man Byron was after he abandoned her. Some women will always lead with their hearts, no matter how many times they are burned.

Before I could return to our chamber with the tea, Anastasia entered the kitchen. I took the opportunity to question her about her voyeuristic behavior.

"Anastasia, about last night. I'm curious as to why you intruded on such a private moment."

She regarded me for a full minute in that strange way of hers before responding, "Watching and learning, Madame Shelley. Watching and learning. That seems to be my mission in life."

She then apologized for her offense, and returned to her work.

Later, I told Percy of our brief conversation in the kitchen, and Anastasia's unexpected statement. He smiled, and said, "She must have wanted to watch a real woman make love. Now she can please George even more."

"From what I heard, Anastasia needs no such lessons."

He looked at me with great anticipation, but I decided to keep him in the dark regarding Byron's opinion of her sexual fortitude.

III

After dinner that evening we all gathered around the fireplace. Outside, lightning flashed and barrages of thunder shook the manor. During dinner, Percy and Byron had talked incessantly about their future writing projects. That conversation waned as we settled into comfortable chairs and pulled the lamps close in an attempt to drive away the gloom.

We had all consumed copious amounts of wine through dinner, and as we sat around a low polished table made of some exotic wood, Anastasia brought us a full decanter of red wine along with clean goblets. Byron surprised us by emptying a vial of a reddish-brown liquid into the wine and stirring it.

"Laudanum," he said before I could ask. "I find it stimulates the imagination, and helps me with my writing."

I had heard of laudanum, of course, as the tincture of opium was credited with great medicinal powers, but I'd never had occasion to sample it. I was more than willing to continue the festive mood, but if I'd known how dramatically the atmosphere would change, I might have reconsidered my actions.

By this time, everyone had taken note of Polidori's amorous attentions to my person, especially Percy, who had nearly come to blows with the physician that afternoon. Tensions were high, and all of us drank of the fortified wine far more than necessary.

After one concussive blast of thunder, Byron exclaimed, "The night is perfect for ghost stories." He had with him a copy of *Fantasmagoriana*, a collection of German ghost stories. Byron insisted we take turns reading from the anthology, which only added to the claustrophobic atmosphere.

I read from Heinrich Clauren's fantastical story, *The Grey Room*, and Byron from Laun's *The Death Bride*, which caused Percy to shiver and pour the remainder of the wine into his glass. He downed it in one long swallow. Anastasia was there within seconds to replace the decanter.

We heard a shutter flapping from one of the bedchamber windows. I felt a cold gust of wind blow through the drafty house, guttering the candles, and casting sinister shadows upon the walls. The odor of smoke hung in the air along with the aura of dread created by the ghost stories.

A frosty shudder advanced from the nape of my neck down my back. I pulled my shawl tighter around my bare shoulders. Polidori shed his jacket and wrapped it around me with a flourish.

"A lovely woman shouldn't suffer from this intemperate weather," he said, squeezing my shoulder affectionately.

Percy started to rise from his chair, his fists balled, but I shook my head and he settled shakily into his seat. It was clear the wine and laudanum had had its effect on my sweet Percy. I could see he was teetering on the ledge of rationality, swaying between belligerent paranoia and unconsciousness.

Byron broke the tension by suggesting we should write our own ghost stories. There ensued some spirited conversation between Polidori and Byron, with Percy coming awake enough to add a few thoughts of his own. I listened as the men talked of long dead spirits molesting unsuspecting maidens. Of human hearts transferred into the bodies of wild primates. Of animals able to change their appearance at will. Of ancient beings surviving on the lifeblood of humans.

Both Byron and Polidori were excited about this last gruesome idea of blood-sucking creatures, but it sent another chill tramping across my back.

Claire had retired to her chambers long before, but I found the discussion fascinating. Anastasia must have also since she had crept closer to the table, and now stood with one hand on the back of Byron's chair, listening with rapt attention. They bantered back and forth, each proposing a chilling premise for their stories. I was left with nagging doubts about whether I could contribute anything worthwhile after listening to the intriguing speculations of these creative minds.

I saw that Percy was nearly asleep, and nudged him. "We should excuse ourselves," I suggested.

"But not before hearing Coleridge's latest," Byron insisted. "I was able to purchase one of the first published copies of his epic poem, *Christabel*."

"I've heard it's his master work," Polidori said. "Read it to us, George. You have just the voice for it."

Percy came awake, as I knew he greatly respected Coleridge, and had many times praised *The Rime of the Ancient Mariner*.

Byron began reading the poem, affecting the tone and dramatic intensity of a Shakespearean stage actor. Considering the turbulent weather with the lightning and thunder rolling off the mountains and across the lake, and the intoxicating effects of the stimulants we'd ingested, Byron's recitation had the effect of unnerving us all.

The shadowed walls seemed to press in on me. I felt a throbbing in my chest, and the taste of bile on my tongue. I had no idea how Byron's reading was affecting the others until he read this passage from the poem:

Like one that shuddered, she unbound
The cincture from beneath her breast:
Her silken robe, and inner vest,
Dropt to her feet, and in full view,
Behold! her bosom and half her side—

Percy's eyes suddenly went wide. He threw up his hands with an eerie scream and dashed from the room, his chair crashing to the floor behind him.

Byron paused momentarily, glancing at me, and then to Percy's fleeing figure.

He shrugged and smiled apologetically.

"I didn't think your recitation was that bad," Polidori said to Byron.

I leaped from my chair, dropping Polidori's coat to the floor, and chased after Percy. Behind me I heard Byron's voice as he commenced reading once again.

I found Percy lying on our bed, a down pillow covering his head. I removed the pillow and asked, "What gave you such a fright?"

He sat up and covered my cheek with wet kisses. "I'm so sorry, but I had the most terrible vision." His hands were trembling.

I couldn't imagine what he saw, but felt it must have been instigated by the wine and laudanum he'd consumed. "Perhaps it would help if you share your vision with me."

He seemed hesitant to tell me, his eyes darting from my face to my bosoms.

"Please tell me," I insisted.

"Promise you won't think me insane."

I promised, and he said, "As Byron read that last passage of the woman dropping her robe to the floor, I saw you in the same state of undress, but …"

"But what?"

"Your breasts were bare, but instead of nipples, there were eyes staring back at me." His face had turned ashen as he spoke.

He may have been shocked by the vision, but it struck me as humorous. To calm him, I said, "I can assure you there are no eyes on my breasts, except those of your own when you look upon me."

He placed a hand on my bosoms. "How can I be sure? You'll have to show me."

And so I did.

IV

I awoke late the next morning to find the storm had cleared some of the clouds away, and patches of blue peered through the overcast sky. Lying there, my thoughts returned to the ghost story we were to write and deliver to the group that evening. A number of fanciful ideas came to me as I lay abed listening to Percy snore, but none of them felt compelling enough to capture anyone's attention. It was time, I decided, to become serious about the project.

Villa Diodati contained a lovely courtyard that had remained unoccupied these last few days due to the inclement weather. Even though the temperature was still brisk, I was determined to sit outside to work on my story. I threw a blanket around my shoulders, and collected my journal, pen and ink well.

On the way to the courtyard Anastasia stopped me to ask if I wished to have breakfast. I told her I was going to sit in the courtyard to work on my story. She offered to bring me croissants and a pot of tea, which I gratefully accepted.

Sitting outside, I struggled to coerce an original idea from my still besotted brain. Most of what I'd heard discussed the night before were variations on the themes of the German stories we'd read. I wished to find something original, not derivative of another's work. I took pen in hand and wrote of a woman who dreams of a monstrous beast with glowing red eyes and coils of snakes wrapped around its body. She awakens to find the beast has come to life and it devours her.

Anastasia brought the tea and croissants to my table as I was writing.

"What is your story about?" she asked.

I told her my idea of the snake-giant and the woman. She remained silent, but I felt she was not overly impressed with my fiction. "What do you think?"

She didn't answer immediately, but was obviously deliberating her reply. She fingered the silver bracelet while looking down at my journal. She shrugged, and said, "Not a bad subject for a ghost story, but the original is much more frightening."

"The original?"

"In Greek mythology, no monster was more feared by the gods than Typhon. He was described as a giant, so tall his head touched the stars, and while he had the head and torso of a man, they were wrapped by coils of snakes, hissing and writhing menacingly."

I thought about that and wondered if I'd previously read about this Typhon monster and somehow pulled it from my subconscious. "I suspect there are many monsters to be found in mythology," I said.

"To be sure," Anastasia replied. "Some of mankind's earliest writings can be found on the stone tablets of Mesopotamia where men wrote stories of heroes journeying to netherworlds, fighting demons, and vanquishing monsters."

By this time nothing Anastasia said surprised me. Her head seemed to be filled with a wealth of arcane knowledge from across the ages. "Then maybe I should use one of these ancient myths as the basis for a contemporary story."

She sat down in the chair opposite me, and poured tea into the cup she'd brought. I took it and inhaled the warm fragrance. "So what do you think?"

This time she didn't hesitate. "If I were to write a story, even a ghost story, I'd want it to touch on the human condition, the universal elements affecting all men. Fear of the unknown is one circumstance you can exploit, but what we fear most of all is something we live with every day."

"And what is that?"

"Death, Madame Shelley, death. Human beings have great potential, but they're constrained by a grotesquely short life span. Think about it. Compared to other organisms, your life is over in the blink of an eye. Some trees live for thousands of years. Even the lowly sponge has been known to survive deep below the sea for fifty or more human generations."

"You're saying I should write about our short life spans?"

"Not directly, but about how to either extend it or ..." She paused and cocked her head, her eyes closed as though listening to an internal voice.

"Or what?" I prompted.

"Or perhaps how to bring people back to life after they've died."

"Now you sound like Byron and Dr. Polidori," I said, remembering their conversation from two nights ago about Galvani's experiments with the frog legs. "Besides, bringing people back from the dead isn't original either. Jesus brought Lazarus to life—at least the Bible declares it so—though every educated person knows the Bible is nothing more than fables and morality tales."

She considered my words, nodding slightly. The sun had broken through the clouds, and diamonds of light danced across her dark eyes. "Jesus commanded his apostles to 'Heal the sick, raise the dead, cleanse the lepers, and cast out devils.' And Peter raised Tabitha from the dead, and St. Paul raised Eutychus."

"Stories told to children and the simple-minded."

"Believe what you wish, but imagine the possibilities if we could bring life to the dead."

She said it with such conviction that I began to think of my own life, and the people I'd lost. I thought about the mother I never knew, of my own daughter, dead within days of leaving my womb. Would I bring them back to life if I could? Deep in my soul I knew I would do all in my power to make it so.

"But how would such a thing be possible?"

"It may not be possible, not in your lifetime, but think of the potential of electricity."

"You mean like Galvani's experiment animating the frog leg?"

"Yes, but on a much larger scale. The power to animate a human body would have to come from a force much stronger than a static charge. Perhaps from a lightning bolt."

Excited by the idea, I scribbled fiercely in my journal. When I looked up, Anastasia was gone, and Percy was wending his way shakily toward the table.

I was reluctant to tell Percy about our conversation, or Anastasia's suggestion for a story. The tale hung by a single delicate thread. It lacked the underpinnings of plot, purpose, and character.

Percy helped me eat the croissants and finish the tea. By then, he seemed refreshed, but I felt seized by a deep lethargy. I knew the night's story telling would go late into morning, and I needed to rest.

I excused myself, saying, "If I don't nap, I'll not stay awake for tonight's debauchery,"

"We can't have that, can we?" He kissed me on the mouth in parting, saying he would find Byron, and maybe they would go sailing if the weather permitted.

Back in the warmth of our bed, I fell quickly asleep, though I found my repose fitful, filled with macabre dreams. One of the dreams was a manifestation so dark and frightful that I woke with a start. As I lay clutching the heavy comforter, the nightmarish actions of the dream came alive once again, and I realized this was the genesis of my story. I later documented the dream in my journal, writing,

I saw the pale student of unhallowed arts kneeling beside the thing he had put together. I saw the hideous phantasm of a man stretched out, and then, on the working of some powerful engine, show signs of life and stir with an uneasy, half vital motion. Frightful must it be; for supremely frightful would be the effect of any human endeavor to mock the stupendous mechanism of the Creator of the world.

That evening I related the central thread of my story. The men seemed surprised by the concept, probably not believing I could create such a ghastly premise by myself. They encouraged me to complete it, and Percy later insisted I expand the ghost story into a novel.

We left Lake Geneva and Villa Diodati behind not long after that night of story telling, but I thought often about the strange Greek girl, and her commanding presence. I am convinced she helped me breathe life into my story of a monster created from the scraps of corpses.

* * *

Two years later, the fragment of a story that grew from a bad dream I had on the shores of Lake Geneva was finally published. I titled the book, *Frankenstein: or, The Modern Prometheus*, and was surprised by the acceptance it received from the reading public.

I decided I should thank Anastasia for her assistance, and thought I'd send her a gift of a few pounds, along with a signed copy of the book. Since Percy remained good friends with Lord Byron, I asked if he would inquire if Anastasia was still in his employ.

Months went by, and I'd all but forgotten my request when Percy entered the study of our apartment one afternoon holding a sheaf of papers.

"She's gone," he said.

"Who's gone?" I had no idea who he was talking about.

"Anastasia. This is a letter from George, in answer to my query about her whereabouts. He said Anastasia returned to her home in Greece shortly after we departed Switzerland. He tried to find her, hoping to entice her to return to his service, but no one knew where she went. He said there had been an influenza outbreak in the region and he feared she may have succumbed."

I was heartsick. "Poor Anastasia. She was such a remarkable individual, striking in so many ways, don't you think?"

Percy agreed and we fondly recalled our holiday on Lake Geneva during the summer that was no summer.

V

And now, dear reader, I move on to the saddest of days, which will move my story to its final chapter. Unfortunately, the beginning of the end starts with another death. The love of my life perished in July of 1822. Always enamored with the sea, it seemed fitting Percy should die in its embrace, but why at such a young age, leaving me alone to raise our son, Percy Florence?

His schooner was caught in a violent summer storm and foundered while returning from a visit with Lord Byron and his friend Leigh Hunt at Livorno, Italy. Poor Percy's body washed ashore several days later, and he was cremated right there on the beach. Byron and Hunt were in attendance in my stead.

They told me his heart refused to burn, and so they delivered it to me. I still hold it among my most precious possessions. Percy's remains were buried in the Protestant Cemetery in Rome, and several years later I had occasion to visit Italy with young Percy Florence. Naturally, I wished to see Percy's final resting place, and show little Percy where his father was buried.

On that warm August afternoon, I bought a bouquet of flowers from a street vendor, and we made our way to the cemetery. We found his grave near an ancient pyramid in the city walls. His gravestone bore the Latin inscription, *Cor Cordium*, "Heart of Hearts," and below that, in reference to his death at sea, were these lines from Shakespeare's *The Tempest*:

'Nothing of him that doth fade
But doth suffer a sea-change
Into something rich and strange'

"He was a man of immense talents," I told my son after we had placed the flowers at the head of the grave.

"You miss him greatly, do you not, Mother?"

I stood quietly with my head bowed for a minute before answering. I felt tears pooling in my eyes and commence streaming down my cheeks. Sniffling, I held my son close, whispering in his ear, "Oh, so much more than you can imagine, sweet child. But I have you to remind me of our love for one another."

We stood together in silence until something caught my eye on the edge of the grave, half-hidden in the shadows cast by a towering cedar. It was a small, neatly wrapped package, the paper nearly the same color as the white marble stone. Before I could retrieve it, however, I heard a movement behind me. I turned to see a man of middle age, dressed in the clothing of an English gentleman, with long waistcoat and high silk hat.

He was leaning against the city wall only ten feet from where we stood. He was a mostly unremarkable man, and I was certain I'd never seen him before, but there was something familiar that compelled me to approach him.

As I neared, I could see he was studying me intently, his head cocked at a curious angle. A slight smile played over his lips, and his dark eyes were alight with an internal glow that belied the shadows surrounding him.

"Excuse me, sir, but do I know you?"

He didn't reply.

"Did you know my husband?"

"You might say I was one of his many admirers." His voice was steady, but I found the tone to be slightly mocking, almost arrogant.

"What are you doing here?" A hint of anger edged my voice.

He gave me another bout of exasperating silence, taking his time digesting my question as if deciding whether to swallow or spit out an answer.

"Watching and learning, Madame Shelley. Watching and learning. That seems to be my mission in life."

I believe my mouth may have fallen open upon hearing his rejoinder. He touched the brim of his top hat and walked away, disappearing through a gate in the city walls.

As I write this now, I must assume you are as shocked by this turn of events as I was. My mind churned as we made our way back to the hotel, turning the matter one way and the other, but never finding a satisfying answer to the enigma. How could it be, I asked myself over and over, that some ten years after Anastasia disappeared, presumably dead, a man nearly twice her age appears with the same mannerisms, reciting the exact same phrase she once did?

It made as much sense to me as if I'd heard Percy's voice hailing me from beneath his gravestone. The matter troubled me throughout our European holiday.

* * *

Back in London later that year, I was invited to a literary gathering to honor the poet Elizabeth Barrett Browning. Among the guests was the scholar Hugh Stuart Boyd. Mr. Boyd was an Englishman, and though blind when I met him, he was still considered one of the most brilliant men of his generation. I'd heard he'd been teaching Greek to Ms. Browning, a kindly woman who had sent me a condolence note after Percy's death.

When speaking with Mr. Boyd that evening, he inquired about the events leading to my writing of the Frankenstein novel. The story of our evenings at Byron's Villa Diodati had spread, growing to scandalous proportions as gossipers added their own salacious, and mostly fictitious, details.

It wasn't the first time I'd been asked about those nights in Lake Geneva, and it wouldn't be the last, but I was eager to set the record straight for Mr. Boyd. I told him about the ghost stories we'd read, and how Lord Byron had challenged us to write our own story. And because Mr. Boyd was a Greek scholar, I mentioned Anastasia's role, and described her amazing knowledge of world history.

He was fascinated by my tale, especially after I told him of the man in the cemetery. He chortled, saying, "Then she has surely lived up to her name."

"Why is that?"

"In the Greek language, Anastasia means, 'One who is reborn,' so your mystery cemetery caller must have been Anastasia paying you another visit."

He laughed heartily at the apparent absurdity of such a thing, and I feigned to join him for I already knew the truth of the matter.

* * *

I sit here today, in the winter of 1851, pen in shaky hand, writing on the last page of what may be the final journal I ever complete. Percy Florence is a grown man. It has been over twenty years since the two of us visited the cemetery in Rome and chanced upon the man in the top hat. The man's words, though, still ring in my ears—

Watching and learning. That seems to be my mission in life.

I can close my eyes and hear the words, picturing not the man's face, but Anastasia as she stood in the kitchen of Villa Diodati that blustery day in 1816. I hear her expound upon Lake Geneva's glacial formation some ten thousand years before. I can see her peering through the doorway into our bedchamber observing Percy and I making love. And I can still hear her voice as we discussed the possibility of bringing the dead to life.

As I write this final chapter, I leave it to you to determine the truth of what you've read here. Was I a participant in a supernatural event, or was it only a riddle of my own making? Before you rush to judgment and assign it all to the bewildered ravings of an infirm woman, let me take you back to the encounter at Percy's gravesite. After hearing the man in the top hat echo those words I'd heard a decade before, I retreated in a state of shock, completely forgetting about the packet I'd spied moments earlier. Unbeknownst to me, my son had retrieved it and slipped it into my coat pocket.

My mind was awhirl with turbulent thoughts. I barely remember walking back to the hotel, and it wasn't until much later that I discovered the small box in my coat pocket, hidden in the folds of a scarf.

Would that Percy had been there when I unwrapped the package and opened the box. He was such a lover of all things mystical and fantastical, he would have cut right to the heart of this queer episode. For you see, what was in that box is the key to this entire drama. It once hung on Anastasia's slender wrist. Now the silver Heracles knot bracelet Percy so admired dangles heavily from my wrist, even as I write these words.

My experiences with Anastasia have taught me all things are possible. I'd like to believe this ancient Greek bracelet contains the power of resurrection. Or perhaps, you might say, my story is no more than the maundering of a mind blighted by death, braced by copious amounts of laudanum, which I consume regularly to help me through bouts of melancholia and failing health.

You can believe what you wish, but for me the choice is a simple one. I choose to believe the bracelet is an offering from beyond the grave, a magical connection to those days we spent in Villa Diodati when a servant girl named Anastasia helped me bring a monster back from the dead, and also opened my eyes to the mysteries of life.

Does the bracelet hold the power to reverse the natural order of things? Like Anastasia's name, will I be reborn if I'm still wearing it after my heart stops beating? Ah, that is the last great question, is it not, and I sense the answer will soon become apparent. My story will either come to an abrupt end, or if perchance Anastasia has passed along the gift of renewal, then there may be more journals to write.

Until the moment of enlightenment, all I can do is watch and learn. That is my final mission in life.

Author's Notes - Parker Francis

Most of what you read in The Strange Case of Lord Byron's Lover is based on historical fact. Researching the events leading to Mary Shelley's writing of *Frankenstein: or, The Modern Prometheus* gave me an appreciation of the historic nature of that meeting between three of the most creative artists of any generation.

Lord Byron hosted Mary and her soon-to-be husband, Percy Bysshe Shelley, along with Mary's half-sister Claire, in June of 1816. Dr. John Polidori was Byron's personal physician and accompanied the poet, keeping a diary of their travels. If the accounts are accurate, the good doctor lusted after Mary and sexual tensions ran high. Not mentioned in my story is the fact that Polidori "borrowed" Byron's idea for a ghost story and used it as the basis for his own tale, *The Vampyre*, the first published vampire story.

This amazing confluence of creative minds in Villa Diodati struck me as the perfect background for my Prometheus story and I took advantage of it for my own dramatic purposes, though I like to think that everything you read in *The Strange Case of Lord Byron's Lover* is true—except the parts I made up.

—*PF*

FIFTEEN DOLLARS' GUILT

I

New York City, June 11, 1880

Maynard hunched over with his knees at his chest, clutched his blanket tighter across his body. It was cold, even for a summer night in New York, and it didn't help any that he was sopping wet. The wreck of the SS Narragansett paddle steamer burned to the waterline. Her fires hung in the dense fog like a blazing corona over Long Island Sound. What few survivors made it to shore scrabbled up the defile along the waterside, where firefighters hauled them up the rest of the way.

A scant few had escaped the blaze. A child clutched at her mother's dress as they both scoured the water for someone. An old man sat on his haunches, bawling with the heels of his hands dug into his eyes. Screams from those still caught below deck cut short as the steamer sank beneath the waves.

Maynard had seen enough. Besides, the police were coming, and it would not do if they asked him for a statement. He offered his blanket to the mother and child, then walked away.

The waterside was astir with activity – firefighters, policemen, and newspaper reporters stumbled over each other in a chaotic race to the scene. It was an easy thing for him to sidle past with all the commotion headed back the way he had come.

A bar up ahead advertised cheap whiskey and nightly shows. Most importantly, it was a dark, out of the way place where he could gather his thoughts. He made a beeline for the counter and propped himself up on a stool. Water poured off his clothes in solid streams.

"Oy now!" The barkeep, a portly Irishman whose flyaway white hair had migrated to his enormous sideburns, slapped his meaty palms against the counter. From the elbows down, he looked like he had hams for arms.

"Ain'cha got any sense, man?" the man went on. "I just mopped the floor!"

Maynard diverted his eyes. "My apologies."

Shaking his head, the barman sighed. "No harm, I suppose. What's your pleasure?"

"Water."

He chuckled. "You've had plenty o' that. Try again."

"Lay off him, Cormac." A haggard man two seats to Maynard's left slapped some money onto the counter. "He's drinking with me." Then, after a moment's reflection, he added, "He looks like he needs a double.

"Women's kisses and whiskey, amber clear," Cormac the barkeep said with a smirk.

The man beckoned Maynard to come closer.

"What's your story, friend?" asked the man, cradling his empty shot glass. His breath reeked of alcohol.

Maynard took the stool next to the man. "My name is Maynard," he introduced himself. He stuck out his right arm – fingers fully extended, hand rigid like the blade of a knife – for a handshake. Water streamed off of Maynard's sodden coat onto the man's trousers.

The man batted Maynard's arm away. "Hey, watch it! What are you, some kind of imbecile?"

Maynard, whose hand so far had been in the same position, retracted his arm. He stuffed his hand into his pocket with all the nonchalance he could muster.

"No," Maynard said.

"No what?" the man responded.

"I answered your question."

"What are you talking about?"

"Your inquiry concerning my purported imbecilic status." He paused a beat. "I am most assuredly not an imbecile."

The man glared at him. "You are a rare breed, mister."

Maynard sighed. "Perhaps more than you know."

Cormac rapped two shot glasses of whiskey against the counter. "There you are, lads. Bottoms up."

The man sitting beside Maynard propped his elbows on the counter and nestled his chin on his palms.

"What is your name?" Maynard asked.

"Charles," he grunted.

"It is a pleasure to meet you, sir."

"Pleasure's mine," he said flatly.

Maynard raised an eyebrow. "Do I detect facetiousness in your tone?"

"Yes." He raised the shot glass to his lips. "If I'd have known you'd be this much trouble, I'd have thought twice before buying you that drink."

"I appreciate it regardless." Maynard held up his glass. "Thank you." He downed it in one go without flinching.

Charles watched him, wide-eyed.

"Shall I repay the favor?" Maynard thumbed through the money in his billfold. He plucked a two-dollar bill and waved it over his head. "Barkeep! More alcoholic beverages, please."

Charles's eyes grew to the size of dinner plates. He grabbed Maynard's arm and pulled it down to his lap, nearly tackling him to the ground in the process.

"What is wrong with you?" Charles asked. "This is New York City – you can't be flashing so much money about. You'll get mugged!" He eased back onto his stool and looked over both shoulders.

"Forgive me," said Maynard. "I am not from here."

"It shows." He eyed Maynard from top to bottom and back again. "Where do you come from, anyway?"

"Europe."

Charles gave a slow, deliberate nod. "What brings you to New York City?"

"Business."

Charles shot Maynard an assaying look. "You don't say much."

"That is not what I am here to do."

"So what are you doing here?"

Maynard turned to face him. He graced him with a smile that was equal parts cordiality and cold aloofness. "I have come to observe and report."

Charles blinked. "You are reporter?"

"Yes. Of a sort."

"Then you're missing the story of a lifetime. Two steamers smashed into each other out in the fog. One got back safely, but the other caught fire and sank."

"Yes, I'm aware," said Maynard. "The Stonington and the Narragansett."

"And have I got a story for your paper. You can interview me if you like. I was on the deck of the Stonington, and I saw everything as it happened."

Maynard put up a hand. "No thank you. I was aboard the Narragansett. It burnt as it sank. There were few survivors."

Charles twirled the glass around in his hands. "I see."

Maynard put on his cold, closed-mouth smile.

"Are you a god-fearing man, Maynard?" asked Charles.

"How do you mean that?"

"I mean… strike that. Sometimes, when a man has so close a pass at death as I have had, his nerves fail him, and he resigns himself to the pursuit of trivial aims. Not me. That I have survived so horrible an event only proves that I am destined for great things."

Maynard, his interest genuinely piqued, cocked his head to one side. "Such as?"

Charles sighed so heavily that his shoulders caved. "For the life of me, I do not yet know." He sipped his whiskey. "But it is not my lot to complain. I persevere."

Maynard took advantage of the pause in their conversation to study his companion. Charles's haggard look was understandable, considering that the man had just minutes ago survived a brush with disaster. That aside, Charles's business suit and tie spoke to his status among the professional gentry.

"Forgive me if I was curt with you before," Charles said. "My name is Charles Julius Guiteau. And you, Mister Maynard?"

"Maynard will do just fine, thank you."

"Yes, right," said Charles, slightly put off. "You say you are a reporter. Well, I liken myself to the polymaths of old." He snapped the lapels of his wool topcoat. "I am a barrister of some renown, an itinerant preacher, and political speechwriter. Why, the speech I've written, entitled 'Grant vs. Hancock', will certainly ensure President Grant is reelected. I would very much like to share it with you, if you would write about it in your paper."

"Thanks, no."

"Oh," said Charles, markedly crestfallen. "I suppose that is fine and good. People will learn of it sure enough. I've printed several hundred copies." He finished his drink in silence. "Well, Mister Maynard, it has been good knowing you. Will you be staying long in the city?"

"Only so long as work requires."

Charles handed Maynard a slip of paper. "My calling card, sir. If ever I may be of service, or if you should feel inclined to grace me with a visit, please do not hesitate to call on me."

"I thank you."

II

New York City, May 24, 1881

Maynard sat at the counter of Cormac's bar, contemplating the double shot of whiskey in the glass before him. This glass was full to the brim, as was another glass, identical to the first, sitting beside it. It would not be long now before Charles would join him at the counter, and he wanted to have their drinks ready for when his friend would arrive. Good manners called for the doing of just these sorts of things. The last thing Maynard wanted was to appear out of place.

Charles blustered in through the bar's front door.

"Greetings," Maynard said, flashing his practiced closed-mouth smile.

"Hello Maynard," Charles groused. He perched on a bar stool and propped his chin in his hand.

"Why do you look so glum?" Maynard asked.

"I am not glum," said Charles, nearly cutting him off. "I am livid. There is a difference."

"I am aware."

Charles fixed a hard stare on Maynard. His eyes drifted to the shot glass on the counter. "What's this?"

"It is for you."

Charles's gaze flitted from Maynard to the glass and back again. "Thank you," he said, but it rang hollow.

"You are welcome." Maynard lifted his glass as if to toast and drank it down in one pull. "Refreshing."

Charles, his shot glass held aloft halfway to his lips, set the glass back down. "Maynard, do you know anything of politics?"

"Yes."

He shot Maynard a sideways glance. "Sometimes, I question whether you know more than you put on."

Maynard shrugged his shoulders.

"I'll tell you what politics means," Charles went on. "It is a compound word come down to us from the ancient Greeks. Poly means many. Ticks are bloodsucking insects."

"That etymological analysis is faulty."

"It was a joke," Charles spoke into his shot glass. He took a sip. The whiskey sent a shudder down his frame. "God, I don't know how you drink this stuff without flinching."

Maynard smiled politely.

"Only," said Charles, "I'm coming to learn that the joke is on me."

"Do tell."

"That speech I wrote last year – that brilliant speech, 'Garfield vs. Hancock'…"

"My apologies for interrupting. Your speech was entitled 'Grant vs. Hancock'. Our current President Garfield defeated the incumbent Grant for the Republican nomination."

Charles's face flushed. "Indeed. Regardless of what it was called, my speech got a Republican elected to the presidential office."

"Point noted."

"You would think the least the man could do is award me an ambassadorship – an assignment to Vienna, or Paris, even. But no!" He slammed his fist on the counter, drawing the attention of everyone at the bar. "President Garfield won't even give me the time of day. And Blaine is all but sick of me."

"I beg your pardon. Who is Blaine?"

Charles rolled his eyes. "James Blaine. Secretary of State." His gaze crossed with Cormac's and Charles held up two fingers, indicating another round of drinks. "Low, consummate jackasses," Charles said under his breath. "Each and every one of them. Garfield threw me out of the White House. Blaine himself told me to my face,

'Never speak to me again of the Paris consulship as long as you live.' The nerve of that man. Of those men."

He brooded over what remained of his drink. "Maynard," he said in little more than a whisper. "My family has abandoned me. My profession is in shambles. My aspirations to public office have been squelched by those Washington ingrates. You are my only friend. Can you, friend, do me a favor?"

"I will consider it."

He took a breath and sighed out his nostrils. "I need fifteen dollars. I know this is a considerable sum of money but I do not ask this lightly of you. Lend me the money and I will repay you, with interest."

"What do you need it for?"

"My calling, sir. Divine providence saw to it that we would survive the terrible steamboat calamity a year ago. Providence was what arranged for us to meet in this bar back then, when we discussed the ultimate aims of our lives. And providence has deemed me worthy to know the point of my existence. Great things are afoot, Maynard. I beg of you, do not stand in their way but help speed them along."

That was more than enough convincing, as far as Maynard was concerned. He pulled the money from his billfold handed it to Charles.

"One last question, my dear friend," Charles said. "Wood, or ivory?"

"I do not understand."

"Which do you think would look best as a museum exhibit?"

Maynard thought on that some. "Ivory has a timeless look to it."

A fiendish smile crept across Charles's face. "I like the way you think."

III

New York City, June 9, 1881

Maynard entered Cormac's bar and was surprised not to see his friend Charles at their usual spot at the counter. Instead, Charles sat at a table off in a corner of the pub. He waved at Maynard from his seat.

"Hello," said Maynard, settling into a chair.

"Hello yourself, my friend," said Charles. His voice was unusually giddy.

Maynard had not noticed it at first, as the table had hidden it from view, but a white sheet was tied around Charles's neck. Charles's left arm hung in the makeshift sling.

"What happened to your arm?"

Charles brushed him off. "I sprained it in a fall, but that's nothing to worry about in the grand scheme of things." He leaned into the aisle and looked both ways. "Want to see what caused it?" he whispered.

Charles looked both ways again, then reached into his pocket with his good hand. In his fist was the biggest revolver Maynard had seen in his life. Its ivory grip gleamed in the light.

"It kicks like a mule," Charles said with a smirk. "It's a .44 caliber Webley British Bulldog revolver. Knocked me down the first time I fired it."

Maynard edged back in his seat. "What do you plan to do with that?"

"Fulfill my destiny, dear Maynard." Charles's grin widened to show teeth. "I am going to remove President Garfield."

Maynard swallowed hard in a dry throat. "This is monstrous."

"This is righteous," he fired back. "Monstrous is what they did to me, friend. They led me by the nose for so long, benefitting through my labors and genius, only to abandon me in the end. Even the least obedient dog gets a bone sometimes. What does Charles Guiteau get? Guiteau gets told to Git-Out."

"I want no part of this," Maynard said. "I wash my hands of you and…"

A solid click from under the table cut him short. Charles had cocked the gun.

"You are my friend, Maynard," said Charles all too coolly. "Friends do not forget their friends. I will not forget you, and would appreciate if you did not forget me so close to when I will be fulfilling my destiny."

"You are insane. How can you justify this?"

"I leave my justification to God." Charles's face softened. There was a rustle under the table as he eased the gun into his pocket.

"Forgive me, friend," said Charles. "I have let my emotions get the better of me. You know me well enough to know there is no malice or madness in what I do."

Maynard's jaw set into a tight line. "You cannot go through with this."

"Washington and Franklin were cautioned similarly, yet today we call them patriots. How am I any different?"

"Murder is wrong."

"Murder is not my aim, dear Maynard. I have thought everything out to exacting detail. I shall shoot to injure, not to kill. When the president dies, it shall be through the doctors' own incompetent attempts to spare him." He gave a wistful smile. "I shall be exonerated."

"That constitutes torture."

Charles shrugged his shoulders. "My aim is not to make him suffer. Still, the fact remains that President Garfield must be removed from the picture."

"I will have no part in this filthy business," Maynard said. "For the sake of our friendship, I ask that you reconsider your actions."

"I am sorry, Maynard." He rested his hands palms-up on the table. Slowly, very slowly, his gaze diverted from Maynard's until his eyes were locked on his hands. "I have made arrangements to repay the debt I owe you."

"Keep the fifteen dollars," he said. "If that is what it takes to buy peace of mind, then it comes cheap enough."

Charles smirked, nodded. He coughed into his fist to clear his throat, but it was little more than a ploy to buy time. "I want you to know something. I have been thinking, and I have come to apprehend there is a chance I may not survive what I must do."

Maynard crossed his arms.

"No matter what happens," Charles went on, "people must be told of my work. My story cannot die with me. Ours is a government of the people, by the people; so help me I will be the one who saves this country even if that means a man must die."

His eyes flew up to meet Maynard's. "I'm entrusting this task to you. My story must stand out as a shocking parable of what happens when those in power impugn their constituents." He paused, motioned toward his pocket with his eyes. "This ivory-gripped instrument of justice will make a fine addition to the National Museum one day. Maynard, my friend, will you tell my story if I cannot?"

Maynard drilled a hard stare into Charles.

"Right. Very good." Charles lowered his head. "I leave for Washington soon. This is goodbye, dear Maynard. If things should turn sour for me, understand that I will disavow your involvement in any of this. Farewell." He shuffled out of the booth and onto the street.

IV

Washington, D.C., July 2, 1881

Hands in his pockets, Charles paced the floor of the Baltimore and Potomac station. He was fidgety, and understandably so, as the president was due to arrive at any moment.

Today was his day. He had practiced this. He had envisioned this moment countless times – draw the gun, pull the trigger, pocket the gun, head for the waiting cab up the street – but as the time drew near, he questioned whether he'd be able to carry out his destiny. A train whistle blast pierced the air and he nearly leapt out of his skin.

The door swung open. Charles's throat went dry. President Garfield entered the station's waiting area. At his shoulder were two of his sons. Secretary of State Blaine followed close behind. Charles's gorge rose at the sight of Blaine. With any luck, he'd spare a bullet for him.

Charles negotiated the crowd to position himself alongside Garfield. He slowed his pace, so the president would be just a step ahead, then rammed the barrel of his pistol into the small of Garfield's back. The president's head whipped around to face Charles. His chin was pinned to his shoulder as his body pivoted with the movement.

Their eyes met.

Charles held his breath and fired twice.

He was sprinting across the station before Garfield's body even hit ground. The hot gun in his pocket burned his leg, but that was the furthest thing on his mind. Escape was paramount. He barreled into a lady and high-stepped over her as she spilled to the floor, he himself nearly toppling over. The collision put him off balance, sending him flailing into the waiting arms of policeman Patrick Kearney.

Any dreams of escape vanished as quickly as they had come on. A full complement of policemen piled onto Charles, snapping him up from the ground and pinning his arms behind his back.

Doubt gnawed at his insides. Everything had happened so fast – had he, in fact, shot the president? The prospects of having come so far only to be caught and have nothing to show for it stung the marrow of his bones.

All around him, the gathering crowd of onlookers shouted: "Lynch him! Lynch him!"

A wry smile snuck across his face, for he knew then he had prevailed.

"I am a Stalwart of the Stalwarts!" he shouted. "I did it and I want to be arrested! Arthur is President now!"

V

The Trial of Charles Julius Guiteau
Excerpts from his Cross-Examination
University of Missouri-Kansas City School of Law
Famous Trials Archives
November 1881

Q: [By the prosecution] You intended to kill [President Garfield]?

A: I thought the Deity and I had done it, sir . . . I never should have shot the President on my own personal account. I want that distinctly understood.

[. . .]

Q: Who bought the pistol, the Deity or you?

A: The Deity furnished the money by which I bought it. I was the agent of the Deity.

Q: Through whose hand was it that you were furnished the money to buy that murderous weapon?

A: It is of no consequence whether it was Mr. Jones or Mr. Maynard, or anybody else . . .

Q: Did he lend it to you?

A: He loaned me money; yes, sir.

[. . .]

Q: The only inspiration that you had, as I understand you, was to use a pistol on the President?

A: The inspiration consisted in trying to remove the President for the good of the American people, and all these details are nothing.

Q: Were you inspired to remove him by murder?

A: I was inspired to execute the divine will.

Q: By murder?

A: So-called; yes, sir; so-called murder.

Q: You intended to do it?

A: I intended to execute the divine will, sir.

Q: You did not succeed?

A: I think the doctors did the work.

Q: The Deity tried, and you tried, and both failed, but the doctors succeeded?

A: The Deity confirmed my act by letting the President down as gently as he did.

[. . .]

Q: Why did you prefer the pistol with the ivory handle? . . . Did you think it would look better in the Patent Office?

A: I do not know about that.

Q: Did you say so?

A: I think I said something of the kind, about putting the pistol in the library of the State Department, in one of my notes. I never mentioned it to a human being.

Q: You thought it would be put there?

A: Possibly it might have been put there.

Q: You thought it would be exhibited in future time as the weapon you used in killing the President?

A: In removing the President; yes, sir. You seem to delight in that word "killing" and "murder." I had no conception of it in that way, and never have had.

VII

A series of newspaper clippings
Maynard's personal files
January through June 1882

The jury returned a unanimous verdict of guilty to the rousing applause of everyone present – everyone, except Charles Guiteau . . . Judge Cox sentenced Guiteau to be hanged by the neck until dead on June 30, 1882. In response, Guiteau loudly berated the judge, jury, and everyone in attendance . . .

Writing from prison, Guiteau posted a letter to the White House in the hopes that President Arthur – who, as Guiteau saw it, benefitted through his slaying of President Garfield – would grant a pardon . . . Arthur refused.

Standing at the gallows, the assassin read fourteen verses from the Gospel of Matthew and a poem he himself had written, entitled: "I Am Going to the Lordy." Guiteau recited several stanzas in singsong manner before his sentence was carried out. Spectators cheered the killer's demise.

VIII

Washington, D.C., early twentieth century

Maynard whistled in the empty warehouse, casually swabbing the concrete floor with even passes of his mop. Incandescent spotlights hung from the ceiling, casting lily pads of light against the thick shadows that played on the ground. It was almost closing time. He wheeled his mop bucket around a stack of crates as tall as he and headed for the janitor's closet. He slowed his pace, listening for nearby footfalls. The warehouse was a cavernous place, but he could not afford a slip-up.

The Guiteau exhibit had just arrived today, destined for the Smithsonian tomorrow. A shipping crate the size of an icebox sat in a dolly. Maynard looked both ways to see if the coast was clear, then lifted the box's lid.

Inside was President Garfield's spinal cord in a display case. Fractures in the vertebra clearly indicated where the man had been shot. Alongside it was a large envelope with Guiteau's collected writings, with the Webley revolver in a hinged glass container. Guiteau's brain sat in a jar of preservative. Maynard lifted it out of the crate with both hands and contemplated it.

To be fair, Guiteau was a killer, but he was also a greatly disturbed individual. Any attempt to study his brain now was misguided. The key to finding out what had gone wrong within his skull had died with him. Maynard shook his head. Guiteau – who Maynard had known as Charles – was a pitiable case. Whether anything the man did was driven by madness or sheer frustration was anybody's guess. But one thing was certain: Maynard could not carry out Charles's final wish. To clear his conscience, he had to ensure Guiteau's legacy was short-lived.

Maynard set the jar down, then looked around again to see if anyone was watching. The contents of the Guiteau exhibit had to disappear, only there was no way to abscond with all of it at once.

A door opened somewhere in the warehouse.

"Quittin' time," a voice called out.

Maynard glanced at the box of Guiteau's effects. The revolver's ivory grip shone in the warehouse's harsh light. Without a second thought, he worked the gun case open and dropped the pistol into the murky water sitting in his mop bucket. Then, nonchalantly as ever, he went to the custodial closet at the warehouse's far end. Once the door had shut behind him, he lifted the grille covering the floor drain and poured the bucket's contents into it.

The drain emptied into the harbor. Within minutes Guiteau's pistol would be at the bottom of a busy shipping channel. It would never be seen again. All the Smithsonian would have was a cataloguing photograph taken around the time the gun was accepted into the museum collection.

For Maynard, it wasn't much, but it brought him some peace of mind knowing that the murder weapon his money had bought would forever be lost to history.

Author's Notes - Antonio Simon Jr.

Charles Julius Guiteau led a sad life, especially considering that his greatest – and arguably only – achievement in his forty years alive was the assassination of a U.S. president.

Guiteau was born on September 8, 1841 in Freeport, Illinois. His grandfather died while Guiteau was in his twenties, and he set his inheritance money aside for tuition at the University of Michigan. He was refused admission. By 1860, at his father's insistence, he gave up on attending the university and moved with his father to New York.

Guiteau's father had connections with a religious sect in New York called the Oneida Community. Much as Guiteau tried to associate himself with the Oneida group over the course of five years, he was rejected. He actually joined and left the group twice. The group's nickname for him was a play on his name – "Charles Gitout." Later, Guiteau relocated to New Jersey, where he inaugurated a religious newspaper. When this enterprise folded, he returned to New York and filed lawsuits against the Oneida Community's founder. Guiteau's father was so embarrassed by his son's fiasco that he wrote letters in support of the religious group, calling his own son irresponsible and insane.

Guiteau moved back to the Midwest, this time settling in Chicago. There, he obtained a license to practice law and focused his practice on debt collection. He was not well liked among the judges and his clients – perhaps mostly his clients, as he was known to charge contingency fees of up to 75% of the claim.

Eventually he shifted his career focus from the practice of law to theology. Guiteau became an itinerant preacher, traveling from city to city to lecture on faith. His view of the faith was contained in a book he had written, entitled *The Truth*. This book was a near-total plagiarization of the Oneida Community's creed. By the late 1870's he was back on the east coast, preaching to communities in major cities.

On June 11, 1880, Guiteau was aboard the SS Stonington. Heavy fog made it near impossible to see. The ship collided disastrously with the SS Narragansett. The Stonington returned to port safely, but the Narragansett caught fire and sank. Few aboard the stricken ship survived the catastrophe. As for Guiteau, he believed the event proved he had some higher purpose in life.

Perhaps thinking that his calling lay in a government job, Guiteau next tried his hand at politics. He wrote a speech in support of incumbent president Ulysses S. Grant which he titled *Grant vs. Hancock*, Hancock being Grant's political opponent at the time. When Grant lost the 1880 presidential campaign to candidate James A. Garfield, he renamed the speech *Garfield vs. Hancock*.

Despite that Guiteau canvassed political offices with copies of his speech, the speech is believed to have been delivered no more than twice. Even so, he thought himself – and his speech – responsible for Garfield's eventual victory at the polls. He wrote a hail of letters to capitol hill, some to the president's cabinet and others to President Garfield himself, requesting that he be appointed to an ambassadorship in Europe. Guiteau traveled frequently to Republican Party offices in New York and Washington, D.C., haranguing politicians about his role in the president's election. Secretary of State James Blaine is reputed to have told Guiteau to his face: "Never speak to me again of the Paris consulship as long as you live."

That was the last straw. Guiteau was flat broke and utterly convinced that he would never be appointed to the consulship. The way he saw it, President Garfield's administration had turned its back on its most loyal supporter. It would pay for this betrayal. Then, in a flash, the idea came to him that he ought to assassinate the president. Finally, Guiteau had found his higher calling – the Republican party he had taken to his breast was shot full of corruption, and it was his God-given duty to set the party straight by cutting off its head.

Guiteau purchased his murder weapon – an ivory-handled .44 Webley British Bulldog revolver – with fifteen dollars borrowed from a Mister Maynard. Who Maynard was remains unclear, as Guiteau only mentions him tangentially during his trial testimony: "It is of no consequence whether it was Mr. Jones or Mr. Maynard, or anybody else . . ." Based solely on Guiteau's answer, Maynard may not actually have existed.

Evidence of Guiteau's mental condition leans strongly toward an indication of mental illness. He went so far as to claim so in his legal defense. Guiteau stated that he was insane "legally" but not "medically". By this, one supposes he meant he was sane from a health standpoint, yet not sane for the purposes of finding him guilty of murder. Even so, if nothing else, Guiteau was natural showman. Prior to shooting the president, he had decided against a wooden grip for the murder weapon because he believed the ivory grip would look better as a museum piece. While in jail, he financed his legal defense by allowing himself to be photographed and then collecting a share on the sale of prints. Newspapers and curious onlookers paid top dollar for his photos, many of which are extant today.

During the legal proceedings, a jury deemed Guiteau sane enough to stand trial and convicted him of murder. He was sentenced to hanging. While standing on the gallows and awaiting execution, Guiteau sang a tune he himself had written, "I Am Going to the Lordy", before the crowd that had assembled to watch him die. He was hanged on June 30, 1882.

President Garfield's spine is housed at the National Museum of Health and Medicine in Washington, D.C. It bears the entry wound where Guiteau's bullet struck the president.

Guiteau's murder weapon was photographed in the early 1900's for inclusion in the Smithsonian Museum. The photo is available to be viewed online. As for the gun itself, some time after the revolver was catalogued into the museum's collection, it mysteriously vanished. It has never been seen since, and the only record of it that remains is the Smithsonian's photo.

—*ASJr*

CRYSTAL NIGHT

How fortunate it was for the world that when these great trials came upon it, there was a generation that terror could not conquer and brutal violence could not enslave.

—*Winston Churchill*

I

Berlin, November 9, 1938

Elsa's voice faltered on the final note of her song. Two men in black trench coats had entered Das Karussell, prowling like panthers through the tables at the back of the nightclub. Applause drifted towards the stage but it soon died when the patrons noticed the men in their midst. The manager, Helga Gartner, waved her hand. Play on, she gestured. Pianist Siggy Katzmann tinkled the keys. Elsa Fischer composed herself, cleared her throat and with a shy smile began, *A Night in May.*

The younger of the two men, tall and athletic, his blond hair swept back, sides shaved in a buzz-cut, wandered through the sparse weeknight crowd, singled out a couple and asked for their papers. The other man, much older, broad-shouldered with a hardened frown, took off his leather coat and settled on a stool at the bar near the club's entrance.

At the end of the bar's long polished counter, a young man in his early twenties emerged from the cellar through a small door. Johann, the bartender, carried a heavy crate of beer bottles. The sleeves of his white shirt hugged his bulging biceps.

"His papers, Helga?" Inspector Oberrisch asked.

Helga stepped between her new bartender and the Gestapo inspector's gaze, hands on hips. She turned, whispered into the young man's ear and he retreated to the cellar.

"Pilsner, *ja*?" She pulled the tap in front of Oberrisch. "Another recruit, Klaus?" She nodded in the direction of the tall blond agent. "How many more agents does the State Police need?"

"My nephew, Heinz Bremer. My sister asked if I could find him a job." Oberrisch took a notepad from his trench coat and glanced around the room.

"Put that away, Klaus. Take the night off for a change."

"You're always grousing about something, Helga."

"Grousing keeps my costs down. Grousing keeps me in business."

"The Gestapo's patronage keeps you in business." Oberrisch sipped his beer. "My notebook keeps you in business. Don't ever forget that."

The front door of the club opened with a rattle. The noise startled Helga. Four men wearing brown uniforms and Nazi armbands stormed in. "What are they doing in my club? Get them out of here!"

Oberrisch rose from his stool, placed his hand on the chest of the lead stormtrooper and ushered the group back to the narrow foyer. "Everything is under control," he said. "Just stay here at the door. Be quiet and let no one leave or enter, *ja*? Not until he arrives, understand?"

Oberrisch straightened his tie, returned to the bar and surveyed the crowd. The patrons had dismissed the presence of the Gestapo and SA stormtroopers as routine, a fact of daily life in Germany. The patrons returned to their hushed conversations and to the singing of Elsa Fischer, an eighteen-year-old as young and as vibrant as they were.

Johann returned from the cellar with an armful of wine bottles. Oberrisch stopped writing in his notebook and looked up. A scowl grew on his face. His eyes squinted. "Papers, Helga."

"Fetch that bottle of schnapps, Johann," Helga said. "With my regrets, inspector, I have a nightclub to run." She cast her eye towards a table where an elderly man was sitting alone. "Pour a glass for Herr Doktor Franz at Table Two."

"His papers, Helga?"

She ignored the inspector again. Johann took the bottle of schnapps to the gentleman at Table Two.

"There's no profit in staying open on a weeknight, Klaus," she said. "So why do I? Just look around this club and you'll see the reason. It's for the young people. The ones who work late at the Reich Ministries making sure Goebbels' latest propaganda is ready for the morning. And what do these young men and women, the pride of Germany, want after a long, hard day working for the Reich? I'll tell you what they want. An out-of-the-way place to enjoy a drink, to listen to some music and to settle their nerves. They want a place where they can exchange a kiss without being judged as to who they're kissing. That's all."

Helga reached for another bottle of schnapps, poured two shots and pushed one towards Oberrisch. "Don't you remember when we were their age? It's not really that long ago."

Oberrisch wrote in his notebook, head down.

"We were no different," she continued. "That's why I keep the club open on weeknights. They make me feel young all over again even if you've forgotten what being young means. In turn, I make them feel welcome. I try to make them feel safe. And then you and your junior Klaus barge in."

"Heinz. His name is Heinz."

"That's what I said. A junior Klaus. If you want a name to put in your notebook, I suggest you get hers." Helga pointed her shot glass to a table partially obscured by a row of potted ferns. A sultry young woman with short blond hair in a wavy coif sat across from an older man. His stuffy shirt, dark necktie and bland jacket suggested he was a civil servant.

Helga downed the schnapps in one gulp. "She comes into the club a lot. Each time in the company of a different male companion. If anyone's name should be in your notebook, Klaus, it's hers. And look at him, he should know better. A department head from the mayor's office? In here with that ... that *slut*? He should be at home with his wife and children."

The woman wore bright red lipstick, a jade-green dress and had eyes like blue crystal. She drank from a near-empty champagne glass with the speed of a ravenous hummingbird. The woman giggled at the civil servant's nervous joke. His fingers pulled on the tight collar of his shirt, his eyes darted about the club, moving from the Gestapo men to the SA stormtroopers guarding the way out.

Oberrisch reached into his jacket and pulled out a thick wad of money. He passed a twenty Reich mark bill across the counter. "Another bottle of champagne for his table, Helga. Tell him it's on the house. Tell them they make you feel young again or whatever words you want to shovel their way."

Helga pushed the note back. "I'm not condoning her kind of business in here."

"She works for me, which means she works for the Reich and for our Führer." Oberrisch grabbed Helga's wrist and thrust the money into her palm, closing her fingers over the bill. "You will do as I say, Helga. Magda is doing her job as a loyal German, helping uncover another traitor. You are a loyal German, aren't you? Give them another bottle of champagne."

Helga winced. "You and your informants, Klaus. You're like red wine stains on a dark carpet. You hope we'll walk right by you without noticing you're there. Your brownshirts patrol Berlin's streets like escaped lions. Those thugs don't belong anywhere near my club. I want them out of here."

"The SA keeps the streets clean."

"Tell that to the women who have to wash the blood off our pavements each morning."

"Watch your tongue. If I didn't know you as well as I do, I'd have Bremer arrest you. And perhaps he should. Young Heinz needs to practice what we've taught him." Oberrisch stiffened and glared at Helga. "Do you have his papers, or not?"

The bartender returned to the bar and was restocking wine. "Champagne, Johann, for Table Seven."

"Yes, Fräulein Gartner."

Johann picked up a bottle of French champagne and as he walked to the end of the bar, he brushed by Klaus Oberrisch. A spark jumped from Johann's arm to the Gestapo inspector's wrist. The inspector glanced at his watch, and then tapped the dial several times. He looked up at the clock above the bar. "Strange, my watch has stopped. And it looks like the clock above the bar has stopped too. What time do you have?"

"Perhaps if your other Gestapo men paid for their beer and schnapps once in awhile, I might be able to afford to have things fixed around here."

"I asked for the time, Helga, not a lecture on your accounts." Oberrisch produced a silver coin from his pocket and rolled it across the counter. "Besides, paying you has never stopped you from complaining. I don't know anyone who grouses as much as you do."

"Tell that to your guests in the cells at Number Eight."

"Careful, Helga."

"You wanted the time, *ja*? It must be at least ten o'clock. Herr Doktor Franz doesn't come in here much before that."

"That late? They will be here soon and we haven't finished. I need to see his papers, Helga."

"*Who* will be here soon?"

Oberrisch gestured to Heinz Bremer who was watching the elderly gentleman at Table Two with suspicion. The inspector had a brief word with Bremer and they walked over to the brownshirts at the door. Bremer and two of the stormtroopers departed in a hurry.

The inspector returned to the bar, eyed Johann as he gathered empty glasses, and said, "I hope for your sake, Fräulein Gartner, that he has papers. Because if you don't produce them this very instant, I will have you arrested."

Helga's face lost its sternness and confidence. She reached below the bar and produced a small metal box, taking out several passport-sized documents. She slapped them on the counter. "These are his, and those are mine. Each with new stamps to employ a foreign worker, approved by the Reich Ministry of Labor."

Oberrisch glanced at Helga's permit and set it aside. "Still greasing that weasel at the Labor Ministry? The one who comes in here to feel *safe*? The one who would stamp a dead dog's paw if it paid him well enough? He's a homosexual, you know. His time, like the rest of his kind, is short. In a few days, the degenerate will be gone and both of us will have to find another weakling to bribe inside the Labor Ministry."

Oberrisch picked up the bartender's passport. He examined every page and stamp in detail, the quality of the watermarks. "It looks genuine enough. If this is a forgery, it's a very good one. In Berlin, Swedish passports are usually found on Jews trying to leave Germany, not on foreigners wanting to stay. He's not Jewish, is he?"

"Look at him, Klaus. He's more Aryan than you are. His hair couldn't be more blond, his eyes more blue."

Oberrisch examined the Swedish passport again. "What's he doing here? In Berlin?"

"Why don't you ask him yourself? His German isn't bad. Just a bit wooden. He's learned some odd phrases."

"Odd?"

"Well, old-fashioned. As if he learned his German by reading literature from the last century. I guess he had a bad teacher in Sweden. I keep correcting him. He learns incredibly fast for a foreigner. He's a smart young man."

"And virile."

"What's that supposed to mean?"

"I've known you for a long time, Helga. Are you paying him like the others with just room and board? You've always had your ways to get what you wanted when you needed it. And you need a real man to help you run this place, not a boy."

"I've told you before, Klaus, what you need is a good Nazi wife, a frau with strong arms and wide hips. Like those on the Party posters with braids wrapped in a bun, a white blouse and a flowery Bavarian frock. Someone dumb and willing."

Oberrisch turned away from her. "Young man," he barked. "Step over here, please. Routine documents check. Fräulein Gartner must have told you about me. It's my job to keep clubs like this from being contaminated by the wrong kind of people. What is your purpose in Germany, Herr...," Oberrisch looked down at the passport, "... Nilsson. Johann Nilsson?"

"I'm here to learn, to study."

"A student? In a nightclub?" Oberrisch chuckled. "Well, yes. I guess you will learn a lot of things in a place like this. But I don't see a student visa in your passport."

"The world is my school, sir."

"The world is your school? And this nightclub is your lecture hall?" Oberrisch let out a belly laugh loud enough to turn nearby heads. "You said he was clever, Helga. You didn't say he was a comedian. What are you here to study?"

"Mankind and his society. His science. His arts. Human psychology. The geography of earth. Its animals and plants. Many things, and all things."

"Much of what you may have learned is being rewritten. The Nazi Party is challenging conventional thinking."

"That's what I've heard and read. I understand German scientists have discovered a species of sub-humans. This discovery sounds very exciting. I'm interested in learning more about these new creatures. I've come to Germany to further my research into human genetics. The instinct for the preservation of one's own species is the primary cause that leads to the formation of human communities."

Oberrisch grunted. "What is that nonsense? Is that the genetics they teach you in Sweden?"

"No. That was written here," Johann replied. "In Germany. By one of your most famous scholars."

"And Herr Oberrisch," a deep voice said from behind the Gestapo man, "if you were a student of *Mein Kampf*, as you should be, and as it appears this young man certainly is, you would know he's quoting the Führer."

Oberrisch looked over his shoulder. "Commander von Kamptz!" He jumped off his stool, clicked his heels and raised his arm in a stiff salute. "Heil Hitler!"

Conversations in Das Karussell went silent. Elsa's voice trailed off and Siggy stopped playing. Patrons rose to their feet. 'Heil Hitler!' rang throughout the room.

The door to the club rattled open. Heinz Bremer entered. Three more SS officers marched in behind him, their shiny black boots clomping on the hardwood floor. The SA brownshirts stood aside and saluted. Bremer led the officers to a table close to the stage.

"Music! Please keep playing. Please, enjoy," SS-Commander von Kamptz announced. His smile was broad and white as if it had been painted on his sour face by an approved Nazi artist.

Elsa gestured to Siggy to resume the song he was playing before the interruption. When they finished, her face was flush. A lump formed in Elsa's throat. Her voice croaking, she struggled to thank the crowd for their applause. She acknowledged the club's new guests with a coy smile, turned to take a drink of water from a glass behind the piano, and whispered to Siggy, "What's going on? Why are the SS here?"

Siggy Katzmann squinted through the glare of the hot stage lights. His face turned pale. He reached for a handkerchief in the pocket of his jacket and wiped his brow.

"Siggy, what's wrong?"

"We can't play *My Golden Baby*," he gulped. "Not now."

"Why not?"

"It's too jazzy. Too negro. They're SS. That's not acceptable. That's the head of the Schutzpolizei at the bar. Commander von Kamptz. And do you see the one in the spectacles at the table? Don't you know who he is?"

"I've been in Berlin less than four weeks. I don't know anybody. Not anybody important."

"His armband," Siggy whispered. "Can't you tell by his armband? And by the way the other two are fawning over him?"

Elsa peered at the table, forcing a smile. Two black-and-silver uniformed officers flanked a slight, bespectacled man with a paintbrush mustache. His Nazi armband had three white stripes.

"Who is he? The lights in my face are so bright I can't tell."

"Reichsführer Heinrich Himmler. Head of the entire SS."

She turned her head away and gasped. "*Mein Gott*, Siggy. *Himmler*? Here?"

Elsa took another sip of water. "All right," she whispered. "How about... oh, *mein Gott*, let me think...how about *My Little Green Cactus*? It's a jolly tune. Surely it isn't banned?"

"*Ja, sehr gut*, Elsa. But we need to take a break after this."

"We're supposed to play two more songs before our next break. Helga will be furious."

"We need to take a break." Siggy mopped a bead of sweat that trickled down his cheek. He keyed the introduction to *My Little Green Cactus*. "Sing," he said.

Elsa cleared her throat. The melody of the popular song bounced easily from her tongue; its light and meaningless words perfect for a fresh-faced innocent to sing in a room whose atmosphere had tensed. The young people in the crowd soon joined in the chorus.

Helga introduced herself to Himmler and his aides, took their order and returned to the SS table with a tray holding three glasses of the finest French cognac she owned. Himmler sniffed his glass and looked pleased at her selection. Elsa's voice had recovered, soaring like a bell, the pleats of her yellow chiffon dress swaying in time with the music. Himmler tapped the table with the palm of his hand, sipped his cognac and smiled to his aides.

Happy that the Reichsführer was happy, Helga nodded her approval to Elsa for the choice of song and returned to the bar. Johann was in the middle of a deep conversation with SS-Commander von Kamptz.

"So you've been to Tibet?" the commander asked.

"Yes. I lived there. Many, many years ago. In Lhasa."

"The Reichsführer, the one sitting at the table over there, has just commissioned an expedition to Tibet. They left in August to study the origins of the Aryan race."

"I studied the people of the region when I was there."

"It's too bad Himmler's expedition has already left. I'm sure they could have used a person of your experience. It is such a remote part of the world and so hard to get into. Sweden sent an expedition to Tibet?"

"No, I traveled there independently."

"You're so young to have traveled so far afield at your age. Very admirable. Perhaps there would be another chance for you to join a similar SS expedition in the future. South America or Africa perhaps."

"I have been to both continents, many times."

"That's incredible. Were your parents diplomats?"

"The ones who created me have allowed me the freedom to do as I wish."

"So you're not close to your parents? That's a pity. But I understand. Many young people are searching to find their place in the world. Searching for purpose. We should talk about the SS and the opportunities it provides young men like you. We can be the family you never had."

"Excuse me, Commander," Helga said. "If I had known I would have to entertain special guests tonight, I would have called in my other staff." She approached Johann and started to lead him away. "I do apologize but I need help from Johann to serve the tables."

"You will have to manage without him." Oberrisch grabbed her arm. "Commander von Kamptz has become quite interested in your young Swede." Oberrisch pulled Helga aside.

"I can't afford to have any more of my staff arrested or, heaven forbid, recruited," she complained.

"Resettlement, Helga. Not arrests. We resettle undesirables. Like your communist friends."

"I have no communist friends."

"That's true. You don't any more. When the commander is finished with Nilsson, I'll let you know. Until then, you have customers to serve, *ja*? Like the one at Table Two who has been so patient."

"You leave Doktor Franz alone."

"And why should I do that?"

"Because I said so." Helga huffed and took the bottle of schnapps from the counter.

The elderly gentleman at Table Two was a man in his seventies. He was wearing a red silk cravat, with white shirt and blue blazer. An Iron Cross medal was pinned to his lapel. His cheeks were ruddy and his thick white hair and handlebar mustache were plumed like the feathers of a swan.

"Elsa's far too young for you," Helga said as she poured him a glass of schnapps.

"Where do you find such larks?"

"I don't, Herr Doktor. They find me."

Heinz Bremer arrived at the doctor's table. "Your papers, please."

"Why do you need to see my papers, young man?"

"Papers, *bitte*. I ask the questions."

"You don't know who you're talking to, do you?" Helga protested. "Doktor Franz is a decorated war hero. He was pulling wounded soldiers out of the trenches while you were still suckling at your mother's breast."

"That was then, Fräulein Gartner," Bremer replied. "This is now. This is a new Germany, a better Germany. A Germany that isn't ashamed of its past. Our Führer no longer wants us to celebrate this gentleman's defeats as if they were victories."

"You despicable little—" Helga bit her tongue.

Oberrisch saw the heated exchange. He excused himself from the conversation between von Kamptz and Johann Nilsson, crossed the room and put a hand on Bremer's shoulder. "Discretion, Heinz. We don't want to make a scene. Don't worry, I can vouch for the Doktor." Oberrisch took his protégé to one side, "Magda is leaving. It's time."

The civil servant from the mayor's office was slipping a mink stole over the shoulders of the sultry woman in the jade-green dress. Her seductive grin was accompanied by a gentle touch of her hand on the man's cheek. The pair passed between the two brown-shirted goons guarding the door and left the club.

"Follow them, Heinz. You know what to do."

Bremer slunk out of Das Karussell. The pair of brownshirts followed.

Oberrisch returned to Table Two. "There, Helga. Satisfied? The lions are back on the street where they belong. Now come. I would like to reminisce with you and the Doktor. Please, I would like you to join us."

"I have work to do and, as you say, patrons to keep happy."

"Sit, Helga."

Her face turned sour. "But Himmler and his officers?"

"They are happy. Their glasses are not empty."

Helga gestured to Johann. More Cognac, she mouthed, pointing to the SS table. Johann excused himself from von Kamptz and picked up the cognac bottle.

"Now sit, Helga, before I drag you off your feet."

She took the chair next to Doktor Franz, her fingers twirling the pearl necklace around her neck as if she was fondling a rosary. "What's this about, Klaus?"

"I want to dispel some unsubstantiated rumors. The gossip that has followed the good Doktor into his old age. I need your help to restore our war hero's unblemished image in the community. I know you want that." Oberrisch turned to Doktor Franz. "Your wife died several years ago. In Leipzig, I believe?"

"It was tuberculosis," the old man said.

"Very sad. And then she was cremated. You wouldn't happen to still have her ashes, would you?"

"What kind of question is that?" Helga asked. "Can't you see how upsetting his wife's death is?"

"Funny, I don't see any concern on his face, Fräulein Gartner. And I think I might know why. Could we still find the presence of arsenic in the ashes of a cremated body, Herr Doktor? If we could test those ashes?"

"My wife was Austrian. At the request of her family, her ashes were spread out on the Danube," Franz replied. "At a riverside park where she spent so many good times in her youth."

"How sweet. How fitting. And how convenient."

"Is that why you came here tonight, Klaus?" Helga protested. "To dishonor a war hero, an innocent old man? With vile rumors? Innuendo, that's all it is. You should be quashing these stories, not propagating them."

"There was a singer in this club after the Great War," Oberrisch said, unfazed. "A singer with a young daughter in her teens. I would think about the same age as Helga was in 1920." Oberrisch leered at Helga.

She turned her head away.

"Those were bad times in Germany," he continued. "Especially hard for a young mother. Unmarried, I'm told."

The notes of Elsa's next song floated over the table.

"Where is this singer now, Herr Doktor? You were seen in her company so many times. Were you helping to support her and her daughter? A wealthy man like you, so kind and generous, owning both an apothecary and a nightclub...yes, Helga I know Das Karussell is not really yours."

"I don't know what you're talking about," the doctor replied. His fingers fidgeted with his mustache.

"Very well, Franz. I really want to put these ugly rumors to rest. I can do that if you will cooperate with me on a certain matter. Together, we can make your past of no further interest to the Gestapo. We have more important things to do these days."

"That's the best thing I've heard you say all night," Helga said.

Oberrisch smiled. "But there is *something* the State is very interested in. You sold the Berliner Apotheke to a Jew, didn't you?"

"He's a good pharmacist. Very competent. And he had the money. Why wouldn't I? His customers are happy. His prices are reasonable."

"This district may need to find a new pharmacist after tonight, Herr Doktor. And until a new one is found, the Ministry of Health would like you to come out of retirement. Just for a short while. To run things. For the people who need their medicine."

"I'm retired from that profession, and happily so."

"Are you saying you won't come to the Führer's aid? To the aid of the German people? At a time of need? You did so before and have the medals to prove it. This is no different. A different kind of war, that's all."

The old man downed his schnapps.

"How can I encourage you, Doktor? Perhaps if you do this for the Reich, you will see all these ugly, unsubstantiated rumors disappear. Just like that. And in a few short weeks, maybe a month, you can return to your retirement knowing you have served a generous Reich; a Reich with a Führer who has vowed to protect you in your old age. Just like you did for that singer and her daughter in their time of need, *ja*?"

"I will consider it."

"Good. Officer Bremer will come to you the day after tomorrow with the keys. There may be some cleaning up needed before we reopen the apothecary."

"Has it been sold?"

"Let's say, the Jew no longer wishes to be in the business. He has volunteered for resettlement to a place where he and his family will find a happier life. In fact, we will all be happier after tonight."

"What's so special about tonight?" Helga asked.

The answer from Inspector Oberrisch was not forthcoming. The music had abruptly stopped. Helga looked at the stage. Siggy Katzmann was not there. Elsa was leaning on the piano to steady herself. She looked frightened. Himmler and his SS officers looked uncomfortable. Their entertainment had ended suddenly. Siggy had taken an early break.

"*Mein Gott*! Not now," Helga said. "What is he thinking?"

Elsa disappeared behind the stage curtain.

"I must see what's wrong." Helga nearly knocked over the bottle of schnapps as she rose. "Please excuse me." She waltzed past the SS table in a flurry, opened the side curtain and scurried back stage where she found Elsa Fischer pacing the tight corridor outside the small dressing room.

"He's locked the door," she said when Helga arrived. "I can hear him rustling around in there. What's he doing?" The girl was shaking. "He said we had to take a break. Every time he looked in the direction of Himmler's table, I could see him getting more and more anxious."

"Stop crying. This isn't the first time he's done something like this," Helga muttered. "Siggy!" She banged on the door. "Siggy! Open this door!"

The door flung open in her face and she was pushed back against the wall. Siggy emerged holding a tatty suitcase bulging at its buckles.

"Where are you going? You can't leave. Not now. What are we supposed to do without you?"

"Sing a cappella!" Siggy shouted as he bolted through the stage door into the alley.

Elsa cried, "What are we going to do now?"

Helga put her arm around her.

"I can't go back there," Elsa sobbed. "What would I sing without a pianist?"

"Take a moment to compose yourself. Surely you know something. A ballad. A lullaby. *Oh Gott*! There must be something you can sing? We'll say he got sick. They'll understand. But you must sing, Elsa. You have to. We have such important guests."

"I don't care if it's the Führer in there! I just can't do it. I feel faint."

Helga held Elsa's hand. Tears streaked the girl's stage makeup; black mascara raced down her cheeks. "I'll get you a chair from the dressing room."

The tinkle of piano keys drifted into the corridor. A string of notes soared high into the air on silky wings then crashed in a crescendo like waves pounding on rocks.

Elsa stopped sobbing. Her mouth gaped open, her eyes wide. "It's Wagner. Fantasia in F sharp. But who? Who's playing it?"

"*Mein Gott*! Someone is playing for Himmler!" Helga rushed out of the corridor. She paused behind the stage curtain and peeked through. "You won't believe this, Elsa. It's Johann!"

"Johann?"

"Himmler is entranced. The whole nightclub is. I've never heard Wagner played like this before. With such precision ... and with such incredible passion. It's as if Johann helped Wagner write it."

II

Helga woke with a start to the sounds of men's voices and dogs barking. At street level, five stories below her top floor apartment, broken glass crashed onto the pavement.

Her skin tingled with the afterglow of Johann's hard young body. She rubbed her eyes and looked at the clock beside the bed. It had stopped at a quarter to midnight.

Johann Nilsson stood on the balcony, naked, staring up at the Milky Way, its stars playing hide and seek with the clouds.

Helga put on her nightgown and lit a cigarette. "What's going on down there?"

He didn't answer.

She plucked his trousers from the floor and stepped through the French doors. "Put these on before the neighbors see you. Aren't you cold? What are you doing out here?"

She stroked his broad back, feeling the scratches on his smooth skin. Her scratches. "I'm sorry about this. Did I hurt you? I couldn't help myself. You were like a machine. I've never—" She wrapped her arms around his waist. "You're not even cold."

He stood silent and rigid, his eyes staring into the night sky.

"Look at me, Johann." She heard a faint crackle at the back of his head. She touched the hair on the nape of his neck and a spark of static electricity pricked her finger.

She stepped between Johann and the railing of the balcony. "Your eyes, Johann. What's happening to them?"

His pupils glowed, pulsing with a soft blue light.

A dog barked, the echo bouncing off the quiet buildings into the crisp night air. A woman screamed. There were more voices, frightened voices. Footsteps, people running, others chasing.

Helga turned. She looked across the rooftops of Berlin and put her hand to her mouth. "*Mein Gott*!"

It was still dark outside but the early light of the new morning's sunrise was showing on the horizon. Another light flickered across the night sky, a reddish orange glow. In the distance, buildings burned. Plumes of black smoke rose from the orange flames, forming dark unnatural clouds in the starry sky.

An open-backed truck full of men rumbled along the street below. The truck turned right at the entrance to the local square and stopped. A dozen men dismounted. The SA, the brownshirts of the Nazi Party, Hitler's devoted army of stormtroopers, were on the prowl again. Some carried petrol cans. Others held clubs.

"The synagogue," Helga gasped. "They're going to burn down the synagogue!"

Helga heard a sizzling sound. A static charge rolled down Johann's back into her nightgown. The shock pushed her away from him.

He turned his head, "Why?"

"Why what?"

"Why destroy buildings that still have purpose? Why smash shop windows? It doesn't make any sense. I've seen so many of this world's wars, so much destruction for no apparent reason. But this? There's been no declaration of a war. Are the German people not prosperous and happy? Why is this happening? What is the purpose of it?"

"Don't be silly. You're in Germany. Where have you been for the past five years? What planet have you lived on?"

Johann put on his trousers and walked back into the bedroom. He found his shirt on the chair.

"These are things we can't control," Helga said as he finished dressing. "It's too late for that. Much too late. But war may be coming sooner than we want. The only thing people like you and I can do now is find a way to survive it."

"Survival? I understand the concept very well. If there are beasts in the forests and jungles, we need to protect ourselves. When wars are declared between kings to conquer each other's lands, men fight against men. It's a wasteful practice I have yet to understand. But its purpose is clear and, when there's war, survival is necessary. But this? Destroying your own city? Where is the enemy? I don't understand any of this."

As he spoke, Helga could feel the electricity in the air around him. In the dimness of the darkened bedroom, sprays of an ethereal blue light were dancing above Johann's head. "I must be dreaming this," Helga said, her body shaking.

She glanced into the study next to the bedroom and gasped. Papers were strewn all over the opened bureau, its drawers still ajar and her Luger removed from its hiding place. She ran into the study and then ran back out, fuming. "Have you been going through my papers while I've been sleeping?"

"It's nothing to worry about. I meant to put them back before you woke up. Then I heard the breaking glass."

"Put them back? You shouldn't have been looking at them in the first place. They're private papers." She stepped away from him. His eyes had stopped glowing but his expression was blank. "What were you doing with them?"

"I'm curious."

"*Curious*?" She pulled on the silk of her nightgown. "I'm beginning to wonder just what kind of fool I've been."

"What do mean?"

"No man with any feeling could have made love to a woman like, like ... *that* and then be like *this*—warm on the outside but cold as ice on the inside. Then I discover you've rifled through my private papers while I've been sleeping. Now I know who you *really* are."

"You do?"

"Only a fool would believe a woman of my age could attract a handsome young man into her bed without the help of Klaus Oberrisch."

"Oberrisch? The inspector? I don't understand what he has to do with this."

She laughed. "You're one of his spies, aren't you? All this nonsense about wanting to see your papers. The fuss over your job at the club. It's all a ruse by Oberrisch to trick me into believing in you. A foreigner? A Swede? A charlatan more likely. And now, tonight of all nights, with Himmler in my club, and you, *you* ... warming my bed with *such* ... I don't even know how to describe it."

"It wasn't nice for you?"

"Of course it was *nice*. It was incredible. But that's the problem. I've never experienced anything like *that*. No woman has. Such stamina. Almost inhuman. And too *perfect*. And now I think I know why."

"You do?"

"Yes. Oberrisch said it in the club, about his new protégé. It's what all of you have been *taught* to do. Your job. Your training. You're just like Heinz Bremer. You're just the same as he is." She sobbed and backed into the study.

"I'm nothing like him. I'm not one of them."

"No? We'll see." Helga glanced at the Luger on the desk and inched herself towards it. She looked up at Johann. His haunting blue eyes were drawn to the pistol as well. Her hand slipped slowly across the top of the desk feeling for steel as she kept her gaze fixed tightly on the muscular young Swede.

"I need answers, Johann," she said. She picked up the Luger and pointed it.

"Answers? What kind of answers?"

Her hand shook. "I don't want to use this," she sobbed. "But I may have to. And I know how to. An hour ago, you made love to me like no man has ever done. And now, you fill me full of dread. I'm frightened of you and of what your kind represents. Unless I get answers, I *will* use this. I know what's inside that head of yours."

"How can you? No one has ever known."

"I understand the way all of your kind thinks. Only too well. I know who you truly are, inside. You can't fool me any longer with this charade, Johann. Your kind thinks you belong to a master race; that you're better than the rest of us? But you all bleed like we do."

"Helga, don't do this."

"I've been such a damn fool. I've risked everything I've worked for. I've risked every hope I've ever had to escape this ungodly mess, and for *what*? A night of lust and pleasure? It was a delusion. A dangerous delusion. I've worked too hard to let something like my past destroy me."

Helga moved towards Johann, gun drawn, trying to steady her aim. "It would be easy to kill you and say you returned to Sweden. I could make up a story that you didn't have the stomach to live in Hitler's glorious Reich. And what would they say? Would they admit you're one of them? I don't think so. You're disposable to the Gestapo and the SS, Johann. Human life in Germany today is as disposable as yesterday's newspaper."

"You have no reason to be afraid of me."

"No? Then I *must* have answers. What does the Gestapo know about me? What do they know about Doktor Franz? If you don't tell me what you know, what's in my file, I'll be forced to… to…" She stepped closer, steadying the Luger in her raised hand.

"I can't let you fire that gun, Helga. No one must ever know about me."

"And I can't let you out of this apartment, alive. I don't think it's your choice, Johann. It's *mine*. Because, I have the gun. Now back away!"

He took a step forward.

Electricity filled the air again.

She pulled the trigger.

The gun jammed.

III

The smell of freshly baked bread swirled in the air. Johann stepped out of the Anhalter Bahnhopf, Berlin's central train station, into a slight drizzle. A man, forty years old, and a girl of sixteen were doing brisk business from a sidewalk stall selling loaves of pumpernickel and rye, brötchen crusted with sesame, and twisted braids of pretzels in all sizes.

Several women filled their wicker baskets. When they moved on to the next stall, Johann handed the bread seller a slip of paper. "Can you help me get to this address?"

The man recoiled, shoving the paper back into Nilsson's hand. "Number Eight Prinz-Albrecht-Strasse? Why do you want to go *there*?"

"I have an appointment."

The man laughed. "People do not make appointments at Number Eight Prinz-Albrecht-Strasse. That's the Reich Security Office. The headquarters of the Gestapo. You don't *make* an appointment."

"But I did. I met an officer last night. A man called Jürgen von Kamptz."

"SS-Commander von Kamptz?"

"Do you know him?"

"Everyone in Berlin knows him. The Gestapo reports to him. Only informers want to meet with von Kamptz. You're not German, are you? Where have you come from?"

"Have you seen the sub-humans?"

"The what?"

"The species of sub-humans. Your newspapers say a rat-like species of sub-humans lives here. They say they are everywhere, in every German city and elsewhere in Europe. But I didn't find any in Sweden. I've only been in Berlin a few weeks but if they are so abundant, I don't understand why I haven't seen any yet. Perhaps they are nocturnal. Are they very small? Where do they hide during the daytime? I need to know. I must find out for my research. Surely you've seen one?"

The man grunted. "What are you talking about, you fool. Appointments with the Gestapo? And now this lunacy? The feeble-minded have no future in Germany. There are asylums that cleanse our population of people like you. Now get away from my stall before I call the police and they make another 'appointment' for you!"

"Just tell me how I can get to Prinz-Albrecht-Strasse. Please?"

"One block north. Turn right. An 'appointment' with the Gestapo?" The man chuckled. "God help you, idiot."

Johann crossed the plaza, following Saarland-Strasse north into the administrative center of Berlin. In a few minutes he came across a crowd lining the sidewalk in front of the Reich Ministry of Labor. Music filled the air. A marching band approached followed by a double column of brown-shirted stormtroopers stomping down the broad avenue carrying Nazi banners on staffs topped with golden eagles. Trumpets blared. Leather jackboots thumped the ground; the sound like a herd of elephants marching to the beat of jungle drums.

Behind the brownshirts, a bedraggled collection of weary men and women, some very old, trudged along, lugging heavy suitcases. Little children carried cloth satchels. Most of the men were bloodied and bruised. The women and children were crying. Stars made from yellow cloth were pinned to their coats.

"What's happening to those people?" Johann asked a stranger, a lady in a finely tailored coat and posh fur hat standing with her young child of about four, a girl waving a small Nazi flag.

"They're being resettled," came the woman's dispassionate reply. She spit into the street.

Policemen with guard dogs herded the group forward. The dogs snapped and snarled at the heels of any stragglers. Then the parade abruptly stopped. The crowd along the sidewalk yelled a torrent of insults. Objects were thrown. A young man, his face already cut and bleeding, was struck in the head by a potato. He fell to his knees and dropped his suitcase. Looking up, he spotted a man in the crowd preparing to heave a brick his way. The young man grimaced, his face contorted in rage, and he charged his would-be assailant. The brick was thrown. The young man ducked. It missed his head and the two men wrestled, falling to the ground.

A policemen released his German shepherd and the eager dog leapt forward, sinking its teeth into the young man's arm. The police dog dragged him back into the street, screaming in pain.

"No!" Johann cried out. "He's done nothing wrong." He pointed at the gruff workman who tried to escape into the anonymity of the crowd. "It was *that* man."

"Are you a Jew?" the lady in the fur hat asked. "You don't look like a Jew. Let the police do their job. It's not your concern."

A gang of three brownshirts broke through the ranks of the police. The dog was called back by its handler so the stormtroopers could club the young man until his protests ended. He lay motionless. A pool of dark blood expanded on the pavement.

The shrillness of a whistle cut the air. The officer-in-charge ordered his policemen to move the group again. In the confusion of swinging clubs and snarling dogs, a little girl, perhaps four or five years old, had lost her doll. It lay on the road ten yards behind the procession. Her mother, her eyes wide, her face pale as a ghost, pulled the child along. A policeman speared the woman in the ribs with his truncheon and the child slipped out of her mother's hand. She ran back for the doll.

The police dog was off its leash, roaming up and down the line of policemen as they marched forward. It spied the girl; its eyes followed the running of little feet as if tracking a wild rabbit. It bowed its head, ears pinned back, teeth bared. Growling with a trained hunger, it charged. Nilsson was standing on the curb, ten feet from the girl. He took a step into the street. The dog was about to pounce on the helpless child when it jolted backwards as if slamming headfirst into an invisible brick wall. It looked in Johann's direction and whimpered, shook its head, and scratched its ears at a sound no one else could hear. With a tremendous yelp, the German shepherd backed away from the frightened child and scurried off with its tail between its legs.

The little girl picked up the doll and stared into Johann's glowing eyes, pausing for a moment as if she and her mysterious savior were the only ones in existence. There was an anxious shout in the procession. The girl turned away from the young man with the blond hair, the smooth unadulterated skin, and the haunting blue eyes, and rejoined her desperate mother on their march into an uncertain future.

The sound of thumping jackboots pounded the street. The police ordered the bedraggled group of men, women and children to move forward again. As soon as the procession passed, the crowd, with its finely dressed ladies and their demure little children, dispersed.

Johann heard the stranger say to her daughter, "Did you enjoy the band, Heidi?"

Cars returned to fill the avenue, veering around the motionless body left in the middle of the road.

* * *

The building with the nondescript exterior sat dwarfed by the massive Air Ministry on the opposite side of Prince-Albrecht-Strasse. It was a building devoid of Nazi banners or flags. Berliners avoided walking past Number Eight, preferring to cross over to the other side of the boulevard.

A black Mercedes stopped in front of the main entrance. People on the street halted their conversations in mid-sentence. They waited just long enough to see if they could recognize who was being hauled out of the car's back seat. A man and a woman in their sixties, and still in their nightwear, were frog-marched into the building. Once the onlookers' morbid curiosity had been satisfied, they went about their business, their one-time neighbors forgotten.

Oberrisch met Johann on the front steps of the Reich Security Office, Number Eight Prince-Albrecht-Strasse. Once inside, a black-and-silver uniformed officer waived the inspector and his 'guest' past the SS guards into the grand foyer. A broad staircase led up to a gallery two stories high, its barrel-arched ceiling and tall windows spreading sunlight into an otherwise grimly lit interior of empty hallways.

"Where is everyone?" Johann asked as they climbed the steps.

"Busy," Oberrisch replied. "We're always busy. Who has time for paperwork?"

Johann looked through the windows of the gallery. A large courtyard lay on the outside hidden from the street by solid wooden gates. SS soldiers, police and non-uniformed Gestapo agents were herding prisoners into and out of the quad. Many of those being arrested slumped to the cobblestones as truncheons fell on their heads.

"Do you like dogs?" Oberrisch asked.

"I don't think they like me."

"Well, if they ask if you want to join a canine unit, you'd better say no. You don't want to fail at your first assignment. That wouldn't look good on your record."

Quick footsteps echoed high into the ceiling. Oberrisch and Johann turned. A young man in a trench coat was running up the stairs. He arrived out of breath. "Herr Oberrisch," Heinz Bremer said, wheezing, "I thought you should know as soon as possible."

"Know what? Spit it out."

"Helga Gartner. Found dead this morning. On the street outside her apartment. It looks like suicide. She threw herself off her balcony."

Oberrisch stepped back. "Suicide? Helga?" His voice choked. "But *why*?"

"This was found on her body, inspector."

Bremer held out a large manila envelope. It was crumpled and dirty and covered with bloodstains. Oberrisch opened it and took out a sheaf of papers. He read through them and as he turned each page, the creases on his face deepened.

"So, the final solution," he said, "to a riddle that has perplexed me for some time. I was right. Helga Gartner was indeed the daughter of the singer who had an affair with Doktor Franz. The reason he poisoned his wife. And these papers prove both mother and daughter were Jewish. Someone must have threatened to report her. Do we know who this informant was, Bremer?"

"No, inspector. I'll continue to investigate in case others are complicit in protecting her Jewish identity. There was the pianist who ran out of the club. Perhaps the singer, Elsa Fischer?"

Oberrisch stuffed the papers into the envelope and handed them back to Bremer. "Take these to Department B, the Jewish registry."

Bremer clicked his heels and left. Oberrisch turned to Johann. "How well did you know Helga Gartner?"

"I had only just started my employment with her. She was strict but generous. She cared very much for her employees."

"She was a bon vivant, Johann. Cocksure and outspoken. That might have let her survive in the decadent old days of the Weimar Republic, but not now in the Third Reich. We are so much purer now than her kind." The inspector looked at his watch, "Damn! Another one has stopped. What is wrong with these watchmakers?"

"We mustn't be late." Head down, Oberrisch navigated the maze of corridors in great haste until they reached a small foyer near the back of the building. A male secretary in SS uniform sat at a desk in front of a set of tall double doors.

"Herr Oberrisch and the Swede," the secretary announced as he ushered them into the office of SS-Commander Jürgen von Kamptz, head of the Gestapo in the Berlin capital district.

The walls of his office were paneled in thickly beveled dark walnut. Spartan chairs sat on a bare wood floor in front of the commander's ornate Bavarian gothic desk. A bright red flag with a black swastika stood on a pole in one corner. Von Kamptz stood by the window. The light of the gray November sky cast a pall over his face.

Von Kamptz sat and gestured to Oberrisch and Johann to do the same. Behind him was a portrait of Adolf Hitler; next to that a photograph of Hitler and Himmler saluting SS troops from a grandstand, Von Kamptz by their side.

"I enjoyed my conversation with you last night, Herr Nilsson," he said. "And Reichsführer Himmler was very impressed. You are quite a talent on the piano. Who would have thought a Swede would be so proficient in Wagner? It proves how much Scandinavians have in common with Germans. Our Führer believes we share a common destiny. He has a vision for a Greater German Reich, an empire that will bring together the Aryan populations of Europe. You have an amazing command of our Führer's teachings. I've never heard anyone recite passages from *Mein Kampf* as precisely as you did last night."

"I have a very good memory."

"You are an articulate, educated young man. There will be a time, coming very soon, when the SS will need officers fluent in many languages. The Waffen-SS has been ordered to form a Scandinavian regiment. The standards we seek in our officers are high. Soldiers in the SS need both physical and intellectual strength. You clearly exceed those standards. The only question is one of loyalty to the Führer and to the Reich. Are you prepared to pledge your loyalty to the Führer?"

"Where are the sub-humans?" Johann asked.

Von Kamptz was taken aback.

"How dare you speak to the commander like that!" Oberrisch said. "Remember who you are talking to!"

"That's perfectly fine." Von Kamptz's dour expression changed to one of amusement. "The Swede is inquisitive and straight forward. I like that about him. When we talked in the club, I sensed a great desire to get to the subject at hand. Too many people dance around the points they try to make without actually making them. I detest flowery conversations. This young man has purpose in his veins. The SS needs more men like Johann Nilsson."

"I want to understand the science of the sub-humans, Herr Commander. Surely you must have captured some of them?"

"Captured some of them? I dare say we have. We have captured thousands of them and are capturing more every day."

"You have?" Johann leaned forward in his seat. "Where are your laboratories? Can you send me to one?"

"Laboratories?" Oberrisch sneered. "We have no laboratories. What we have are resettlement camps."

"Don't dampen this young man's enthusiasm, Oberrisch. Laboratories? Yes, perhaps we do have some and you're not aware of them, inspector. I'm thinking Johann would be ideal for Reichsführer Himmler's newest scientific undertaking. Our young Swede's expertise in genetics can be of great benefit to the Reich. So many of our own German scientists are, shall we say, too 'squeamish' at the prospects of the kind of research Himmler wants the SS to conduct, to further the genetic progress of the Aryan race. Our young man seems to have no such aversion to that, do you?"

"It is essential to my mission on earth to learn as much about every species."

"You are just the kind of man the SS needs." Von Kamptz opened his desk drawer and took out several forms. "It will be an honor to draw up your enlistment documents. The best place to send you is the medical research unit at the resettlement camp of Dachau, northwest of Munich. There, you will find plenty of sub-humans to work on."

"That is outstanding, Commander. Finally, I will get my hands on these elusive creatures."

Von Kamptz and Oberrisch laughed.

"You really don't have to go that far," the SS-commander said. "Come with me."

Von Kamptz rose and went to the window. His office overlooked a courtyard smaller than the one at the entrance to Number Eight, a quad surrounded on three sides by doors with iron bars. The fourth wall of the yard was bare brick. Bloodstains ran down its surface. He opened the window and shouted down an order. Four guards arrived with Mauser rifles and stood in a line. The officer in charge of the firing squad ordered another group of soldiers to open the cells. Four prisoners were hauled into the courtyard, hands tied behind their backs, their gaits disoriented and weak.

Von Kamptz looked at his watch. Puzzled, he turned and asked, "Does anyone know what time it is? My watch has stopped."

"Two minutes and three point six seconds before twelve o'clock noon, Central European time," Johann replied.

"Such precision, young Swede," the SS-commander said. "I like that."

Von Kamptz shouted another order to the officer in the courtyard. The four prisoners were led face first towards the wall and forced to their knees. Rifle barrels were pressed against the back of their heads. Von Kamptz signaled to the officer. A single shot rang out. One of the men slumped forward like a sack of potatoes.

"I gave them until noon to identify the other conspirators in their plot. These men now have two more minutes to improve their motivation and do what is right."

The officer-in-charge walked behind the remaining three prisoners, prodding them in the ribs with a truncheon and yelling into their ears. He struck one of them across the back of the head then yelled up to the window, "Nein, Herr Oberführer."

"Is it noon, Johann?"

"Yes."

Von Kamptz lifted his finger into the air. Another shot rang out. Another body fell.

"This courtyard is a microcosm of the world we live in today, gentlemen," the SS-commander said. "Down there, things must be done to advance the justness of a cause. We must do what is right. And so must those other men, our enemies. The strong must survive to perpetuate the species. Am I not right, young scientist?"

"Yes, commander. Darwin told me that himself."

"In your readings, of course? Well, you should read what our Führer has to say on that subject some time at your leisure. But what we see here and now, below us, are the bonds that men share. These men are being tested. They are being asked by the barrel of a gun to prove to their comrades they can be trusted with the justice of their cause. Who will break that trust? Personally, I admire the men we shot. They did not betray their comrades' trust. Will you be able to do the right thing for the SS when that time comes, Johann?"

"Loyalty to some kind of cause is the nature of the human condition, commander. Or so I have learned during many travels to every point on this planet. It has been that way for mankind as long as I can remember. An eternal concept, or so it seems. True for several millennia by my count."

"Good. You are also a student of history. Then you understand what I'm talking about."

Von Kamptz signaled again. Another shot rang out. A third body fell face first onto the cobblestones.

"Three foolish men with a lost cause. Only one remains," Von Kamptz said as he turned to Oberrisch. "Come with me. We'll take Johann down to the courtyard to prove his loyalty to the Führer."

* * *

The firing squad stood to attention with their rifles by their sides, their faces cast like stone statues as SS-Commander Jürgen von Kamptz inspected their ranks.

"The finest young men the Reich will ever produce," he said to Johann. "They honor Germany with their service."

Von Kamptz stopped by the last soldier, took his Mauser from his hands, thrust the rifle sideways into Johann's chest and gestured to the final prisoner kneeling next to the three bodies, a man trembling and coughing up blood.

"You would do me a great honor, young Swede, if you would end this charade."

Johann gripped the Mauser's stock, opened the bolt and looked at the stripper clip of bullets inside. A pigeon flew across the courtyard. With incredible speed, Johann reloaded the rifle, followed the flight of the bird, and downed it in an explosive burst of feathers.

"What a shot!" Oberrisch exclaimed.

Johann approached the kneeling prisoner.

The man turned around and looked up at Johann. It was Siggy Katzmann, the pianist from Das Karussell. His right eye was bruised and nearly closed. His lip was puffed and split open.

"Nilsson!" he sneered. He spat out a bloody tooth. "I knew you must be an informant. I told Helga that, but she didn't believe me."

Johann pressed the end of the rifle barrel into Siggy's forehead.

"You want to look into my eyes, don't you, Swede? You want to see the life leave them."

"I'm doing the right thing."

"For who?" Siggy said. "Go ahead. Pull the trigger, you filthy Nazi!"

Johann looked back at von Kamptz and Oberrisch. The SS-Commander nodded. Johann looked down. The sweat was beading off Siggy's forehead onto the gun barrel.

As Johann pulled the trigger, a tiny ripple of electricity ran into the cold hard steel of the rifle.

The gun jammed.

He stepped away from Siggy and passed the Mauser back to the soldier. "This gun needs cleaning. There's too much oxidation in the chamber."

"But I cleaned it this morning," the soldier replied.

Von Kamptz slapped the soldier hard. "Liar! This young man knows more about weapons than you will ever know. Why else would it jam? Huh? Tell me!"

Von Kamptz drew the Luger from his holster. "Here, Nilsson. Use this."

Johann opened the chamber and looked inside.

"Everything in order?"

Johann didn't answer. He racked the bolt of the pistol, stepped towards Siggy and placed the Luger to his head. He looked back at von Kamptz. "Commander, this man plays the piano."

"And he is also a traitor to the Reich."

"I would like to understand how the sub-humans respond to music while I conduct my experiments. But I can't play the piano at the same time. I would like to take this man with me to Dachau."

Von Kamptz thought for a moment, and then chuckled. He looked over at Oberrisch. The inspector shrugged.

Von Kamptz smiled; that faux-jolly, painted smile he had worn at the nightclub to keep the music playing. "*Ja, sehr gut*, Johann. You have shown you can be trusted. Very well then."

Von Kamptz peered at the disheveled pianist, the Gestapo's pathetic blood-soaked prisoner. "I guess you have a savior after all, Katzmann. Congratulations. This has been your lucky day."

The SS-Commander patted Johann on the back as Siggy was hauled back to his cell. "You are indeed one of a kind, young Swede, and will be of great service to the Reich at Dachau. Your research will make a considerable contribution."

"This planet amazes me with its complexity."

"The Führer intends to simplify things very soon. History will be written, and you'll be there to help write it."

"I'll be satisfied with observing and learning. I'm sure I'll be doing lots of both in the Third Reich."

"Excellent. What say, we all go back to my office and have a cognac? To celebrate the great accomplishments of our Führer last night, *Kristallnacht.* And to toast our new recruit, SS-Lieutenant Johann Nilsson, and his out-of-this-world curiosity."

Author's Notes - Charles A Cornell

The night of November 9, 1938 was a night of violence that came to be known as *Kristallnacht* or Crystal Night, the Night of Broken Glass. No event in the history of German Jews between 1933 and 1945 was so widely reported as it was happening, and the accounts from the foreign journalists working in Germany sent shock waves around the world.

The *Daily Telegraph* correspondent, Hugh Greene, wrote this of events in Berlin:

Mob law ruled in Berlin throughout the afternoon and evening and hordes of hooligans indulged in an orgy of destruction. I have seen several anti-Jewish outbreaks in Germany during the last five years, but never anything as nauseating as this. Racial hatred and hysteria seemed to have taken complete hold of otherwise decent people. I saw fashionably dressed women clapping their hands and screaming with glee, while respectable middle-class mothers held up their babies to see the "fun".

Kristallnacht was followed by additional economic and political persecution of Jews, and is viewed by historians as the beginning of the Final Solution and The Holocaust. From November 9 to November 10, the SA—the paramilitary wing of the Nazi Party known as the brown-shirts or stormtroopers—shattered the storefronts of about 7,500 Jewish stores and businesses, and damaged or destroyed about 200 synagogues. Some Jews were beaten to death while others were forced to watch. More than 30,000 Jewish men were arrested by the Gestapo and SS and taken to concentration camps; primarily Dachau, Buchenwald, and Sachsenhausen. Counting deaths in the concentration camps, around 2,000–2,500 deaths were directly or indirectly attributable to *Kristallnacht*.

DACHAU

Dachau was the concentration camp in operation the longest from March 1933 to April 1945; nearly all twelve years of the Nazi regime. From 1933 to 1938, Dachau held Communists, Socialists and other 'enemies of the state'. Over time, the Nazis began to send German Jews to the camp. In 1938 after *Kristallnacht*, more than 10,000 male Jewish citizens of Germany and Austria were deported to Dachau. As the German military occupied other European states, citizens from across Europe were sent to concentration camps. Subsequently, Dachau was used for prisoners of all sorts, from every nation occupied by the forces of the Third Reich. In 1940, Dachau became filled with Polish prisoners, who constituted the majority of the prisoner population until Dachau was officially liberated.

Hundreds of prisoners suffered and died, or were executed in medical experiments conducted at Dachau. Dr Sigmund Rascher, an SS doctor based at Dachau, reported directly to Reichsführer-SS Heinrich Himmler. Prisoners were coerced into participating; they did not willingly volunteer and there was never informed consent. Typically, the experiments resulted in death, disfigurement or permanent disability, and as such are considered examples of medical torture.

Inmates were subjected to various experiments designed to help German military personnel in combat situations, develop new weapons, test experimental vaccines for infectious diseases, and to advance the racial ideology backed by the Third Reich. Experiments on hypothermia were conducted on captured Russian troops; the Nazis wondered whether their genetics gave them superior resistance to cold.

On 19 August 1947, SS doctors captured by Allied forces were put on trial in *USA vs. Karl Brandt et al.*, which is commonly known as the Doctors' Trial. At the trial, several of the doctors argued in their defense that there was no international law regarding medical experimentation.

* * *

For more information on *Kristallnacht*, and the Nazis' concentration camps, Wikipedia has excellent reference material and was the source for these author notes.

http://en.wikipedia.org/wiki/Kristallnacht
http://en.wikipedia.org/wiki/Dachau_concentration_camp
http://en.wikipedia.org/wiki/Nazi_human_experimentation

I would also encourage you to visit the website of The United States Holocaust Memorial Museum at www.ushmm.org. Through its work to document the causes and horrors of the Holocaust, the Museum inspires citizens and leaders worldwide to confront hatred, prevent genocide and promote human dignity.

—*CAC*

STRANGERS ON A PLANE

August 1969

Somewhere in the clouds between Toronto and Vancouver

What great luck. Our flight was only half full.

Wyatt and I managed to score three seats in a row to ourselves. I laid him out across the window and middle seats, placed my hand on his tummy, and rubbed it in soothing circles. Even before we were airborne, Wy was sound asleep. Perhaps he was already a great little traveler, even at the tender age of three months. Go figure—because he was a perfect ogre at home where he often refused to fall asleep.

Long distance plane travel never fazed me. In fact, I loved it. Our itinerary showed the flight from Toronto to Vancouver took four hours. That was a snap—nothing compared to my flying from Houston to Moscow for a summer course studying Russian. Travel was in my blood, and I hoped it would be in Wyatt's too.

I positioned our paraphernalia in an orderly fashion around us. Bulging tote bag under the middle seat in front of Wyatt. My macramé purse under the aisle seat in front of me. Pacifier, water bottle, burp cloths, tissues tucked beside Wyatt. Settling back in my seat, still rubbing my baby's tummy, I waited impatiently for takeoff. My friend Larissa was in deep trouble, thousands of miles west of Toronto, out on the edge of North America, in Vancouver, British Columbia. The plane could not get there fast enough to suit me.

At takeoff, Wyatt awoke. He gave only one piercing shriek before I plopped his pacifier in his mouth. Again, luck was with me. He settled right down and sucked happily away on it, lulling himself back to slumber land. After a few minutes, satisfied he would stay asleep, I unfurled the front section of the *New York Times.* When another traveler had left it behind in the Toronto airport, I pounced and slipped the jewel inside my tote. Living in Canada in self-imposed exile with my draft-resisting husband, I seldom got a chance to read this magnificent newspaper, and counted my newest possession as my third piece of luck. Three small, seemingly inconsequential pleasures reassured me that the trip would be successful.

I opened the *Times* to the front page. Above the fold, a large photo of America's moon men showed them rejoining their families in Houston, Texas—the Armstrongs, Aldrins, and Collinses. The headline read: "No Germs Are Found So Quarantine is Ended; Men in Good Health." The dateline was the day before, August 10, 1969.

Ah, Texas, my home state. I sighed, pushing fond memories away, refusing to wallow in self-pity. My life was now an exercise of seeing the glass—any glass—half full, rather than each half empty.

When I returned to the newspaper and glanced over the rest of the articles, I noticed the other stories were not so upbeat.

The news out of Saigon was as usual—dismal. "North Vietnam troops attacked two United States Marine bases along the demilitarized zone, killing nineteen and wounding eighty..."

Thank heavens my husband David's draft number hadn't been called up yet. I was glad we were safely ensconced in Toronto, Canada. The war in Vietnam was a mess with no clear goals. It was nothing like the one our fathers fought in Europe and the Pacific during World War II.

Okay, never mind. Don't think about Vietnam. Keep reading.

I moved on to another article that described a murder spree that had taken place in Los Angeles on August 9. Police were frantically hunting suspects for the murders of actress Sharon Tate, the pregnant wife of film director Roman Polanski, plus four of her friends.

Oh man, so many deaths, on just the front page.

I began musing about murder and mayhem and didn't notice the stewardess when she suddenly appeared. I jumped when the petite woman in her early twenties touched my arm.

"Sorry," she said, although her dark look and snarky tone belied her apology. "Didn't mean to startle you, but you must either hold your infant on your lap or use the belt to strap him to the seat, Mrs.—?"

"Starr. Call me Austin." I nodded and picked up Wyatt.

"How old is he, Mrs. Starr?" she asked.

"Three months," I said.

She frowned. "He's beautiful, but I can't imagine what it's like to be tied down to a baby. Never being able to go places, see friends, or party much. Bet you don't get a chance to party."

I opened my mouth to answer, but she was already moving away. I watched as she flipped her bleached-blonde hair and sashayed her way down the aisle.

Wyatt squirmed in my arms, arched his back, and let out a scream. "Shush, little Wy," I said. My eyes darted around, looking for signs that he had disturbed the other passengers. No one looked in our direction.

So much for my chance to devour the *Times* in tranquility. Oh well, most of the news was grim anyway. I turned my full attention to Wyatt, rocking him until he fell back to sleep again in my arms.

I must have dozed off too, because sometime later I awoke with a start. The plane hit an air pocket and fell a few feet. No, actually, my stomach announced it felt more like fifty, as it lurched and tightened. My heart thudded and my breathing grew rapid.

Wy still slept—a small miracle for which I was grateful.

I chewed on my lip and tapped my foot. This wasn't like me to have the jitters during a plane ride.

Who was I kidding? My nerves weren't coming from the bumpy ride.

What was I about to plunge into? It wasn't only friendship that propelled me across the continent. Curiosity drove me. I couldn't stand a mystery. I sought answers, and if someone near and dear was the focus of a criminal investigation, I'd be compelled to meddle. Larissa needed me.

Back home in Texas my grandmother often tut-tutted when she thought I was inordinately nosy. "Austin, remember this. Curiosity killed the cat." Despite her warnings, she never kept me from trying to uncover secrets.

A second adage about another type pet came to mind. Mother had told me over and over—which is why all this stuff stuck in my head, rolling around eternally, even when I wanted to get rid of it—"You're like a dog with a bone, Austin."

Then she'd offer up the killing zinger, the coup de grace. "That's not appropriate behavior for a proper young lady." As if that were enough to stop me! All she did was instill guilt. She never seemed to recognize that I inherited my dog-plus-bone trick from *her*.

Now I felt a tiny doubt about having pushed David so hard to let me make this trip. I sensed for the first time what danger could lie ahead for me, out in Vancouver by the shimmering sea. I must refrain from total entanglement in the murder Larissa supposedly committed. I began to wonder about details surrounding the murder. Dang it all. I was at war with my own mind. Besides, I had to remember the promise I made to David.

After two years of marriage, the constant claims that my two guys—father and son—made on my time kept surprising me. Was I selfish to want to do my own thing sometimes? Mother, who set the standard for my life's endeavors, never complained about spending all her time tending her family's needs. She made such devotion look easy and fun. But I wasn't built that way. I wanted to do what I wanted to do. And in this case, I was lucky that Wy could travel with me—and also lucky his daddy had agreed.

And yet, now my guilt suffocated me, made me feel like gagging.

I tried to shake off the feeling and replace it with a sense of duty to repay my debt to Larissa and her family. They had sheltered and supported me while I fought to prove David's innocence when he had been jailed for murder. If flying across the continent for moral support would help them, then I was more than happy to do it. I only hoped I'd be useful.

I thought back to my last case.

"Case?" I said aloud.

Embarrassed at my outburst, I looked across the aisle to see if anyone had noticed, but the elderly woman seated across the aisle kept on snoozing. I think she was snoozing, anyway. I had the sneaking suspicion that it was almost for show. Her head lay against her spouse. He looked much younger than she did. Well, maybe her spouse. Then again, the couple could also be—what?—cousins? Aunt and nephew? No. Those ideas couldn't be right. The thoughts were almost kinky.

I routinely tried to guess people's situations when I watched them in public. Maybe people-watching was a bad habit, but sometimes my theories turned out to be correct. Now, wiggling in the confined airplane seat, I wondered what lay ahead for Wyatt and me in British Columbia.

To my right across the aisle, the female septuagenarian stirred and climbed over her snoring mate. She headed for the restroom.

The plane hit another air pocket. We dropped what felt like hundreds of feet, down, down through the air. My chest grew tight, and bile rose in my throat. Seemingly unperturbed, the elderly passenger continued to glide down the aisle. She never wavered or bobbled. I admired her agility—more nimble than I would have been. And at her age, too. Imagine that.

Turning my head, I looked out the window. Even from the aisle seat, this was not a great idea. Taking in great gulps of air, I surveyed the scene below. The vast expanse of Saskatchewan prairie was gone. Now we flew over steep mountains, the likes of which I'd never seen. Even viewed from the air, the Rockies in Alberta were spectacular.

Thoughts of the plane falling from the sky and crashing onto the rugged landscape below suddenly swamped my brain. I glanced at Wy. While he remained asleep and looked fine, I clearly wasn't. I started to pant.

"Are you ill, my dear?" The old lady, back from the restroom, stood beside me and patted my shoulder. "Shall I ask the stewardess to bring you some water?"

How embarrassing. I had never flipped out on a plane before. What was wrong with me?

"Thank you," I said. "I'm fine, just fine." The lie rose so easily to my lips.

"All right, dear. But do let me know if you need anything. I have some Dramamine in my purse. It might help and—"

"Thank you, no. I'll try to read now."

Get a grip, Austin. I willed myself to calm down and forced my breathing to slow. Breathing in, breathing out—oh so slowly—I pondered what the old lady's accent was. It was strange, one I could not place. Usually I was good at figuring out where a person had grown up. This was a first.

Beside me, Wyatt woke up.

As I fished in my bag for his baby bottle, the voice of the Canadian Pacific stewardess interrupted. "Fasten your seatbelts. Our pilot says there's more turbulence ahead."

What a drag. I suspected my good luck had ended. The easy part of our journey was past, and trouble lay ahead. Beside me, Wyatt kicked off his blanket and began to cry. I tried to quiet him, but his wails persisted. I felt my cheeks grow warm. We must not disturb the other passengers.

"Let me help, dear."

I felt a feathery touch on my shoulder. The elderly woman was standing in the aisle and looking down at me. Her eyes held mine—steadily, calmly. I tried to turn away but found my gaze locked onto hers.

A few moments passed. Who knows how many—mere seconds, five minutes? I had no idea. But then suddenly my shoulders relaxed. And Wyatt, miracle of miracles, stopped crying. A feeling of peace washed over me as my eyes stayed on the woman's. I couldn't even turn my head to look at my son. Somehow, I sensed he was all right.

"There now, there, there." Her voice was lush and melodious like the wind. I swear it had not sounded like that before. "You and your son Wyatt will be all right now."

How did she know my son's name? Had I told her earlier? Surely not.

The stewardess hustled down the aisle towards us, a determined look on her face. Her eyes narrowed and her mouth spread in a tight line. "Did you hear my announcement, madam? You must sit down in your seats with your belts fastened. Now, sit."

The stewardess took hold of the elderly woman's arm. There was a sharp crackle. I smelled something that reminded me of burned rubber. *Where did that come from?*

The eyes of the stewardess bulged. She stepped back, running her hand through her hair. Her bouffant style, no longer smooth, now looked more like a Mohawk, standing straight up on her head.

"Pardon me." The stewardess turned toward the old woman and bowed from the waist. "I had no idea who you were. May I get you something to drink, madam? Coffee, tea? No? Then some wine perhaps?" She backed up a few steps. I guessed she had lost interest in getting her passengers to prepare for a bumpy ride.

I tried to hide my amusement at the stewardess's changed demeanor and failed. No matter how firmly I pressed my lips together, a giggle escaped.

The elderly woman straightened up to her full height.

How strange. I could have sworn that earlier she appeared to be of diminutive stature. Now, only inches from me, she seemed to be positively Amazonian in height. I had to tilt my head back to see her face.

Her regal look was heightened by her voice, which sounded low and assured. "I want nothing. I have all I require, thank you. Now I shall sit with these young people, here." She gestured at the row in which Wyatt and I were sitting. "We shall not need your services again." She flapped a hand at the stewardess. "Now, be gone."

The stewardess mumbled something that sounded like an abject apology and backed up several rows. All the while, she kept her eyes focused on the old woman.

I obeyed also. Picking up Wyatt, I scooted over to the window seat and placed him in the middle one. "I presume you would prefer the aisle, yes?"

Her smile was gentle. "Thank you, Austin. How kind of you." She sank into the seat I had vacated.

She knew Wyatt's name. She knew my name, too. How was this possible? Had she read the flight manifest?

A shiver of nerves ran through me. What—or who—was I dealing with? "How do you know my name? And my son's?"

"You said them to the stewardess, dear," she said. "I confess, I listen to people nearby. A bit nosy, some have told me. Call me Promethea."

She searched through several pockets on her long jacket. Finally, she drew out a passport. Its cover had a strange seal on it, one I did not recognize.

"You are not from America or Canada then, I take it?" I tilted my head toward her passport.

She closed her eyes and fingered a necklace at her throat, then turned to me, her eyes open again. "No, my dear. Not originally. But indeed I have been here before—in fact many, many times." She flipped through her passport and returned it to her pocket.

Smoothing the lapels on her jacket, she swiveled to face me. "You have the look of a stranger in a strange land. Is something the matter?"

I'm not one to open up to strangers, especially one on a plane. But something compelled me. "I'm going to Vancouver to help out a... friend in trouble."

I blurted out something about the accusation of murder, and Larissa's innocence. I'm not even sure what exactly I said, and my stammer caused me to blush with embarrassment.

"I see. Please, do not worry about it. You worry too much. Worry is bad for your health."

I looked down at my ragged cuticles. I routinely tore them to shreds in fits of nerves when all my efforts to stay in the half-full position failed me. "That's true. But I don't know how to stop myself." I looked back up and met her eyes. They acted like a truth serum. "I make a joke of it. I like to say that worrying is my favorite hobby."

As she leaned across Wyatt and put her face closer to mine, she seemed about to impart a great truth to me. The plane's sudden drop in altitude stopped her, though.

And I must confess I let out a shriek.

Wyatt startled and uttered one short cry.

Promethea was ready. She laid two fingers of her left hand on his chest, and he ceased crying at once.

With raised eyebrows, I looked at her. "How are you able to do that?"

She shrugged. "Years and years of practice."

"So you have children of your own then?"

She turned her head away for a moment, then turned back and cast her forceful gaze on me once again. I stopped breathing and held her eyes, transfixed.

"No, no children of my very own, no. But I have helped many, many mothers with their infants. You might say I have, well—I must admit that I do have a gift."

How odd. Where and how had she acquired her expertise if she had no children of her own?

A feeling of peace flowed over me like a slow-moving river. All tension left my neck, my shoulders, right down to my toes. I no longer needed to fly in a plane. I felt as light as a canary's feather, able to waft through the air.

Beside me, Wy burbled and blew a tiny bubble. He smiled, then chortled. His tiny hand curled into a fist and reached out to touch Promethea's arm. Then he made a cooing noise.

I gasped. "Did you hear that? That was his first laugh, his very first."

A broad smile spread across her wrinkled face. "I am honored to witness this grand event. The advancement of a baby human is a wondrous thing to behold."

A baby human? What an odd way to talk about a baby. My baby.

I squirmed in my seat. "Yes, um, it's fun watching Wyatt grow and change. I just wish my husband had been able to hear his son's first laugh."

Promethea fingered her necklace again. I noticed it looked like a locket and wondered what it held inside. She said, "Many times I am amazed by watching the two sexes raise their offspring. The roles of the males and the females are so distinct. That amuses me. The patterns seem archaic, out of date, and no longer relevant." She reached across the aisle at her sleeping companion, tapped him on the arm. "Darling, can you fetch Betty?"

After a moment, he raised his head, stared at her, then stood up and stretched. He picked up a handbag, stepped into the aisle, and passed the bag to Promethea. They smiled at each other, and he returned to his seat. Promethea opened her purse, pulled out a book, and passed it to me.

I looked at the cover. *The Feminine Mystique* by Betty Friedan.

"Have you read this?" she asked.

I shook my head. "It's famous, but I've never read it."

"Well, you should. It offers a new perspective, one you may find helpful." She paused, cocking her head and eying my hands on her book. "You keep it. If you read it and digest its messages, you will find your undertaking easier to handle."

"What do you mean?"

"A great mystery awaits you in Vancouver. Your ability to solve it will be enhanced by Friedan's writings."

My curiosity was running rampant through my skull. I had to know more about this strange lady. "Are you a—well—something like an anthropologist? Is that what you do for a living?"

She glanced across the aisle at her male companion, who was sleeping again. To me, she said, "He's such a sweet young man. Yes, my traveling companion and I are something akin to anthropologists. We go around the continent and see what people are up to."

This information excited me. I also liked to watch human behavior. "Where are you from?"

"Oh, my dear, I'm not exactly sure myself. I'm something of an orphan."

"Well, let's try and figure it out. I am good at geography and—"

A violent shudder shook the plane. People cried out in fear. Automatically, I reached out to Wyatt, but Promethea had already picked him up and was holding him to her chest. He opened his large blue eyes and gazed up at her, blinking.

A male voice came over the loud speaker. "Ladies and gentlemen, do not be alarmed. Our instruments show that one of our engines has a problem. However, I assure you that everything is under control. Nothing is wrong with the other engine. Just relax and we will be at our destination soon."

Promethea uttered a small snort, totally unexpected from someone of her age and demeanor. She seemed to be assessing the situation, listening keenly. "The pilot is wrong, I believe. He should pay more attention to all of his gauges." She suddenly turned my way to peer out the window, then jerked her head, startled. "Austin," she said softly, "you must do up your seatbelt."

Fear squeezed my heart. Stunned to see my belt undone, I fumbled with the buckle and snapped it on. I reached out for my baby. "Let me hold him, please."

Even to my own ears, my tone sounded desperate. I doubted she understood a plane's mechanism, but her words had scared me nevertheless.

As soon as Promethea handed Wy to me, I embraced him.

"Promethea, what is—?"

"Please hush, dear. I must concentrate. This is important."

Now the captain's voice: "All passengers, please remain in your seats and fasten your seatbelts."

The plane shuddered again. People shrieked. I looked out the window. The mountaintops seemed to rise up to meet us. We were going down. We were going to crash.

The cabin was in turmoil. The stewardess tried to give instructions, but she was hardly audible over the cries of frightened passengers.

Beside me, Promethea undid her seatbelt, rose in a beautiful, fluid motion, and glided down the aisle toward the front of the plane. Wyatt raised his little hand towards her back, as if he were sorry to see her go.

My eyes strained to follow Promethea's progress and were able to watch the stewardess try to check her onward march to the front of the cabin. I witnessed the older woman turn her penetrating gaze on the younger one, who promptly bowed and let her pass. Even when I was no longer able to see Promethea, I was spellbound and watched intently to see what would happen next.

Time passed. I had no idea how much. Seconds? Minutes? Perhaps even hours?

The row of seats in front of me suddenly seemed to be higher.

Was our plane regaining altitude? I prayed that it was. I held Wyatt more tightly. Probably too tightly, but despite that, he did not make a sign of protest.

A high-pitched sound registered in my ears. I could not tell if the noise was coming from inside my head. Was it the plane's intercom that made that noise? Was it the plane itself? All I knew was that the sound engulfed me.

I must have fallen asleep. When I awoke, Promethea was back in her aisle seat in my row, calmly reading my copy of the *New York Times*. The plane was descending towards an airport visible in the distance beside a tranquil sea, and Wyatt still slept in my arms.

I rubbed my eyes with my right hand, the one not clutching Wyatt. "What happened?" I asked Promethea.

"I'm not sure," she said. "A while back, the pilot announced we had a bit of engine trouble, but everything appears to be fine now. He just notified us a few minutes ago that we would land shortly. The warning must have been what woke you up."

Why had she gone to the front of the plane? I had to know.

I leaned across the middle seat that separated us. "What happened when you—?"

She stretched out her hand to me. In it was the necklace that she had been wearing. "Here, I want you to have this. I have enjoyed talking to you so much. I learned so much too."

"What, what did I do, or say? We hardly talked." I stammered as I said this. I was rarely so incoherent.

"Oh, but you did just enough. And now I want you to have this as a memento of our meeting."

I let the necklace fall into my hand. "Well, if you are sure, then I thank you for this gift." I peered at it closely and admired the thick gold chain with a bauble hanging from it. "It looks like a really old locket. Is there anything inside?"

"Indeed I am sure you must have it, and yes, that locket is old," she said. "Open it. The contents should help you remember what I told you."

With fumbling fingers, I opened the locket, and when I saw what lay inside, I tried to hide my confusion. "I'm sorry. What does this lock of hair signify and how can it help me?"

"That hair once grew on the magnificent, wise head of Susan B. Anthony. I told you that patterns between men and women are now out of date. They need revision since they no longer make sense. If you will keep this in mind, it will serve you in good stead for the rest of your life. Most importantly, this idea will help you make sense of what you will find when you help your friend in Vancouver."

I tried to reply, but my mouth was incapable of moving. All I managed to do was nod.

Promethea seemed satisfied. She smiled. "Now I must return to my companion. We will land soon." She unstrapped her seatbelt and returned to her original place across the aisle.

I must have dozed off again. When I awoke, the plane held very few passengers. Promethea was no longer on board. I stood with Wyatt in my arms and looked down the aisle towards the front of the plane. Both strangers were gone.

I fingered the necklace Promethea had given me. This action drew Wyatt's attention to the golden object, and he grabbed it in his chubby little fist. I gently undid his hold and pushed his hand away.

I never saw her again. Somehow, I knew I would never forget her.

THE BLURRED MAN

I

The area was a complete disaster. Smoke billowed and smothered the air, casting a shadow across a sky that should have been glowing with morning light. Rubble lay everywhere, the ruins strewn across the landscape more like the remnants of some ancient civilization than a modernized milling facility.

Agent Dylan Plumm strode across the chaotic landscape, her oversized rubber boots sucking in the thick mud with every step. The boots were loaners from one of the many firefighters that swarmed the scene. Ambulances, police cars and other emergency vehicles were present as well, creating a pulsing lightshow that would have been visible for miles had it not been for the blanket of choking smoke.

The local force was a small, bewildered group obviously out of their comfort zone in a situation of such destructive magnitude. She imagined that the small town of Adamsville, Alabama didn't see anything remotely like the eruption that destroyed the flour mill. Small wonder they appeared so discomforted. The man in charge was Captain Forrester, who appeared a bit more experienced than the men that worked under him. Dylan studied him briefly, assessing his facial features, build, age, posture and mannerisms.

Ex-military, more than likely the US Army. Served well, but lacked ambition. Most likely topped out at lieutenant before retiring and entering law enforcement. Modest means, but proud of his accomplishments. Still married to first wife with multiple children and grandchildren. Alabama fan.

Agent Chen Lee debriefed the Captain, leaving Dylan free to survey the scene. While it would take days or weeks for the survey and investigation teams to come to a conclusion, her eyes saw past the damage. The quantum computer in her brain analyzed the pattern of debris, the totality of the damage, the affect on the surrounding area. She concluded that a powerful explosive was purposely triggered from the top of the building, causing enough damage to the core of the structure that it basically imploded on itself. The initial explosion triggered secondary ones on account of the compressed air, dust, and enclosed spaces, furthering an already catastrophic eruption.

"What do we got, Plumm?"

She brushed a stray strand of her pulled-back blond hair from her face as Agent Lee approached. Like Dylan, he was dressed in dark slacks and an FBI jacket over his rumpled dress shirt. He wore his customary deadpan expression, scrubbing his hand across his bristly, short-cropped hair.

She paused from recording the imagery with her tablet computer. "Massive explosion. The entire building is history. Don't see these very often anymore."

"Anyone got a theory on the cause?"

"Not yet. With dust and enclosed spaces there's always a risk of explosions in mills like this, though all the modern ones are constructed to reduce that chance as much as possible."

She slid some pages over on the tablet, looking at the data projections. "Still, something like an overheated bearing in an elevator leg might ignite the dust and cause an explosion. That could cause a chain reaction, but–"

"But that wouldn't bring down the entire building, would it?"

Dylan shook her head. She briefly considered offering her full analysis, but realized it wouldn't matter. Agent Lee didn't think much of working with women, and it showed in his attitude. In their short time working together he proved to be a chauvinistic dinosaur of an agent, cutting off her sentences, claiming credit for her finds and ignoring her every chance he could. He would pretend to listen, then dismiss everything she told him unless it agreed with his own assessment. In view of that, she gave him the response he expected.

"All estimates indicate negative on that. Best guess is that an explosive was detonated. No evidence to support that yet, but–"

Lee grunted. "Yeah, well it's a hell of a mess. How many dead?"

Dylan continued to scan the intel from the dossier on her tablet. She had no need, but reciting everything from memory only attracted unwanted attention. "Six unaccounted for. There's a crew trying to salvage any body parts for identification. Not going to be easy, with the exception of one."

"How's that?"

"You're going to have to see it."

He sighed and followed her. As they picked their way past debris and salvage teams, he slipped and just managed not to embarrass himself. "Dammit! Muddy as hell."

Dylan nodded. "The fire department had a time stopping the fire from spreading."

"What did they do, drop a few loads by helicopter? This place is saturated."

"I noticed. It's possible the explosion could have ruptured the main water line." She omitted that only a massive storm could have dropped so much water at once. It was too bizarre for Agent Lee to believe because all weather reports in the area claimed fair skies. She couldn't properly explain the phenomenon without more data, so she filed it in her mental database as a quandary to examine in full detail later.

She led Agent Lee to the far end of the collapsed mill where an emergency crew gathered around a corpse laid upon a gurney.

"One of the day shift supervisors identified him as Guy Mann, employee of six months."

Lee snorted. "Guy Mann? Guess that's better than John Doe. You guys have a cause of death?"

One of the medics looked up. "Flatline. That's all I can tell. No sign of stroke or heart failure. All organs seem to be intact. Almost as if his brain just... shut off."

Dylan surveyed the body. The man could have blended in anywhere without standing out. In fact, he was the most nondescript person she had ever come across. It actually took concentration to focus on his perfectly average features, as if his face was purposefully meant to be dismissed. His clothes were scorched and torn in a few places. He lay as though asleep; his lips slightly curved in a peaceful smile.

Lee scratched his head. "Ok, what's so strange about a dead guy?"

Dylan gave him a sideways glance. "Don't you find it strange that the body is almost completely unharmed? Only a few lacerations and bruises. There's hardly a scorch mark even though he was found in the middle of this wreckage."

Lee shrugged. "Stranger things have happened."

Another medic spoke up. "He was covered in some black substance when we found him. We thought he was severely burned. But it was some type of... covering. Appeared organic. It deteriorated as soon as we peeled it off of him. We just managed to get a few samples for the lab before the wind blew it all away."

"Some kind of fireproof shield, maybe," Lee said. "Maybe he was responsible for the explosion."

"It will be hard to prove that now," Dylan said. "What do you want to do?"

Lee gestured indifferently. "Process him. Maybe an autopsy will give us a few answers. Check if he had any psych records, mental illnesses. Known associates. Find out what kind of person he was."

He turned away as the medics zipped up the body bag. An emergency worker ran their direction, gesturing frantically. "Over here! We have someone!"

They saw a group of emergency workers supporting a tall blond man. He was smothered in soot and bruises. A bloody bandage covered one of his shoulders.

Agent Lee shared a smile with Dylan. "I'll be damned." The entire group scrambled toward the man, leaving the gurney unattended.

* * *

"So can you please explain how a dead body just… vanishes?"

Philip Dirk drummed his thick fingers on the weathered surface of his oak desk. Like the desk, the Field Director had seen better days. The years of running ops, public relation spins, and bureaucratic wrangling had paid off with interest in premature scowl lines, heavily bagged eyelids, and a graying hairline in the process of rapid retreat.

Dylan created the façade of nervousness by shifting uncomfortably in her chair. Most people approached a summons from the Director like an invitation to their own funeral, so she felt it only appropriate to feign the proper sense of anxiety. Not that it mattered. Having hacked the FBI system long ago, she had downloaded all of their personnel files into her mental data banks, including medical records. Instantaneous recall of Dirk's last physical exam revealed a near-certain likelihood for a major heart attack or stroke, whichever caught him first. His intake of medication for high blood pressure and related maladies didn't seem to buffer the onslaught of stress from upper management demands, budget slashes, personnel disasters, and a rather aggressive smoking habit.

"A dead body belonging to the only real suspect behind this explosion, by the way," he continued. "A dead body under the watch of the FBI, not to mention the local police force and emergency crews.

Yet somehow this 'Guy Mann' pulls a resurrection act and nobody notices? How is that possible, Agent Plumm?"

Dylan hesitated for a moment. "I thought Agent Lee was the lead on this case, sir. Shouldn't he be debriefing you?"

Dirk frowned and sat back in his chair. His eyes shifted away as the words reluctantly dragged out. "Agent Lee has been taken off the case."

"Taken off the case? Why?"

"Incompetence." Dirk's fingers tapped a staccato across his desk again. Itching for a cigarette, Dylan figured. The Director went through an average of a pack and a half a day. Unless it was a bad day, when he'd smoke until he ran out.

"Agent Lee can be called many things," she said. "Incompetent isn't one of them."

Dirk glared at her. "What do you want, the official report?" He picked up the tablet on his desk. "Says here that his 'mental state no longer warrants field work. Intensive psychiatric evaluation recommended.' You ask me what that means, I say incompetent. Now that we got that out the way, why don't we get back to the original topic: the dead body of a main suspect disappearing into thin air?"

"I have nothing to tell you that's not in my report, sir. We left the body for the forensics crew to handle. Standard procedure. Our main focus was on the lone survivor, Michael McDonald." Her memory core automatically pulled the dossier: The tall, blond man that they recovered at the scene was currently in an agency psychiatric ward in San Francisco, recovering from severe mental and emotional trauma.

Dirk's mouth twisted. "Another loony toon. Know what he spouts when he's not heavily medicated?"

"I've seen the videos, sir."

Dirk went on as if she hadn't spoken. "Keeps going on and on about faceless monsters. Giant spiders and rats. Doorways to another dimension. Your average horror movie feature. I swear, the shit these guys pull to get a crazy card. This case will never make it to court, mark my words. It'll just go on and on…"

Dylan nodded as thousands of possibilities for the conversation's outcome processed through her neural net. Less than a second later she chose the appropriate query to bring the discussion to an end. "What do you want me to do, sir?"

Dirk's attention refocused. "Bodies don't just disappear, Agent Plumm. My best guess is that Mr. Mann took some kind of sedative cocktail that put him in a temporary coma state. Once it wore off he slipped away with none the wiser. I'd say that makes him the main suspect in this bombing. You find him and bring him in."

"That might take some time, sir."

"It's your case now, Agent Plumm. It doesn't close until you get some results. The top brass are breathing down my neck on this one. Do what you have to do to get it done."

"Yes, sir."

"Oh, and one more thing." He flicked the tablet screen over to a file of case photos. "Try to keep your hands from shaking when you take pictures, Agent Plumm. Every shot of Guy Mann's face is blurred."

Dylan hesitated only for a moment before delivering the appropriate response. "Yes, sir. I'll try, sir."

* * *

Dylan reviewed the case photos carefully in the privacy of her apartment. It was just as Director Dirk stated, despite knowing every shot she took was strikingly focused. In fact, the only obscured part of any of the photos was Guy Mann's face. That meant only one thing: the Blurred Man was real.

Dylan knew the urban legend. Bits and pieces were readily available on the internet, touted by fly-by-night bloggers with less than credible sources. A CIA case file was reported to exist on the subject, but if so it was buried somewhere in the same vault with Area 57 data. But like Bigfoot and Elvis, the sightings never truly went away.

"Chip, pull up all relevant data on the Blurred Man."

Her palm-sized, synthetic assistant whirred from its position on her desk. "The Blurred Man. Chasing ghosts in the night, are we? Very well." The pyramid-shaped automaton emitted a holographic screen flooded with scrolling data from its apex. Dylan's sparsely furnished studio apartment flooded with light as statistics and pictures flickered, absorbed by her optic receptors and processed by her quantum core at inhuman speed. Seconds later she digested all that was available on both public and private online databases.

"Unfortunately, credible information is quite scarce," Chip said.

Dylan nodded. "Worldwide intelligence agencies only reluctantly acknowledge the existence of an individual or group of operatives possibly responsible for manipulating a number of catastrophic events."

Light pulsed across Chip's allowed surface. "The implications are frightening if true. Such events include the Trinity explosion and the WWII atomic bombing of Nagasaki–which many conspiracy theorists claimed was never supposed to be a target after Hiroshima. The 1980s Chernobyl meltdown disaster was also supposedly instigated by the Blurred Man, along with other less threatening but still disastrous events since that time."

Dylan interacted with the holographic screen, sliding over to a photo of a young black man sitting in front of a computer. "Strange that a conspiracy theorist blogger would be the person to connect the dots. What do we know about Nathan Ryder?"

Chip whirred. "He had been blogging for several years with only a small following before he turned his attention to government conspiracy. His early work details mostly his life growing up as a young black man with a stereotypical background of low income and poor schooling, separated from his peers because of his mental gifts.

Instead of feeling alienated, he embraced his solitude, excelling scholastically and earning a scholarship from Yale, where he distinguished himself in law, mathematics and psychology."

"How did he discover his information on the Blurred Man?"

"A combination of luck and obsessive behavior," Chip said. "He has a passion for photography, which led to a study of its history, particularly of catastrophic and wartime events. His detailed examination of thousands of photographs revealed a disturbing aberration: more than a few photographs displayed a man's image, always with his face obscured despite the clarity of the photo. At times more than one person's face was blurred, but it was never more than two at a time. Ryder stuck with the singular label of 'Blurred Man', a term that instantly caught on with the fringe elements of the blogging community."

Dylan motioned with her hands, enlarging a college newspaper article. "He published his work two years ago, insinuating the intelligence agencies covered over proof of the Blurred Man's existence. His findings created a firestorm of controversy as mainstream media leaped on the bandwagon."

"National attention came soon after." Chip's beam flickered, switching the holographic display over to a collage of news articles. "A six-figure book deal, speaking engagements, even movie and television offers."

"What's interesting is what didn't happen," Dylan said. "Ryder didn't take any of those lucrative propositions. He accepted an offer for a consulting position with Chimera Global instead."

"A global corporation with a number of umbrella operations including nuclear energy, international arms supply, military science, and mercenary employment." Chip switched the display to a screenshot of the imposing Chimera Global headquarters building. "Ironic since Ryder blogged many times about the danger of such operations."

"What are you up to, Mr. Ryder?" Dylan processed each data point almost instantaneously, her algorithms mapping and eliminating thousands of different scenarios. "Which branch of Chimera is he currently stationed at?"

"A military institution just outside of San Francisco," Chip said, switching the screenshot over to a satellite image of the area. "Currently funded and staffed by Chimera Global operatives. I'm accessing their records." Tiny dots of light winked across Chip's frame. "This is interesting." He exhibited the information on the holographic display.

"Michael McDonald is being held there," Dylan said. "The only survivor of the mill explosion where Guy Mann was last seen. It's all connected somehow. The fact that Chimera has sequestered this investigation only confirms it. That means I have two goals to accomplish: discover what Chimera wants with Michael, and find out what Nathan Ryder knows about the Blurred Man. Fortunately I know a way to accomplish both tasks at the same location."

Chip shut off the display and rose from the table, its tiny repulsors firing as it drifted over to land in the palm of Dylan's hand. "I believe that means that I have work to do."

Dylan glanced in the mirror and focused, accessing the portion of her mind that manipulated self-image. A tingling sensation was the only indicator of the slight alteration in her optical receptors to visualize herself with darker hair and eye color. Picking up a pair of thin-rimmed glasses off the table, she tried them on and studied her reflection. "That's right, Chip. I need an additional profession. One that can get me access to Michal McDonald. It will have to be able to withstand a thorough investigation and background check. I'll be using chestnut hair color and hazel contact lenses to give me a slightly different look, so make sure to include that in the ID photos."

"Not much of a challenge," Chip said. "Consider it done. May I suggest caution this time? Chimera is known for ruthless maneuvering to achieve their goals."

"That's why you won't be coming," Dylan said. "I need you to prepare another safe house. My calculations indicate a eighty-six percent chance of this expedition turning disastrous. Dylan Plumm may no longer be a valid alias afterward."

Chip buzzed in a distressed manner. "I'll purchase your airline tickets."

II

Dylan studied Nathan Ryder as he leaned back in his cushioned office chair. It didn't appear to be a relaxed gesture at all. He also avoided eye contact for the most part, glancing anywhere but her as they exchanged formalities. Merging his behavior with the personality exams Dylan had already downloaded allowed her to run an analysis in her mind.

The retreating posture is his unconscious indication that he feels uncomfortable in my presence. Combined with his irritated expression and terse manner of speech, it reveals his social handicap. Although gifted with brilliance in logical thinking, he is at odds with basic personal interaction. Schizoid personality disorder would best account for his behavior. His preference is isolation, being able to operate individually with little or any supervision. His office is his comfort zone, and I'm intruding simply by being here.

He was younger than he appeared in photos, in his mid-twenties with a slim physique and carefully crafted appearance. His suit was stylish without drawing attention to the fact, personally tailored to his build. His mustache and short-cropped hair were perfectly lined, indicating his penchant for orderliness. The quality was reflected in his polished office furniture and orderly arrangement of his desktop.

"You appear a bit out of place in a military institution, Mr. Ryder," she said. "But I suppose your interest here is more academic than gung ho."

"My interest here is none of your concern, Agent Plumm." Ryder didn't appear to care or even notice his discourtesy. "Let's cut to the chase and get to the point where you tell me why an FBI agent is suddenly interested in this facility."

Dylan crossed one stocking-clad leg over the other. Although her skirt wasn't short, the movement did allow the exposure of a generous amount of her lower leg. "Let's say that I have an interest in an individual that's being detained here."

Ryder shifted uneasily, his eyes flicking to the safe zone of the office wall. "We have a number of detainees here, Agent Plumm."

"True. But only one directly related to a case I'm assigned to. His name is Michael McDonald. The only survivor of a mill explosion. I'm quite sure you know of him."

"You want access to Michael McDonald? Impossible." He peered at her suspiciously from behind black-rimmed eyeglasses, his expression clearly indicating he wished she would just vanish into thin air. "Mr. McDonald is for all intents and purposes a prisoner of the state. He doesn't receive visitors and doesn't give interviews. I'm afraid that you'll have to present more than an FBI badge to be granted access, Agent Plumm."

She fixed him with her best dubious stare. "There are certain legal channels that appear to be trampled on by his imprisonment, Mr. Ryder. We both know that detainment by private sectors allows the government loopholes to deny prisoners their civil and lawful rights. This facility isn't administered or funded by any US agency. Chimera pays the bills here, leaving me to wonder what branch of the government, if any, has authorized Mr. McDonald's imprisonment."

Ryder's mouth curved in amusement. "That's something you'll have to take up with your branch of the government, Agent Plumm. I assure you that we have legal matters properly arranged to handle this special circumstance. If you wish to debate the matter, I suggest you bring a lawyer with you next time."

Dylan pulled up a file on her tablet and placed it in front of him. "As a point of interest I happen to be a lawyer, Mr. Ryder. Michael McDonald's, in fact."

She smiled at his stunned expression. "I can assure you that the legalities of my position are properly arranged. Now if you don't mind, I'd like to speak with my client."

* * *

Michael McDonald was tall and well built, his blond coif just unruly enough to be roguishly likeable, with eyes blue and clear as a bay in the Bahamas. He didn't look at all like a man who would kill his coworkers by way of massive explosion. He was what women called a stunner, though that meant little to Dylan. She had long ago accustomed herself to recognize what was considered attractive without being able to experience the thrill of the sensation in a personal manner. There was still some connection she was not able to make, some intangible spark that never ignited within her, despite the ages she had spent in the form of both genders.

She put those thoughts away, assessing her subject. He smiled when he spoke, shaking her hand gratefully when she introduced herself.

"Thank God," he said as he sat down. "I thought they'd never allow me to contact a lawyer. They're treating me like a terrorist, Ms. Plumm. I didn't do the… things that they're saying I did. I've answered all their questions, but they just keep telling me that I'm crazy." He locked gazes with her the entire time as though trying to channel his honesty through his eyes. "I'm not crazy, Ms. Plumm. I know what I saw that night and as unreal as it sounds, every word is true."

"I've read the transcripts, Mr. McDonald." She glanced down at her tablet. "You claimed the mill was enveloped by a massive rainstorm that prevented the employees from leaving, despite local weather reports indicating clear skies that evening. You then state that faceless, shape-shifting beings invaded and slaughtered everyone inside except you and a fellow employee with the implausible name of Guy Mann, who you claim planted an explosive as a failsafe to prevent an event called an 'Aberration' from engulfing our world."

"Well, it does sound a bit crazy when you say it like that. But you didn't see what I——" Michael narrowed his eyes. "Wait a minute. You were there. I remember you. Your hair was blond, but it was you. You and the other guy... Agent Lee." He leaned back and sighed heavily. "You're not really my lawyer, are you? You're just another damn suit who thinks I'm a terrorist."

"I was there, yes." Dylan allowed her eyes to widen and parted her lips slightly in order to convey empathy. "I saw the aftermath of the blast. I saw the remains of people that would never see their loved ones again. And I saw you, Michael. I saw you dazed and confused, with no idea what happened. Isn't it possible that you—"

"No, no, *no!*" Michael punctuated each word with a fist pound on the table. "Don't play mind games with me, lady. You weren't there when everything went to hell." His face distorted as though battling the memories. "You can't help me. No one can. No one will believe me." His shoulders sagged as he stared at the floor.

"Not even your friend? The one you claimed saved your life?"

"Guy?" Michael lifted his head. "You've... seen him?"

"That's proven impossible He disappeared from the crime scene right after we found you. We've found no records aside from his brief employment at the mill. No digital footprint, no public history. It's almost as if he never existed. Anything that you can tell me about him would do a great deal toward finding out where he might possibly be."

"I can't help you, Ms. Plumm." Michael slouched in his chair, his expression downcast. "I can't even help myself. I'm stuck in this joint being deprived of my rights and all you can do is interrogate me about a man that the shrinks claim I made up in my head."

"You're being told Guy is a fabrication?"

"That's right." Michael leaned forward, his voice dropping to a near-whisper. His eyes glistened; the tears quivered in expectation of their release. "They want me to believe that I bombed the mill. That everything I saw was just my own mind shielding me from the truth. That I'm a crazy man that murdered my coworkers, and Guy never existed."

* * *

Dylan heard footsteps behind her. Ryder caught up with her in the hallway, matching her stride as she made her way to the exit. "You didn't want to help Mr. McDonald at all," he said, thrusting an accusing finger her direction. "You wanted info on the Blurred Man."

She glanced at him. "You believe that Guy Mann is the person in those photos you published on your blog?"

"I think he is one of their agents," Ryder said. "This is an organization, not an individual. If it was simply one or two people then they would have to have very long lives in order to have appeared at so many historical disasters. My data has found instances of their existence since the invention of the camera. There's no telling how long they've operated before they were actually caught on film."

He nodded to the guard at the exit, who opened the doors to the parking deck. Dylan expected Ryder to remain behind, but he followed her out.

She smiled. "I'm afraid I can't afford to abduct Chimera's prize paranormal consultant."

Ryder glanced behind him. "A gentleman walks a lady to her car. I'm a stickler for decorum."

"I wouldn't have thought of you as a romantic, Mr. Ryder."

He shrugged. "Nobody's perfect."

As they approached her SUV, his voice lowered. "I don't know what you're looking for, or who you really are. An FBI analysis expert and a top-rated lawyer? I ran a check on you, Agent Plumm. Your file says you were a child prodigy, but it still takes time to accomplish everything you've done."

Dylan smiled. "I'm flattered by the interest. Let's just say that time is a luxury for me, Mr. Ryder. Unlike most people, I have all the time I need to accomplish whatever it is I need to do."

He opened her door for her, his voice still carefully low-pitched. "We seem to be looking for the same thing, Ms. Plumm. Just going about it different ways. Piece of advice: be very careful. You don't know how dangerous these people are."

"The Blurred Man organization?"

"No." His hand flicked forward, expelling an SD card that landed neatly in her cup holder. "I'm talking about Chimera. Take care, Ms. Plumm." He closed the door. Dylan watched from the rearview mirror as he turned and strode back to the compound entrance without a backward glance.

* * *

It took only seconds for Dylan to discover that Ryder was right. Chimera had remotely installed spyware on her tablet. Dylan didn't know if it was a standard tactic or if she was targeted specifically, but either way it enforced the corporation's ruthless reputation. She tapped her ruby-studded earring, automatically enabling a call from the hidden Bluetooth to her new safe house.

"Chip, I need a clean sweep of my tablet."

"Infiltrated already? Not even dinner first?"

She ignored Chip's banter while it remotely downloaded the appropriate spyware eliminator. Afterward, she installed the SD card. Among the data files was a video clip labeled *Play Now*. She clicked on it. Nathan Ryder's image popped up on the vehicle's digital heads-up display as Dylan cruised into the busy San Francisco streets.

"If you're seeing this, I must be close," Ryder's recorded image said. He appeared far less guarded in the video, his face displaying genuine anxiety. His expression was haggard, as though suffering from a lack of sleep.

"I also must be in grave danger," he continued. "Since I might not make it out of Chimera alive, this is the compilation of what I've discovered so far."

His message listed a number of illegal activities Chimera Global was involved in, such as illegal arms trafficking and mercenary aid to nations in dispute with the US. On the political front Ryder provided hacked emails that revealed Chimera's tampering of US congressional and presidential elections that included threats, blackmail and murder. The corporation also bankrolled votes on both sides of the political floor in order to press legislature that benefitted the company's interests. Pushing their agenda abroad, they armed militants and revolutionists in the Middle East and Africa, bolstering their financial gain in the process of manipulating chaos.

"But make no mistake: empowering itself monetarily is only the secondary agenda of Chimera," Ryder said. "They possess ambitions that go far beyond fiscal domination. Their outright confiscation of Michael McDonald from under the FBI's very nose is proof of both their reach and their future plans. Hiring me as a consultant was no mistake either. Although ostracized by the blogging community as just another fringe conspiracy theorist, I was one of the few compiling real data on the event that Michael referred to as the 'Aberration.' My data indicated a powerful energy surge of extraordinary magnitude that didn't register on normal instruments, therefore going unnoticed by investigative agencies. If what Michael has stated is true, this energy not only has tremendous destructive potential, it can also open a threshold to another dimension."

"I hate to interrupt," Chip's voice buzzed in her ear. "But I've been tracking you via a friendly satellite tag. Have you noticed you've been followed since you left the Chimera compound?"

"Of course." Dylan paused the recording and glanced in the rearview mirror. A black BMW followed exactly two cars behind, tailing her every lane change, yet staying behind a safe distance. The windows were fully tinted, allowing no glimpse of who or how many were inside.

"Hopefully nothing to be concerned about," she said. "This will be an easy day if all I have to do is lose a tail." She resumed the recording.

"This power is what Chimera Global is after," Ryder's message continued. "The dark energy registering from the Aberration has endless potential for uses both benevolent and malevolent, untapped possibilities ripe for experimentation and exploitation. Chimera is willing to overlook the other side of the equation: the likelihood of a dimensional break, where the energies of two separate worlds collide. This is where the Blurred Man factors in. I believe he is a guardian from that neighboring dimension, a gatekeeper to prevent the catastrophic event of a dimensional break into our world. He cannot appear in photographs because he is not of this world."

Ryder's face drew closer to the camera. His expression was agonized; the desperation clearly audible in the tone of his voice. "I know this sounds bizarre, but all the data I've compiled supports my theory. The Blurred Man not of our world, an alien surely as if arrived from another planet. Yet he may well be all that stands between us and imminent destruction. Chimera has neither the willingness nor perhaps even the ability to see beyond their greed as they strive to harness what may destroy us." He hesitated, taking a wary glance around. "I'm out of time. If you have this transmission, you may be the only one aware of what is happening. You may be the only one who can stop this. I've compiled as much information as I could on this memory card. Use it to stop Chimera if you can. If not... we may all be doomed."

The video ended. Dylan kept an eye on the car tailing her as she considered Ryder's discovery and warning.

"That was... ominous," Chip said in her ear.

"It's nearly unbelievable," Dylan said. "If Ryder's warning is true, the entire world is in jeopardy. And the idea of an intruding dimension..." Her voice trailed off at the concept. The notion was staggering, containing so many variables that even her computer-guided mind had difficulty mapping out the nearly endless range of possibilities.

"Interdimensional beings and multiverses have been purely theoretical by human research up until now," Chip said. "Yet even in theory the effects of dimensions interacting are nearly always catastrophic. Warped reality, collisions of natural forces–the possibilities are endless for cataclysmic aftereffects. That's if Mr. Ryder isn't as insane as Michael McDonald reportedly is, of course."

"I doubt either of them are mentally deficient." Dylan flicked a few of the files from the tablet to the heads-up display. "The data that Ryder compiled appears surprisingly sound. The energy surges that he discovered was picked up on sensors constructed by paranormal fanatics to detect ghostly disturbances. It makes sense that their ghosts were really intrusions from a neighboring dimension."

Chip's humming buzzed in her ear. "I'm backing up your files here at the safe house. The rest of the card contains data compilations and hacked files on an island lab constructed by Chimera Global somewhere in the Bermuda Triangle. Supposedly it's one of the few locations on earth where a dimensional break can be artificially created."

"Chip, do you know what this means?"

"That the end of this world might arrive a bit prematurely?"

"No, I'm talking about all of this. Everything." Dylan hesitated, surprised by the increased rate of her heartbeat. "Ryder's discovery is earth-shattering. Everyone on the planet will be affected by it. An otherworldly encounter with Earth was always a possibility in view of my existence, but a threat from interdimensional means is something that can possibly affect both my mission and my very presence here. I've experienced several bizarre encounters in the time I've been on this planet, but evidence that any of them originated from beyond this world has been–"

"Dylan?" Chip's voice crackled with alarm. "Look out for the–"

Dylan's brief distraction cost her. An armored Humvee swerved in from her blind zone, slamming into her SUV with the force of a runaway freight train.

Safety glass shattered into glittering cubed shards, floating across the confined space. Dylan increased her reaction rate, body going limp to absorb the impact. The entire right side of the vehicle crumpled with an agonizing metallic groan; airbags simultaneously deployed like exploding popcorn kernels. The safety belt dug into her flesh as her body swung to the left, her head struck the driver's side window, shattering the glass from the force of impact. The world turned upside down, over and over as her SUV flipped until it skidded to a halt somewhere near the edge of the median after leaving a trail of wreckage in its wake. Blaring horns and screeching tires were the only sounds as other vehicles reacted to the crash. The scent of heated rubber and scorched metal smothered the air.

Dylan hung upside down, held in place by her seat belt. Her body throbbed, pulsing with the agony of her damaging wounds. Her left leg did not respond, her ribs were fire, and every breath took extra effort. *Punctured lung, broken ribs, fractured left fibia* was the initial analysis, minus the less-threatening bruises and lacerations. She felt the surge of adrenaline as platelets multiplied at an accelerated rate to speed the healing process, allowing her body to immediately begin repairing the damage.

"Chip?" Her voice was barely audible against the ringing in her ears. The coppery tang of blood laced her injured tongue, creating another check on her list of agonizing sensations. There was no response from Chip. Judging by the crash, both her Bluetooth and the vehicle's smartphone receiver sustained too much damage for a valid connection.

The pain was too distracting. Her quantum core responded to her mental command, identifying the sensory receptors sensitive to pain and dulling them to the point of near-nonexistence. The throbbing sensation faded quickly, allowing her to better focus on her predicament. She stretched, pulling a short knife from the sheath strapped to her leg. Slashing through the seat belt, she fell on her back, neck bent awkwardly. Her hands began a blind search for the metal box that had been lying in the passenger seat.

Voices became audible as the ringing in her ears lessened. The shattered windshield registered kaleidoscopic images of movement. She was barely able to identify urban camouflage pants and military boots running toward her ruined vehicle.

A squad leader's authoritative baritone barked out orders. "Make sure she's finished, then check the vehicle for personal effects. Double time it so we can blow this soup sandwich."

The movement drew closer. Dylan's hand found the field kit, snatching it from under the crushed passenger seat. Inside were her firearm and a few other necessities. Her free hand snatched out the frag grenade. Pulling the pin, she flung it directly at the approaching unit. Their alarmed shouts were punctuated by frantic feet running the opposite direction before the inevitable explosion. Not bothering to assess the damage, Dylan snatched the H&K VP9 handgun out of the kit and crawled out of the driver side window, dragging her ruined leg.

Opposing lane traffic had gridlocked the intersection of Market and Octavia as onlookers stopped to stare at the chaos, the mid-day traffic at full swing before everything went to hell. Dylan ducked as she limped across the opposite lane, heedless to the shouts of passersby offering help or asking questions. They became insubstantial blurs as she gauged her surroundings, mentally calculating the quickest route to escape her pursuers.

A young man in an Oakland Raiders cap stared at her, mouth open. "Lady, you look like shit! You wanna–" His sentence was cut off by a bullet shredding his neck area. Blood spattered his face as he toppled with a shocked expression.

Dylan turned in the direction of the shot, spotting the sniper lying on the roof of the Humvee. She dropped to the pavement before his next shot shattered the car window behind her. People screamed and tires squealed as cars careened into one another in their haste to escape the firefight. Bullets whined overhead as her assailants unloaded, shredding the car Dylan used for cover. It rocked from the impact of the shots, showering her with shattered glass.

The brief respite gave her the time to calculate her response and reassess her damage. Her re-inflated lung made breathing easier, and her ribs felt less quivery as well. The leg fracture was mending, but the progress was hampered by her movement. She switched her focus on her counterattack.

Another mental command allowed her to manipulate the nerve impulses that translated sound to the circuits in her brain. Background noise filtered out, allowing her to clearly focus on the retorts of gunfire. Mapping out the trajectory of the shots based on the sounds allowed her to predict the position of the shooters. Her retaliation projections were accurate to ninety-eight percent, making it relatively easy to roll, rise, and get a shot on the sniper before he could react. His body jerked as her shot shattered his rifle scope and exited out the back of his skull.

Dylan had already turned, firing twice in a continuous motion. Two more soldiers toppled before their comrades could react. She dropped, staying low as the remaining two assailants responded with panicky response fire. She accelerated despite her injury, the burst of adrenaline propelling her faster than their reaction rate as she dove behind a large Mercedes SUV.

"Who the hell is this bitch?" one of the soldiers shouted. His neck snapped back as Dylan's next shot took him out. His body went limp, lost to sight as a stream of running bodies blocked her view.

The last soldier ducked behind a bullet-riddled car. His voice nearly broke as he screamed into his radio. "Repeat: my unit is down, the mission is fubar, and where the hell is my backup?"

The chaos spread to the surrounding city blocks as people fled their gridlocked vehicles for the safety of nearby buildings. Wailing sirens announced the presence of emergency vehicles approaching the scene. Dylan stayed low, blending in with the fleeing crowds. The woman beside her shrieked hysterically, eyes wide with panic. Dylan seized her by the arm, using the woman's broad body to conceal herself from view.

The black BMW that had tailed her earlier screeched to a halt, ejecting four near-identical dark-suited men wearing sunglasses and toting submachine guns. Their heads swiveled as they surveyed the scene. One of them gestured, and they broke into teams of two. Shoving people aside, they swept through the crowd.

Dylan released her unwitting partner as they passed an alley between buildings. Limping forward, she advanced as quickly as possible. Her leg had nearly knit itself back together, but the tendons were still tender. She estimated she had a seventy-two percent chance of making it to the end of the alley and before her pursuers could make it through the throngs of fleeing people.

"There she is!"

Her percentages were off. The new squad was better than the previous one. She turned, kneeling in the same motion to throw off their initial shots. She would be able to at least take the first team down, but not without sustaining major damage. The second would surely overcome her. It was too bad. She had rather enjoyed being Dylan Plumm.

A loud horn blared from behind her. She rolled to the side as a black van barreled down the alley at full speed, tinted windows reflecting the shocked faces of the men it rumbled toward. Dylan flattened herself against the alley wall as the van whipped past. It met a hail of bullets before striking the armed duo head-on with a sound like raw meat slung against asphalt. More bullets whined as someone inside the van exchanged fire with the second team. Men grunted and cried out as they died.

Dylan steadied her hand and aimed at the rear doors of the van as they opened. A black-clad man emerged, critically studying the steaming, bullet-perforated vehicle. He turned, revealing his face. He was the most nondescript person she had ever come across. Just like the last time she saw him.

"No need for the gun," Guy Mann said. "I'm not here to harm you. But I do think we need to leave quickly. Both of us will want to avoid unnecessary questions. I understand that you've been looking for me. The irony is I've been looking for you as well. For a very long time."

III

The smell of redwood giants lingered, perfuming the afternoon air. Dylan sat at a bench in the midst of their majesty, just another insignificant speck loitering in their imposing shadows. The ramshackle cottage behind her was deep in the forest, far enough from the city to make civilization irrelevant. She saw no technology other than solar receptors, placing the abode completely off the grid. She wondered who, if anyone knew of its existence. It had taken a drive in a stolen car, a ride on ATVs, and then a three-day hike just to get to the place.

The Blurred Man served ginger green tea in china mugs that were almost certainly thousands of years old. He sat on the opposite side of the weathered bench, his form seemingly morphing with the shadows until it was hard to determine if he was physically there. Steam from the tea obscured his face when he lifted the mug for a sip.

"You heal remarkably well," he said.

Dylan did not respond, recognizing the ages-old casual approach to prod her into talking about herself. She gazed at the forest behind him. For some reason the ancient trees were full of ravens, in far greater numbers than she had ever seen before. They peppered the branches high as she could see, silently peering down as though waiting to pronounce judgment. Of what, Dylan could not fathom. The fall of man, perhaps.

Guy carefully set his mug down. "Your partner, Agent Lee. I expect his mental health will continue to deteriorate. An unfortunate side effect of exposure to an Aberration. Everyone within a five-mile radius will be affected to one extreme or another, from terrible dreams to full-blown insanity. Fortunately these side effects are not contagious. Not that you're in any danger from any of that, of course. Being... who you are."

Dylan toyed with the handle of her mug. "And who am I?"

"You're not human," Guy said. "Your body might be made of similar DNA, your appearance might be spot on, but you do not originate from this planet. You've been here a long time. How long I don't know, but almost certainly longer than I have. I don't believe that you are from another dimension. And if so, I don't believe that you're a threat to humanity."

"How can you be so sure?"

"Because if you were, I would have surely been ordered to kill you by now." He took another sip, expressionless. Dylan realized that like her, time was not a hindrance to Guy. He would wait patiently for her response, whether it took seconds or months.

"Why the last name Mann?" she asked. "At first I thought you had a sly sense of humor, but you don't seem to be the type."

"Antenor was the one with the sense of humor," Guy said. "He was my handler, the one who created the many aliases I've used over the years."

"And where is he now?"

"Dead." The word hung in the air, the echo almost audible from a thousand raven minds.

"You say that you're from another dimension." She sipped her tea. It was quite good, sweetened with honey she was sure was from the neighboring forest. "That agrees with the information I've gathered."

"That you gathered? Or that Nathan Ryder gathered?" Guy smiled at her expression. "I try to keep track of all of my potential allies, Ms. Plumm. Or did you truly believe that Mr. Ryder simply stumbled on information about the Blurred Man on his own?"

Dylan hesitated at the revelation. "Regardless, it explains why you can't be captured on film. There's something lost in the translation of capturing a being from another dimension." She studied him over the rim of her tea mug. "Your task is grueling. The exhaustion has taken its toll on you. You have lost your sense of humanity, alienated and alone to the point that emotion is a foreign concept to you. Human lives become mere numbers, statistics that you tally up as either acceptable losses or not."

He seemed to smile. "That last part. Were you talking about me… or were you talking about yourself?"

She didn't respond. Her analytics of the outcome of the conversation surprised her with their inconclusiveness. The algorithms were off the charts, unable to decisively chart what Guy's intentions were. It was as if his motives were as blurred as the photographs of his face.

He leaned back and inhaled deeply. "Ah, do you smell that air? So... clean. And this forest: a marvel beyond description. You can take a million photographs, paint a billion pictures, and it would never be enough. They would never convey the awe and humility of actually being here. It's amazing to think despite the population overload on this planet, there are still so many places where most humans simply avoid. So many places one can live an entire lifetime with little or no interaction, should they so desire."

"Is that what you desire?" she asked.

"More than anything." His nondescript face was clearly visible when he leaned forward, yet somehow still hard to focus on. "You might have the luxury of living through the ages, but things play out differently for me. I don't live through time, I basically flow across it. I am taken from one potential catastrophe to the next, never having time to recover or find a moment's peace. I exist for a singular purpose, and it is not to smell the roses."

"I don't understand." Dylan set her empty mug down. "How are you able to travel across time? What type of place is this dimension that you come from?"

His expression darkened. "A ruined one. And as far as how I do it…" He glanced above. "I go wherever the ravens take me."

She looked up. "The ravens?" The birds met her gaze, intelligence sparkling from their inky eyes as they perched like obsidian statues, their feathers gleaming in the patches of sunlight that streamed through the canopy of branches.

Guy smiled. "It's hard to explain. More tea?"

The forest darkened as the sun lowered into its depths. The wind swayed raven-laden branches, stirring the aroma of ancient bark and evergreen needles. Steam wafted from the freshly-poured tea. Guy closed his eyes, rocking slightly as if concentrating on absorbing it all.

"Have you ever planted a tree, Ms. Plumm?"

Dylan slowly nodded. "Yes."

"Tell me about it." He was a shadow among shadows, eyes gleaming as he stared more intently than the ravens.

"I planted a giant sequoia once." Memories emerged from her data banks, as palpable as the moments when they happened. "From seed to sapling to fully grown tree, I kept watch. I checked in, studied its growth as the years passed and I went through several manifestations. I watched as it towered toward the sky, forming an ecosystem of its own that supported a diverse amount of insect and animal species. I came back time after time, until a millennium passed. The entire world changed, but the tree was still there, a king among kings, pressing on to eternity."

"And then one day you returned to find the tree gone," Guy said.

Dylan nodded.

"They cut it down, didn't they?"

Dylan looked into the distance as the memory resurfaced. "They cut down the entire forest," she said softly.

Guy shook his head. "Such a simple statement. Yet somehow it epitomizes the very spirit of humanity. The exact same sentiment dominated my world. The same destructive greed reduced our world to ash and darkness."

She looked at him. "You don't like them, do you?"

His face was expressionless. "No."

"Then why do you do it? Why protect them?"

He raised the mug to his lips. "Because I'm exceedingly good at following orders."

"That's all? That's your answer?"

He exhaled softly. "We can't all be kings, Ms. Plumm. As you know very well, some of us must be foot soldiers. There is more to it, of course. A distinctively valid reason for my role in this travesty. I'm afraid I'm not willing to reveal everything about myself." A small smile touched his lips. "Unless you're willing to do the same."

Dylan did not immediately respond. She analyzed the entire conversation, compiled data and predicted various outcomes. "You want me to help you," she said.

A raven cawed loudly. Its call was answered by its brethren, thousands of raucous cries exploded from the birds and echoed through the darkened forest. The noise went on, as though the ravens were trying to make up for their earlier silence.

Guy raised a finger toward the branches. "*They* want you to help me."

"Do what?"

"Save their world." Guy steepled his fingers. "You've personally experienced how Chimera operates. They have an agenda, one they value so highly that they're willing to unleash mercenary units in broad daylight on the city streets in order to protect their interests. They are so fixated on capturing this source of energy that they are blind to the associated dangers. Opening a doorway to my dimension will unleash forces so destructive it's beyond imagining. When that happens, the forest gets cut down again, Ms. Plumm. This time you get to do something about it."

She shook her head. "You're talking about completely altering the face of this world. That goes far beyond the parameters of my mission. That's not what I'm here to do."

The ravens cawed as though mocking her. Guy smiled knowingly. "You can't spend millennia among a people without forming some sort of attachment, Ms. Plumm. You brought up emotion earlier. The mere fact that you would mention it indicates that at some level you understand it. You've... developed it. Absorbed it into your system despite any notions of detachment. That tree you planted. It meant something to you. All the memories you've absorbed: they mean something to you. This world means something to you."

"I have my orders," she said. "I have a role to play. Like you said, we can't all be kings."

"You have your orders," he said. "You keep watch. I understand that. You keep watch, you transmit, you experience. You keep watch." He smiled. "And sometimes you act."

Dylan shook her head. "I don't know what you're talking about."

"Oh, but you do. You've intervened before. Like in London, near the turn of the twentieth century. 1888, to be exact. Does that ring any bells?"

Dylan remained silent.

"It should. It was a year to be remembered, and it has been to this day. It's not every year that someone as infamous as Jack the Ripper is born, is it?"

He flicked a coin on the table. It spun for a long time. Dylan recognized the alternating faces of the 1888 sovereign coin: Queen Victoria on one side, and on the other a depiction of St. George and the Dragon.

Guy spoke softly. "You were 'observing' from the role of a prostitute named Sally, if I'm not mistaken. That put you close to the plight of the victims. Did your time in that role make you empathetic to those used and battered women, Ms. Plumm? Did you grow to care for them? Or were they mere numbers, statistics that you tallied up as either acceptable losses or not?"

Dylan studied him. "*You* were the Ripper. You murdered those women, didn't you?"

The sun went missing. The resulting darkness transformed the forest into something raw and ethereal. The brush crackled from nocturnal footpads. Somewhere in the distance a wolf howled. The ravens cackled as though appreciating the sound.

"Murder?" Guy's silhouetted figure tilted its head slightly. "You know as well as I what those women had become."

Dylan exhaled into the chilly air. "Monsters. They turned into some sort of twisted creatures."

"Others," Guy said. "As we refer to them. In a rather ingenious scheme, one of the Others infiltrated the barrier. It sought to spread its corruptive influence though sexual interaction. Prostitutes were an obvious choice. They were widely abundant and could have quickly and easily spread the infection across the city. The good people of London would have experienced grotesque transformations in no time. Widespread panic would have occurred, and the entire city would have been overrun by the monstrosities."

"But you stopped the possibility of infection by killing the hosts."

He shrugged. "What was I to do? You know what I was up against. I may have killed the infected, but it was you who removed their organs, wasn't it?"

Blood slicked her arms as she removed the steaming kidney from Catherine Eddowe's freshly slain body and placed it in a glass container for later examination. She paid no heed to the grisly stab wounds or the rank, clotted stench of death. She had to work quickly. It was only a matter of time before the body was discovered...

Dylan shifted uncomfortably. "I wanted to know. I suspected there was more to the killings, but needed additional information. My intricate knowledge of human physiology gave me an advantage the investigators of that time did not possess. The autopsies I performed revealed a new and frightfully aggressive virus had infected those women."

"Then you butchered your own work to make it seem like the mindless mutilation of a depraved killer. Rather gruesome, that."

"They were already dead," Dylan said. "You know that because you killed them."

Guy made a circular gesture. "And so it goes. But you did more than that, Ms. Plumm, didn't you?"

Dylan remained silent.

"I left the last one for you," he continued. "I'd ascertained that someone else was investigating the killings. Someone smarter than the police. It wasn't hard to find out who you were. I was watching you, even as you searched for me. I wanted to see what you would do. I left enough clues for you to figure out who the last infected girl was." He paused "You know who I'm talking about."

"Mary Jane Kelly," she whispered.

He nodded. "After Annie Chapman I realized I was chasing the symptoms. I needed to find the source, the creature responsible for the infection. I was so caught up that I nearly missed Elizabeth Stride and Catherine Eddowes. Had to take both of them down in one night. You know that because you did Ms. Eddowe's quick autopsy, removing her kidney and uterus for inspection. But you didn't get a chance to investigate Ms. Stride's corpse, did you?"

"I didn't have time," Dylan said. The women's dead, ghastly faces resurfaced from her memory banks. "I didn't realize two women were killed that night."

"That left only Mary Jane Kelly." The darkness had swallowed Guy's face completely, leaving it a shadowy blur. "Lovely girl, wasn't she?"

Dylan recalled Mary Jane's beguiling smile, the perfect ginger shade of her long wavy hair, her green eyes that sparkled with when the light struck them. In Dylan's form of Sally the prostitute, she had shared street corners with Mary Jane, split meager meals of oily stew, consoled the tears of her sometimes companion after she had been abused by another brutal customer. "Yes, she was."

"Until you saw. You witnessed what the virus did to her."

What had been Mary Jane Kelly whirled around, lank twisted locks of oily black hair flailed across its face, if a face it could still be called. It was more a misshapen lump of raw sentient meat, its mouth

a phlegm-coated cavity lined with jagged tusks. The thing shrieked as
it lunged with claw-tipped, elongated fingers...

"Yes." The memory was still jarring. The complete distortion of
face and limbs was impossible for any virus. "It was... inhuman.
Something not of this earth at all. There was no logical explanation,
nothing my compilation of data could have anticipated or even
rationalize. I could only react."

"And you reacted by killing her. It was the only rational thing to
do. The only option that would prevent a widespread infection. You
didn't just watch, Ms. Plumm. You didn't simply observe and report.
You knew what needed to be done and you did it. And I simply can't
believe that moment was the one and only time you acted outside of
your parameters."

Dylan remained silent.

"And after the monster reverted back to human form after dying,
you spent much more time with the autopsy. You needed to prove that
what happened had some rational explanation. But there were no
logical answers. What you witnessed could not be explained. You had
to mutilate your work and leave it to the legend of Jack the Ripper."

"But you caught the original host of the virus," Dylan said. "You
put an end to it."

He nodded. "Your intervention pulled the Other out of the
shadows. You see, it was watching you too. It and I had been playing
cat and mouse the entire time, but I could never precisely nail down its
location. I caught sight of it trailing you after the Mary Jane killing.
After that, it was only a matter of takedown. Of course by then the
Ripper persona had been created by newspapers trying to drive their
sales. Copycat murderers sprang up and dissipated. But the main thing
is that London was spared an infection that would have wiped it off
the map and very possibly spread to other cities. And you had a hand
in that, Ms. Plumm."

"That was... a mistake," she said. "There are repercussions to
consider."

Light bloomed from inside the cottage as the power from the solar generator cranked on. Shadows were shoved backward, yet the Blurred Man remained nearly indiscernible. The ravens that had overrun the trees had vanished completely, gone without a rustle of a feather to mark their passing.

"Inaction is the only mistake, Ms. Plumm," Guy said. "You unwittingly helped me then because you knew it was the right thing to do. All I'm asking now is that you consider the current situation. It's not a single tree that's in jeopardy here, Ms. Plumm. The entire forest is at risk."

"You've had help in the past. From your own kind, I've seen the photos. More than one blurred face."

"True." Guy raised an eyebrow. "But it's hard to remain alive in this type of work, I'm afraid. The mortality rate is quite high, and unfortunately not everyone was as resilient as I have been."

He placed a cell phone and a flash drive on the table next to the antique coin. "You don't have to do anything you don't want to, Ms. Plumm. I'm aware of that. But realize this: what I'm facing now is much worse than that silly London situation. What Chimera proposes to do will open a Threshold and allow the Others complete access to this world. You have the option of doing nothing, that's your right. Just as it's your right to casually observe the end of this world." He gazed intently at her. "Perhaps that is what you desire. Perhaps like me, you're just waiting for your assignment to finally end."

Dylan looked at the objects. "What are these for?"

"On the drive is information about the energy signatures Chimera has been chasing. Far more detailed than what they already have. You start leaking that and they will be sure to come to you. You'll be able to infiltrate their organization and work your way into their secure circle. You can do the most damage from there, should you so choose."

"Where will you be?"

Guy stood up and stretched. Although he was of average height and weight, his body was lined with lean muscle, as though fashioned by a bodybuilder's dream. "I'll have infiltrated another way. Chimera leans heavily on mercenary teams to do their dirty work. My experience will allow me to work my way into their ranks. By the time they ready their expedition, I'll be on the team."

Dylan let the phone and flash drive remain on the table. "I can't promise you anything. You know that, don't you?"

"I understand." Guy turned and strode toward the woods. "You have to compile data. Analyze all possible outcomes. Check with your superiors, perhaps. Take your time, Ms. Plumm. You may stay here as long as you wish. No one will bother you."

"You're leaving already?"

Guy's disembodied voice drifted from the shadows. "It's like I told you. My work is never finished. Farewell, Ms. Plumm."

The woods exploded with the harsh cries of a thousand raven tongues. The myriad sound of fluttering wings swept through the forest like a rushing wind. The forest grew hushed after the sounds faded, leaving Dylan alone with her conflicting thoughts.

* * *

Three months later

Dylan Plumm was for all intents and purposes a dead woman. Another star on an agency wall, another unsolved mystery to drive her former superiors mad. A new woman emerged from the gestation pod in the new safe house. She was shorter than Dylan, her body more sinuously curved than the slender FBI agent. Her wavy hair was the perfect shade of ginger; her green eyes sparkled when the light struck them.

Yet Dylan still existed, reduced to data stored in the new woman's memory core. Her FBI career, her life, and most importantly her encounter with the Blurred Man remained intact, digitally logged along with thousands of other lives and personas she lived in the past.

"Welcome back," Chip said. The synthetic assistant hovered above the pod, humming quietly. "I see you've chosen the alias of Mary Jane Kelley, a thermodynamic physicist. Interesting name choice."

"I find it appropriate," Mary Jane said.

"How so?"

"It was before your time, Chip. The name and form is to honor someone I knew a long time ago, although I'm sure I will miss being Dylan Plumm. How are things progressing with the alias insertion?"

Chip's beacon lit up, projecting a holographic screen scrolling with data. "As you directed, I took one of your stock aliases and activated it when you retired to begin your metamorphosis. Since then I've been hard at work implanting you into the infrastructure of society."

Mary Jane absorbed the flickering data and pictures, downloading the new personality profile into her memory core in seconds. "You've outdone yourself this time, Chip."

The automaton buzzed in a pleased manner. "As you can see, after publishing your theories on a possible new energy source you are now the talk of the science community. Your face graces the Person of the Year cover of Time. Not bad for someone who didn't exist ninety days ago."

Mary Jane scanned the magazine's interior. Inside was a lengthy article covering her research and reclusive personality. Her research was considered brilliant and remarkable. Her personal life was reportedly so cloistered that practically no details existed.

"Excellent idea to make me a reclusive enigma," Mary Jane said. "No known friends or family, no social footprint. I'm sure that makes it easier for your work. This alias creation must become more difficult the more technology advances."

Chip's humming sounded distinctively smug. "Not so much. Actually the more humans lean on technology, the easier it is to create a history complete with full records of one's existence. All I have to do is insert the data in the correct places."

"That doesn't make up for human memory," Mary Jane said. "All this attention could be a slippery slope. More than a few people would recall a young lady this brilliant, no matter how reclusive she was."

"And some people do. Or at least they believe so. I purposely created some high school and university photographs that resemble several other shy and introverted girls. Several people from those schools have already given interviews 'recalling' you as withdrawn, a loner, enigmatic, etc. I'm constantly amazed how easy it is for the human mind to fool itself."

"The wonder of memory deception," Mary Jane said. She flicked across the various screens. "My face seems to be everywhere in the media."

"All the more to make you enticing," Chip said. "Your beauty has Cover Girl desperate for an endorsement deal, and your research has attracted invitations from the most powerful organizations wanting to conference, share resources, or offer employment deals starting in the seven figures."

Mary Jane enlarged the screen displaying a myriad of emails from various companies offering employment. One of the organizations was Chimera Global. She clicked on it.

"Excellent work, Chip. Keep at it. The more we cement my identity, the harder it will be to cross-examine it."

"Considering a bit of espionage, are we? How exciting." Lights danced around Chip's surface.

Mary Jane sat down on her leather sofa and gazed at the lights that winked from beyond her floor-to-ceiling windows. The Manhattan skyline glimmered, its nighttime display a lightshow that created dancing shadows in her penthouse apartment. Her mental circuits analyzed the flood of probabilities. Her entire life had altered in a ninety-day period, changing every variable established while living as Dylan Plumm. Yet something more difficult lay before her as well. An unavoidable choice awaited her decision, one unlike any she faced before.

A buzzing sound interrupted her introspection. The phone on the nearby table vibrated softly. She looked at the ID displayed. The profile's face was obscured.

Mary Jane picked up the phone.

"Hello again," the Blurred Man said.

THE PISCES AFFAIR

Minsk, Belarus, 2015

I learned about the shocking assassination plot on a Friday night in Minsk, Belarus. I was debriefing Ivan Lysenko, a senior official in the Russian defense ministry and a key asset whom we'd turned because of his one-too-many extramarital indiscretions. I'd expected the debriefing to yield only mundane intelligence until Lysenko revealed that a radical, anti-American faction of the Separatists intended to commit a terrorist attack at a summit among heads of state scheduled to take place the following evening in Dubai.

Lysenko had been providing information about the true motivations behind a proposal for peace talks among Russia, the pro-Russian Ukrainian Separatists, and the Ukrainian government. With the Russians reviving Cold War methods, the Agency had stepped up counterintelligence to gauge whether the Russians were our enemies again. Although the Russians said they wanted peace, Lysenko had confirmed that their true goal was to force a Ukrainian withdrawal from the east, which would hand the Separatists, and hence Russia, full control of Donbass. Still he didn't think the Russians were behind the planned terrorist attack—*didn't think*. I hoped he was right, because if the Russians were behind the plot, we would be facing World War III.

The moment Lysenko revealed this startling information, I stopped the interview and telephoned Sean "Snake" Bridges, Director of CIA Field Operations.

"We have an issue," I said to Snake.

"What now, Jakes?" he asked in his familiar Texas drawl. Snake never began a conversation with *hello*, but then again, neither did I.

"Lysenko says that some Ukrainian rebels have planned a hit. It's supposed to take place tomorrow night at *Atlantis The Palm*."

Snake exhaled loudly, just short of a gasp. "They're targeting Mallory Hamilton?" Mallory Hamilton was the Secretary of State and the frontrunner in the next presidential election.

"That's what Lysenko claims."

"This is the last damn thing I thought I'd be hearing, Jakes. Why Dubai? It's a little out of their neighborhood, not to mention the place will be sewn up with security. Give me details."

"It's sketchy. We've been at this debrief for six hours and counting. Lysenko shows no signs of lying, but he's withholding something because he just started asking for asylum."

"No way. He's staying right where he is. Just remind him that if he doesn't cooperate, we have dozens of photos of him cavorting with those women."

"You sure he'll care anymore? He says he's getting divorced."

"The girls were French spies."

I hadn't heard that one.

"If it comes out, he'll be sent to a Siberian labor camp," Snake continued. "Or worse. No asylum."

"Got it."

"Look, we don't have much time. Get the facts out of Lysenko and then head to Dubai."

"The Secret Service isn't going to like me crowding their party."

"We're in our realm with this threat. The new Under Secretary of Defense for Intelligence, Maxwell Brodowski, is planning to be there."

"I've heard some things about Brodowski."

"What things?"

"That he's a self-centered politician who puts his ambitions over anything else. That he's a playboy, irresponsible."

"Take it from me, Max is trustworthy. I know his father. I'll arrange for you to go as his date. Class it up, play it like Angie."

"Not funny, Snake."

"I'm serious."

"Snake, I—"

"Just do it."

That wasn't what I wanted to hear. Me, Jordan Jakes, playing sex-kitten in the style of Angelina Jolie. I hated standing out in a crowd, so this would *not* be my favorite gig. If I had my choice, I'd be in Army fatigues crawling around a desert, or dodging bullets through the streets of Tehran. But I could do this, too. It helped that when I slapped on a little lipstick and let down my hair, people would say I resembled Angie more than a bit. The big difference between us was that my natural hair color was dark auburn, though I always had to cut it or dye it for one operation or another. If I'd had a say on this assignment, I'd be moving inside and out of the kitchen dressed as a server, free to roam around the room, rather than look like a painted-up floozy who's supposed to be window dressing on some guy's arm. Still, why not take a shot at getting Snake to reconsider?

"I'll have more flexibility as a waiter, Snake."

"Those jobs are already filled by other agents. *Angie* it up."

* * *

A day later, Dubai, United Arab Emirates

After the flight to Dubai, courtesy of the U.S. Air Force, and then an Army escort to the hotel, I hurried to get ready for the formal dinner. I chose the black evening gown with the low cut scoop-back and a pair of Christian Louboutin heels. I popped in a pair of dark contact lenses flecked with pinpoints of gold, and flat-ironed my hair so it fell tightly down my back and swirled into a slight wave at my waist. My dangly black and gold earrings—my grandmother, Mimi, would've said that they weren't suitable for a nice girl—conveniently contained an earpiece. My clutch concealed a sexy but deadly red tube of lipstick that sat next to my true friend, the one I counted on most in a pinch—a P320 Sig Sauer. I was safe, and so was Siggy, since no one would be looking me in the eye or checking out the contents of my purse—not wearing this outfit. And fortunately, Snake had taken care of getting me past security.

Someone knocked on my door just as I was putting on my pumps. I slipped on the second high-heel, took a quick look at my reflection in the mirror, and winked at Angie. "Let's get to work, sister."

When I opened the door, Maxwell Brodowski uttered something that sounded like "wow." In his tux, he looked pretty great himself. He appeared to be in his early forties, with the physique of a guy ten years younger, and had the handsome, open face of a politician—square jaw, cobalt blue eyes, dark hair just starting to gray at the temples. A lot of women would've swooned over him at first sight—not only because of his good looks but because of his political power. But he wasn't my type. The only man who'd ever turned my head was the nerdy but hunky NASA scientist and pub owner, Benjamin Johnson. I did hope Ben never found out about this assignment.

"Hello, Jordan," Maxwell said in the suave voice of a practiced diplomat. "You look ravishing. Snake didn't tell me you were drop-dead gorgeous. Maybe when this is over, we can get an after-dinner drink."

I shook my head and said, "Keep it professional." I never accepted baloney from some good-looking, smooth-talking snake oil salesman.

He shrugged. "It was worth a try." He offered me his arm.

Secretary Hamilton had been briefed earlier on the situation—that we'd received information of a potential terrorist attack, and that Max had been assigned a CIA escort for the evening to put another set of eyes in the room. We'd go to the cocktail party first, which was being held outside on the central terrace near the Royal Pool and water fountain, and then finish the evening with dinner inside the formal dining room.

I gripped my Gucci clutch, placing a finger over the cloth where I could feel the outline of Siggy's trigger—just to be sure I knew the gun's exact location. Then I took Maxwell's arm.

"I assume Snake told you I was a Navy Seal," he said.

"Good for you. But I'm in charge now. If anything goes pop, hit the deck, and if you're in reach, take Secretary Hamilton down with you. Otherwise, no heroics."

"You're the boss."

I didn't believe for a moment that he thought I was the boss.

We walked out of the lobby and joined the cocktail party now in session. There was merriment and laughter, and why wouldn't there be? The word *lavish* didn't describe the hotel *Atlantis The Palm*. The edifice and grounds were more opulent than any palace on earth, challenging any grandiose notion of what the legendary Atlantis might have resembled.

The hotel complex sat at the apex of a series of manmade islands shaped like—what else?—a palm tree, which was surrounded by a ring of a dozen or so smaller islands. A central road, like the trunk of the tree, ran the length of the main island. Sixteen peninsulas, shaped like sprawling leaves, eight on each side, extended into the lagoon. Each peninsula had a one-lane road running through it. Rows of luxury homes with access to one's own private beach lined each side of the road. A high-speed elevated train from the mainland ran the length of the "tree trunk" and over the water to the outer island, where *Atlantis The Palm* hotel sat on the peak. I didn't let the opulence distract me. I couldn't, but then I'd never been taken in by glitter.

When we'd refused asylum to Lysenko, he clammed up. I would've thrown him to the wolves had he not disclosed that the perp was planning on taking a shot at the Secretary of State, not using a suicide bomber to blow the place and everyone in it to shreds. Trained sharpshooters usually take every step toward a target with extreme caution and calculate the odds of failure with precision. Much smarter than most would-be suicide bombers, in other words. Since Lysenko had no idea whether the assassin was male or female, I had to consider everyone.

The place was sweltering, the hot desert wind blowing off the mainland only raising the temperature. The sun hadn't set, so I had a clear visual of the area. With security tight, the other guests from the hotel weren't allowed anywhere near the reception. The Union Defence Force, the armed forces of the United Arab Emirates, was present at full strength to discourage curious onlookers. But I couldn't count on them. One of their members might have been the assassin.

Once we were past security, I said to Maxwell, "Give me a minute to have a look around before we mix with the crowd."

I stepped to the side, tapped into the Secret Service's radio frequency, and identified the agents' locations. They had the interior of the hotel already covered, so I wasn't worried about anything that might go down in there. I planned to circulate and identify suspects among the guests.

I identified the dignitaries: our hosts, along with a closely connected network of wealthy Arab royalty and diplomats from a number of countries. I spotted the Russian Foreign Minister, Anton Volokh, and his Ukraine counterpart, Artem Gurka, who stood at opposite corners of the courtyard. Representatives from NATO members Germany, France, the UK, and Italy, were present. UN representatives mingled amongst the crowd, most prominently the new Secretary General, Marco Dominico of Mexico.

The people who caused me most concern were the underlings and extras whom I didn't recognize—like the waiter who now offered us some vintage Veuve Clicquot champagne. There was something blank behind his stare. His eyes were a faded green and his pupils were wide—oddly so. He looked like he'd been nipping at the stuff himself, but I detected no alcohol on his breath. Maybe he'd been smoking hashish, but I couldn't smell it on him.

I raised a hand to pass on the bubbly, but Maxwell took two glasses and handed me one. That was the problem with the *Angie* approach—I had to drink, or pretend to. It wasn't that I couldn't hold my liquor, but when you're trying to stop an assassination, every ounce of awareness counts. If I'd been disguised as staff, I wouldn't need to pretend to be some fun-loving, flighty girl. *Whatever.* I reluctantly took two small sips of the champagne.

The waiter lingered for no apparent reason.

A large, doughy man with a double chin and a salt-and-pepper beard approached us. He wore a waiter's tux. In Arabic, he said to our waiter, "Get back to the kitchen, Oklar. You're not supposed to be out here now."

Oklar started to walk away. His boss threw his hands in the air and snapped, "Leave the champagne with me!"

Oklar nodded mechanically, handed his boss the tray, and walked away.

"I'm Mahaz, the head waiter, at your service," the larger man said in decent English. "Is everything adequate? I'm only asking because Oklar is new. Unsure of his job responsibilities. My apologies if he was rude."

"There's nothing to apologize for," I said.

He picked up the bottle of champagne. "May I freshen your drink?"

I started to say, "No thank you," but he was already pouring. I reflexively took another sip. As soon as he left us, I tapped into my wire to get a read from the Secret Service guys on these two jokers.

"This is Jakes. I've got an oddball waiter, goes by the name Oklar. He just served Brodowski and me champagne. Eleven o'clock, heading inside the kitchen. Check out the headwaiter, too."

There was a pause. Finally, the agent said, "Mahmet Oklar. He's a recent hire, three months ago. Turkish. No contact with the Russians, Ukrainians, or with any Islamic terrorist group. The headwaiter is Mahaz Toma, a Saudi. He's worked at the hotel for three years. Brought over by the chef. He also checks out."

"Maxwell," a man said in a high-English accent as he approached us from the side. He extended a hand, which Maxwell clasped.

"How's the Prime Minister, Richard?" Maxwell asked.

"Fine, fine. I was hoping to catch you for a chat."

"Richard Robertson, this is my girlfriend, Jewel Johnson. Jewel, Sir Richard is the British Home Secretary."

I gave him my warmest fake smile, but thought *Jewel*? My alias was supposed to be *Jacqueline* Johnson, and yet Maxwell gave me a name better suited to a stripper. What was he up to?

I extended my fingertips to Sir Richard and curtsied. He bowed. But something distracted me. Across the crowd I saw a familiar face—Sonya Roth, a high-level Russian intelligence agent. I trusted her only because I knew her weakness—her love for my boss, Snake. Or maybe Sonya was *Snake's* weakness.

I slid my hand into Maxwell's and squeezed. Then I brushed my cheek against his, playing the infatuated girlfriend. I didn't dare kiss him, not in this crowd. Public displays of affection could land you a trip to lockup in a Muslim country. "I'll be back in a few, babe."

He nodded like the doting lover.

I aimed a little finger-wave at Sir Richard and slipped into the crowd.

As I made my way to Sonya, I recognized someone else, a woman I'd come in contact with during an operation in Germany. She was five-feet-eleven with broad-shoulders, a square jaw, and a finely chiseled nose with flaring nostrils. Her dark hair was wrapped in an updo. She wasn't a person whom an average man would want to tangle with. Using the name Ute Mossbacher—an alias, undoubtedly—she worked for a company called Ascension, which provided private security at the highest levels. Most people didn't know that Ascension also employed a crew of hired killers. Somehow, the corporation had managed to evade prosecution for its hit squad.

As I made a beeline for Mossbacher, that waiter, Oklar, blocked my passage and offered me an hors d'oeuvre. I waved him off and tried to go around him, but he mirrored my movement, not letting me pass.

"Move over *now*," I said in a tone that had often intimidated men twice this guy's size.

He just stood there.

I repeated the command in Turkish, but still to no effect.

I gently rolled my neck as though flipping my hair so that I could more thoroughly study him. He was solid, all muscle, but I knew I could take him in an instant. One blow to his throat and he'd never breathe again. I was tempted to get forceful, but couldn't at a state dinner.

I glanced across the room to Sonya Roth, who nodded. I activated my microphone to call in the Secret Service to deal with Oklar when a loud noise attacked my eardrums, leaving me immobile. Then it dropped in decibels to a mesmerizing murmur, almost as if the wind were whistling. It was evocative, haunting. How could one note create such a beautiful melody? I glanced toward the small band near the fountain. The musicians weren't playing, weren't even tuning their instruments. I suddenly felt as though I were intoxicated, but how could that be on a few sips of champagne?

Unless I'd been drugged.

My heart skipped a beat. I'd forgotten to dip one of my varnished fingernails into the liquid to test for the presence of drugs. My God, was this waiter the assassin? Would everyone be drugged? With what? Some hallucinogenic or a debilitating hypnotic that made the room float and sing? My cheeks began to flush, and soon my face burned like white-hot coal.

I looked into Oklar's eyes. There was still that blankness there, but paradoxically also something truly meaningful—what, I couldn't define. The hair on my arms rose, but I didn't feel frightened. I felt unnerved yet completely at ease.

A wave crashed on the shore, and then I was struck with the memory of standing on the banks of a river near Ketchum, Idaho. We were on a family vacation. I was eight years old.

I reached out with that thought, clutched the memory, and drew it forward into the now...

My father is holding my hand, and with his other arm, he's carrying a fishing pole with half-a-dozen fish hooked onto the end. I giggle and laugh wildly as we catch them. What a wonderful game! Back at the rental house, as I watch him fillet the fish, I'm silent, spellbound... horrified. Fish guts, scales, blood. No longer vibrant and alive.

Reading my expression, my father says, "Sometimes killing is justified, JJ. Like when you have to do it to survive. We only caught what we could eat."

I force a smile, but the tears flow down my cheeks.

He begins singing, the melody his own, the words from Elizabeth Barrett Browning's poem A Drama of Exile:

> *And here fantastic fishes duskly float,*
> *Using the calm for waters, while their fires*
> *Throb out quick rhythms along the shallow air.*

Then my father vanished. I reached out for him, but there was only the waiter, and when I looked into his eyes, I sobered. The heat in my face faded. My heart rate slowed. No more than a second had passed.

And yet, I was badly shaken. My parents, who'd also been in the Company, died when I was young—murdered by enemies unknown. That my time with them was short made my memories all the more precious. This vision was all too vivid.

I forced myself to focus and looked at the others around me. Nothing seemed unusual. I couldn't have been drugged. If I had, I wouldn't have recovered so quickly. Maybe this was only a result of the jet lag and the desert heat combined with the sips of champagne. I glimpsed the shoreline. The water was completely calm, like glass.

When I turned back, Oklar was gone.

Sonya stepped around a group of Saudi men. "I see you have a new boyfriend," she said, giving me her best smirk. "The Under Secretary of Defense. What happened to your scientist?"

"It's just for the evening. Speaking of boyfriends, did Snake call you on this one?"

"We have our own sources. Better than yours."

"I just wonder whose side you're on."

"Our countries have our differences, it is true. But do you honestly believe we want to see anything happen to Secretary Hamilton? Russia gets blamed, and then we have an international incident on our hands. We want to stop this as much as you do."

I hoped that she was telling the truth, but I couldn't rule out anything. Sonya Roth was as lethal as any assassin. For the moment, though, I'd take her at face value.

"Do you have any intelligence on your end?" she asked. "Because we only know that there is to be an attempt on Hamilton's life."

It wasn't a time to play games, so I told her what I had, leaving out Lysenko's part in it. "I spotted a hired gun from the Ascension Corporation. Ute Mossbacher."

"Yes, I saw her, too."

"What's she doing here?"

"Seems she is playing bodyguard for the Foreign Minister of Kyrgyzstan."

"One of Russia's closest allies is in bed with Ascension? Does that mean you approved of the hiring?"

"Never. I do not know why they hired those fascists."

I searched the crowd. The Kyrgyzstani Minster, with Mossbacher at her side, was speaking to Secretary of State Hamilton. Before I could say Merry Christmas, Mossbacher reached a hand inside her jacket.

"*Eto yeye*," Sonya said, which meant, "It's her."

I started to go for my Sig Sauer, but Mossbacher pulled her arm out of her jacket, empty handed.

It didn't matter, she was still a threat.

"I'll confront her head on," I said. "You take her from behind. Let's see if we can get her out of here quietly so we don't create an incident."

We were already moving, doing our best to avoid making a spectacle of ourselves. I tapped my earpiece and spoke to the Secret Service. "Female. North of the fountain at ten o'clock. Very tall. She goes by the name Ute Mossbacher. We're doing this quietly. Cover me."

"Jakes, stand down," the man over the wire said. "We'll move in and take her."

"That's not the way it's happening," I said into my earpiece. "She'll already have made you. We can't risk her taking a shot at Hamilton."

"One false move, and she goes down."

"Don't worry. We can do this without a scene."

"Who's *we*?"

"Sonya Roth and me. Just cover us."

"Don't tell me you're working with the Russians."

"Get over it."

We waited for some separation between Mossbacher and the dignitaries. Seconds later, I stepped in front of Mossbacher, shielding Hamilton. Mossbacher instantly slid a hand back inside her jacket and took a step back.

"I wouldn't do that," Sonya said, sliding her arm through Mossbacher's and discreetly nuzzling a handgun into the woman's ribs.

"Let's all go freshen up, Ute," I whispered.

Mossbacher glared at Sonya and started to protest, but when Sonya jabbed her with the gun, Mossbacher nodded.

I slid beside Mossbacher and took her free arm. Sonya and I quickly escorted her through the lobby and into a private office, where half a dozen Secret Service agents were waiting. Any desire that Mossbacher might have had to resist disappeared once she saw what she was up against. A chair had already been placed in the center of the room, with agents surrounding it. As soon as Sonya and I disarmed the woman—she was, indeed, packing—an agent motioned for her to sit down.

"We know why you're here and what you're doing," I said.

"I don't know what you're talking about," Mossbacher said. "But I can assure you that as soon as I speak to the Kyrgyzstani Minister and Dubai authorities, there will be repercussions. You have no right—"

"Enough!" Sonya said in German.

"Who hired you?" I asked.

Mossbacher gave Sonya a sharp look. "I'm here to protect the Kyrgyzstani Minister—your country's close ally." She tilted her head toward me. "*She's* your enemy, not I."

"*Fignya!*" Sonya said, which meant *bullshit* in Russian.

"Listen carefully, Ute," I said. "You can make this real simple or you can make it hard. Who hired Ascension to assassinate Mallory Hamilton?"

Her eyes widened in shock. She was either truly surprised or a superb liar. "I don't know what you're talking about. Kyrgyzstan retained us because they don't have the manpower to guard the minsters at state dinners like this." She began spilling her guts, giving us plenty of references that seemed legit. But I wasn't about to let her go before we checked out her claims. If she was telling the truth, we couldn't hold her for long, not without incurring the wrath of the Minister of Kyrgyzstan.

Before our guys could run that check, the selfsame Kyrgyzstani minister, followed by the Russian minister and Dubai authorities, burst through the door.

Mossbacher shot to her feet. "These people are insane," she said. Looking at the officials from Dubai, she pointed to me and added, "Typical American arrogance."

The Russian minister pulled Sonya aside, and after a heated exchange, Sonya stormed out. Then none other than my "date" for the evening, Maxwell Brodowski, walked in.

Maxwell pointed to Mossbacher. "Let this woman go," he said to the Secret Service agents.

I started to object, but Maxwell's glance made me think better of it. In the end, he was my superior.

"My weapon," Mossbacher said. "I was cleared by security."

Maxwell nodded again, and one of our agents returned Mossbacher's gun.

"You won't speak of this," Maxwell said to her.

She looked at the Russian and Kyrgyzstani ministers for affirmation. Fortunately, they nodded in agreement. Mossbacher pranced out of the room, making sure to flash me her most condescending victory smirk.

When we left, I pulled Maxwell into a corner. "What was that about?" I asked. "She's a trained assassin and was no more than two feet from Secretary Hamilton. And you let her walk out of here? With her weapon?"

"Right, she was that close to the Secretary and yet she didn't shoot her," Maxwell said. "You can't go around acting like you're a gunslinger in the Wild West. This isn't our country."

"But—"

"If you don't do a better job of being *sub rosa*, you're going to cause a real mess."

I didn't reply, only thought about what had just happened. What Maxwell said made sense, and yet he'd agreed to let a trained killer loose. I didn't really know if Mossbacher was the assassin or not, but why take chances? And what about Sonya? She'd always been a great actress, and I knew she played my ally only when it suited her country's interests. As far as I knew, she never diverged from the party line. Was the quarrel she had with the Russian minister real, or rather an act? The group that was supposedly trying to kill Secretary Hamilton was staunchly pro-Russian. They'd already been responsible for downing a commercial airline bound for the Middle East, killing one hundred and forty passengers.

Maxwell took my arm, and we returned to the party—even though, at that moment, I couldn't stand his touch. Not only that, his breath smelled of alcohol.

* * *

Maxwell and I were seated at one of the standalone circular tables that sat away from the long banquet table, which spanned the length of the room and hosted all the major dignitaries. Secretary Hamilton was seated prominently toward the center and next to the Minister of Ukraine, Artem Gurka. On her other side sat U.N. Secretary-General Dominico. My stomach turned once I saw the set up. Any shooter who wanted to take out Hamilton could also dispose of one or both of the others.

I tapped my earpiece to speak with the Secret Service. "I thought Hamilton was supposed to be sitting toward the end of the table."

"Hamilton insisted on the change," one of the Secret Service agents replied. "She didn't want the Americans to be relegated to the outskirts. We couldn't talk her out of it. She's not what you'd call *compliant*."

"Not good."

"Agreed. But we've got her covered from all angles."

I didn't like the set up with the Secretary, but at least I was nicely positioned with my back to the wall, which gave me an unobstructed view of her and the rest of the circular tables in the center of the room. Better yet, I had a clear line of sight to the kitchen through which staff entered and left the room—the perfect entrance or escape route for any shooter. And since our table hosted lesser players—the Chinese, Italians, and Omanis—I'd have more flexibility.

Across the room were Sonya and the lesser lights of the Russian delegation. They weren't sharing a table with anyone else. But Sonya was conversing intensely with a man I didn't recognize. I looked toward the stage and noticed that the Russian Foreign Minister Anton Volokh, had changed seats, too. He was now closer to the center of the long table on the opposite side to Hamilton. The new arrangement had undoubtedly happened because the Russians insisted on as much prominence as the Americans.

Maxwell leaned close to me. "Jewel Johnson, let me introduce you to our dinner companions."

At first I thought, here we go with this *Jewel* bit again, but then I got another whiff of his breath. He reeked, which made me wonder whether he'd ordered the Secret Service and me to release Mossbacher because he was drunk and not thinking clearly.

"Jewel is my fiancée," Maxwell continued.

I started to choke, thinking, well, Johnson would be the correct last name, but Maxwell was *not* the right guy. Ben Johnson was my true fiancé. I glanced down and noticed that my hand was missing the requisite artifact. I hoped that no one would notice this *faux pas*. We were bombarded with congratulatory remarks by the other guests, which forced me to play along. I'd heard rumors that Maxwell liked his liquor, but I'd never expected him to get tight at a state dinner, especially where lives were at stake. I smiled at everyone like a devoted fiancée. Then, luckily, the first course arrived and the gourmet Middle Eastern delicacies silenced the crowd.

Oklar and one of his colleagues were waiting the tables in our area. They served us a beetroot salad topped with stuffed wine leaves, and garnished with walnuts and feta cheese. A third waiter brought a platter filled with freshly prepared hummus and stuffed pastries, including spinach *fatayer* and meat *sambousek*. I kept an eye on Oklar because his unusual affect had me on edge, and I noticed that the headwaiter Toma always seemed to be on his case.

Once everyone had focused in on the spectacular cuisine, I leaned close to Maxwell and whispered, "What's with this engagement crap?"

Through a forced smile, he whispered in my ear, "You almost made a fool of yourself back there, almost blew your cover. I'm trying to help cover you up again."

As much as I didn't want to, I let it go. I didn't trust a drunk, Assistant Secretary of Defense or not. But there was something else—Maxwell might have been right.

We'd finished the next course, lentil soup, when we were served a cold 22-carat gold tea embellished with mint leaves in a glass teacup with an accompanying saucer. I'd heard of the tea, which was all the rage.

The sheik from Oman raised his glass. "Not only is the tea delicious, but it helps the body to relax."

I hesitated, not sure that I actually wanted to drink real gold. But Maxwell gave me a sharp look indicating that it would be an insult if I didn't drink. I tried the tea and had to admit that it had a delicate, yet complex flavor. It was mild but at the same time tasted like a fragrant flower—not at all what I'd expected. I took another sip, and when I set it down, looked through the clear glass of the teacup to examine the color of the tea.

A moment later, I became hyperaware of the light clanking china, like gentle chimes, or maybe a soft strum of a harp. Only one note but exquisite. Then I realized that it was happening again: the loss of control, the mental confusion, the drug-like curtain clouding my awareness. I squeezed my eyelids shut, trying to shake myself out of it. Another all-consuming memory entered my thoughts …

The sharp smell of ammonia permeates the air—a strong, disinfectant. I'm lying in bed asleep, and suddenly bolt up, wide awake. I look around, but all I can see is white, an indoor blizzard. I'm so cold. I'm in the hospital. My mother is in a chair next to the bed. She's asleep, although the expression on her face is strained. It's daytime, maybe early morning. But I don't know the time, I can't even say how long I've been here. The last thing I can remember is trying to blow out the five candles on my birthday cake—no, six candles (one to grow on). It was a chocolate cake covered in a light purple frosting, made at the new bakery near the Mayfair Market.

"Make a wish before you blow out the candles," my mother says.

I wish to see the ocean. Then I blow. But I miss one. "I wanted to see the ocean," I said, sighing.

Now, my stomach suddenly lurches. I feel queasy and then vomit, covering the hospital blanket in greenish-brown bile.

My mother springs from her chair. "JJ, honey!" She hurriedly calls for the nurse and then takes me into her arms. I fold into the comfort of my mother's love.

When the nurse rushes in, her face and body covered, she notices my mother. "You took your mask off," she scolds. "You should be wearing your mask."

My mother looks defiant. "I'll be fine."

"Mama, I don't feel good," I say. She gently rocks me, smoothing back my hair. I'm all sweaty. "Am I going to die?"

"No, of course not, baby girl."

But my mother looks scared, like she's going to cry, and I extend my arms to hug her but can't quite reach her ...

The memory faded, and like awakening from a dream, I'd returned to the dinner party, now aware of a hubbub taking place near the long banquet table. Volokh and Gurka seemed to be embroiled in a heated debate—or maybe it was already a full-blown argument. The Vice President, Prime Minister and Ruler of Dubai, His Highness Sheikh, Nasser Hassan Albudoor, who was seated front and center, rose and raised his arms. Fortunately, the Russian and Ukrainian ministers pulled back, and the entire room fell silent. Sheikh Albudoor welcomed the guests and began his speech on peace and goodwill among nations.

I glanced around the room, caught the attention of a few of our Secret Service agents, and looked at them questioningly. Each replied with an *all-clear* nod. I relaxed briefly. Had my informant, Lysenko, given us a fake tip, trying to buy himself a new home in America? I hoped so.

After Sheikh Albudoor finished his speech, the waiters filed into the dining room again and began serving the main course: grilled seafood, sautéed vegetables, and vermicelli rice, along with all the traditional condiments.

Then I looked at Mossbacher, probably for the twentieth time. It unnerved me that she still sat in this room carrying a gun. Yet, she'd had plenty of opportunities to shoot and hadn't. And to do so would've been suicide. Had Sonya played me on Mossbacher as part of a Russian attempt to embarrass the United States? It had taken no time for the Russian and Kyrgyzstani ministers to catch up with us. Had Sonya conspired with them so that we Americans would look like bullies? Maybe it was a good thing that Maxwell had come into the room when he did. Maybe he *had* spared our country from diplomatic humiliation—humiliation that I would've caused. And yet he'd allowed a known hit-woman to roam free.

I looked for Sonya, but she wasn't at her table.

Maxwell placed his hand on my arm. "Are you feeling okay, sweetheart?" he asked. "You look a little pale." He leaned toward me, obscuring my view of Hamilton and the Russians. "Why don't you go freshen up?"

My ears echoed with that tinkling single note. *Not again*! I pushed him away so I could see around him, my heart rate accelerating.

"Jewel," he said, quietly but adamantly. "Do not make a scene." He sounded completely sober.

There was a loud crash in the kitchen. I looked over just in time to see Toma, the headwaiter, grab a tray away from his underling, Oklar. By all appearances, it looked as though Toma was reprimanding Oklar yet again.

"Go splash some water on your face," Maxwell whispered harshly. "You've had too much to drink. When Snake told me about you, he didn't tell me you drank on the job."

"Look who's talking."

"Having a drink is part of a diplomat's job. I consume mineral oil before I come to these things. It absorbs the alcohol before it reaches the bloodstream. Now, go on."

"I'm fine. Back off."

He clasped my arm and tried to pull me to my feet.

I pressed against him, trying to look affectionate while at the same time pushing him off me. "If you don't let go of me now, I'll scream."

He sat back in astonishment. I think he expected me to threaten to break his nose or even shoot him, not to act like a hysterical girl. And on another occasion, I might've gone after him. But in my line of work, you have to choose the right weapon for the right circumstance.

"Just don't do anything crazy," he whispered.

There was a buzzing in my ears, as if someone had infiltrated the air with some kind of white-noise technology. I looked around to figure out where it was coming from.

"Do you hear it?" I asked Maxwell.

"Do I hear what? I really think you should…"

Annoyed, I rose from my seat. It didn't matter what Maxwell said he did or didn't hear. He wasn't trustworthy. I forced myself to touch him lovingly on the shoulder, and said loudly enough for others to hear, "You know, babe, I think I will freshen up after all."

"I'll be waiting, Jewel," he said.

I started toward the kitchen to see if I could find some audio-visual control room—I knew federal courthouses used this kind of white-noise technology for judge's sidebar conversations—but as I passed the kitchen, I bumped into Oklar.

"You are going the wrong way," he said in surprisingly well-articulated English.

"What do you mean, *I'm going the wrong way?*"

His eyes were stone cold, but somehow also incisive and intelligent. He pointed behind me. I turned my head, glancing over my shoulder only to realize that his arm was aimed directly at Secretary Hamilton. The headwaiter, Toma, was about to serve her a plate of food.

I turned back to Oklar. He began humming. One note, one frequency. The tinkling sound. Or was I imagining it? Maybe I *was* going crazy. I tried to clear my head.

"What did you mean when you said, '*I'm going the wrong way*'?" I asked.

He didn't reply.

I looked back toward Hamilton and the others, and then over at the Russians. Sonya was still missing. I searched for Mossbacher. She was gone, too.

Oklar tried to walk around me.

I took a step to block him. "Talk to me."

He hesitated a moment and stared at me.

I was flooded with the memories again—my father and the fish, my mother and the hospital. And then I finally understood.

As I sprinted back toward Secretary of State Hamilton, I shouted, "Madame Secretary, don't eat anything more!"

She'd been about to take her first bite of the fish course, but she suspended her fork in midair and gaped at me.

The whole room fell silent. Maxwell Brodowski got up from the table and started toward me, an angry scowl on his face.

When I was no more than six feet away from Hamilton, Toma spun on his heels. In a surprisingly agile move, he came around and drew a gun from his vest. Before he could fire, Maxwell leapt over the banquet table and tackled him. A shot rang out, and people screamed and dove for cover. Then the Union Defence guards, our Secret Service guys, and Russian intelligence all swarmed on the headwaiter and Maxwell like players in a rugby scrum.

I wanted to know if Maxwell was okay, I really did, but instead I watched Oklar walk over to Secretary of State Hamilton. She was, remarkably, still holding her forkful of fish in the air. He grabbed the fork out of her hand. One of the Secret Service guys aimed his gun at him, but I pulled the agent's arm down. We both watched the waiter eat the fish from the Secretary's fork. With his hands, Oklar scooped up the entire piece of fish left on her plate and swallowed it whole, like a cobra devouring its prey. Oklar took the plate and hid it in his shirt.

I looked over to find Maxwell sitting on the floor, dazed, but alive, thankfully. Blood trickled down his arm. Meanwhile, one of the many agents had handcuffed Toma.

Then I noticed that all the agents had their guns trained on Oklar.

All at once, Oklar bolted for the exit, faster than an Olympic sprinter.

"Hold your fire!" I shouted.

One of the agents fired a shot anyway, but the guy moved so quickly that it missed. I followed, though I couldn't keep up with him. He left the building and headed across the courtyard, miraculously evading the Union Defence Forces who were trying to stop him.

"Wait," I called. "We just need to talk to you."

But he kept running.

I pulled out my Sig Sauer. "Stop, or I'll shoot!" I didn't want to fire, because this man had surely saved the Secretary of State's life. Still, I couldn't let him get away. We had to contain him, at least until I truly understood what was going on.

I didn't know how, but he'd communicated to me that Hamilton's fish had been tainted. Those memory flashbacks I'd experienced: my father and catching fish, my fifth birthday and being hospitalized for something never diagnosed, but that the doctors speculated was an unknown virus or severe food poisoning. Had my parents communicated with me? Or was this simply how my instincts took hold on this occasion? I'd never believed in the supernatural, but I hadn't believed in many things that had come true—like falling in love with Ben Johnson.

The monorail train crossing the lagoon was just leaving the island. Oklar turned toward the train and raced after it.

"Wait!" I shouted again.

But he didn't stop. He ran so fast that he'd actually managed to catch up with the train. In my astonishment, I dropped my gun.

Oklar jumped in the air, or was he flying, because the leap was almost superhuman. Then he latched onto a handle at the back of the train.

I watched the train fade out of sight. Shaking myself back into reality, I called for backup. The authorities had to be alerted so they could stop the train and catch this guy. But who would believe my story?

* * *

When the Dubai authorities stopped the train, there was no sign of the waiter or anyone fitting his description.

My superiors at the Agency would've thought I'd gone crazy, except that once Toma was interrogated, he sang like a warbler. He was a radical Islamist who'd joined forces with pro-Russian Ukrainians to spike Hamilton's fish—with Ebola. They had been working with an African-Islamic terrorist group that had access to the tainted fluids in an unsecure hospital in Liberia. Their goal was to infect, not only Secretary Hamilton, but also the President and his entire cabinet.

Which means I should have shot Oklar, because he'd eaten the Ebola-tainted fish and could've caused a deadly epidemic. Hospitals worldwide were waiting for him to check in. But no one who looked like him ever did. After the twenty-one-day incubation period passed, everyone breathed a sigh of relief.

Lysenko had turned out to be a good source. And fortunately, Maxwell Brodowski had stopped me from rousting Ute Mossbacher and creating an international incident. When Maxwell got out of the hospital, he asked me again to have that drink with him. He was a hero, but I refused. I had my own hero at home—Dr. Benjamin Johnson.

* * *

Shedding the identity Mahmet Oklar—as he'd shed thousands of identities before—Prometheus had jumped from the train, landing in the water on the ocean side of the island. He dove, pumping his arms and legs to reach the bottom depth of twenty-six meters. The air in his lungs had completely dissipated by the time he reached the bottom. He activated a remote control, and a mound ballooned upward. A shimmering golden-hulled submersible emerged from the sand. The double-sealed hatch opened, and Prometheus slid inside the craft. He felt the comfort of the womb he never knew. He would heal his now-damaged lungs, ponder the next move, and regenerate. In three months, the world would change, and so would he, but for now he was safe. A new identity would protect him. Just like all the other times, he would start over again.

He rarely interfered with the natural progression of humanity, no matter how monstrous. On this occasion, he'd violated that order. The intelligences that created him would not approve. But he simply could not let the humans be slaughtered by a horrible virus—a concept that he understood only intellectually, because he was immune to their illnesses. And yet, in a previous identity he'd gone to Africa and had witnessed the horror. The disease had no conscience, no mercy.

The submersible began moving through the water with an almost other-worldly stealth, the craft's path strangely beautiful. A single tone radiated, humming.

ABOUT THE AUTHORS

ELLE ANDREWS PATT
DACO AUFFENORDE
BRIA BURTON
M.J. CARLSON
CHARLES A. CORNELL
BARD CONSTANTINE
DOUG DANDRIDGE
PARKER FRANCIS
KAY KENDALL
JADE KERRION
KEN PELHAM
ANTONIO SIMON JR.

ELLE ANDREWS PATT

Elle Andrews Patt has long pondered Manteo's role with the Lost Colony. He stood witness to all three of Sir Raleigh's expeditions. As a native American, he held a unique perspective on colonization. There is very little hard fact on Manteo. He disappeared from the historical record along with the colonists. Elle's take on him is drawn directly from John White's writings and her imagination.

Elle received an Honorable Mention from Writers of The Future for ***Prelude To A Murder Conviction*** in 2013. She won the First Place Royal Palm Literary Award for Published Short Fiction from the Florida Writers Association in 2013 and 2014. She was invited to join the Alvarium Experiment during its 2014 inception and first published ***Manteo*** in 2015 as a stand-alone e-novella within the AE's first project, ***The Prometheus Saga***. It is still available with bonus research notes included.

In between the many hours spent keyboard-pounding, computer-screen staring, and workshopping fiction since 2001, Elle has unschooled her kids, team-mom'ed for softball, volleyball, and golf, sweated through stints as a veterinary technician, horse-show manager, pizza maker, business phone packer, baseball bat seller, boarding barn manager, and equine semen collector, rejoiced at finding wi-fi far afield, and ridden all sorts of horses, both evil and golden, over cross country jumps, across un-mowed hunt country, and all gussied up into the dressage arena.

She currently lives with her husband and two daughters in the breeziest part of Florida she's ever been to and is grateful for it every day.

WORKS by ELLE ANDREWS PATT

PUBLISHED NOVELLA

Manteo
(2015 RPLA Finalist)

SHORT STORY PUBLICATIONS
(as Laura Andrews)

Karl's Last Night (2014 RPLA Winner) – The Rag Literary Magazine
Becky's Story (2013 RPLA Winner) – Saw Palm: Florida Literature
The Legend of Johnny Bell – Solarcide Anthology
Coming of Age – FWA Collection #6- First Steps

UPCOMING NOVELS

Billie Mae – Paranormal Murder Mystery
(2015 RPLA Finalist)

The Year of the Bear – Mainstream Literature

www.elleandrewspatt.com

DACO AUFFENORDE

Born at the Naval hospital in Bethesda, Maryland and raised in Wernher von Braun's Rocket City of Huntsville, Alabama, Daco holds a B.A. and M.A.S. from The University of Alabama in Huntsville and a J.D. from the Cumberland School of Law. She is a member of the International Thriller Writers, Romance Writers of America, Author's Guild, Florida Writers, and the Alabama State Bar.

Daco's debut novel, *The Libra Affair*, an international spy thriller with romantic elements, became an Amazon #1 Bestseller of Suspense, Romantic Suspense, and Romance in 2013. The novel was included in 2014 in a limited-time only suspense bundle entitled *Racing Hearts: 10 Thrilling Suspense Novels*.

The Pisces Affair, a science fiction thriller also featuring Jordan Jakes, is a double gold medalist in the *2015 Global Ebook Awards* for Thriller Fiction and Science Fiction. It is also a finalist for the *2015 Royal Palm Literary Awards* short story genre. The next Jordan Jakes story, *The Virgo Affair*, will be released Fall 2015 as part of an anthology compiled by Clay Stafford's *Killer Nashville* that will also include stories by best-selling authors Jeffery Deaver, Robert Dugoni, and Mary Burton, among others.

"Jakes is a lively and witty narrator with the wits and skills of James Bond, and readers will savor her fresh perspective on being a woman in the male-dominated spy world."—*Publishers Weekly*

The Libra Affair is "A complex spy game, rather like a Jason Bourne movie – only instead of the usual male secret agent, we get Jordan Jakes. And she is more than capable of rocking your world."— *RT Book Reviews*

"Daco's romantic thriller debut intrigues with fast-paced, high-stakes action that forces the take-charge heroine to balance her clandestine mission with obligations to her heart ... The keenly sharp intelligent female characters soar in this edge-of-your-seat adventure..."—*Publishers Weekly*

PUBLICATIONS by DACO AUFFENORDE

JORDAN JAKES THRILLERS

The Libra Affair

The Scorpio Affair (coming soon)

JORDAN JAKES SHORT STORIES

The Pisces Affair

(2015 RPLA Finalist)

(2015 Global Ebook Awards Double Gold Medalist)

The Virgo Affair (coming soon)

www.authordaco.com

BRIA BURTON

Bria Burton has been inventing stories since she first learned how to write words and form sentences. She lives in St. Petersburg and is blessed with a wonderful husband who loves her despite her writing habit.

While she writes, her dog and cat do their best to distract her, which is why they now star in her family-friendly short story collection, **Lance & Ringo Tails**. Her novella, **Little Angel Helper**, a 2015 Royal Palm Literary Award Finalist, was written for her sisters, one of whom has special needs like a character in the story. She also writes speculative fiction stories, which have been featured in anthologies such as **Welcome to the Future** edited by Christina Escamilla, and in magazines such as **The Colored Lens**.

In January 2015, she was a contributor to **The Prometheus Saga**, an experimental short story collection of the Alvarium Experiment, a by-invitation-only consortium of award-winning authors. Each short story in the Saga was individually published in the Kindle Store and is still available. Bria is thrilled that the anthology version is now in your hands.

Her novel, **Sprinter**, a hybrid of inspirational women's sport fiction, is a 2015 RPLA Finalist in the unpublished women's fiction category. In 2011, she was awarded a First Place RPLA for her epic fantasy manuscript, **Livinity**. In October 2015, she'll find out if **Little Angel Helper** or **Sprinter** earn any awards at the RPLA Banquet hosted by the Florida Writers Association. She's been a member of FWA since 2008. She currently leads the St. Pete FWA Writers Group.

At St. Pete Running Company, she's employed as a blogger and customer service manager.

WORKS by BRIA BURTON

SHORT STORY COLLECTION

Lance & Ringo Tails

NOVELLA

Little Angel Helper
(2015 RPLA Finalist)

SHORT STORY PUBLICATIONS

The Wheels Must Turn – Broken Worlds anthology
On Both Sides – The Prometheus Saga
In Line at the DMYV – Welcome to the Future anthology
The Darkness Below – The Colored Lens
Switching – The Dunesteef Audio Fiction Magazine
Ligeia – The Journey Into… podcast
The Mute Girl - eFantasy
This is Hollywood – FICTION on the WEB

Several short stories featured in FWA Collections

UPCOMING SHORT STORY PUBLICATIONS

Empty Girl – Revisions: Stories of Starting Over
Tight Pants – Page & Spine

www.briaburton.com

M.J. CARLSON

M.J. Carlson's first novel, *The Alien Who Fell*, was a finalist in the Unpublished Science Fiction Novel Category from the Florida Writers Association in 2010 and his short story, *Wish Upon A Falling Star* was also a finalist the same year. Two short stories, *A Simple Breach of Etiquette* and *Paradox Effect* received honorable mentions in the international Writers of The Future contest in 2012 and 2013.

His debut novel, *Changed* is a post-cyberpunk story that blends action and hard-core science with psychological suspense. Layering hidden meaning inside the protagonist's story, *Changed* explores what it means to be human in an increasingly technological society.

M.J. was invited to join the Alvarium Experiment at its inception in 2014 with *Ever After*, a stand-alone e-short story within The Prometheus Saga universe. *Ever After* explores the concept of disseminating standardized myths throughout history in order to monitor each individual culture's influence on the tales. It is still available for individual download with research notes included.

M.J.'s home for nearly half a century is the Florida of scrub palms and sand spurs; of cool December beach breezes; forty-minute, four o'clock August thunderstorms; sultry, honeysuckle-scented summer nights; John D. MacDonald's Slip F-18; and where the road ended for Jack Kerouac. He's watched the sun rise over the Atlantic and drop into the Gulf of Mexico on the same day; walked the heat-shimmered backroads; raced motorcycles across the Everglades under a full April moon; and awoken, bleary-eyed and cotton-mouthed, on Key West's Duval Street more than once. He shares this life with Sparkle, his wise-reader and muse.

WORKS by M.J. CARLSON

NOVELS

Changed
Natural Selection (coming soon)
Engines of Destruction: Book 1 of the Nicole Piricelli series
(coming soon)
The Alien Who Fell
(2010 RPLA Finalist)

NOVELLAS

Paradox Effect
(2013 Writers of the Future Honorable Mention)

SHORT STORIES

Ever After – The Prometheus Saga

A Simple Breach of Etiquette
(2012 Writers of the Future Honorable Mention)

Wish Upon A Falling Star
(2010 RPLA Finalist)

Anna 101a

www.mjcarlson.com

BARD CONSTANTINE

Bard Constantine doesn't believe he's living in the right world, so he creates ones he feels more comfortable in. He was born in Chicago, raised in California, and currently dwells in Alabama with his wife and unrestrained imagination. He has a love for books, cinema, travel, and most creative outlets. More often than not he's chained to his desk in a dank basement pounding out tales of gritty futures and far-flung fantasy under the overprotective watch of a vengeful muse. If you see him outside, please contact the nearest psychiatric ward for immediate retrieval.

NOVELS BY BARD CONSTANTINE

THE ABERRATION SERIES
The Aberration
Torment of Tantalus (coming soon)

THE TROUBLESHOOTER SERIES
The Wise Man Says (short story)
Red-Eyed Killer
New Haven Blues
The Most Dangerous Dame

THE SHADOW BATTLES SERIES
City of Glass (short story)
The Eye of Everfell
The Darkest Champion (coming soon)

SOLO NOVELS
Silent Empire
The Blurred Man (Prometheus Saga)

POETRY COLLECTION
Immortal Musings

www.bardwritesbooks.com

CHARLES A CORNELL

Charles A Cornell was born in England, raised in Canada and now divides his time between Michigan and Florida. He started writing seriously more than ten years ago.

His first published novel, *Tiger Paw*, won the 2012 Royal Palm Literary Award for Best Thriller from the Florida Writers Association. His newest work, a 2014 Royal Palm Literary Award Finalist in Science Fiction, *DragonFly* is a retro-futuristic collision of science fiction and fantasy with a generous dash of alternative history.

Regardless of what genre he's writing, Charles aims to provide a unique perspective in his fiction, layering hidden meaning inside the protagonist's journey. His debut FBI thriller, *Tiger Paw* blends action and intrigue with psychological suspense, and asks the questions, how far will someone go to sell his soul to the Devil? And what if the Devil seeks revenge?

His new dieselpunk series, *DragonFly* explores the incredibly turbulent times during the 1940s and the 'what ifs' that might have been. *DragonFly* follows the journey of Veronica Somerset as she battles the odds to become Britain's first female fighter pilot. Packed with full color illustrations and black and white 'retrographs', *DragonFly* conjures up a whole new world of fantastic technology, dangerous fighting machines and wizards battling across the boundary between good and evil in a World War re-imagined like never before.

Charles lives in Michigan with his wife, rock musician son, and a cat. Most of the time, the cat wonders what the hell is going on as they lead such busy lives. He must write about that some day. From the cat's point of view, of course.

WORKS by CHARLES A. CORNELL

SCIENCE FANTASY NOVELS:

MISSIONS OF THE DRAGONFLY SQUADRON

DragonFly - Illustrated Edition
(2014 RPLA Finalist)

DragonFly Part I: To Hell and Back
DragonFly Part II: Victory or Death

Spies in Manhattan (coming soon)

COMPANION SHORT FICTION:

DRAGONFLY - BEHIND ENEMY LINES

Die Fabrik / The Factory
Escape From The Zauber Korps (coming soon)

MYSTERY THRILLERS
Tiger Paw
(2012 RPLA Winner)

www.CharlesACornell.com
www.DragonFly-Novels.com
www.Cornell-SciFi.com

DOUG DANDRIDGE

Doug Dandridge has written novels in just about every area of the fantastic; Urban Fantasy, High Fantasy, Steampunk, Hard Science Fiction, and of course, Space Opera. A graduate of both Florida State University (Psychology/Biology) and the University of Alabama (Clinical Psychology), Doug is an avid sports fan as well. A veteran of the US Army and the Florida National Guard (infantry), as well as a voracious reader of military history and fiction, he is well known for his ability to create realistic strategy, tactics and logistics in his stories.

Doug has to date twenty-seven books on Amazon, and has sold over 140,000 copies of his work in slightly less than three years. His *Exodus Empires at War* series has placed six consecutive books on the Amazon Best Seller Genre lists in the US and UK in Space Opera, Space Fleet and Military Science Fiction. *Exodus Books 3-7* all hit the number one spot in Space Opera in the UK, and were top five selections in the US. He has made his living as a full time author since March of 2013. *Exodus 1-3* are currently available in audiobook versions, with *Exodus Book 4* coming soon. Doug has appeared in Kevin J Anderson's *Five By Five Military Scifi Anthology*, and is due to appear next year in the *Fiction River Anthology Apocalypse*.

Doug lives in Tallahassee with his five feline friends, and attends a variety of men's and women's sports throughout the year. He is active in Kenpo Karate, and is still an avid reader of science fiction, fantasy and history.

NOVELS by DOUG DANDRIDGE

SCIENCE FICTION

EXODUS: EMPIRES AT WAR
Books 1 & 2; Book 3: The Rising Storm
Book 4: The Long Fall; Book 5: Ranger
Book 6: The Day of Battle; Book 7: Counter-Strike
Book 8: Soldiers; Book 9: Second Front
Exodus: Machine Wars: Book 1

***

The Deep Dark Well
To Well and Back
Deeper and Darker
Afterlife
Diamonds in the Sand
The Scorpion
We Are Death, Come For You

FANTASY

REFUGE
The Arrival: Book 1 & 2
Book 3: The Legions; Book 4: Kurt's Quest
Doppelganger
Aura
Daemon
The Hunger

NONFICTION

How I Sold 100,000 Books On Amazon

PARKER FRANCIS

Like the shape-shifting Prometheus character, Victor DiGenti, writing as Parker Francis, is a bit of a shifty character himself. After an education at the University of Florida, DiGenti followed a haphazard career path including a gig as a Top 40 radio DJ, door-to-door vacuum salesman, studio cameraman at a CBS affiliate, producer/director of public affairs programs and award-winning documentaries, and producer of the Jacksonville Jazz Festival for eight years.

DiGenti then turned to his first love—writing. He found inspiration in his household of four-legged critters and wrote three award-winning adventure/fantasies featuring a feline protagonist. His *Windrusher* trilogy went on to win multiple awards and attracted readers of all ages.

Writing as Parker Francis, DiGenti now writes hard-boiled suspense novels. The first in the Quint Mitchell Mystery series, *Matanzas Bay*, won the 2007 Josiah W. Bancroft Sr. Award and was named Book of the Year in the 2009 Royal Palm Literary Awards competition in the Pre-Published category. ***Bring Down the Furies*** won the Gold Medal in the 2013 Florida Authors & Publishers Association's President's Award Competition, and his most recent, ***Hurricane Island,*** is a Finalist in the 2015 Royal Palm Literary Awards competition (as is ***The Strange Case of Lord Byron's Lover***).

Vic (aka Parker) is a frequent speaker at libraries, book festivals and conferences, as well as leading his popular Novel in a Day workshop. He's a longtime Regional Director of the Florida Writers Association and the former Co-Director of the Florida Heritage Book Festival and Writers Conference. Vic and his long-suffering child bride live in NE Florida with three unimpressed cats.

NOVELS by VICTOR DIGENTI

WINDRUSHER ADVENTURE FANTASIES
Windrusher
Windrusher and the Cave of Tho-hoth
Windrusher and the Trail of Fire

NONFICTION
The Crafty Writer's Guide to Strong Beginnings,
Effective Middles & Satisfying Endings

The Crafty Writer's Guide to Writing Compelling Scenes
– Then Revising Them

NOVELS by PARKER FRANCIS

MYSTERIES
Matanzas Bay
(2009 RPLA Winner & Book of the Year)
Bring Down the Furies
(2013 FAPA Gold Medal)
Hurricane Island
(2015 RPLA Finalist)

SHORT FICTION
Ghostly Whispers, Secret Voices
Blue Crabs at Midnight

www.parkerfrancis.com
www.windrusher.com

KAY KENDALL

While growing up in the bucolic Flint Hills of Kansas, Kay Kendall dreamt of returning to her father's ancestral home of Texas and becoming a latter-day Nancy Drew or John Le Carré. Instead, higher education and circumstance led her down a long and winding road (footnote, the Beatles) to Harvard, Canada, international corporate communications, and, finally, back again to her beloved Texas.

While enjoying her peregrinations around the globe and garnering awards for her public relations work—most notably when McDonald's opened its first restaurant in the Soviet Union AKA Russia—she was haunted by the feeling that something was missing. There was another activity she was certain she'd been set on earth to do. That longing was fulfilled when she began to write historical fiction. In the spring of 2013, Stairway Press of Seattle published her historical mystery, ***Desolation Row—An Austin Starr Mystery***. Its sequel, ***Rainy Day Women***, came out in the summer of 2015. Kay now works on her third mystery at her home shared with her Canadian husband, three house rabbits, and spaniel Wills. Kay's husband Bruce is a lifelong fan of science fiction, and their forty years together discussing the genre's tropes helped her participate in ***The Prometheus Saga.***

Kay is the president of the Southwest Chapter of the Mystery Writers of America, a member of International Thriller Writers and contributing editor to its online magazine, ***The Big Thrill***. Other memberships include Crime Writers of Canada, Writers League of Texas, Houston Writers Guild, and the Texas Association of Authors. She earned degrees in Russian history and studied the Russian language in the Soviet Union, which accounts for her being a student of the Cold War and an aficionado of Russian culture. Watch for Austin Starr to tangle with Cold War spies in Vienna in Kay's next mystery.

NOVELS by KAY KENDALL

AUSTIN STARR MYSTERIES

Desolation Row

Rainy Day Women

Tombstone Blues

www.kaykendallauthor.com

www.austinstarr.com

JADE KERRION

Jade Kerrion defied (or leveraged, depending on your point of view) her undergraduate degrees in Biology and Philosophy, as well as her MBA, to embark on her second (and concurrent) career as an award-winning science fiction, fantasy, and contemporary romance author.

Her debut novel, *Perfection Unleashed*, published in 2012, won six literary awards and launched her best-selling futuristic thriller series, *Double Helix*, which blends cutting-edge genetic engineering and high-octane action with an unforgettable romance between an alpha empath and an assassin.

Earth-Sim and *Eternal Night* won first place Royal Palm Literary Awards in the Young Adult and Fantasy categories respectively. Readers have clamored for sequels, and Jade will get around to them when her To Do list opens up (sometime after 2020.) *Life Shocks Romances*, Jade's sweet and sexy contemporary romance series, features unlikely romances you will root for and happy endings you can believe in. They prove that, at the very least, she knows how to alphabetize books.

If she sounds busy, it's because she is. Jade writes at 3:00 am when her husband and three sons are asleep, and aspires to make her readers as sleep-deprived as she is.

Visit Jade at www.jadekerrion.com for a free copy of *Perfection Unleashed*.

NOVELS by JADE KERRION

THE DOUBLE HELIX COLLECTION

Perfection Unleashed

Perfect Betrayal

Perfect Weapon

Perfection Challenged

When the Silence Ends

Miriya

Zara

Xin

Carnival Tricks

OTHER SCIENCE FICTION AND FANTASY

Earth-Sim

Eternal Nigh

LIFE SHOCKS ROMANCES

Aroused

Betrayed

Crushed

Desired

Ensnared

Flawed

Graced

Haunted

www.jadekerrion.com

KEN PELHAM

Ken Pelham's debut novel, **Brigands Key**, a winner of the Royal Palm Literary Award, was published in hardcover in 2012, in softcover in 2014, and in audiobook in 2015. The prequel, **Place of Fear**, a 2012 first-place winner of the Royal Palm, was released in 2013. A short story, "The Wreck of the Edinburgh Kate," garnered a second-place award in 2014.

He has twice been a judge in literary awards contests.

Although his primary literary love is fiction in general, and suspense fiction in particular, Ken often gives seminars on the craft and publication of writing. His nonfiction book on writing in viewpoint has been translated into Italian, Spanish, and Portuguese, and his book on building and maintaining suspense has been translated into Italian. He's also a licensed and dangerous landscape architect, with a background in park and open space planning and design. He's written, published, and presented numerous times on the natural and built environments. Audiences usually stick around until the end.

He grew up in the small South Florida town of Immokalee, and lives with his wife, Laura, in Maitland, Florida. A member of the International Thriller Writers and the Florida Writers Association, writing keeps him off the streets and out of trouble, although he's sometimes spotted cycling, fishing, or scuba diving, seldom simultaneously.

NOVELS by KEN PELHAM

MYSTERY THRILLERS

Brigands Key
(2009 RPLA Winner)
Place of Fear
(2012 RPLA Winner)

NONFICTION BOOKS

Out of Sight, Out of Mind: A Writer's Guide to Mastering Viewpoint
Great Danger: A Writer's Guide to Building Suspense

SHORT STORY COLLECTIONS

Treacherous Bastards: Stories of Suspense, Deceit, and Skullduggery
A Double Shot of Fright: Two Tales of Terror
Tales of Old Brigands Key

"SOUNDTRACKED" SHORT STORIES

"The Wreck of the Edinburgh Kate"
(2014 RPLA Finalist)
"Familiar"

www.kenpelham.com

ANTONIO SIMON, JR.

Antonio Simon, Jr. was born and raised in Miami, Florida. He holds a law degree from Saint Thomas University School of Law and two undergraduate degrees (Political Science and History) from the University of Miami. He has been writing since 2002 and has published four books, collaborated on two, and authored dozens of short stories. His contribution to this anthology, *Lilith*, is a 2015 Royal Palm Literary Award finalist.

His debut novel, *The Gullwing Odyssey*, published in 2013, is a four-time award-winning fantasy/comedy about being the hero you never wanted to be. The novel is chock full of pirates, dragons, wizards, and everything that can make a hero of anyone quick, if they don't kill him first. It was the first-place winner of the prestigious 2014 Royal Palm Literary Award in the category of Humor/Satire. A sequel is currently in the works.

Antonio's interests are as varied as his literary repertoire. He is a local historian and has written *Miami Is Missing*, which delves into the hidden history of the Magic City, with all its glitz and scandal. His public appearances on Miami's history never fail to enlighten and entertain. He is also an avid tabletop gamer and the author of *R.A.G.E.: Roleplay Adventure Gaming Engine*, a fun, innovative, and original role-playing game system.

BOOKS BY ANTONIO SIMON, JR.

The Gullwing Odyssey
(2014 RPLA Winner)

Miami Is Missing

R.A.G.E.: Roleplay Adventure Gaming Engine

Transit Dreams: A Collection of Short Stories

Forgotten Spaces: Poetry For A Pensive Mood
(with Steven M. Fonts and R. Perez de Pereda)

Learn more about the Gullwing series at:
www.GullwingOdyssey.com

Find Antonio's books at:
www.DarkwaterSyndicate.com